The *Mountain* of adventure

and

The *Ship* of adventure

Enid Blyton, who died in 1968, is one of the most successful children's authors of all time. She wrote over seven hundred books, which have been translated into more than forty languages and have sold more than 400 million copies around the world. Enid Blyton's stories of magic, adventure and friendship continue to enchant children the world over. Enid Blyton's beloved works include The Famous Five series, the Malory Towers series, the Faraway Tree series and the Adventure series.

Titles in the Adventure series available as double editions

The Island of Adventure *and* The Castle of Adventure

The Valley of Adventure *and* The Sea of Adventure

The Mountain of Adventure *and* The Ship of Adventure

The Circus of Adventure *and* The River of Adventure

The Mountain

of adventure

and

The Ship

of adventure

Enid Blyton

MACMILLAN CHILDREN'S BOOKS

The Mountain of Adventure first published 1949 by Macmillan Children's Books
The Ship of Adventure first published 1950 by Macmillan Children's Books
First published as a double edition 2002 by Macmillan Children's Books

This double edition published 2010 by Macmillan Children's Books
a division of Macmillan Publishers Limited
20 New Wharf Road, London N1 9RR
Basingstoke and Oxford
Associated companies throughout the world
www.panmacmillan.com

ISBN 978-0-330-39837-4

17 19 18

A CIP catalogue record for this book is available from
the British Library.

Typeset by Intype Libra Ltd
Printed and bound in the UK by CPI Mackays, Chatham ME5 8TD

The *Mountain* of adventure

Contents

1. All set for a summer holiday   1
2. At the farmhouse   10
3. The first morning   20
4. Up on the mountain-side   28
5. Arrival of the donkeys   37
6. Off to the Vale of Butterflies   46
7. On the way   55
8. First night in camp   64
9. A different world   73
10. A disturbing night   82
11. A strange happening   91
12. Wolves in the night!   100
13. The face in the tree   109
14. Plenty of things happen   118
15. Behind the green curtain   127
16. Inside the mountain   136
17. Philip again   145
18. A little exploring   154

19. The king of the mountain   163
20. An amazing secret   172
21. On the mountain-top   181
22. The helicopter   190
23. The wonderful wings   199
24. The helicopter comes again   207
25. A thrilling night   216
26. Flight through the mountain   226
27. Escape at last   235
28. Trailed by the dogs   245
29. The tables are turned!   254
30. The end of it all!   263

All set for a summer holiday

Four children were singing at the tops of their voices in a car that was going up a steep mountain-side road.

A parrot was also joining in, very much out of tune, cocking up her crest in excitement. The man at the wheel turned round with a grin.

'I say! I can't even hear the car hooter. What's the matter with you all?'

Philip, Jack, Dinah and Lucy-Ann stopped singing and shouted answers at him.

'It's the beginning of the hols!'

'And we're going to have a donkey each to ride in the mountains!'

'Pop goes the weasel!' That was Kiki the parrot, of course, joining in.

'We've got eight weeks of fun all together.'

'And you'll be with us, Bill, as well as Mother! Mother, aren't you excited too?'

Mrs Mannering smiled at Philip. 'Yes – but I hope

you're not going to be as noisy as this all the time. Bill, you'll have to protect me from this rowdy crowd of children.'

'I'll protect you all right,' promised Bill, swinging the car round another bend. 'I'll knock all their heads together once a day at least – and if Lucy-Ann starts getting tough with me I'll . . .'

'Oh *Bill*! said Lucy-Ann, the youngest and least boisterous of the lot. 'Jack's always saying I'm not tough *enough*. I ought to be by now, though, considering all the adventures I've been through.'

'Tough enough, tough enough!' chanted Kiki the parrot, who loved words that sounded alike. 'Tough enough, tough . . .'

'Oh, stop her,' groaned Mrs Mannering. She was tired with their long car journey, and was hoping it would soon be over. She had eight weeks of the children's holidays before her, and was quite sure she would be worn out before the end of it.

Philip and Dinah were her own children, and Jack and Lucy-Ann, who had no parents, lived with her in the holidays and loved her as if she were their own mother. Bill Cunningham was their very good friend, and had had some hair-raising adventures with them.

He had come with them on these holidays to keep them out of any more adventures – or so he said! Mrs Mannering vowed she was not going to let them out of her sight for eight weeks, unless Bill was with them –

then they couldn't possibly disappear, or fall into some dreadful new adventure.

'They ought to be safe, tucked away in the Welsh mountains, with both you and me, Bill, to look after them,' said Mrs Mannering. Mr Mannering had been dead for many years and Mrs Mannering often found it difficult to cope with so many lively children at once, now that they were growing older.

Philip loved any animal, bird or insect. His sister Dinah didn't share this love at all, and disliked most wild animals, and hated quite a number of harmless insects, though she was certainly better than she used to be. She was a hot-tempered girl, as ready to use her fists as Philip, and they had many a battle, much to gentle Lucy-Ann's dismay.

Lucy-Ann and Jack were brother and sister too. Kiki the parrot was Jack's beloved parrot, usually to be found on his shoulder. In fact, Mrs Mannering had once actually suggested that she should put a little leather patch on the shoulders of each of Jack's coats to stop Kiki from wearing thin places there with her clawed feet.

Jack was fond of birds, and he and Philip spent many an exciting hour together bird-watching, or taking photographs. They had a marvellous collection of these, which Bill said was worth a lot of money. They had brought cameras with them on this holiday, and, of course, their field-glasses for watching birds at a distance.

'We might see eagles again,' said Jack. 'Do you

remember the eagle's nest we found near that old castle in Scotland once, Philip? We might see buzzards too.'

'Buzz-z-z-z-z-z,' said Kiki at once. 'Buzz! Buzz off!'

'We might even have an adventure,' said Philip, with a grin. 'Though Mother and Bill are quite certain they will guard us from even the smallest one this time!'

Now here they were, all set for a wonderful holiday in the Welsh mountains, in a very lonely spot, where they could wander about with cameras and field-glasses wherever they liked. Each child was to have a donkey, so that they could ride along the narrow mountain paths as much as they wished.

'I shan't always come with you,' said Mrs Mannering, 'because I'm not so thrilled with donkey-riding as you are. But Bill will be with you, so you'll be safe.'

'Ah – but will Bill be safe with *us*?' said Jack, with a grin. 'We always seem to drag him into something or other. Poor Bill!'

'If you manage to pull me into an adventure in the middle of some of the loneliest of the Welsh mountains, you'll be clever,' said Bill.

The car swung round another bend and a farmhouse came into sight.

'We're nearly there,' said Mrs Mannering. 'I believe I can see the farmhouse we're going to stay at. Yes – there it is.'

The children craned their necks to see it. It was a

rambling old stone place, set on the mountain-side, with barns and out-buildings all around. In the evening sunset it looked welcoming and friendly.

'Lovely!' said Lucy-Ann. 'What's it called?'

Bill said something that sounded like 'Doth-goth-oo-elli-othel-in.'

'Gracious!' said Dinah. 'What a name! Not even Kiki could pronounce that, I'm sure. Tell her it, Bill. See what she says.'

Bill obligingly told the name to the parrot, who listened solemnly and raised her crest politely.

'Now you just repeat that,' said Jack to Kiki. 'Go on!'

'This-is-the-house-that-Jack-built,' said the parrot, running all the words together. The children laughed.

'Good try, Kiki!' said Jack. 'You can't stump Kiki, Bill – she'll always say something. Good old Kiki!'

Kiki was pleased by this praise, and made a noise like the car changing gear. She had been doing this at intervals during the whole of the journey and had nearly driven Mrs Mannering mad.

'*Don't* let Kiki start that again,' she begged. 'Thank goodness we are here at last! Where's the front door, Bill – or isn't there one?'

There didn't seem to be one. The track went up to what appeared to be a barn and stopped there. A small path then ran to the farmhouse, divided into three and went to three different doors.

The children tumbled out of the car. Bill got out and stretched his legs. He helped Mrs Mannering out and they all looked round. A cock near by crowed and Kiki promptly crowed too, much to the cock's astonishment.

A plump, red-faced woman came hurrying out of one of the doors, a welcoming smile on her face. She called behind her to someone in the house.

'Effans, Effans, they have come, look you, they have come!'

'Ah – Mrs Evans,' said Bill, and shook hands with her. Mrs Mannering did the same. A small man came running out of the house, and came up to them too.

'This iss Effans, my husband,' said the plump woman. 'We hope you will be very happy with us, whateffer!'

This was said in a pleasant sing-song voice that the children liked very much. Everybody shook hands solemnly with Mrs Evans and her husband, and Kiki held out a claw as well.

'A parrot, look you!' cried Mrs Evans to her husband. 'Effans, a parrot!'

Mr Evans didn't seem to like the look of Kiki as much as his wife did, but he smiled politely.

'It iss very welcome you are,' he said in his sing-song voice. 'Will you pleass to come this way?'

They all followed Effans. He led them to the farmhouse, and, when the door was flung open, what a welcome sight met the children's eyes!

A long, sturdy kitchen table was covered with a snow-white cloth, and on it was set the finest meal the children had ever seen in their lives.

A great ham sat ready to be carved. A big tongue garnished round with bright green parsley sat by its side. An enormous salad with hard-boiled eggs sprinkled generously all over it was in the middle of the table. Two cold roast chickens were on the table too, with little curly bits of cold bacon set round.

The children's eyes nearly fell out of their heads. What a feast! And the scones and cakes! The jams and the pure yellow honey! The jugs of creamy milk!

'I say – are you having a party or something?' asked Jack, in awe.

'A party! No, no – it is high tea for you, look you,' said Mrs Evans. 'We cannot do dinners for you at night, we are busy people! You shall have what we have, and that is all. Here is high tea for you today, and when you have washed, it iss ready!'

'Oh – have we got to wash?' said Philip with a sigh. 'I'm clean enough. Golly, look at that meal! I say, if we're going to have food like this these hols I shan't want to go donkey-riding at all. I'll just stay here and eat!'

'Well, if you do that you'll be too fat for any donkey to carry,' said his mother. 'Go and wash, Philip. Mrs Evans will show us our rooms – we can all do with a wash and a brush – and then we can do justice to this magnificent meal.'

Up some narrow winding stairs went the little party, into big low-ceilinged rooms set with heavy old-fashioned furniture. Mrs Evans proudly showed them a small bathroom, put in for visitors to the farmhouse.

There were four rooms for the party. Bill had a small one to himself. Mrs Mannering had a big one, well away from the children's rooms, because they were often so noisy in the mornings. Philip and Jack had a curious little room together, whose ceiling slanted almost to the floor, and the girls had a bigger one next door.

'Isn't this going to be fun?' said Jack, scrubbing his hands vigorously in the bathroom, whilst Kiki sat on a tap. 'I'm longing to get at that meal downstairs. What a spread!'

'Move up,' said Dinah impatiently. 'There's room for two at this basin. We shall have to take it in turns to come in in the morning. Oh, Kiki, don't fly off with the nail-brush! Jack, stop her.'

The nail-brush was rescued and Kiki was tapped on the beak. She didn't mind. She was looking forward to the food downstairs as much as the children. She had seen a bowl of raspberries which she meant to sit as near to as possible. She flew to Jack's shoulder and muttered loving things into his ear whilst he dried his hands on a very rough towel.

'Stop it, Kiki. You tickle,' said Jack. 'Are you ready,

you others? Aunt Allie! Bill! Are you ready? We're going downstairs.'

'Coming!' cried the others, and down they all went. Now for a proper feast!

2

At the farmhouse

That first meal in the Welsh farmhouse was a very happy one. Mrs Evans was excited to have visitors, and Effans, her husband, beamed all round as he carved great slices of ham, tongue and chicken. There were a lot of 'look yous' and 'whateffers', and Kiki was especially interested in the up-and-down song-like way the two Welsh folk talked.

'Wipe your feet, whateffer,' she said to Mrs Evans suddenly. Mrs Evans looked surprised. She hadn't heard the parrot speak before.

'Shut the door, look you,' commanded Kiki, raising her crest. The children squealed with laughter.

'She's speaking Welsh already!' said Dinah. 'Hey, watch her, Jack – she's absolutely wolfing those raspberries!'

Jack put a plate over the bowl, and Kiki was angry. She made a noise like the car changing gear and Effans looked startled.

'It's all right – it's only Kiki,' said Jack. 'She can make all kinds of noises. You should hear her give her imitation of a train whistling in a tunnel.'

Kiki opened her beak and swelled up her throat as if she was about to make this horrible noise. Mrs Mannering spoke hastily. 'Jack! Don't let Kiki make that noise. If she does you'll have to take her upstairs and put her in your bedroom.'

'Bad Kiki, naughty Kiki,' said the parrot solemnly, recognizing the stern tone in Mrs Mannering's voice. She flew to Jack's shoulder and cuddled there, eyeing the plate that he had put over the bowl of raspberries. She gave his ear a little nip.

What a meal that was for six very hungry travellers who had had nothing but sandwiches all day long! Even Mrs Mannering ate more than she had ever eaten before at one meal. Mrs Evans kept beaming round as she filled the plates.

'There iss plenty more in the larder, look you,' she said. 'Effans, go fetch the meat-pie.'

'No, no!' said Mrs Mannering. 'Please don't. We have more than enough here – it's only that we are extra hungry and the food is so very very good.'

Mrs Evans was pleased. 'It iss plain country food, but it iss very good for the children,' she said. 'They will soon have good appetites in this mountain air, look you.'

'Indeed to gootness they will,' agreed Effans. 'Their appetites are small yet. They will grow.'

Mrs Mannering looked rather alarmed. 'Good gracious! I've never in my life seen them eat so much – if their appetites get any bigger I'll never be able to feed them at home!'

'And we shall *starve* at school,' grinned Jack.

'The poor boy!' said Mrs Evans. 'It iss a big ham I must give him to take back, whateffer!'

At last nobody could eat any more. They sat back from the table, looking out of the wide, low windows and the big open door. What a view!

Great mountains reared up their heads in the evening light. Deep shadows lay across the valley, but the mountains still caught the sunlight, and gleamed enchantingly. It was all so different from the country round their home, and the children felt that they could never look long enough on the mountain-tops and the shadowed valleys below.

'You are very lonely here,' said Bill. 'I can't see a single house or farm anywhere.'

'My brother lives on the other side of that mountain,' said Mrs Evans, pointing. 'I see him at the market each week. That is ten miles away, or maybe eleven. And my sister lives beyond that mountain you can see there. She too has a farm. So we have neighbours, you see.'

'Yes – but not next-door ones!' said Dinah. 'Don't you ever feel cut-off and lonely here, Mrs Evans?'

Mrs Evans looked surprised. 'Lonely? Indeed to gootness, what iss there to be lonely about, with Effans by my side, and the shepherd up on the hills, and the cow-herd and his wife in their cottage near by? And there iss plenty of animals, as you will see.'

Hens wandered in and out of the open door, pecking up crumbs fallen from the table. Kiki watched them intently. She began a warm, clucking noise, and the hens clucked back. A cock came strutting in and looked round for the hen that had a cluck he didn't quite know.

'Cock-a-doodle-doo!' suddenly crowed the cock defiantly, catching sight of Kiki on Jack's shoulder.

'Cock-a-doodle-doo!' answered Kiki, and the cock immediately jumped up on to the table to fight the crowing parrot.

He was shooed down and ran out indignantly, followed by a cackle of laughter from Kiki. Effans held his sides and laughed till the tears ran down his cheeks.

'That is a fine bird, look you!' he said to Jack, quite losing his heart to Kiki. 'Let her help herself to the raspberries again.'

'She's had enough, thank you very much,' said Jack, pleased at Effans' praise of Kiki. People sometimes didn't like the parrot, and when she went away with him Jack was always anxious in case anyone should object to her.

They all wandered out into the golden evening air, happy and well satisfied. Bill and Mrs Mannering sat on an old stone wall, watching the sun sink behind a mountain in the west. The four children went round the farmhouse and its buildings.

'Pigs! And what a marvellous clean pig-sty,' said Dinah. 'I've never seen a clean pig before. Look at this one, fat and shining as if it's been scrubbed.'

'It probably has, in preparation for our coming!' said Philip. 'I love these little piglets too. Look at them rooting round with their funny little snouts.'

'Kiki will soon have a wonderful collection of noises,' said Lucy-Ann, hearing the parrot giving a very life-like grunt. 'She'll be able to moo and bellow and grunt and crow and cluck . . .'

'And gobble like a turkey!' said Dinah, seeing some turkeys near by. 'This is a lovely farm. They've got everything. Oh, Philip – *look* at that kid!'

There were some goats on the mountain-side not far off, and with them was a kid. It was snow-white, dainty and altogether lovely. Philip stood looking at it, loving it at once.

He made a curious little bleating noise and all the goats looked round and stopped eating. The kid pricked up its little white ears, and stood quivering on its slender legs. It was very young and new.

Philip made the noise again. The kid left its mother and came leaping to him. It sprang right into his arms and nestled there, butting its soft white head against Philip's chin.

'Oh, Philip – isn't it sweet!' said the girls, and stroked the little thing and rubbed their cheeks against its snow-white coat.

'I wish animals came to me like they come to you, Philip,' said Lucy-Ann enviously. It was amazing the attraction that Philip had for creatures of any kind. Even a moth would rest contentedly on his finger, and the number of strange pets he had had was unbelievable. Hedgehogs, stag-beetles, lizards, young birds, mice, rats – you never knew what Philip would have next. All creatures loved him and trusted him, and he in turn understood them and loved them too.

'Now this kid will follow at his heels like a dog the whole time we're here,' said Dinah. 'Well, I'm glad it will be a kid, not a cow! Do you remember that awful time when Philip went into a field with a herd of cows in, and they all went to him and nuzzled him and followed him about like dogs. They even tried to get over the gate and through the hedge when he went out. I was awfully scared they would.'

'You ought to be ashamed of being afraid of cows,' said Philip, stroking the kid. 'There's no reason to be, Di. It's surprising you're not afraid of this kid. I bet you'd run if the goats came near.'

'I shouldn't,' said Dinah indignantly, but all the same she moved off hurriedly when the herd of goats, curious at seeing the kid in Philip's arms, began to come nearer to the children.

Soon they were all round Philip, Lucy-Ann and Jack. Dinah watched from a distance. The kid bleated when it saw its mother, but as soon as Philip put the little thing down to run to her, it leapt straight back into his arms!

'Well! You'll have to take it to bed with you tonight, there's no doubt about that,' said Jack, grinning. 'Come on – let's go and see the horses. They're the kind with shaggy hooves – I just love those!'

The goats were shooed off, and the children went to look at the great horses standing patiently in the field. There were three of them. They all came to Philip at once of course.

He had put down the little kid, and now it followed so close to his heels that, every time he stopped, it ran into his legs. At the first possible chance it sprang into his arms again. It followed him into the farmhouse too.

'Oh! You have found little Snowy!' said Mrs Evans, looking round from her oven with a face redder than ever. 'He has not left his mother before, look you!'

'Oh, Philip, don't bring the kid in here,' said Mrs Mannering, seeing at once that yet another animal had attached itself to Philip. She was afraid that Mrs Evans would object strongly to the kid coming indoors with Philip – and once it had felt the boy's attraction nothing would stop it from following him anywhere – even upstairs!

'Oh, it iss no matter if a kid comes into the house,' said Mrs Evans. 'We haff the new-born lambs in, and the hens are always in and out, and Moolie the calf used to come in each day before she was put in the field.'

The children thought it was a wonderful idea to let creatures wander in and out like that, but Mrs Mannering thought differently. She wondered if she would find eggs laid in her bed, or a calf in her bedroom chair! Still, it was a holiday, and if Mrs Evans like creatures wandering all over her kitchen, the children would like it too!

Lucy-Ann gave an enormous yawn and sank down into a big chair. Mrs Mannering looked at her, and then at the grandfather clock ticking in a corner.

'Go to bed, all of you,' she said. 'We're all tired. Yes, I know it's early, Philip, you don't need to tell me that – but we've had a long day, and this mountain air is very strong. We shall all sleep like tops tonight.'

'I will get ready some creamy milk for you,' began Mrs Evans, 'and you would like some buttered scones and jam to take up with you?'

'Oh, *no*,' said Mrs Mannering. 'We simply couldn't eat a thing more tonight, thank you, Mrs Evans.'

'Oh, *Mother*! Of *course* we could eat scones and jam and drink some more of that heavenly milk,' said Dinah indignantly. So they each took up a plate of scones and raspberry jam and a big glass of creamy milk to have in bed.

There came the scampering of little hooves, and Snowy the kid appeared in the boys' bedroom. He leapt in delight on to Philip's bed.

'Gosh! Look at this! Snowy's come upstairs!' said Philip. 'Have a bit of scone, Snowy?'

'I say – did we hear the kid coming up the stairs?' said Lucy-Ann, putting her head round the door of the boys' room. 'Oooh, Philip! You've got him on your bed!'

'Well, he won't get off,' said Philip. 'As soon as I push him off, he's on again – look! Like a puppy!'

'Maa-aa-aa!' said the kid in a soft, bleating voice, and butted Philip with its head.

'Are you going to have it up here all the night?' asked Dinah, appearing in her pyjamas.

'Well, if I put it outside, it'll only come in again – and if I shut the door it will come and butt it with its head,' said Philip, who had quite lost his heart to Snowy. 'After all, Jack has Kiki in the room with him all night.'

'Oh, *I* don't mind you having Snowy,' said Dinah. 'I just wondered what Mother would say, that's all – and Mrs Evans.'

'I shouldn't be at all surprised to hear that Mrs Evans has got a sick cow in her room, and half a dozen hens,' said Philip, arranging Snowy in the crook of his knees. 'She's a woman after my own heart. Go away, you girls. I'm going to sleep. I'm very happy – full of scones and jam and milk and sleep.'

Kiki made a hiccuping noise. 'Pardon!' she said. This was a new thing she had learnt from somebody at Jack's school the term before. It made Mrs Mannering cross.

'I should think Kiki's full up too,' said Jack sleepily.

'She pinched a whole scone, and I'm sure she's been at the raspberries again. Look at her beak! Now shut up, Kiki, I want to go to sleep.'

'Pop goes the weasel, look you,' said Kiki solemnly and put her head under her wing. The girls disappeared. The boys fell asleep. What a lovely beginning to a summer holiday!

3

The first morning

The next day the two girls awoke first. It was early, but somebody was already about in the yard. Lucy-Ann peeped out of the window.

'It's Effans,' she said. 'He must have been milking. Dinah, come here. Did you ever see such a glorious view in your life?'

The two girls knelt at the window. The sun was streaming across the valley below through the opening between two mountains, but the rest of the vale was in shadow. In the distance many mountains reared their great heads, getting bluer and bluer the further they were away. The sky was blue without a cloud.

'Holiday weather – real holiday weather!' said Dinah happily. 'I hope Mother lets us go picnicking today.'

'There's one thing about *this* holiday,' said Lucy-Ann, 'we shan't have any awful adventures, because Aunt Allie is absolutely determined to go with us, or send Bill with us, wherever we go.'

'Well, we've had our share of adventures,' said Dinah, beginning to dress. 'More than most children ever have. I don't mind if we don't have one this time. Hurry, Lucy-Ann, then we can get to the bathroom before the boys. Don't make too much row because Mother doesn't want to be wakened too early.'

Lucy-Ann popped her head in at the boys' room on the way to the bathroom. They were still sound asleep. Kiki took her head from under her wing as she heard Lucy-Ann at the door, but she said nothing, only yawned. Lucy-Ann looked closely at Philip's bed.

Snowy the kid was still there, cuddled into the crook of Philip's knees! Lucy-Ann's heart warmed to Philip. What an extraordinary boy he was, to have every creature so fond of him, and to be able to do anything he liked with them. The little kid raised its head and looked at Lucy-Ann.

She fled to the bathroom and washed with Dinah. They soon heard the boys getting up, and Kiki's voice telling somebody to wipe his feet.

'She's probably teaching a few manners to Snowy,' giggled Lucy-Ann. 'Kiki always tries to teach things to all Philip's pets. Oh, Dinah – do you remember how funny she was with Huffin and Puffin, the two puffins we found when we had our last adventure?'

'Arr,' said Dinah, making the noise the puffins used to make. Kiki heard them. 'Arrrrr!' she called from the boys' bedroom. 'Arrrrr!' Then she went off into a cackle of laughter, and Snowy the kid stared at her in alarm.

'Maa-aa-aa!' said the kid.

'Maa-aa-aa!' said Kiki, and the kid looked all round for another kid. The boys laughed.

Kiki, always encouraged when people laughed, swelled up her throat to make the noise of a car changing gear, her favourite noise of the moment, but Philip stopped her hurriedly.

'Stop it, Kiki! We've had enough of that noise. Do forget it!'

'God save the Queen!' said Kiki, in a dismal voice. 'Wipe your feet, blow your nose.'

'Come on,' said the girls, putting their heads in. 'Slowcoaches!'

They all went downstairs just as Mrs Evans was setting the last touches to the breakfast-table. It was loaded almost as much as the supper-table the night before. Jugs of creamy milk stood about the table, warm from the milking, and big bowls of raspberries had appeared again.

'I shan't know what to have,' groaned Jack, sitting down with Kiki on his shoulder. 'I can smell eggs and bacon – and there's cereal to have with raspberries and cream – and ham – and tomatoes – and gosh, is that cream cheese? Cream cheese for breakfast, how super!'

Snowy the kid tried to get on to Philip's knee as he sat down to breakfast. He pushed him off. 'No, Snowy, not at meal-times. I'm too busy then. Go and say good morning to your mother. She must wonder where you are.'

Kiki was at work on the raspberries. Mrs Evans had actually put a plate aside for Kiki's own breakfast. She and Effans beamed at the bird. They both thought she was wonderful.

'Look you, whateffer!' said Kiki, and dipped her beak into the raspberries again. It was rapidly becoming pink with the juice.

The children had an extremely good meal before Bill or Mrs Mannering came down. The Evans' had had theirs already – in fact they seemed to have done a day's work, judging by the list of things that Evans talked about – he had cleaned out the pigs, groomed the horses, milked the cows, fetched in the eggs, been to see the cow-herd and a dozen other things besides.

'Mrs Evans, do you know where the donkeys are that we arranged to have, for riding in the mountains?' asked Philip, when he had finished his breakfast and Snowy was once more in his arms.

'Ah, Trefor the shepherd will tell you,' said Mrs Evans. 'It iss his brother, look you, that has the donkeys. He is to bring them here for you.'

'Can't we go and fetch them and ride them back?' said Jack.

'Indeed to gootness, Trefor's brother lives thirty miles away!' said Effans. 'You could not walk there, whateffer.

You go and see Trefor today and ask him what has he done about your donkeys.'

Mrs Mannering and Bill appeared at that moment, looking fresh and trim after their good night's sleep in the sharp mountain air.

'Any breakfast left for us?' said Bill with a grin.

Mrs Evans hurried to fry bacon and eggs again, and soon the big kitchen was full of the savoury smell.

'Golly, if I stay here and smell that I shall feel hungry all over again,' said Philip. 'Bill, we're going up to see Trefor the shepherd to ask about our donkeys. Mother, can we have a picnic in the mountains as soon as the donkeys come?'

'Yes – when I'm sure I can keep on my donkey all right,' said his mother. 'If mine's a very fat donkey I shall slide off!'

'They are not fat,' Effans assured her. 'They are used in the mountains and they are strong and small. Sometimes we use ponies, but Trefor's brother breeds donkeys, and they are just as good.'

'Well, we'll go and have a talk with Trefor,' said Philip, getting up and letting Snowy fall off his knee. 'Come on, everyone! Kiki, do you want to be left with the raspberries? You greedy bird!'

Kiki flew to Jack's shoulder, and the party set off up the path that Effans had pointed out to them. Snowy bounded with them, turning a deaf ear to his mother's bleats. Already he seemed one of the company, petted by them all, though Kiki was not altogether pleased to have another creature taking up so much of the children's attention.

They went up the steep little path. The sun was up higher now and was hot. The children wore only thin blouses or shirts, and shorts, but they felt very warm. They came to a spring gushing out of the hillside and sat down to drink, and to cool their hands and feet. Snowy drank too, and then capered about lightly on his strong little legs, leaping from place to place almost as if he had wings.

'I wish I could leap like a goat,' said Jack lazily. 'It looks so lovely and easy to spring up high into the air like that, and land wherever you want to.'

Philip suddenly made a grab at something that was slithering past him on the warm bank. Dinah sat up at once. 'What is it, what is it?'

'This,' said Philip, and showed the others a silvery-grey, snake-like creature, with bright little eyes.

Dinah screamed at once. 'A snake! Philip, put it down. Philip, it'll bite you.'

'It won't,' said Philip calmly. 'It's not a snake – and anyway British snakes don't bite unless they're adders. I've told you that before. This is a slow-worm – and a very fine specimen too!'

The children looked in fascination as the silvery slow-worm wriggled over Philip's knees. It certainly looked very like a snake, but it wasn't. Lucy-Ann and Jack knew that, but Dinah always forgot. She was so terrified of snakes that to her anything that glided along must belong to the snake family.

'It's horrible,' she said with a shudder. 'Let it go, Philip. How do you know it's not a snake?'

'Well – for one thing it blinks its eyes and no snake does that,' said Philip. 'Watch it. It blinks like a lizard – and no wonder, because it belongs to the lizard family.'

As he spoke the little creature blinked its eyes. It stayed still on Philip's knee and made no further attempt to escape. Philip put his hand over it and it stayed there quite happy.

'I've never had a slow-worm for a pet,' said Philip. 'I've a good mind . . .'

'Philip! If you dare to keep that snake for a pet I'll tell Mother to send you home!' said Dinah in great alarm.

'Dinah, it's *not* a snake!' said Philip impatiently. 'It's a lizard – a legless lizard – quite harmless and very interesting. I'm going to keep it for a pet if it'll stay with me.'

'Stay with you! Of course it will,' said Jack. 'Did you ever know an animal that wouldn't? I should hate to go to a jungle with you, Philip – you'd have monkeys hanging lovingly round your neck, and tigers purring at you, and snakes wrapping themselves round your legs, and . . .'

Dinah gave a little scream. 'Don't say such horrible things! Philip, make that slow-worm go away.'

Instead he slipped it into his pocket. 'Now don't

worry, Dinah,' he said. 'You don't need to come near me. I don't expect it will stay with me because it won't like my pocket – but I'll just see.'

They set off up the hill once more, Dinah hanging back carefully. Oh dear! Philip *would* go and spoil the holiday by keeping something horrible again!

4

Up on the mountain-side

Trefor the shepherd had a small cabin-like cottage a good way up the mountain-side. Around him for miles grazed the sheep. Nearer in were that year's lambs, now grown into sturdy little beasts, their woolly coats showing up against the sheared bodies of the older sheep.

The shepherd was having a simple meal when they got to his hut. He had bread, butter, cream cheese and onions, and beside him a great jug of milk that he had cooled by standing it in the stream that ran down the mountain-side near by.

He nodded his head to the children as they came up. He was a curious-looking old fellow, with longish untidy hair, a straggling beard, and two of the brightest blue eyes the children had ever seen.

He spoke Welsh, which they didn't understand. 'Can you speak English?' asked Jack. 'We can't understand what you say.'

Trefor knew a few words of English, which, after much thought and munching of onions, he spoke.

'Donkeys. Tomorrow.'

He added something the children didn't understand, and waved his hand down the mountain-side towards the farmhouse.

'He means the donkeys will arrive tomorrow at the farm,' said Jack. 'Good! Perhaps Aunt Allie and Bill will come for a picnic on the donkeys.'

Trefor was very interested in Kiki. He had never in his life seen a parrot. He pointed at Kiki and laughed a hoarse laugh. Kiki at once copied it.

Trefor looked startled. 'Wipe your feet,' said Kiki sternly. 'How many times have I told you to shut the door? Three blind mice!'

Trefor stared at the parrot, amazed. Kiki cackled loudly. 'Look you, whateffer, look you, whateffer, look . . .'

The children laughed. Jack tapped Kiki on the beak. 'Now, now, Kiki – don't show off.'

Snowy butted against Philip's legs. He didn't like so much attention being given to Kiki. Philip turned, and the little creature leapt straight into his arms. Trefor seemed most amused and sent out a flood of Welsh words that nobody could understand at all. He tapped Philip on the arm, and then pointed to the ground to show the children that he wanted them to sit down.

They sat down, wondering what he wanted. He went

a little way down the hillside, making a soft baaing noise. From everywhere around the woolly lambs looked up. They came running to the shepherd, bleating, and even little Snowy left Philip and ran too. The shepherd knelt down and the lambs crowded round him, nuzzling against him. Trefor had had them when they were tiny – he had looked after them, even fed some of them from bottles if their mothers had died – and when they heard his soft call that once they had known so well, they remembered and came to him, their first friend.

A lump came into Lucy-Ann's throat. There was something very touching in the sight of that solemn, lonely, long-haired old shepherd, calling to his lambs and being answered. Snowy the kid, eager to get close to him, leapt on to the woolly backs of the lambs, and butted his head against him.

'Look at Snowy! Isn't he a cheeky rascal of a kid!' said Dinah. 'My goodness, you can hardly see Trefor now, he's so surrounded by lambs!'

Trefor came back, smiling, his eyes very blue in his old brown face. He offered the children some bread and onions, but the onions were big and strong-smelling, and Jack felt certain Mrs Mannering wouldn't approve if they all came back smelling strongly of Trefor's onions.

'No, thank you,' he said politely. 'Will you be down to see your brother tomorrow, when he brings the donkeys?'

Trefor seemed to understand this. He nodded. 'I come. Tomorrow. Donkeys.'

'Getting quite talkative, isn't he?' said Jack to the others. 'Right, Trefor. See you tomorrow then.'

They set off down the hill again. They stopped once more at the little spring to drink. They sat on the grass, looking at the towering mountains round them.

'Effans says that all those mountains over there have hardly anyone living on them, because they are difficult to get at,' said Jack. 'I bet there are some interesting animals and birds there. Wish we could go and see.'

'I don't see why we shouldn't if Bill and Mother would come with us,' said Philip, trying to stop Snowy from walking on his middle. 'Stop it, Snowy. Get off my tummy. Your hooves are sharp. It would be fun to go off into the mountains on donkeys and take food with us for a few days.'

'And have tents, do you mean?' said Jack. 'I say – that's an idea, Philip. We could take our cameras and get some fine pictures. I might see some rare birds.'

'I bet you would!' said Philip. 'Hallo, here comes Sally Slither!'

Out of his pocket glided the slow-worm, and curled itself up in the crook of Philip's elbow, in the sun. Dinah removed herself to a safe distance at once. Kiki looked down with interest from her perch on Jack's shoulder.

'Sally Slither! What a nice name!' said Lucy-Ann,

running her finger down the slow-worm's silvery back. 'Look – my finger's tickling her – she's going all dithery!'

'Slithery dithery,' said Kiki, at once. She had a real talent for putting together words of the same sound. 'Dithery slithery, slithery dithery . . .'

'All right, all right,' said Philip. 'We don't want to hear it again, Kiki. You're a clever old bird, we all know that. Jack, look at this slow-worm. It's not a scrap frightened now.'

'I do think you're mean to keep it,' began Dinah, from a safe distance. 'You know how I hate snakes. All right, all right, I *know* it isn't a snake – though I wouldn't be a bit surprised if it bit me if I came near it, so there!'

'I wouldn't be surprised at anything biting you when you're so nervous,' said Philip crossly. 'I feel like biting you myself. Come here, Dinah. Run your fingers down Sally Slither's back – look at her sharp little eyes . . .'

Dinah gave a scream. 'I couldn't bear it! No, don't come near me, Philip. It's worse than those awful white rats you had a few months ago. But at least they grew up and you let them go!'

'Sally can go whenever she wants to,' said Philip. 'I never keep any pet when it wants to go. Do you want to go, Sally Slither?'

'Slithery dithery, musty dusty fusty,' said Kiki, trying to remember the various collections of words she had picked up at one time or another. 'Huffin and Puffin.'

'Come on – let's go,' said Dinah. 'Perhaps that horrible thing will go back into your pocket if we go. And I'm getting hungry.'

The slow-worm slid back somewhere in Philip's clothes. He got up and Snowy bounded round him. 'Now just see if you can walk without getting your head between my legs all the time,' said Philip to Snowy. 'You'll send me flying in a minute. You're a bit *too* friendly at times, Snowy.'

They went back to the farmhouse, enjoying the sunshine and the constant breeze that blew over the mountain-side. By the time they reached the farmhouse they were all terribly hungry, and visions of ham, chicken, salad and raspberries and cream kept coming into their minds.

Bill and Mrs Mannering had been for a walk too, but down the mountain, not up. They had been back for a little while, and were just beginning to wonder where the children were. Snowy went bounding up to them.

'He's a pet!' said Mrs Mannering. 'I suppose we shall have him at our heels the whole of this holiday now. It's a pity kids have to grow up into goats. Don't think you're going to take Snowy back home with you, Philip. I'm not going to have a goat in the garden, whilst you're at school, eating the vegetables out of the beds, and the clothes off the line!'

'Mother, Trefor says his brother will arrive at the farmhouse tomorrow with the donkeys,' said Philip. 'Can we each choose our own? How many will there be?'

'Yes, you can choose your own if you want to,' said Mrs Mannering. 'I don't know how many there will be – six, I suppose. I only hope I choose a sure-footed one!'

'They'll all be sure-footed,' said Jack. 'As sure-footed as goats. But not so leapy. I shouldn't care to ride one of these mountain goats, and find myself leaping about from rock to rock.'

'Good gracious, what a horrible thought!' said Mrs Mannering. 'I shall choose the quietest, staidest, placidest, best-tempered donkey of the lot – one without a single bound or leap in him.'

Everyone laughed. Effans came over to them, beaming to see them happy. 'It iss dinner-time,' he said. 'Mrs Effans has it ready.'

'I shall soon begin to talk in a sing-song voice myself,' said Lucy-Ann, getting up from the stone wall. 'Indeed to gootness I shall!'

They all laughed at the lilting way she spoke. Snowy galloped ahead into the kitchen. Mrs Evans didn't seem to mind at all, but she shooed him down when he leapt into a chair. A hen scuttled out from under the table. Kiki went up to a rafter, sat on a ham wrapped up in a cloth, and cocked her eye down to the table to see what fruit there was.

'Pop goes the weasel,' she announced, and made a popping noise like a cork coming out of a bottle. Effans looked up in admiration.

'Such a bird!' he said. 'Never have I seen such a bird, look you!'

Kiki began hiccuping, and Effans went off into a roar of laughter. Mrs Mannering frowned.

'Kiki! Stop that! How many times am I to tell you I don't like that noise?'

'How many times have I told you to wipe your feet?' retorted Kiki, and screeched. Effans almost died of laughter. Kiki began to show off, snapping her beak open and shut, putting her crest up and down and making peculiar noises.

'Kiki! Come here!' said Jack sternly, and Kiki flew down to his shoulder. Jack tapped her smartly on her beak. 'Any more nonsense from you and I'll shut you in the bedroom upstairs. Bad bird! Silly bird!'

'Poor Polly! Bad Polly!' said Kiki, and nipped Jack's ear. He smacked her on the beak again.

'Be quiet! Not another word!' he ordered. Kiki put her head under her wing in disgrace, and various whispering sounds came to everyone's ears. But nobody could hear what she said, though Effans strained his ears hopefully. What a bird! He wished he could have one like it.

The dinner was as good as the high tea and breakfast had been. The children set to work and Mrs Evans felt very pleased to see how much her good food was appreciated. She kept pressing second and third helpings on everyone, but soon even the boys could eat no more.

'There iss no four o'clock tea,' she kept saying. 'Nothing till six o'clock. So eat, look you, eat!'

'Dithery slithery,' announced Kiki suddenly, and Dinah gave a scream. The slow-worm was gliding out of Philip's sleeve! He pushed it back hurriedly, hoping that no one had seen it. Bill had. His sharp eyes had caught sight of it at once. He grinned.

'Another member added to the family?' he said. 'Very nice too! What with Snowy and Kiki and – er – Slithery, we look all set for a most interesting holiday.'

5

Arrival of the donkeys

The next excitement, of course, was the arrival of the donkeys. The children had waited expectantly for them all the following morning, not liking to go for a walk in case they missed the donkeys' arrival. Lucy-Ann saw them first.

She gave a yell that sent the slow-worm back into Philip's pocket, and startled Snowy so much that he leapt four feet in the air. Even Kiki jumped.

'The donkeys!' cried Lucy-Ann. 'There they come, look, up the mountain path.'

Soon all four children were tearing down the path to the donkeys. There were eight of them, strong, sturdy little creatures, with big bright eyes, and long tails that whisked the flies away. They were all grey, and their long ears twitched to and fro as they came steadily up the steep path.

Trefor's brother David was with them, an elderly man rather like Trefor but with tidier hair and beard. He had the same bright blue eyes, but he looked timid and shy, as if the world had not been kind to him.

He smiled faintly at the lively children. 'Can we ride four of the donkeys now?' asked Philip. 'We know how to ride. Come on, Lucy-Ann, up with you!'

He gave Lucy-Ann a shove and she was up on a donkey's back. Dinah needed no help. With a leap like Snowy's she was up at once.

The donkeys ambled up the steep path with the children, refusing to trot now that they had heavy weights on their backs. Snowy galloped beside Philip's donkey, half jealous of it, butting it in the legs.

'Hallo! Here we are!' cried Jack, ambling up to Mrs Mannering and Bill. 'Eight donkeys to choose from! Which are you going to have, Aunt Allie?'

David stood by smiling whilst his donkeys were examined and tried. Trefor the shepherd arrived, and the two old brothers chatted together in Welsh. Effans and his wife came along, and soon there was quite a company in the farmyard, discussing the donkeys.

'We badly want to go off on the donkeys into the mountains, Mother,' said Philip coaxingly. 'Can we? With you and Bill, of course. To stay a few nights, I mean. Jack and I think there should be a fine lot of rare birds over there in those lonely mountains – and there will be lots of animals too.'

'It *would* be rather fun,' said his mother. 'I haven't

camped out for ages, and in this weather it would be lovely. What do you say, Bill?'

'I say yes!' said Bill, who loved outdoor life and was an old hand at camping. 'Do you good, Allie. We could take a couple of extra donkeys to carry the things we want.'

'Oh, *Bill!* Can we really go?' said Lucy-Ann, overjoyed, and Dinah danced round him too. To go off on donkeys into the mountains, and take tents and food – what could be more fun?

'It will be an adventure!' said Dinah. 'Not one of our usual ones, of course, but a really nice one. You'll like that, Lucy-Ann, won't you?'

'Oh, *yes*,' said Lucy-Ann, who never really enjoyed a proper adventure whilst it was happening. 'I'd like *that* kind of adventure. When can we go?'

'Well, we'd better get used to our donkeys before we think of going,' said Bill. 'I'm not used to donkey-riding, nor is Aunt Allie. We shall be stiff at first, so we'd better get over that stage before we go. Say next week?'

'Oh – I can't wait that long!' said Dinah, and the others laughed at her long face.

'Effans, where is a nice place to go?' asked Jack, turning to him. Effans considered. He spoke to Trefor in Welsh and the old shepherd answered him.

'He says the Vale of Butterflies in a good place,' said Effans. 'It is full of birds as well as butterflies.'

'The Vale of Butterflies – that sounds gorgeous,' said Jack, pleased.

'Super!' said Philip. 'Absolutely wizard! We'll go there. Is it far?'

'Two days on donkeys,' said Effans.

Bill calculated. 'We shall want a guide – either Trefor, Effans or Trefor's brother – and two donkeys at least to carry our tents and food – and six donkeys for ourselves. That's nine. We've only got eight here. Effans, ask this fellow if he's got another donkey.'

It turned out that Trefor's brother had meant to ride home on a donkey himself, and take another donkey back with farm produce to sell, leaving only six. Effans bargained with him to come back the next week, complete with three donkeys to add to the six left behind.

'Then you can act as guide to these people, look you,' he said. 'That will be money. You will have one donkey, they will have six, and there will be two for loads. That is much money for you, David, indeed to gootness!'

David agreed. He would come on the Wednesday of next week, bringing three donkeys to add to the six he would leave behind. Two to carry loads, one for himself, and six for the children, Mrs Mannering and Bill.

The children were very excited. They ran round the donkeys, patted them, rubbed their long noses and sat on their broad backs. The donkeys seemed to like all the fuss. They stood stolidly there, their tails whisking, following the children with their eyes. Snowy darted about, running under first one donkey and then another, acting like a mad thing.

Trefor helped his brother to load up a donkey with packages of all kinds. Heavier and heavier grew the load, but the donkey stood patiently, seeming not to mind at all. Then, eager to be gone, it suddenly brayed.

Kiki had never heard a donkey bray before and she sailed straight up into the air with fright.

'Ee-ore, ee-ore!' brayed the donkey, and stamped his foot.

'Gracious! Now I suppose Kiki will practise braying too,' said Jack. 'We shall have to stop her firmly if she does. It's bad enough from a donkey – but brays from Kiki would be frightful.'

The donkey was loaded at last. David mounted his sturdy little beast, said a polite goodbye to everyone and rode off down the path, the loaded donkey being led after him by a rope he held in his hand.

'Now we can choose our own donkeys!' said Lucy-Ann in delight. 'Aunt Allie – you choose first.'

'Well, they all look *exactly* alike to me!' said Mrs Mannering. Bill spoke to Effans, asking him if he knew which donkey was the quietest. Effans turned to Trefor.

Trefor knew. He pointed out a little creature with a patient expression in its eyes, and said a few words in Welsh.

'He says that is the one for you,' said Effans. 'It is quiet and good. Its name is Patience.'

'Oh, good – I'll choose her then,' said Mrs Mannering. 'This is mine, children – the one with the black mark on her forehead.'

'I want this one,' cried Lucy-Ann, pulling at a sturdy animal that threw his head back continually, and stamped now and then. 'I like him. What is his name, Trefor?'

Trefor said something nobody understood. Effans translated. 'His name is Clover. This one is Grayling, and that one is Dapple. The other two are Buttercup and Daisy.'

Lucy-Ann had Clover. Jack had Grayling, and Dinah had Dapple. Bill had Buttercup, and Philip had Daisy. Each of them was delighted with his or her own special donkey.

'Let's ride them now,' said Jack, mounting his little beast. 'Come on, Bill. Aunt Allie, get on. We'll go for our first ride now – up the path and back again.'

With Effans and his wife looking on in delight, the six rode off on their donkeys. They would not go fast uphill, and Bill warned each child not to try and make them. 'They'll trot coming down all right,' he said. 'But it's heavy going for them uphill, with our weight on their backs.'

It was great fun riding the grey donkeys up the steep mountain path. Mrs Mannering was nervous at first when she came to the rocky bits, but her donkey was as sure-footed as the others, and went steadily along on even the stoniest parts.

Bill rode close by in case Mrs Mannering needed help, but she didn't. The four children, of course, would have scorned any help. They were all used to riding horses, and the donkeys were very easy to manage.

'Now we'll turn back,' called Bill. So they all turned and went homewards. Snowy came too, of course, having leapt and bounded ahead of them all the way, apparently under the impression that he was leading them.

'That was fun,' said Lucy-Ann, as they trotted homewards, the donkeys going faster now that they were on a downhill road. Mrs Mannering didn't like the trotting so much as the ambling.

'My donkey is a very bumpy one,' she said to Bill. 'When I go down he comes up and when I go up he goes down, so we keep meeting with a bump!'

Everyone laughed. They were all sorry when they reached the farmhouse, for by that time they felt as if they could go trotting on for ever. But a meal was ready for them on the table, and Mrs Evans was beaming at the door, so they didn't lose much time in taking the donkeys to the field and carrying their harness to the stables.

'You'll be quite used to riding a donkey by next week,' Bill said to Mrs Mannering. 'By the time Wednesday comes you'll be ready to set off and you'll feel as if you'd ridden a donkey all your life!'

'Oh, yes, I'm sure I shall,' said Mrs Mannering. She

felt something pecking at her foot and looked under the table. She saw a fat brown hen there and pushed it away. 'Shoo! Stop pecking my foot!'

The hen shooed, only to be replaced by Snowy, who, pushed off Philip's knee as he sat at table, was amusing himself by trying to eat shoe-laces under the table. Mrs Mannering pushed him him away too, and Snowy went to chew the hem of Mrs Evans' dress. She never noticed things like that, so Snowy had a nice long chew.

The next day the girls and Mrs Mannering were so stiff with their donkey-ride that they could hardly walk. The boys and Bill were all right, but Mrs Mannering groaned as she came down the stairs.

'Good gracious! I feel like an old old lady! I'll never be able to ride a donkey again!' she said.

But the stiffness wore off, and the six of them soon got used to riding their donkeys day after day into the mountains. There were some lovely rides and magnificent views. Snowy came with them always, never tired, leaping along gaily. Kiki rode on Jack's shoulder, occasionally taking a flight into the air to scare any bird that happened to be flying overhead. They flew off quickly, full of astonishment when Kiki told them to wipe their feet.

'Two days more and it's Wednesday,' said Lucy-Ann happily. 'We'll be quite ready then – able to ride for hours and hours.'

'Yes – off to the Vale of Butterflies!' said Jack. 'I

wonder what it's like! I imagine it to be full of wings of all colours. Lovely!'

'Oh, hurry up and come, Wednesday!' said Dinah. 'Only forty-eight hours – and then, off we go!'

But something unexpected happened in that forty-eight hours – something that quite upset their lovely plans!

6

Off to the Vale of Butterflies

It happened the very next day. It was when Mrs Mannering had gone with Mrs Evans to the big barn. The door suddenly blew shut, and caught her hand in it, trapping it tightly.

Mrs Mannering screamed. Mrs Evans ran to open the door, but poor Mrs Mannering's hand was badly bruised and crushed.

Bill was very concerned. 'I must take you down to the doctor,' he said. 'I'll get the car. Where are the children? Out on their donkeys? Tell them where we've gone, Mrs Evans, when they come back. They needn't worry. I'll have Mrs Mannering's hand seen to, and properly bandaged. I don't expect it will be very much, but I'd like her to have it X-rayed in case any small bone is broken.'

Looking rather white, Mrs Mannering was driven off by Bill, down the steep mountain road to the town that lay some way off in the next valley. It was about fifteen miles and soon Mrs Mannering was in hospital having her hand X-rayed and bound up.

The children were very upset when they heard what had happened. 'Poor Mother!' said Philip. 'It must have hurt dreadfully when her hand got caught in that heavy door.'

'Indeed to gootness, it did,' said Mrs Evans, who looked quite upset too. 'She gave one scream, poor soul, and then made not a sound, whateffer. Now don't look so sadly – she'll be back tonight.'

'Will she be able to go off to the mountains tomorrow?' asked Lucy-Ann. 'How can she ride with a bad hand?'

'Well, there now, she can't,' said Mrs Evans. 'But she can stay here with me and I'll look after her for you. You can go with Mr Cunningham and David.'

'But will Bill go if Mother's hurt?' wondered Philip. 'He thinks the world of her. Oh, blow! It's bad luck for this to happen just when we had such a lovely plan. Poor Mother! I do hope her hand's better now.'

Mrs Mannering arrived back in Bill's car that evening, just before high tea. She looked better, and made light of her hand.

'We've had it X-rayed,' said Bill. 'She's broken a tiny bone just here,' and he showed them where, on the back of his hand. 'It's got to be bandaged and kept at rest. I'm to take her down to have it seen again in three days' time.'

'I'm so sorry, dears,' said Mrs Mannering. 'And Bill, you don't need to take me down, you know. I'm quite able to drive myself down even with an injured hand. Take the children on their trip tomorrow. I can't bear to have them disappointed.'

'What! And leave you like this!' said Bill. 'Don't be silly, Allie. I shall take you down myself in the car on Friday. The children can go with David, if he'll take them on by himself. It's a perfectly ordinary trip, and they'll be back in a few days' time. They can all ride their donkeys as easily as David – and probably they'll enjoy a trip without us!'

'We'd *much* rather you and Aunt Allie came,' said Jack. 'But as you can't, it's decent of you to let us go alone. We'll be perfectly all right, Bill. David knows the way, and we can all look after ourselves.'

So it was settled that the four children should go by themselves on the donkeys with their guide David, taking with them tents, bedding and food. Philip questioned Bill to make sure that his mother's hand was not seriously hurt.

'Oh, no – it will soon be right,' said Bill. 'But I want to be sure she doesn't use it, and I want to take her down to the doctor in three days' time. I'm sorry not to come with you – but you'll be all right by yourselves. I don't see that you can get into any trouble, or any startling adventure, going donkey-riding in the mountains with David. Maybe we can all go together, later on.'

The children were very excited that night, getting ready the things they wanted to take. They had two small tents, a sleeping-bag each, two ground-sheets, cameras, field-glasses, a change of clothes – and food.

The food was Mrs Evans' care. Bill watched her packing up what she thought they would eat in the next few days.

'I didn't like to stop her,' he told the others. 'But, honestly, she's packed enough for a month. She's put in a whole ham!'

'Golly!' said Jack. 'What else?'

'A tongue or two, hard-boiled eggs, tins of all kinds, plum-cake and goodness knows what!' said Philip. 'We shall feast like kings.'

'Well,' began Lucy-Ann, 'I always think that we eat twice as much in the open air, because food tastes so . . .'

'Much nicer!' chorused everyone. Lucy-Ann always said that at least a dozen times each holidays. She laughed.

'Well, anyway, it will be nice to have as much as ever we can eat. There's David too – we've got to take food for him as well.'

'He doesn't look as if he'd eat much,' said Dinah. 'Skinny little fellow, he is!'

'You'd better go to bed early, children,' said Mrs Mannering a little later. 'You'll have a long ride tomorrow, according to Effans.'

'All right. It'll make tomorrow come all the sooner!' said Lucy-Ann. 'How's your hand feel, Aunt Allie?'

'It's quite comfortable, thank you,' said Mrs Mannering. 'I'm sure I could have gone with you to-morrow, really!'

'Well, you couldn't,' said Bill hastily, half afraid that Mrs Mannering would try to be foolish and go with the others after all. She laughed.

'Don't worry! I'm going to be sensible – and, dear me, it will be quite a change to be rid of four noisy ruffians and an even noisier bird for a few days, Bill, won't it?'

All the children were awake very early the next day. Snowy the kid, who was a real sleepy-head in the mornings, didn't want to wake up at all, and snuggled deeper into Philip's blankets as the boy tried to get out of bed.

Kiki took her head from under her wing and scratched her poll. 'Dithery Slithery,' she remarked, which meant that she had spied Philip's slow-worm. It was coiled up in a corner of the room. It would very much have liked to sleep on Philip's bed, but it was afraid of Snowy, who had a habit of nibbling anything near him.

The boys got up and looked out of the window. It was a really perfect day. The mountains towered up into the fresh morning sky, as beautiful as ever.

'They look as if someone had just been along and washed them,' said Jack. 'The sky looks washed too – so very very clean and new.'

'I like the feel of an early morning,' said Philip, putting on his shorts. 'It has a special *new* feel about it – as if it was the first morning that ever happened!'

Snowy went over to the corner where Sally the slow-worm was, and the slow-worm at once wriggled away under the chest of drawers. Philip picked her up and she slid gracefully into his pocket.

'Have to get you a few flies for breakfast, Sally,' said Philip. 'Shut up, Kiki – you'll wake the rest of the household with that awful cough.'

Kiki could give a terrible, hollow cough at times, which she had copied from an old uncle of Jack's, and she was practising it now. She stopped when Philip spoke to her, and hopped to Jack's shoulder.

'Funny bird, silly bird,' said Jack affectionately, scratching her neck. 'Come on, Philip – let's see if the girls are up.'

They were just getting up, both of them thrilled at the fine day and the idea of going camping in the mountains. 'Have you got that horrid slow-worm on you?' asked Dinah fearfully, looking at Philip.

'Yes, somewhere about,' said Philip, feeling all over him. 'There's one thing about Sally Slithery – she does get about!'

Dinah shuddered and went to wash in the bathroom. Snowy the kid was there, nibbling the cork bath-mat, which he evidently thought was delicious.

'Oh, Snowy! Mrs Evans won't be at all pleased with

you!' said Dinah, and shooed the kid out of the door. He went to find Philip. He was quite one of the family now.

Mrs Mannering's hand was stiff and sore that morning, but she said very little about it, not wanting to upset the children. She was glad it was such a lovely day for them, and watched with amusement as Mrs Evans carefully packed up all the food she had prepared for the children to take with them.

'If you eat all that you'll never be able to ride home on the donkeys,' she said. 'You'll be too fat.'

'They must not go hungry,' said kind Mrs Evans. 'There! I think I have thought of everything. Children, you must use one donkey for the food and the other for everything else, look you. I will see that David straps everything on well.'

The children listened to her kind, lilting voice as they sat at breakfast. They felt very happy, and the only thing that spoilt their pleasure was the fact that Bill and Mrs Mannering were not coming with them. On the other hand, they would be freer without grown-ups!

Kiki gave a hiccup, with one eye on Mrs Mannering. She looked at the parrot severely. 'Kiki! You did that on purpose. Do you want your beak smacked?'

'Pardon,' said Kiki, and went off into a cackle of laughter. Effans choked over his bacon, trying to laugh with his mouth full, and went purple in the face. His bacon went down the wrong way, and he got the hiccups too.

'Pardon, look you!' he said to Mrs Mannering, with such a horrified look on his face that everyone roared with laughter.

'Now here is David, all ready for you!' cried Mrs Evans from the door, where she had gone to chase away a turkey that had suddenly appeared. It made a gobbling noise that scared Snowy terribly. Kiki, of course, at once gobbled too, and the turkey looked into the kitchen in amazement. 'Shoo!' said Mrs Evans. 'Good morning, David, it's early you are, and a nice day you have brought with you!'

'Indeed to gootness I have,' said David and smiled timidly at the company in the big kitchen. His donkeys crowded round him, sturdy and patient, their harness clinking and glinting.

'Come on!' yelled Jack, suddenly feeling too excited to sit at the table any longer. 'Come on! Let's pack the things on the donkeys and go!'

They all rushed out. Soon David and Effans were strapping everything on two donkeys. One donkey had big panniers each side for food. The other had the things strapped across his broad little back. They stood perfectly still, their ears twitching as a fly or two settled on them.

'Well – are we ready to start?' said Philip. 'I think we've got everything. Oh, gosh, where are my field-glasses?'

At last everyone and everything was ready. It had been

explained to David that Bill and Mrs Mannering could not come, and Effans had said he would care for the two extra donkeys till the children came back. David did not seem too pleased to think he was to go alone with the children. He looked rather alarmed, Bill thought. Poor fellow! Bill wished it was Effans who was going with the children, not David. Still, the children were used to camping out and could be trusted to be sensible.

'Goodbye!' called everyone. 'See you in a few days' time. Take care of your hand, Mother! Now we're off – off to the Vale of Butterflies! Goodbye, everyone!'

7

On the way

With Bill, Mrs Mannering, Effans and Mrs Evans
waving and calling goodbye, the party set off on their
donkeys. They had to go up by Trefor the shepherd's
little cabin, and the donkeys picked their way steadily
up the steep hillside.

Snowy ran beside them, bobbing about under the
donkeys' bodies as he pleased. They seemed to like him,
and Dapple kept putting his head down to the kid whenever he came near. Kiki was perched as usual on Jack's
shoulder, jogging up and down contentedly, snapping
her beak, and making a few quiet remarks into Jack's ear.

They came to Trefor's cabin. He was on the hillside,
seeing to a sick sheep. He came to meet them, his untidy
hair blowing in the wind, and his eyes shining as blue as
forget-me-nots.

There was a conversation between the two men in
Welsh. David sounded rather complaining. Trefor
seemed to be pooh-poohing what he said. David got out

a map that Bill had given him, and appeared to be saying that he didn't understand it at all.

Trefor then spoke earnestly, pointing in this direction and that, poking David with his finger every time he wanted to make a point go home. The children thought he must be telling David the exact way to go.

'I hope David really does know the way,' said Jack. 'He might have thought Bill would help him with the map if Bill had been going. It looks to me as if he's telling Trefor he's not too certain of the way.'

'Well, what does it matter?' said Philip, pushing Snowy off with his hand as the kid tried to jump up on to his donkey with him. 'I'd *like* to see the Vale of Butterflies – but so long as we go off camping in those gorgeous mountains, that's all that matters.'

'Yes. We shall see heaps of birds and animals anyway,' said Jack, feeling that Philip was right. 'Come on, David! Let's go!'

David leapt on to his donkey at once. He called goodbye to Trefor, and the little company set off once more, taking a narrow path along the mountain-side that went neither very far up, nor very far down.

It was glorious riding there, so high, looking down on the valley far below. It was partly in the sun and partly in the shadow, for the sun was not yet high. Swallows flew round them catching flies, their steel-blue wings gleaming in the sun. Kiki watched them out of her sharp eyes. She had often tried fly-catching herself, but she knew she was no good at it. Anyway, flies didn't taste as good as fruit!

They ambled on until everyone felt hungry and thirsty. They came to a copse of birch-trees with a small stream near by.

'Let's picnic here,' said Philip, sliding off his donkey. 'In the shade of those trees. I'm absolutely cooked with the sun.'

David saw to the donkeys, taking them to the stream for water. He then let them wander free, for they came most obediently at his call, and could be trusted not to go too far away. They went to the shade of the trees and stood there, swishing their long grey tails, enjoying the rest.

Snowy ran to them, and behaved like a spoilt child, letting the donkeys fuss him and stare at him. Dapple put down his big head to the little kid, and nuzzled him in the neck. When Snowy ran to the next donkey Dapple followed him.

'Dapple wants to be friends with Snowy,' said Dinah, unpacking the lunch parcel from one of the enormous panniers. 'Here, Lucy-Ann – take this tin and fill it with water from the stream. It must be absolutely pure, I should think. We can put some of this lemonade essence with it. I'm so dreadfully thirsty!'

David was drinking at the stream, so the children felt that it must be all right. It gurgled along, fresh and clear, running through the pebbles and down the hillside at top speed. Lucy-Ann went to fill the tin.

There was a lovely lunch. The children had to call David to share it because he suddenly seemed shy. He came and sat down a little way away from them.

'No, David. Come here with us,' called Jack, patting the ground. 'We want to learn Welsh! Come and talk to us!'

But the old Welshman was very shy, and it was as much as the children could do to persuade him to eat his share of the lunch. It was such a good lunch too!

There were five different kinds of sandwiches, fresh lettuce wrapped in a damp cloth, hard-boiled eggs to nibble, and great slices of jam tart. Washed down with cold lemonade it was the finest lunch anyone could wish.

'Nobody in the whole world, not even the very richest king, can possibly have a nicer lunch than this,' said Lucy-Ann, munching a chicken sandwich.

'Or a nicer place to eat it in,' said Philip, waving his sandwich at the magnificent view before them. 'Look at that! No king could have a better view from his palace than that! Valleys and mountains, and yet more mountains, and then the clear blue sky! Marvellous!'

They all gazed at the unbelievable view that lay in front of them. A rustle of paper made them look round.

'Snowy! You greedy little kid! Look here, he's eaten the rest of the chicken sandwiches!' cried Jack indignantly, forgetting all about the lovely view. 'Philip, smack him. We can't let him do that or our food won't last out. He can jolly well eat the grass.'

Philip gave Snowy a smart tap on the nose. The kid retreated in a huff, taking with him a mouthful of sandwich papers, which he proceeded to eat with apparent enjoyment. But soon he was back with Philip, pressing against him affectionately, anxious to be back in his good books. Dapple the donkey moved over to Philip too, to be near the kid. He lay down beside him, and Philip at once leaned back against him.

'Thanks, old man! Very nice! Just what I wanted!' said Philip, and everyone laughed as he settled himself against the donkey's side.

'Have another sandwich, David?' asked Lucy-Ann, holding out a packet to him. David had not eaten nearly as much as they had, either through shyness or because he hadn't such an enormous appetite. He shook his head.

'Let's have a bit of rest now,' said Philip sleepily. 'There's no hurry. We can take all the time we like to get anywhere.'

Jack began to ask David the names of things in Welsh. It was silly not to be able to talk to David. David apparently understood more English than he spoke, but even the few English words he said were pronounced so differently that the children found it hard to puzzle out what he was saying.

'Come on, David, talk,' said Jack, who did not feel as

sleepy as the others. 'What's this in Welsh?' He held out his hand.

David began to realize that Jack wanted a lesson in Welsh, and he brightened up a little. He was a trifle embarrassed by Kiki, who insisted on repeating all the words he said too, and added a few nonsense words of her own for good measure.

The girls and Philip fell asleep in the shade, Lucy-Ann sharing Philip's donkey to lean against. Dinah would have liked to do the same but she was afraid that Sally the slow-worm might come out of Philip's pocket if she did, and nothing would make Dinah go near the silvery creature!

Jack patiently tried to learn a few Welsh words, and then got tired of it. He threw a few pebbles down the mountain-side, and gazed round at the many summits towering up in the distance. There was one odd one, shaped like three teeth, that amused him. He decided to look it up on the map.

The map, however, was rather disappointing. It showed very few names in the district where they were, probably because it had been very little visited, and there were no farmhouses or other buildings to put on record. Jack found a name that seemed to him to fit the mountain. 'Fang Mountain,' he read. 'That might be it. Gosh, what a lot of mountains there are about here! I bet nobody has ever explored them all. I'd like to fly over them in an aeroplane and look down on them. We

haven't seen a plane since we've been here. Off the route,
I suppose.'

David had gone to round up the donkeys. Jack woke
up the others. 'Come on, lazy things! We'd better get on,
or David will think we mean to camp here for the night.
There's a heavenly wind got up now. It will be gorgeous
riding this afternoon.'

Soon they were all on their donkeys again, jogging
along round the mountain-side, enjoying the wind and
the sun, gazing on the different vistas that opened up
before them round every bend of the track. New mountains reared up far-away heads, new skylines appeared.
For long stretches the children said nothing at all to one
another, but simply drank in the beauty around them,
and the sun and wind.

They travelled until six o'clock, having decided to
keep to the high tea that Mrs Evans had at the farm. Jack
spoke to David when six o'clock came.

'David! We stop at half-past six. Do you know a good
place to camp for the night near here?'

David did not understand and Jack repeated it more
slowly. David smiled and nodded.

'Iss! Iss!' This meant 'yes', and Jack looked as David
pointed to a wooded spot some way ahead. David said
something else in Welsh, and Jack caught a few words
here and there which he understood. One was 'water',
the other was 'trees'.

'David says there's a good place to camp in a little way

off!' Jack shouted back to the others. 'There's water there, and trees.'

'Gosh! However do you understand him?' said Philip in admiration. 'Jolly clever of you, Jack!'

Jack grinned all over his freckled face. 'Oh, I just caught the words "water" and "trees", that's all! Come on, let's get there in time to watch the sun sink over the mountains. I'd like to have a sunset with my sandwiches!'

Philip laughed. They all ambled on towards the spot pointed out by David. It was a little further than they thought, but when they got there they all agreed it was just the right place to camp for the night.

A spring gushed out beside the small wooded patch, as cold as ice. The trees sheltered the campers from the night-wind, which could be very chilly at times. The donkeys were to be tied to trees so that they would not wander in the night. Everything was perfect!

The children were tired but happy. They slid off their donkeys' backs, and the little beasts, tired now too, were taken to the spring to drink. They stood patiently waiting their turn, whilst Snowy skipped about like a mad thing, not in the least tired with his long trip.

'We'll put up the tents after we've had a meal and a rest,' said Philip. 'Get out the food, Lucy-Ann and Dinah. There's a nice flat stone here we can use as a table.'

Soon the supper, or high tea, was spread out on the big flat stone, and mugs of lemonade were set by each plate. The children drained them at once, and Jack was sent to get more ice-cold water from the spring.

They all ate quickly, for they were very hungry again. They said very little until the first edge of their appetite had worn off, then they all talked with their mouths full, eager to make the others remember the lovely day.

David ate too and listened. The donkeys pulled at the grass. Snowy was with Dapple, and Kiki was eating a tomato and dripping the juice down Jack's neck. They all felt as if they couldn't possibly be happier.

'Now we'll put up the tents,' said Jack at last. 'Come on, Philip! It'll be dark before we've put them up if we don't make haste!'

8

First night in camp

The girls washed the dirty crockery in the cold spring water whilst David and the boys unpacked the tents from the donkey that carried them. They took off the whole of his pack, and also unstrapped the heavy panniers from the other donkey. Both were delighted to be rid of their loads. They lay down on the ground and rolled, kicking their legs up into the air.

Kiki couldn't understand this at all, and flew up into a tree. 'She thinks they've gone mad,' said Jack. 'It's all right, Kiki, they're only feeling glad because their packs have gone!'

Kiki made a noise like a train screeching in a tunnel, and the two rolling donkeys leapt to their feet in alarm and raced some way down the hill. David also jumped violently, and then called to the donkeys.

'Kiki, if you do that again I'll tie your beak up!' threatened Jack. 'Spoiling this lovely peaceful evening with that horrible screech!'

'Wipe your feet, wipe your feet!' screamed Kiki and danced from foot to foot on her branch.

The tents were soon put up, side by side. David did not want to sleep in one. He preferred to sleep outside. He had never slept in a tent, and he thought they were quite unnecessary.

'Well, I'd just as soon he slept outside,' said Jack to Philip. 'I don't believe there'd be room for one more in here, do you?'

'Let's leave the tent-flaps open,' said Lucy-Ann, coming up with the clean crockery. 'Then we can look out down the mountain-side. I wouldn't mind a bit sleeping in the open air, like David, as a matter of fact.'

'Wind's too cold,' said Jack. 'You'll be glad to have a cosy sleeping-bag, Lucy-Ann! David must be very hardy – he's only got a thin rug to cover himself with, and he's apparently going to sleep on the bare ground!'

The sun had now disappeared completely. It had gone behind the mountains in a perfect blaze of colour, and all the summits had gleamed for a while, and then darkness had crept up to the very tops, leaving only a clear sky beyond. Stars were now winking here and there, and a cold wind was blowing up the mountain.

The donkeys were tied loosely to trees. Some of them were lying down. Dapple was looking out for Snowy, but the kid had gone to Philip, and was waiting for him to go into his tent.

They all washed at the spring – but David seemed

rather astonished to see the four children solemnly splashing themselves with the cold water. He had drawn his thin rug over him and was lying quite still, looking up to the starry sky.

'He's not what you might call a very *cheerful* companion, is he?' said Jack. 'I expect he thinks we're all quite mad, the way we joke and laugh and fool about. Buck up, Philip, and get into the tent.'

The girls were already in their tent. They had slid down into their sleeping-bags and tied them up loosely at the neck. Each bag had a big hood to come over the head. They were comfortable, quite roomy, and very warm.

Lucy-Ann could see out of the tent opening. Stars twinkled in the sky, looking very big and bright. There was no sound at all, except of the trickle-trickle of the spring, and the sound of the wind in the trees.

'We might be alone in the world,' said Lucy-Ann to Dinah. 'Dinah, imagine that we are. It gives you an awfully queer feeling. It's wizard!'

But Dinah hadn't got Lucy-Ann's imagination and she yawned. 'Go to sleep,' she said. 'Are the boys in their tent yet? I wish they were a bit further away. I've got an awful feeling that slow-worm will come slithering here in the night.'

'It won't hurt you if it does,' said Lucy-Ann, snuggling down in her sleeping-bag. 'Oh, this is super! I do think we have lovely hols, don't you, Dinah?'

But Dinah was asleep already. Her eyes had shut and she was dreaming. Lucy-Ann stayed awake a little longer, enjoying the sound of the running spring and the wind. She still felt rather as if she was on her donkey, jogging up and down. Then her eyes closed too.

The boys talked for a little while. They had thoroughly enjoyed their day. They gazed out of the open flap of the tent. 'It's pretty wild and desolate, here,' said Jack sleepily. 'It's surprising there's a track to follow, really. Decent of Bill and Aunt Allie to let us come by ourselves!'

'Mmmmmmm!' said Philip, listening, but too sleepy to answer.

'Mmmmmmm!' imitated Kiki from the top of the tent outside. It was too hot for her in it.

'There's Kiki,' said Jack. 'I wondered where she was. Philip, aren't you hot with Snowy on top of you?'

'Mmmmmmm!' said Philip, and again there came the echo from the tent-top. 'Mmmmmmm!'

Snowy was almost on top of Philip. He had tried his hardest to squeeze into the boy's sleeping-bag with him, but Philip was quite firm about that.

'If you think you're going to stick your sharp little hooves into me all night long, you're wrong, Snowy,' he said, and tied up his bag firmly at the neck, in case Snowy should try any tricks in the night. The slow-worm was somewhere about too. Philip was too sleepy to bother to think where. Sally slid about where she pleased. Philip was now quite used to the sudden slithering movement that occurred at times somewhere about his body, which meant that Sally was on the move again.

There were a few more quiet remarks from Kiki, who was apparently talking to herself. Then silence. The little camp slept under the stars. The night-wind nosed into the tent, but could not get into the cosy sleeping-bags. Snowy felt too hot, walked over Philip, trod on Jack and went to lie in the tent opening. He gave a tiny bleat and Kiki bleated in answer.

David was up and about before the children the next day. He was looking at his donkeys when Philip put a tousled head out of the tent opening to sniff at the morning. 'Lovely!' he said. 'Stop butting me, Snowy! Your little head is jolly hard! Jack! Stir yourself. It's a gorgeous morning.'

Soon all the campers were out of their sleeping-bags and running about. They splashed at the spring, laughing at nothing. Snowy bounded everywhere, quite mad too. Kiki hooted like a car, and startled the donkeys. Even David smiled to see such early-morning antics!

They had breakfast – tongue, cream cheese and rather stale bread, with a tomato each. There was no lemonade left because they had been so lavish with it the day before, so they drank the cold spring water and vowed it was just as nice as lemonade.

'David! Shall we get to the Vale of Butterflies today?' asked Jack, and then repeated it again slowly, flapping his arms to show David that he was talking about butterflies. It took David a minute or two to realize this. Then he shook his head.

'Tomorrow?' asked Philip, and David nodded. He went to strap the packs on the donkeys again and to put on the big pannier baskets. All the little grey creatures were waiting impatiently to set off. Already the sun was getting well above the mountains, and, for David and the donkeys at any rate, it was late!

They set off at last, though Jack had to gallop back to get his field-glasses which he had left behind, hanging from a tree-branch. Then they were all in a line, one donkey behind the other, ambling over the mountains with the wind in their hair.

Jack felt sure he saw a couple of buzzards that day and rode most of the time with his field-glasses in his hand, ready to clap them to his eyes at the first sight of specks in the sky. The others saw red squirrels among the trees they passed, shy but tame. One shared the children's lunch, darting up for tit-bits, but keeping a wary eye for Kiki and Snowy.

'It wants to come with you, Philip,' said Lucy-Ann, amused when the red squirrel put a paw on Philip's knee.

Philip stroked the pretty little thing gently. It quivered, half frightened, but did not bound away. Then Kiki swooped down and the squirrel fled.

'You *would* spoil things, you jealous bird!' said Philip.

'Go away, I don't want you. Go to Jack, and let the squirrels come to me.'

Swallows flew round them once again, not attracted by the food, but by the flies that pestered the donkeys. The children could hear the snapping of their beaks as they caught the flies.

'We ought to get Jack to tame a few swallows and take them with us to catch the flies,' said Lucy-Ann, slapping at a big one on her leg. 'Horrid things! I've been bitten by something already. You wouldn't think there'd be any as high up as this, would you?'

Sally the slow-worm came out to eat the fly that Lucy-Ann had killed. She was getting much too tame for Dinah's liking. She lay in the sun, gleaming like silver, and then slid under Philip as Snowy came up enquiringly.

'Keep your nose out of things,' said Philip, pushing the kid away as it tried to nose under him to find the slow-worm. Snowy butted him hard and then tried to get on his lap.

'Too hot, too hot,' said Philip. 'Why did we ever bring a little pest like you, Snowy? You breathed down my neck all night!'

Lucy-Ann giggled. She loved Snowy. They all did. The kid was mischievous, given to butting, and didn't mind treading on anyone – but he was so lively, so full of spring and bounce, so affectionate that it was impossible to be cross with him for long.

'Come on,' said Philip at last. 'David's clearing his throat as if he's going to tell us we're too lazy for words.'

David had a habit of clearing his throat about a dozen times before he spoke. It was a nervous habit which Kiki copied to perfection. She would sit near him, and make a noise as if she was clearing her throat every time he did the same thing. Then she would go off into a cackle of laughter. David always stared at her solemnly when she did this.

They travelled well that second day, and went a long way. When the time came to camp again, David looked earnestly over the mountains as if he was searching for something.

'Lost your handkerchief, old chap?' said Jack, and everyone laughed. David looked solemnly at him, not understanding. Then he suddenly began to flap his arms like wings, and to say a few words in Welsh.

He looked comical standing there, flapping like that. The children had to turn away, trying not to laugh. 'He says tomorrow we shall see the butterfly valley,' said Jack. 'Good! It ought to be a real sight, if it's anything like I imagine it to be!'

They had a meal and prepared to camp out again. The evening was not so fine as the day. It had clouded over and there was no sunset to watch, and no stars to come gleaming out, one by one.

'If it rains, you'll get wet, David,' said Jack. David shrugged his shoulders and said something in his Welsh voice, then wrapped himself in his rug on the bare ground.

'It won't rain,' said Philip, looking at the sky. 'But it's much colder. Brrrrr! I'll be glad of my sleeping-bag tonight.'

'Good night!' called the girls. 'Sleep well.'

'Good night! It will be a lovely day again tomorrow! You just see!' called back Philip, who thought himself a good weather forecaster.

But he was wrong. When they awoke the next morning, they looked out on a completely different world!

9

A different world

Lucy-Ann awoke first. She was cold. She snuggled down into her sleeping-bag, and then opened her eyes. She stared out of the open tent-flap, expecting to see the green mountain-side, and the distant mountains towering up into the sky.

But they weren't there! Instead, a white mist swirled past the tent-flap, some of it putting thin cold fingers into the tent itself.

There was nothing to see at all except this mist. The mountains had gone, the trees by the camp were blotted out, even the donkeys couldn't be seen.

'What's happened?' said Lucy-Ann, astonished. 'Golly! It's a thick mist come up!'

She awoke Dinah and the girls peered out in dismay at the misty mountain-side. Now and again a tiny bit of view could be seen as the mist thinned a little – but it grew thick again at once.

'It's a cloud,' said Dinah. 'You know how we see

clouds resting on mountain-tops – well, this is one. It's resting on *us*! It's like a thick fog we can't see through. Blow!'

The boys woke up then and the girls could hear their dismayed voices. They called to them.

'Jack! Philip! Isn't this sickening! We can't see a thing!'

'It may clear when we've had breakfast,' said Philip cheerfully, appearing out of the mist with Snowy at his heels. 'Gosh, it's chilly! I'm going to put on a warm jersey.'

David also appeared, looking very doleful. He swung his arm out towards the valley and poured out a torrent of Welsh.

'He's quite excited about it, isn't he?' said Jack. 'I wish I could follow him when he talks like that. I just don't understand a word.'

They decided to have breakfast in one of the tents because the mist made everything damp and chilly. David preferred to stay outside. Dinah didn't want to come into the tent because of Sally, and only agreed to if she was allowed to sit in the doorway, ready to escape if the slow-worm appeared.

It was not so cheerful a meal as usual. The children missed the magnificent view they had been used to, and were afraid perhaps David wouldn't take them on their way that day. But the mist cleared a little in an hour's time, and David seemed quite willing to go.

They loaded up the donkeys, mounted and set off

down the track. They could see some way ahead of them now, for the sun was rising higher, and trying to dissolve the mist with its heat.

'It'll be all right,' said Jack. 'I *almost* caught sight of the sun then!'

But then the mist came down again and it was only just possible to see the donkey in front.

'I feel as if I ought to hold your donkey's tail, in case you disappear in the mist!' shouted Jack to Dinah. 'You know – like elephants do in circuses when they come into the ring all holding on to one another's tails!'

The mist thickened even more, and the little company stopped to discuss what to do. It was difficult to get anything intelligible out of David, who seemed suddenly to have forgotten any English words he knew.

Jack flapped his arms, raised his eyebrows and pointed in front of him, meaning to ask if they were near the Butterfly Valley. David understood, but he hesitated.

'I hope he hasn't lost the way,' said Jack to Philip. 'He seemed sure enough of the direction yesterday – now he doesn't seem very certain. Blow!'

'Well, we can't stop here,' said Dinah, shivering in the clammy mist. 'There's no shelter and it's jolly cold. Oh for the sun again!'

'Ride on!' said Jack to David. 'It's the only thing to do till we find some kind of shelter. It's too cold to hang about till the mist has gone. If we go the wrong way we can turn back and go right when the mist goes.'

So they went on, following David's donkey through the wet mist. Kiki was very silent. She didn't understand the mist and was afraid of it. Snowy kept close to Philip's donkey, and was not nearly so full of spring and liveliness. Everyone disliked the mist thoroughly.

'When we find a sheltered place we'll stop for lunch,' said Philip. 'I'm sure we're all getting frightfully hungry now, but we seem to be on quite a bare bit of mountainside, hopeless to picnic in. We'd all be down with colds tomorrow!'

They ambled on, nose to tail, pulling their jerseys close, glad of their coats too. Jack began to look rather worried. He stopped his donkey and went to walk beside Philip's.

'What's up?' said Philip, seeing Jack's serious face.

'We've left the track,' said Jack. 'Haven't you noticed? We've followed some kind of track up till an hour or two back – but now I'm pretty certain we've lost it. Goodness knows where David's heading for. I doubt if he's even noticed we're not on any track at all.'

Philip whistled. 'Don't let the girls hear you. They'll be scared. Yes, you're right. There's not the vestige of a track here. David's lost the way.'

'Better ask him,' said Jack and rode to the front of the line. 'Is this the right way?' he asked David slowly, so as to be understood. 'Where is the track?' He pointed downwards to the ground.

David was looking solemn too. He shrugged his

shoulders and said something in his sing-song voice. Jack
rode back to Philip.

'I think he knows he's off the track, but he's hoping to
pick it up further on. Anyway he doesn't seem inclined
to stop or go back.'

'Well – he's our guide,' said Philip, after a pause.
'We'll have to trust him. He knows these mountains
better than we do.'

'Yes. But he's so shy,' said Jack. 'He wouldn't be able
to tell us we were lost. I wouldn't put it past him to go
on losing us deeper and deeper in these mountains, once
he'd begun! He just wouldn't know what else to do.'

'What a horrible idea!' said Philip. 'Good thing we've
got so much food with us, if that's what he means to do!'

They came at last to a big outcrop of rocks, which
would give them shelter from the wet, chilly wind.
'Better have a meal here,' said Philip. 'I'd like something
hot to drink. Did Mrs Evans put in a kettle?'

'Yes. If we can find a stream or spring, we'll build a
little fire and boil some water for cocoa or something,'
said Jack.

But there was no spring and no stream. It was most
annoying.

'Considering the *dozens* we've passed this morning,
and waded through, I call it a bit hard that there's not
even a tiny one here,' said Dinah. 'I'm jolly thirsty too.'

They had to have a meal without anything to drink.
They were very hungry, and the food seemed to warm

them a little. They played a game of Catch to get themselves thoroughly warm after the meal. David looked as if he thought they had gone mad. Snowy joined in wildly, neatly tripping everyone up. Kiki rose in the air and screamed.

'Look at David's face! He thinks we're all crazy!' giggled Lucy-Ann. She sank down on a rock. 'Oh, I can't run any more. I've got a stitch in my side.'

'Stitchinmyside, stitchinmyside,' chanted Kiki, running all the words together. 'Pop goes the weasel!'

'The mist's clearing! Hurrah!' suddenly cried Jack, and he pointed upwards. The sun could quite clearly be seen, struggling to get through the clouds of mist.

Everyone cheered up at once. Even David looked less dismal. 'Let's try to get to the Butterfly Valley before the evening,' said Jack to David, doing the flapping business vigorously to make sure David understood. David nodded.

They mounted the donkeys again and set off once more. They could see much further in front of them now. Quite a big stretch of mountain-side was spread before them. The world suddenly seemed a much bigger place.

They rode on steadily. The mist thinned more and more rapidly, and the children felt the heat of the sun on their heads. They took off their coats, revelling in the warmth, after the chilliness of the mist.

'Look – we can see the nearest mountain-tops now,'

called Jack. 'And the distant ones will soon be uncovered too. Thank goodness!'

'We ought to see the Vale of Butterflies soon,' said Lucy-Ann, eagerly. 'David said we'd get there today. I wonder where it is. Look, there's a butterfly, Philip.'

Philip glanced at it. 'Only a meadow-brown,' he said. 'We've seen heaps of those.' He looked before him searchingly and then put his field-glasses to his eyes.

'There's a valley which *might* be it,' he said, pointing. 'Hey, David! Is that the Vale of Butterflies?'

David looked where Philip was pointing. He shrugged his shoulders. 'Iss. No,' he said.

'Yes, no! Whatever does he mean by that?' said Philip in disgust. 'I suppose, in plain English, he means he hasn't the faintest idea. Well, we'll go on and hope for the best. It looks a nice sheltered kind of valley, the sort that might be hot enough for all kinds of insects and flowers.'

Picturing a perfect paradise of brilliant flowers and equally brilliant butterflies, the children rode on and on down towards the valley in the far distance. It was much further than they thought. That was the worst of travelling in mountains. Everywhere was about twice as far as you imagined it to be. Most disappointing!

It was late when they rode into the valley, which was really more of a shallow depression between two high mountains than a real lowland valley. Certainly it was sheltered, and certainly it had more flowers in it than they had so far seen – but there were no butterflies!

'This can't be it!' said Philip in disappointment. 'Is it, David?'

David shook his head. He was looking round in a puzzled manner, and it was quite clear that he really didn't know where he was.

'If this is *not* the butterfly place, where is it?' asked Jack slowly and clearly. David shook his head again. It was really maddening, not being able to speak Welsh.

'Well,' said Philip, 'he's brought us the wrong way, to a place he doesn't know, but it's quite warm and sheltered, so we'll make the best of it tonight. Tomorrow we'll get the map from David, see if *we* can find out the way, and set off with ourselves as guides. He's as much use as Kiki to guide us in these mountains!'

They set up their camp again, feeling rather disappointed. They had so hoped to come to the place they wanted that night, and set up camp properly for a few days, to revel in hordes of common and uncommon butterflies. Now they would have to ride on still further, and goodness knew if they would ever find it!

They crawled into their sleeping-bags and called good night, just as the stars gleamed out. David was sleeping as usual outside.

But in the night the boys woke up suddenly. David was crawling into their tent. He was trembling with fright. 'Noises,' he said, in English, and then poured out something in Welsh. He was very frightened. 'Sleep here,' he said, and crept between the boys. They were amused and puzzled.

Whatever *could* have scared David so much?

10

A disturbing night

The sun was shining brightly when the camp awoke next day. It made them all feel cheerful and lively. Snowy, who had resented David sleeping with Philip and Jack the night before, and had butted him continually, bounded about lightly everywhere, butting David whenever he met him.

'What happened to you last night, David?' asked Jack, when they were all having a meal. 'Why were you so frightened?'

'Noises,' said David.

'What sort?' asked Philip curiously. '*We* didn't hear any.'

David made some surprising noises that sent Kiki sailing into the air and Snowy bounding away in fright. The children stared at David in astonishment.

By means of odd words and gestures David managed to convey to the children that he had gone to see if the donkeys were all right in the night, and had heard these noises near by where they were tethered.

'That explains why *we* didn't hear them, I suppose,' said Jack. 'David makes them sound like animal noises – fierce and savage!'

Lucy-Ann looked scared. 'Oh! You don't think there are wild animals anywhere about here, do you, Jack? I mean, *fierce* wild animals?'

Jack grinned. 'Well, if you are thinking of lions and tigers and panthers and bears, I think I can say you needn't be afraid of finding *those* here. But if, like Dinah, you include snakes, foxes, hedgehogs and so on in your list of fierce wild animals, then I should say, look out!'

'Don't be silly, Jack. Of course I don't mean those,' said Lucy-Ann. 'I don't quite know what I *did* mean. I just felt scared – and wondered what animal had made the noises David heard.'

'Probably his own imagination,' said Philip. 'Or a bad dream. That could scare him.'

David did not seem to want to go any further. He kept pointing back over the way they had come. But the children were not going to let their trip come to such a disappointing end. They meant to go and find the Butterfly Valley, if it took them all week! There was a lot of flapping to make David understand this.

He turned even more silent, but mounted his donkey to go with them. Jack now had the map, and examined it very carefully. It was annoying that the Butterfly Valley wasn't marked. Perhaps very few people knew about it.

They all set off across the valley and up into the mountains again. Perhaps the next valley would be the one they wanted, or the one after that. But although they travelled hopefully all the day, they did not find any valley full of butterflies. The children began to think it was all a fairy-tale.

There was no track to follow now, though they kept a keen look-out in case they should come across one again. When they camped that night, they discussed what they had better do next.

'If we go on any further we shan't know our way back,' said Jack. 'David would, perhaps, because he was born and bred among mountains, and, like a dog, could follow his own trail well enough, if we had to go back. But he's lost us once and I don't like to trust him too much. I wouldn't be surprised if he lost the way going back, if we take him much further!'

'Had we better go back then?' asked Lucy-Ann in disappointment.

'Or camp here for a few days,' said Jack, looking round. 'It's quite a good place.'

They were halfway up a steep mountain that rose very sharply from where they were, and looked quite unclimbable.

'What a peculiar mountain!' said Dinah, gazing up. 'I

shouldn't think anyone ever climbed that to the top. It's all crags and rocks and jutting-out bits.'

'We'll camp here,' decided Philip. 'The weather looks quite settled. There's a spring near by. We can mess about with our cameras and field-glasses.'

They told David. He did not seem pleased, but went off to tether the donkeys for the night. They were all tired that evening, children and donkeys both, for they had had a very long day. They cut the big ham that Mrs Evans had provided for them, afraid that it might go bad if they didn't eat it soon.

David looked as if he thought he would sleep in the tent again that night, for he cast various longing glances in that direction. However, the night was hot, and he felt he couldn't bear to be under cover. So he arranged himself under his rug in the open, fairly near to the two tents. The donkeys were some way away, tethered to trees by long ropes.

That night there was a snuffling around the camp. Lucy-Ann awoke suddenly and heard it. She went right down to the bottom of her sleeping-bag, frightened. What could it be? Was it the wild animal that David had heard?

Then she heard a howl! The boys heard it too, and awoke. David, outside, was awake, having heard both the noises. He was shivering with fright, all kinds of fears coming into his mind at once.

The moon was up and everywhere was silvery bright.

David sat up and looked down the hill. What he saw made his hair rise straight up on his head.

Wolves! A pack of wolves! No, no, it couldn't be wolves! He was dreaming! Wolves had not been known in the mountains for hundreds of years. But if those creatures were not wolves, what were they? And that noise of snuffling he had heard. That must have been a wolf too! No, not a *wolf*. It couldn't have been such a thing.

David sat there, hugging his knees, his mind going round and round – wolves or not? Wolves or not? What were they doing near the donkeys?

Another howl came – half a howl, half a bark, a horrible noise. David shot into the boys' tent and gave them a terrible start.

He stammered something in Welsh, and then in English, 'Wolves!'

'Don't be silly,' said Jack at once, seeing that the man was badly scared. 'You've had a bad dream.'

David dragged him to the tent opening and pointed with a trembling finger to where the pack of snuffling animals stood, not far from the donkeys.

The boys stared as if they could not believe their eyes. They certainly *looked* like wolves! Jack felt a cold shiver down his back. Good gracious! Was he dreaming? Those creatures were more like wolves than anything else!

Snowy the kid was trembling as much as David was. The trembling somehow made the boys feel scared too.

The only person who was not in the least scared was Kiki.

She too had caught sight of the wolves. She sailed out of the tent at top speed to go and investigate. Anything unusual always interested Kiki. She flew above the animals, whose eyes gleamed green as they turned at her coming.

'Wipe your feet!' screamed Kiki, and made a noise like a mowing-machine cutting long grass. It sounded really terrible in the still night air of the mountain-side.

The wolves started in fright. Then with one accord they all galloped away down the hillside into the night. Kiki shouted rude remarks after them.

'They've gone,' said Jack. 'Gosh, were they real? I can't understand it!'

When it was dawn, David got up to see if the donkeys were all right. Neither he nor the boys had slept again that night. David had been too scared to, and the boys had been too puzzled.

Daylight was almost on the mountain. David crept down quietly to the donkeys. They were all there, safe and sound but uneasy. David untethered them to take them to the stream to drink.

The boys were looking out of their tent, down the hillside to watch. There was no sign of any wolf now. Birds sang a little, and a yellow-hammer cried out for a little bit of bread and no cheese.

Suddenly something happened. David, who was

taking the donkeys in a line to the stream, gave a terrified yell and fell to the ground, covering his face. The boys, holding their breath, thought they saw something moving in the bushes, but they couldn't see what.

David gave another yell and got to his feet. He mounted a donkey and rode at top speed up to the tent.

'Come!' he cried in Welsh, and then in English. 'Black, black, black!'

The boys had no idea at all what he meant. They stared at him in amazement, thinking he must have gone mad. He made a violent gesture to them, pointed to the following donkeys as if to tell the boys to mount and follow him, and then galloped off at breakneck speed.

They heard the hooves of his donkey echoing on the mountain-side for some time. The other donkeys looked doubtfully at one another, and then, to the boys' dismay, trotted after David!

'Hi! Come back, David!' yelled Jack, scrambling out of the tent. 'Hi, hi!'

One donkey turned and made as if to come back, but he was pushed on by the others behind. In a trice they had all disappeared, and the sound of their hooves grew fainter and fainter as they galloped away after David and his mount.

The two boys sat down suddenly. They felt faint. Jack turned pale. He looked at Philip and bit his lip. Now they were in a terrible fix.

They said nothing for a moment or two, and then the girls' two scared faces looked out from their tent.

'What's happened? What's all the yelling? Was that David galloping away? We didn't dare to look!'

'Yes – it was David – running away from us – and all the donkeys have gone after him,' said Philip bitterly. 'We're in a pretty fix now!'

Nobody said anything. Lucy-Ann looked really alarmed. No David! No donkeys! What were they going to do?

Jack put his arm round her as she came and sat down beside him. 'It's all right! We've been in worse fixes than this! At the worst it only means a few days here, because as soon as he gets back to the farm, Bill will come and look for us.'

'Good thing we unloaded the donkeys and have got plenty of food,' said Philip. 'And our tents and sleeping-bags. Blow David! He's a nuisance.'

'I wonder what he saw to make him gallop off like that,' said Jack. 'All I could make out was "Black, black, black!"'

'Black what?' asked Dinah.

'Black nothing. Just black,' said Jack. 'Let's go down to the place where he got his fright and see if we can see anything.'

'Oh *no*!' said the girls at once.

'Well, I'll go, and Philip can stay here with you,' said Jack, and off he went. The others watched him, holding their breath. He peered all round and then turned and shook his head and shouted.

'Nothing here! Not a thing to see! David must have been seeing things! His bad night upset him.'

He came back. 'But what about those animals in the night?' said Philip, after a pause. 'Those wolves. We both saw those. *They* seemed real enough!'

Yes – what about those wolves!

11

A strange happening

It wasn't long before Dinah suggested having something to eat, and went to the big panniers that had been unloaded from the donkeys the night before. She pulled out some tins, thinking it would be a change to have sardines, and tinned peaches, or something like that. Anything to take their minds off David's flight, and the disappearance of the donkeys!

They sat down rather silently. Lucy-Ann kept very close to the boys. What with wolves and David's fright she felt very scared herself!

'I hope this won't turn into one of our adventures,' she kept saying to herself. 'They always happen so suddenly.'

Snowy the kid bounded up to Philip and knocked a tin flying from his hand. He nuzzled affectionately against him and then butted him. Philip rubbed the furry little nose and then pushed the kid away.

'I'm glad *you* didn't go off with the donkeys too!' he

said. 'I've got used to having you around now, you funny aggravating little thing. Take your nose out of that tin! Lucy-Ann, push him off – he'll eat everything we've got!'

Kiki suddenly flew at Snowy, screaming with rage. She had had her eye on that tin of sliced peaches, and to see Snowy nosing round it was too much for her. She gave him a sharp peck on the nose, and he ran to Philip, bleating. Everyone laughed and felt better.

They sat there, eating by the tents, occasionally glancing up at the mountain that towered up so steeply above them. It had no gentle slope up to the summit, as most of the mountains around had, but was steep and forbidding.

'I don't much like this mountain,' said Lucy-Ann.

'Why?' asked Dinah.

'I don't know. I just don't like it,' said Lucy-Ann. 'I've got one of my "feelings" about it.'

The others laughed. Lucy-Ann often had 'feelings' about things, and really believed in them. It was just like her to start having 'feelings' about the mountain, when everyone was also having uncomfortable ideas about wolves and other things.

'Well, you needn't have any "feelings" about mountains,' said Philip. 'Mountains are all the same – just tops, middles and bottoms, sometimes with sheep on and sometimes without!'

'But not many have wolves,' said Lucy-Ann seriously, and that made the others feel uncomfortable again.

'What are we going to do today?' asked Jack, when they had finished their meal. 'I suppose we *must* stay here till Bill comes to find us. We can't try to walk back home, because for one thing we don't know the way, and for another we'd never be able to carry enough food to get there without starving.'

'We'd far better stay here,' said Philip at once. 'It's ten chances to one David will know his way back here all right, and can bring Bill and the donkeys. Whereas if we start moving about, they'll never find us.'

'Yes – it does seem the most sensible thing to do,' said Jack. 'We've got our camp here – tents set up and everything – so we might as well make the best of it, and enjoy the camping. I wish there was somewhere to bathe though. It's so jolly hot. That little stream's too small to do anything but paddle in.'

'Let's all keep together,' said Lucy-Ann. 'I mean – we could frighten those wolves away perhaps if we all screamed at them – but one of us alone might be – might be . . .'

'Gobbled up!' said Jack, and laughed. 'What big *eyes* you've got, Granny! And, oh, what big TEETH you've got!'

'Don't tease her,' said Philip, seeing Lucy-Ann's alarmed face. 'It's all right, Lucy-Ann. Wolves are only really hungry in the winter-time and it's summer now.'

Lucy-Ann looked relieved. 'Well – I suppose if they'd been really hungry they would have attacked the donkeys, wouldn't they?' she said. 'Oh dear – I do think it's most extraordinary to find wolves here.'

They were just about to get up and clear away the picnic things when something curious happened that froze them to the ground.

First of all there was a grumbling, rumbling noise that seemed to come from the heart of the mountain itself – and then the ground shook a little. The four children distinctly felt it quivering beneath them, and they clutched at one another in alarm. Kiki flew straight up into the air, screaming. Snowy leapt to a high rock and stood there, poised on his four little legs as if to take off in the air like a plane.

The ground stopped shaking. The noise died away. But almost imediately the rumbling began again, a little louder, but very muffled as if great depths of rock separated it from the listeners. The ground quivered once more and Snowy took a flying leap into the air, landing on another rock. He was really terrified.

So were the four children. Lucy-Ann, very pale, clung to Jack and Philip. Dinah, forgetting all about the slow-worm, held on to Philip too.

There were no more rumblings, and the earth beneath them stayed still. The birds, which had stopped singing and calling, began to chirp again, and a yellow-hammer gave his familiar cry.

Snowy recovered himself and came bounding up to

the others. Kiki landed on Jack's shoulder. 'God save the Queen,' she said, in a relieved voice.

'What in the *world* was that?' said Philip at last. 'An earthquake? Gosh, I *was* scared!'

'Oh, Philip! This mountain isn't a volcano, is it?' said Lucy-Ann, gazing up at it fearfully.

'Of course not! You'd know a volcano all right if you saw one!' said Jack. 'This is a perfectly ordinary mountain – and goodness knows why it should have rumbled like that, and trembled beneath us. It gave me a horrible feeling.'

'I told you I had one of my "feelings" about this mountain,' said Lucy-Ann. 'Didn't I? I feel very peculiar about it. I want to go back to the farmhouse and not stay here.'

'So do we all,' said Philip. 'But we shouldn't know the way, Lucy-Ann. It isn't as if we'd followed a track – we left the track as you know, and part of the way we were in thick mist – we shouldn't have the faintest idea of the way.'

'I know you're right,' said Lucy-Ann. 'But I *don't* like this mountain – especially when it starts to rumble and shake! What made it?'

Nobody knew. They got up, cleared away the meal and went to splash in the little stream. The wind suddenly began to blow rather chilly, and, looking up, the children saw that big clouds were coming up from the south-west.

'Looks like rain,' said Jack. I hope the wind doesn't get up much more, or it will blow our tents away. Do you remember how they were blown clean away from over us on our last adventure – on the Island of Birds? That was an awful feeling.'

'Well,' said Philip, 'if you really think the tents might blow away, Jack, we'd better find a better place to camp than this – somewhere not too far, though, because we don't want to miss seeing Bill and David when they come for us. A copse of trees or a cave or somewhere like that – right out of the wind.'

'Let's look now,' said Dinah, pulling on her coat. It was extraordinary how cold it got as soon as the sun went in and the wind blew up the mountain. 'We'd better take Snowy with us, or he'll eat everything we've left!'

Snowy had every intention of coming with them. He capered along by Philip and Jack, as mad as ever. He was now very annoyed with Kiki, and leapt at her whenever she came within reach, wanting to pay her back for nipping his nose.

When the girls had been left a little way behind, Philip spoke in a low voice to Jack. 'We'd better find a cave, I think, Jack – I don't like the idea of those animals prowling around us at night – wolves, or whatever they are. If we were in a cave we could light a fire at the entrance and that would keep any animal off.'

'Yes. That's quite a good idea,' agreed Jack. 'I hadn't thought of that. I can't say *I* like the idea either of wolves nosing round our tents when we're asleep at night! I'd feel much safer in a cave!'

They hunted about for some kind of rocky shelter or cave, but there seemed none to be found. The mountain was so steep that it really was difficult to climb, and Lucy-Ann was afraid of slipping and falling.

Snowy leapt ahead of them, as sure-footed as ever. The boys wished heartily that it was as easy for them to leap about the mountain as it was for the kid.

'Look at him up there, standing on that rock!' said Jack, feeling exasperated and far too hot with his climbing. 'Hey, Snowy, come and give us a leg up! If only we had four springy legs like yours!'

Snowy stood there, whisking his little tail, and then ran back and disappeared. 'Where's he gone?' said Jack. 'Oh, there he comes again. Philip, there must be a cave or overhanging rock up where he is – he keeps going back and disappearing into it, whatever it is!'

They climbed up to where Snowy was, and sure enough, just at the back of the overhanging rock was a long low cave, its roof made out of another overhanging rock, its opening fringed with ferns of all kinds.

'This would do awfully well for us,' said Jack, going down on hands and knees and looking in. 'We could light a fire on the rock outside – the one Snowy stood on – and feel quite safe tonight. Clever little Snowy! You found us just what we wanted!'

'But how in the world are we going to get everything

up here?' said Philip. 'It was such a climb. It's not as if we are donkeys or goats, able to scramble up steep places quite easily, even with a load to carry. We need our hands to help us.'

This was certainly a problem. The boys hailed the girls and helped them up on to the rock where Snowy stood. 'Look,' said Jack, 'here's a good place to sleep in tonight. We can quite well see from here if Bill and David come – see what a good view we have from this rock – and we'd be safe from the wolves if we lighted a fire at the entrance to the cave.'

'Oh, *yes*!' said Lucy-Ann, pleased. She went into the cave. She had to bend her head at the opening, but inside the roof grew higher. 'It's not *really* a cave!' she said. 'It's just a space under that big jutting-out rock – but it will do awfully well.'

They all sat down on the rock, wishing the sun would come out. Snowy lay down beside them and Kiki sat on Jack's shoulder.

But suddenly she rose up into the air and screeched loudly. Snowy leapt up and stood looking downwards. What was the matter?

'Is it the wolves again?' asked Lucy-Ann in alarm. They listened. They could hear a noise of some animal or animals down below in the thick bushes, under the birch-trees.

'Get back into the cave,' said Jack to the girls. 'And keep quiet.'

The two girls went silently back into the darkness of the cave. The boys listened and watched. What animal was it down there? It must be big, by the noise it made!

12

Wolves in the night!

Snowy suddenly bleated loudly and took a flying leap off the rock before Philip could stop him. He disappeared into the bushes below – and then a loud and welcome sound filled the air.

'Ee-ore! Ee-ore! Ee-ore!'

'Goodness! It's a donkey!' cried Jack and scrambled down to see. 'Have they come back? Is David with them?'

They soon found what they were looking for. Dapple the donkey was in the bushes, nuzzling Snowy, evidently full of delight at seeing him again. But there was no sign at all of the other donkeys or of David.

'Dapple! You darling!' said Lucy-Ann, running up to him in joy. 'You've come back to us.'

'Come back to *Snowy*, you mean!' said Philip. 'He was always fond of Snowy, weren't you, Dapple? So you came back to find him. Well, we're very very glad to see you, because you will solve a very knotty problem for us – how to get all our goods up to that cave!'

Dapple *had* come back to see Snowy, but he was also very pleased to see the children again. He was a quiet, stout little donkey, hard-working and patient. He kept close to the children, and had evidently made up his mind he was going to stay with them. Snowy was sweet with him, and trotted by his side all the time.

'Here, Dapple!' called Philip. 'Come and help us with these things, there's a good fellow.'

Dapple stood obediently whilst the boys strapped things on to his back. He took all the bedding up to the cave first, scrambling up the steep bits with difficulty, but managing very well indeed. Then he took up the panniers of food.

'Thanks, Dapple,' said Jack, giving him a pat. 'Now come and have a drink!'

They all went to the stream and drank and splashed. The sun had come out again and immediately it was very hot. The children flung off their coats and lay about, basking.

'We must collect wood for the fire tonight,' said Jack. 'We shall need a good lot if we're going to keep the fire going all night long. We'll stack it in the big panniers and get Dapple to take it up for us.'

'Good old Dapple!' said Dinah.

They collected as much wood as they could, and soon it was all piled up on the rock outside the cave. The boys made a fire but did not light it. There was no need to do that till night.

The day soon went, and the sun sank behind the mountains in a blaze of crimson. As soon as darkness fell on the mountain-side, the children retired into the cave. The thought of wolves kept coming into their minds, and David's scream of terror, when he had seen something in the bushes, 'Black, black, black!' What *could* he have seen?

The children hadn't thought much of these things during the bright daylight, but they came back into their minds now it was dark. They debated whether or not to have Dapple in the cave with them.

But Dapple settled that idea by firmly refusing to go under the overhanging rock. He just stood outside stubbornly, his four legs set firmly on the ground, and no amount of pushing or pulling made the slightest difference. He was *not* going into that cave!

'All right, Dapple,' said Jack crossly. 'Stay outside and be eaten by wolves if you want to!'

'Oh, *don't* say things like that,' said Lucy-Ann. 'Dapple, do come inside! Please!'

Dapple lay down firmly outside, and the children gave it up. There would be no difficulty about Snowy or Kiki. One would want to be with Philip, the other with Jack.

'Now we'll light the fire,' said Jack, as stars began to

glimmer in the sky. 'It's getting very dark. Got the matches, Philip?'

The fire soon burnt up, for the twigs and branches were very dry. The cheerful flames leapt and flickered, and the fire crackled merrily.

'That's very very nice,' said Lucy-Ann, pleased. 'I feel safe tucked away in this cave with a fire at the entrance. Philip, make Snowy go the other side of you. He's sticking his hooves into me. I wish he'd wear bedroom slippers at night!'

Everybody laughed. They all felt safe and comfortable, tucked up in their sleeping-bags, with the fire lighting up the cave, filling it with jumping shadows. Snowy was pressed against Philip, Kiki was on Jack's middle. Somewhere outside was Dapple. Lucy-Ann wished he was in with them, then the whole family would be safe.

They all watched the flames for a while and then fell asleep. The fire flickered down as the wood was burnt up, and soon only the embers glowed.

Philip woke up with a start a few hours later. He saw that the fire had died down, and he got out of his sleeping-bag to put on more wood. It would never do to let it go out!

Dapple was still outside, lying quietly. Philip saw him when the flames leapt up to burn the wood he piled on. The boy went back to his sleeping-bag. He found that

Snowy had crept inside it whilst he was piling wood on the fire.

'You little scamp!' he whispered. 'Get out. There's not room for us both.'

There was quite a scuffle as he tried to get Snowy out of the bag. Fortunately the others were so very sound asleep that they didn't wake. Philip got Snowy out at last and slid in himself. He hastily laced up the neck of the bag before Snowy could try to squeeze in again. Snowy gave a sigh and lay down heavily right on Philip's middle.

Philip lay awake, watching the fire. The wind sometimes blew the smoke towards the cave, and for a moment or two the smell made Philip want to cough.

Then he heard Dapple stir outside, and he got up on one elbow to see why. His heart began to beat very fast.

Silent dark figures were slinking up to the cave! They did not pass beyond the fire, but they did not seem to be afraid of it. Philip felt breathless, and his heart beat even faster, as if he had been running.

What were those figures? Were they the wolves? The boy caught sight of two gleaming eyes, shining like the headlights of a distant car – but green as grass! He sat up quietly.

The wolves were back! They had smelt out the little company. What would they do? They had not attacked Dapple, thank goodness – and the donkey did not seem to be unduly frightened. He was only moving uneasily.

The slinking figures moved to and fro behind the fire.

Philip couldn't think what in the world to do! He could only hope that the fire would frighten them enough to keep them out of the cave.

After a while all the animals disappeared. Philip breathed again! Gosh, what a horrible fright he had had! What a blessing they had thought of that fire! Philip made up his mind that he wasn't going to sleep again that night, in case the fire went out. At all costs he must keep that up.

So the boy lay wide-eyed, thinking of wolves, rumblings, earthquakes and 'Black, black, black'. There was something very unusual about all these things. Did they fit together, or didn't they? *Was* there something peculiar about this mountain?

The fire was dying down again. Philip got up cautiously to put more wood on. The moon was up now and he could see for miles. He piled wood on the fire and the flames shot up. He slipped out of the cave to Dapple.

Then the boy heard a sound. He looked up – and to his horror he saw a wolf between him and the cave! He had gone to pat Dapple – and in that moment the wolf had slunk in between fire and cave. Would he go in?

The wolf stood still, looking at Philip in the moonlight. Philip gazed back, wondering what to do if the creature attacked him – and as he looked, a very peculiar thing happened.

The wolf wagged its long tail! To and fro it went, to and fro, like a big dog's! Philip's heart leapt. The animal wanted to be friendly! All animals were attracted to Philip – but a wolf! That was extraordinary.

The boy held out his hand, half afraid, but bold and daring. The wolf trotted round the fire and licked Philip's hand. It gave a little whine.

The moon shone down brightly on the animal's dark coat, pointed ears and long muzzle. *Was* it a wolf? Now that he was close to it Philip began to doubt.

And then quite suddenly he knew what this friendly animal was!

'Why, you're an Alsatian *dog!*' he cried. 'Aren't you? Why didn't I think of it before? I *knew* there weren't wolves in this country! Where are the others? You're all Alsatians! Good dog! Fine dog! I'd like to be friends with you!'

The big Alsatian put his paws up on Philip's shoulders and licked his face. Then he lifted his head and howled. It was a wolf-like noise, but Philip no longer minded that!

It was a call to the other dogs, the rest of the pack. There came the sound of feet in the bushes below, and a crowd of dogs leapt up on to the rock. They clustered round Philip, and, seeing that their leader was so friendly with the boy, they pawed him and licked him.

The howl awakened all the three children in the cave, and they sat up in fright. To their unspeakable horror they saw, outside the cave, what looked like Philip being attacked by wolves!

'Look! They've got Philip! Quick!' yelled Jack.

All three children slid out of their sleeping-bags and rushed to Philip's aid. The dogs growled at the sudden commotion.

'Philip! We're coming! Are you hurt?' cried valiant little Lucy-Ann, picking up a stick.

'It's all right, it's all right!' yelled Philip. 'They're not attacking me. They're friendly. They're not wolves, but Alsatians! Dogs, you know!'

'Goodness gracious!' said Dinah, and came out into the moonlight, so glad that the dogs were not wolves that she didn't even feel afraid of so many big dogs!

'Oh, Philip!' said Lucy-Ann, almost in tears with the shock of delight at knowing the wolves were only dogs. 'Oh, Philip! I thought you were being attacked.'

'You were a darling to come to my rescue then,' said Philip, smiling when he saw the little stick that Lucy-Ann had meant to attack the wolves with. 'The leader of the dogs made friends with me – so all the others are doing the same!'

The dogs had apparently made up their minds to stay for the night. Philip debated what to do. 'We can't possibly go back into the cave,' he said. 'The whole pack will come crowding in, and it would be impossible to breathe.'

'Quite impossible,' said Dinah, filled with horror at the thought of so many dogs sleeping with them.

'So we'll bring our sleeping-bags out here on the rock

beside Dapple, and sleep there,' said Philip. 'The dogs can stay if they want to – they'll be good guards! And if they don't want to, they can go. There are about ten of them! I wonder how it is they're wandering about here wild. Ten of them! It's extraordinary.'

They dragged out their sleeping-bags, and got into them. The dogs sniffed round in wonder. The leader sat majestically down by Philip, as if to say, 'This boy is my property. Keep off!' The others lay about among the children. Snowy was afraid of the big leader-dog and dared not even go near his beloved Philip. He went to Jack instead. Kiki stayed up in a tree. There were altogether too many dogs for her!

It was a curious sight the moon looked down on: four children, one goat, one parrot, one donkey – and ten dogs!

13

The face in the tree

When the morning came, Dapple awoke the children by giving a mighty sneeze. They woke with a jump, wondering what it was. Dapple gave another sneeze, and they knew!

'It's Dapple! Have you got a cold, Dapple?' asked Lucy-Ann anxiously. Then she remembered the happenings of the night, and looked round.

Everyone said the same thing at once.

'Where are the dogs?'

They had disappeared. Not one was there. The children looked at one another, puzzled. Where had they gone, and why?

'We couldn't *all* have dreamed them,' said Dinah, answering everyone's unspoken thought. 'They really were here. Ten of them. Most peculiar.'

'Yes, it *is* peculiar,' said Jack. 'Personally, I think they must belong to somebody. They didn't strike me as being a pack of *wild* dogs.'

'Nor me,' said Philip. 'But who could they belong to? There's not a house for miles! And why should anyone in this desolate mountain country keep ten man-hunting dogs?'

'Oooh – are they man-hunters?' said Lucy-Ann, startled.

'Well, the police use them for that,' said Philip. 'Don't they, Jack? They hunt criminals with them. Those Alsatians can smell them out and capture them. But there can't be any police here, with hunting-dogs! I mean – Bill would have had it reported to him, if they were. He's high up in the police organization himself, and there's not a thing he doesn't know about what's going on in the police world.'

'Where do the dogs come from then?' asked Dinah. 'Would they be kept as guards for anything – to frighten anyone off, or give the alarm, for instance?'

'Yes – but what is there to guard here, among these mountains?' said Jack. 'Nothing at all, as far as I can see!'

'Give it up!' said Philip, sliding out of his sleeping-bag. 'I'm going for a splash in the stream. Coming?'

'Yes. Then we'll open a tin or two,' said Dinah. 'I wish we'd thought of giving that ham-bone to the dogs, Jack. The ham's gone bad now – but they wouldn't have minded.'

'We'll give it to them next time we see them,' said Jack. 'I've no doubt they'll be along again!'

They all splashed in the stream, Snowy and Dapple

too. Kiki sat apart, making sarcastic remarks, for she was not fond of water.

'Pooh! Gah!' she shouted, trying to remember all the rude words she knew. 'Gooh! Pah!'

'That's right. Mix your words up, Kiki,' said Jack. 'What about "piffle" and "bunk"? You used to know those too.'

'Pifflebunk,' said Kiki, and thought that was a good word. 'Pifflebunk, bifflebunk, pop goes the pifflebunk.'

The children laughed. Kiki laughed too and then began to give an imitation of Dapple braying. This was much too lifelike and Dapple started up, looking all round for the other donkeys.

'Ee-ore, ee-ore, ee-ore,' went on Kiki, till Jack threw a towel at her to make her stop. It fell over her head and she screamed in rage. Dapple and Snowy stared solemnly at her, puzzled and surprised.

They had a meal. Lucy-Ann volunteered to go down to the stream again and wash the dishes, whilst the others looked at the map, trying to find out exactly where they were. She went off to the stream, humming.

She knelt down by the water, scouring a dish, when a sound made her look up. She had heard something in the tree above, just by the water.

There was a big, leafy tree there, growing almost out of the stream. Lucy-Ann, thinking there must be a bird in the tree, peered up into the branches.

She got a terrible shock. Looking down at her was a face – and it was black.

The little girl sat there, petrified, the dish in her hand, unable to move or speak. The branches moved and she saw that the face was topped by black, thick hair, and had bright eyes and a cheerful expression.

'It's a black man!' she thought to herself. 'But here! Up this tree! What shall I do?'

The black face looked down on the little girl, and then the man's lips parted in a smile. The head nodded amiably. Then a black finger came up from among the leaves, and was put to the lips.

'Don't you make a sound, l'il gal,' said the man, in a hoarse whisper. He sounded like an American! 'Don't you say I'm here. I'm just a poor man, lost and alone.'

Lucy-Ann couldn't believe her ears. She felt that she simply must call the others. But they didn't hear her, and as soon as she had shouted, the man frowned fiercely and shook his head.

'L'il gal, you gotta git away from here. It's a no-good mountain, full of bad men. They'll git you if you don't git away. There's bad things here, l'il gal.'

'What are you doing here?' asked Lucy-Ann, in a scared voice. 'How do you know all this?'

'I've been in that there bad mountain, l'il gal. I've gotten away. But this poor fellah's gotten no place to go – and he's surely scared by those big dogs. I'm staying right here in this nice big tree. You git away, l'il gal, git far away!'

Lucy-Ann felt odd, standing there talking to a black stranger up a tree. She suddenly turned and ran back to the others. She ran fast, and arrived absolutely out of breath.

'What's the matter, what's the matter?' cried Jack, seeing from Lucy-Ann's face that she had had a shock. Lucy-Ann could only gasp out one or two words. She pointed back to the stream.

'Black man!' she gasped. 'Black!'

'Black! That's what David said!' cried Philip. 'Get your breath, Lucy-Ann! Tell us what you saw. Quick!'

Lucy-Ann panted out what she had seen and heard. The others listened in astonishment. A black man hiding in a tree – from the dogs! A man who said the mountain was bad – an American – whatever did it mean?

'Come on – we'll ask him what he knows!' cried Jack. 'There's something going on here. We'd better find out and then we can tell Bill when he comes. Quick!'

They all ran back to the stream and peered up the tree. But there was nobody there. The man had gone.

'Blow!' said Jack, in disappointment. 'He must have seen you scuttle back to us, Lucy-Ann, to tell us you had seen him – and he's scared, and now he's gone.'

'It's a wonder the dogs didn't find him last night – and before that, when David saw him up this very same tree,' said Jack.

'Well, he's been rather clever, I think,' said Philip, looking at the stream. 'You know, dogs can't follow scent through water. They lose it. And I reckon that chap was clever enough to wade up or down the stream to that tree, and hop up it from the water. The dogs couldn't possibly follow his scent through the stream. They would lose it wherever he entered the water. Still, he must have felt pretty scared when he saw the dogs milling around near here!'

'Were they hunting for him, do you think?' asked Lucy-Ann fearfully. 'He must have been awfully afraid. I should be terrified if I thought a pack of Alsatian dogs was after me.'

The children hunted for the strange man, but he was nowhere to be seen. They wondered what he ate. There was not much to eat on the mountains except bilberries, wild raspberries and grass.

'Do you think he really meant there were men inside this mountain?' asked Dinah, when they had tired themselves out looking for the American.

'It seems incredible – but if you remember those noises of rumbling we heard yesterday – and the way the earth shook beneath us – it seems as if there *might* be men working underground,' said Jack.

'What – as miners or something?' asked Dinah.

'I don't know. Possibly. Though goodness knows what could be mined inside this mountain, or how they would get the machinery there. There would have to be a road – and then everyone would know.'

'It's very mysterious,' said Dinah.

Lucy-Ann sighed. 'It's another adventure, that's what it is. It's fatal to go off together like this. We go to look for birds, or butterflies or something – and we always stumble into something peculiar. I'm getting tired of it.'

'Poor Lucy-Ann!' said Philip. 'We certainly do happen on strange things. *I* think it's very exciting. I love adventures.'

'Yes, but I don't,' said Lucy-Ann. 'I don't like that kind of thing at all.'

'*I* do,' said Dinah at once. 'I've enjoyed every single one of our adventures. And this one seems more mysterious than any other. What *is* going on inside this mountain? How I'd love to know! If only we could see that chap again, we could ask him to tell us all about it.'

'Oh, listen – I do believe that rumbling's going to start again,' said Lucy-Ann suddenly. 'See how frightened Snowy is! Yes – there it comes.'

They sat and listened. Jack put his ear to the ground. At once the rumblings became magnified, and sounded more puzzling than ever. Was something exploding down there, far in the heart of the mountain?

Then the earth quivered as it had done before and Lucy-Ann clutched at Jack. It was horrible to feel the firm solid earth quivering like a jelly.

It soon stopped. Dinah glanced up at the steep mountain, rearing up just behind them, wondering what its secret was. She suddenly stiffened, and caught hold of Philip's arm.

'Look!' she said, and pointed upwards.

They all looked. Out of the side of the mountain was drifting a small cloud of smoke. One puff came. Then another. But it was not ordinary smoke. It was a curious crimson colour, and it did not drift away like mist on the wind, but hung like a solid little cloud, close to the mountain, for some time. Then it suddenly became lighter in colour and disappeared.

'Well – whatever was *that*?' said Jack, in amazement. 'I never in my life saw smoke like that before. There must be a vent or something in the side of the mountain there, that lets out smoke or gases.'

'What's a vent?' asked Lucy-Ann, her eyes looking as if they would drop out of her head.

'Oh – a sort of chimney,' said Jack. 'Somewhere with a draught that will take up smoke or gases to the outer air. Whatever's going on in the mountain produces that smoke, which has to be got rid of. I wonder what else is being produced inside there!'

Nobody could imagine. They couldn't seem to fit together all the curious facts they knew – the pack of man-hunting dogs – the poor runaway – the noises, the earth's shaking, the crimson smoke. It didn't make any sense at all.

'If only Bill would come!' said Philip. 'He might be able to fit this jigsaw together.'

'Or if we could get hold of that chap Lucy-Ann saw,' said Philip. 'He could tell us a lot.'

'We may see him again,' said Dinah. 'We'll watch out for him.'

They did see him again, that very evening – but alas, he didn't answer any of their questions!

14

Plenty of things happen

They decided to go for a walk that evening. They would leave Dapple tied up to a tree by the stream, with a note on his harness to say they would soon be back – just in *case* Bill came when they were away.

'Though he couldn't *possibly* be here yet,' said Jack. Still, you never knew with Bill. He had a remarkable way of doing impossible things extraordinarily quickly.

They went off together, Snowy capering about, and Kiki on Jack's shoulder. They climbed up past the cave where they had slept the night before. Their sleeping-bags were still there, pulled into the cave out of the sun. They meant to sleep in them up on the rock again that night.

'Let's follow Snowy,' suggested Dinah. 'He always seems to know a way to go, thought I expect he only follows his silly little nose! But he usually chooses quite possible paths for us.'

So they followed Snowy. The little kid took it into his

head to climb up the mountain, but at last they all came to such a steep cliff of rock, almost sheer, that they had to stop. Even Snowy was brought to a halt!

'I'm frightfully hot,' said Dinah, fanning herself. 'Let's sit down under those trees.'

The trees were waving about in the wind. Jack looked longingly up into the wind-blown branches. 'It would be lovely and cool up there, in the windy boughs,' he said. 'What about climbing up? They look pretty easy to climb.'

'A wizard idea!' said Philip. 'I love swinging in the branches at the top of a tree. Want a leg-up, Lucy-Ann?'

Lucy-Ann got a leg-up and soon they were all settled into forking branches, letting themselves be swung about in the wind, which was very strong just there.

'This is lovely,' said Dinah. 'Heavenly!'

'Super!' said Jack. 'Don't clutch my shoulder so tightly, Kiki. You won't fall off!'

Snowy was left down below, bleating. He tried his best to leap up into the tree but he couldn't. He ran round and round Philip's tree and then, in a rage, he tore up to a rock and leapt up it and down it without stopping. The children watched him, laughing at his antics.

Then, quite suddenly, a hullabaloo broke on their ears. It was the sound of excited barking and snarling, howling and yelping.

'The dogs!' said Jack, straining his eyes to see where the noise came from. 'I say – they're after that man!'

There came the crashing of bushes and twigs far below them on the mountain-side, accompanied by more howls and barks. Then the children caught sight of a man running across a bare stony part of the mountain-side below them – about half a mile away.

The dogs poured after him. Lucy-Ann almost fell out of her tree in fright at seeing a man chased by dogs. The children watched without a word, their hearts beating fast, anxious for the man to escape.

He came to a tree and flung himself up it just as the first dog reached him. He pulled himself up, and was lost to sight. The dogs surrounded the tree, clamouring loudly.

Lucy-Ann gulped. Tears ran down her face. She felt so sorry for the hunted man that she could hardly see through her tears. The others watched grimly. Philip debated whether to go down and see if he could call the dogs off.

Then another man appeared, walking leisurely across the mountain-side towards the tree and the dogs. He was too far away for the children to see what he was like, or to hear his voice.

But on the crisp air of the mountain came the shrill sound of a whistle. The dogs at once left the tree, and trotted back to the man. He stood not far off the tree, and evidently gave orders for the man to come down. But nobody came down from the tree.

The man waved his hand to the dogs and at once they

streamed back to the tree again, clamouring and howling like mad. The man turned to go back the way he came.

'Oh! He's left the dogs to keep the poor man up the tree till he starves, or comes down to be set on!' sobbed Lucy-Ann. 'Philip, what shall we do?'

'I'll go down and call the dogs off,' said Philip. 'I'll give the man a chance to get right out of sight, so that he won't see me. Then I'll see if I can get the dogs away and give that chap a chance to escape from the tree.'

He climbed down his tree, after he had waited for twenty minutes, to give the second man a chance to go back to wherever he had come from. He made his way cautiously through the tall bushes.

And then something happened. A rough hand pounced down on his shoulder and he was held in a grip like iron. He was swung round – and came face to face with the man who had ordered the runaway to come down from the tree!

Philip wriggled, but he couldn't possibly get away. He didn't dare to yell for the others in case they got caught too. Blow! Why hadn't he waited longer before going off to the black man's rescue!

'What are you doing here?' said the man, in a strange, foreign accent. 'Who are you, boy?'

'I've only come to look for butterflies,' stammered Philip, trying to look as if he knew nothing about any-thing but butterflies. He didn't like the look of the man at all. He had a fierce hawk-like face, overhanging eyebrows, and such a sharp look in his black eyes that Philip felt sure he would be difficult to deceive.

'Who are you with?' asked the man, digging his steel-like fingers into Philip and making him squirm.

'I'm alone, as you can see,' said Philip, hoping the man would believe him. The man looked at him searchingly.

'My dogs would have got you if you had been here for long,' he said. 'And all your friends too!'

'What friends?' asked Philip innocently. 'Oh, you mean Snowy, my kid? He always comes with me.'

Snowy had bounded up at that moment, to the obvious surprise of the man. 'He's like a dog – never leaves me. Let me go, sir. I'm looking for butterflies. I'll be gone tonight.'

'Where did you come from?' asked the man. 'Do your parents know where you are?'

'No,' said Philip truthfully. 'I just went away to hunt for butterflies. I came from over there.'

He nodded his head vaguely behind him, hoping that the man would think he was a harmless nature-lover, and let him go. But the man didn't.

Instead he tightened his fingers on Philip's shoulders, and turned towards the tree where the black man was still hiding, surrounded by the dogs.

'You'll come with me now,' he said. 'You've seen too much.'

Just then there came a yelling and shouting from the

tree. Evidently the runaway had given in. The man, still clutching Philip by the shoulder, and followed by a puzzled Snowy, went towards the tree. He took a whistle from his pocket and blew on it shrilly. As before, the dogs at once left the tree and came to him. The man shouted for the runaway to come down.

The poor man came down in such a hurry that he half fell. The dogs made no attempt to go for him. Philip saw that they had been extremely well trained.

The man fell on his knees and began to jabber something. He was terrified. The man told him to get up, in cold contemptuous tones. Surrounded by the dogs, the prisoner walked stumblingly in front of the man, who still held Philip firmly by the shoulder.

Up in their trees the children watched in horror, hardly believing their eyes when they saw Philip held by the man. 'Sh! Don't make a sound,' commanded Jack. 'It's no good us being captured too. If the dogs go with Philip, he'll be all right. He'll have ten friends he can call on at any time!'

The little procession of men, boy, dogs and kid passed almost beneath the trees the children were in. Philip did not glance up, though he longed to. He was not going to give away the hiding-place of the others.

Jack parted the branches of his tree and followed the procession anxiously with his eyes. They were going in the direction of the steep wall of unclimbable rock. Jack took up his field-glasses, which were slung round his neck as usual, and glued them to his eyes, following the company closely. Where exactly were they going? If he knew, he might be able to go and rescue Philip and Snowy.

He saw Philip taken right up to the steep wall. Then, before his eyes, the whole company seemed to vanish! One moment they were there – the next they were gone! Jack took his glasses from his eyes and rubbed the lenses, thinking something must have gone wrong with them. But no – he saw exactly the same thing – a steep wall of sheer rock – and nobody there at all, not even a dog!

'Jack! Can you see what's happened to Philip?' came Lucy-Ann's anxious voice. 'Oh, Jack – he's caught!'

'Yes, and he's been taken into that mountain,' said Jack. 'Though how, I don't know. One moment they were all there, the next they were gone! I can't understand it.'

He looked through his glasses again but there was nothing to be seen. He suddenly realized that the sun had gone down and it was getting dark. 'Girls! It'll be dark soon. We must get down and go to the cave, whilst we can still see our way!' said Jack. They all climbed down quickly. Lucy-Ann was trying to blink back tears.

'I want Philip to come back,' she said. 'What's happened to him?'

'Don't cry,' said Dinah. 'Crying won't help him! You always burst into tears when anything happens!'

Dinah spoke crossly because she was very near tears

herself. Jack put his arm round both of them. 'Don't let's quarrel. That won't help Philip. Come on, let's get back quickly. I'll fetch Dapple from the stream, and bring her up to the rock.'

They made their way back to the cave they had left their sleeping-bags in. Jack fetched the patient Dapple. Kiki sat silently on his shoulder. She always knew when things had gone wrong with the children. She nipped Jack's ear gently to tell him she was sorry.

It was almost dark when they reached the cave. There was no need to make a fire tonight – they did not fear wolves any more. Indeed they would have been very glad indeed to see dark figures come slinking up to the cave. They would have welcomed the dogs eagerly.

'I miss Snowy,' said Dinah. 'It's queer without him leaping about everywhere. I'm glad he's gone with Philip. I'm glad the slow-worm's gone too!'

They didn't want to get into the sleeping-bags and go to sleep. They wanted to talk. A lot of things seemed to be happening very suddenly. Oh dear – when would Bill come? They could manage quite well without grown-ups in many ways – but just at the moment all three would have welcomed even David!

'Well – let's get into our bags,' said Jack. 'Isn't the moon lovely tonight?'

'Nothing seems very nice when I think of Philip being captured,' said Lucy-Ann dismally. All the same, the moon was glorious, swinging up over the mountains, and making everywhere as light as day.

They were just about to slide into their bags when Lucy-Ann's sharp ears caught an unfamiliar sound.

'Listen!' she said. 'What's that? No, not a noise underground this time – somewhere up in the sky!'

They went out and stood on the flat rock, listening, their faces upturned to the moonlit sky.

'What a peculiar noise!' said Jack. 'A bit like an aeroplane – but *not* an aeroplane. What *can* it be?'

15

Behind the green curtain

The noise came nearer. 'Like a motor-bike in the sky,' said Jack.

'Or a sewing-machine,' said Dinah. 'Jack, look! What's that? That tiny speck up there?'

Jack fumbled for his glasses, which were still round his neck. He put them to his eyes, straining to focus the little black speck up in the moonlight. It came nearer.

'Well – whatever it is I do believe it's going to land on this mountain!' said Dinah. 'Isn't it going slowly? *Is* it an aeroplane, Jack?'

'No,' said Jack. 'Gosh – it's a helicopter! You know – they are just the thing for travelling in mountains. They don't fly fast but they can land in a very small space – on a lawn, or a roof even!'

'A *heli*copter!' cried Dinah, and took the glasses from Jack. 'Let me see.'

It was now near enough for Dinah to be able to see it clearly with the glasses. Jack and Lucy-Ann watched it with screwed-up eyes. It hovered over the mountain-top, and then flew slowly round it, appearing in sight again after a few minutes.

It then flew up a little higher, and descended slowly, almost vertically, its engine making a curious sound in the night. Then there was silence.

'It's landed,' said Jack. 'But where? Gosh, I wouldn't like to land on a mountain as steep as this one.'

'Perhaps there is a proper landing-place,' said Lucy-Ann. 'Right on the very top!'

'Yes. There may be,' said Jack. 'What a thing to do, though – land a helicopter on the very summit of a mountain like this! What for?'

Nobody knew the answer to that.

'Well,' said Jack, at last, 'if that helicopter *did* land up on top, that would be one way of bringing food and stuff to the men who are at work inside the mountain – they'd have to have food, and there's no way of getting it round about here!'

'I feel as if all this must be a dream,' said Lucy-Ann, in a small voice. 'I don't like it at all. I wish I could wake up.'

'Come on – let's get into our bags,' said Jack. 'We can't *do* anything. We'll just have to wait for Bill. We can sleep out on the rock tonight, if you like. It's got very warm again, and we're snug enough in our bags.'

Nibbling bars of chocolate the three of them slipped into the bags. Kiki flew up into a near-by bush. She cleared her throat as David had often done. 'Look you, whateffer, look you, whateffer,' she began, meaning to have a little practice of the new words she had learnt.

'Kiki! Shut up!' said Jack.

'Whateffer!' said Kiki, and hiccuped very loudly. 'Pardon!' she gave a cackle of laughter and said no more for a moment. Then she took her head out from under her wing. 'Pifflebunk,' she said, delighted at having remembered it, and put her head back again.

Jack woke several times in the night, wondering about Philip. He also puzzled his head to think how the whole company of dogs, men and boy could possibly have vanished as they did, under his very eyes. He felt that he really would have to go and explore that steep wall of rock the next day. Perhaps he would find out where the company had gone – and *how* it had gone.

'Do you think Bill will come today?' asked Lucy-Ann, next morning. Jack reckoned up and shook his head. 'No – perhaps he will tomorrow, though, if David got back quickly, and Bill came at once. Still – if we go far away from the stream, we'd better leave a note for Bill, in case he comes and we're not there. Like we did yesterday.'

They had taken the note off Dapple's harness the night before, when they had brought the donkey back from the stream, up to their sleeping-rock. Now Jack set to work to write another. In it he told the story of Philip's disappearance by the wall of rock, and he also wrote about the helicopter he had seen. He had a feeling that he had better tell all he knew in case – just in *case* – something happened, and he and the girls were captured too. So many strange things had happened on this mountain. It was quite likely that if the man got out of Philip the fact that he had friends near by the mountain, they would send to capture them too.

He took Dapple back to the stream, putting him in the shade, in some long lush grass, and near enough to the stream to stand in it, or drink if he liked. Dapple liked this kind of life well enough, but he stared anxiously all around, missing Snowy. Where was his tiny friend?

'Snowy will come back soon, Dapple,' said Jack, rubbing his hand up and down the long grey nose. 'You wait and see!'

'What are we going to do today?' asked Lucy-Ann, when Jack came back. 'I don't feel like doing anything now Philip's gone!'

'Well – would you like to come with me to the steep rocky wall the others went to last night?' said Jack. 'Just to see if we can find out how they disappeared so suddenly. But if you come we'll have to keep a jolly good look-out in case we're taken by surprise!'

Lucy-Ann looked as if she didn't want to come at all, but nothing would stop her being with Jack if she thought there was any likelihood of danger. If they were going to be taken by surprise, then she would be there too!

So, taking some tins with them in case they didn't feel inclined to go all the way back to the cave in the heat of the day for a meal, the three of them set off. Kiki flew over their heads, annoying the swallows, and crying 'Feetafeetit, feetafeetit!' just as they did. They took not the slightest notice of her, but went on with their fly-catching deftly and serenely.

The three came at last to the little copse of trees where they had swung in the wind the evening before. 'Wait here a minute,' said Jack, and he leapt up into a tree. 'I'll just have a look round to make sure the coast is clear.'

He balanced himself in branches near the top of the tree and swept the countryside around with his glasses. Not a sound was to be heard except the wind, the trees and the birds. There was no sign of any human being, or of any of the dogs.

'It seems all right,' said Jack when he got down to the foot of the tree again. 'We'll go. Come on.'

Kiki began to bray like Dapple, and Jack turned on her fiercely. 'Kiki! Stop it! Just when we want to be quiet! Bad bird! Silly bird!'

Kiki raised her crest up and down, snapped her beak angrily, and flew up into a tree. It was almost as if she had said, 'All right then – if you speak to me like that, I won't come with you!' She sat on a branch, sulking, keeping one eye on the three children walking towards the wall.

They reached it and looked upwards. It towered up,

steep and sheer. Nobody could climb that, not even Snowy!

'Now where were the others when they disappeared?' said Jack. 'About here, I think.'

He led the way to an uneven slab of rock. Hanging down in front of it, over the rocky wall, was a thick curtain of greenery, half bramble, half creepers of some kind, all matted together.

The children thought this mass of green was actually growing on the wall, in the same way that many other little plants and ferns grew. It was only when the wind blew strongly, and the curtain-like mass swung backwards and forwards a little that Lucy-Ann guessed it wasn't growing out of the wall – it was hanging down, covering it!

She caught hold of it. It swung back like a curtain! Behind it was the wall, right enough – but there was a split in it, a great crack that reached up about twenty feet.

'Look!' said Lucy-Ann. 'This is a kind of curtain, Jack. And look at the big crack in the wall behind. Is this where they went yesterday?'

'Gosh, yes! They must all have gone quickly behind this curtain of creepers,' said Jack. 'And I thought they had vanished! Hold it up, Lucy-Ann. Let's see the crack. I bet they went through that!'

All three passed easily behind the swinging curtain of creeper and bramble. They could slip through the crack without any trouble at all. Once through it they found themselves in an immensely high cave, very round, and with no roof that could be seen, though Jack flashed his torch up as far as he could manage.

'It's like a hole in the mountain,' he said. 'It goes up goodness knows how high!'

'Did the others come in here?' asked Dinah, staring upwards. 'Where did they go then?'

'Can't think,' said Jack, puzzled. 'I say, look here – look what's in the middle of the floor! I almost went into it!'

He flashed his torch on to the floor of the cave – but there was hardly any floor to be seen! Most of it was taken up by a silent black pool, whose surface had no wrinkle or ripple!

'It's not a nice pool,' said Lucy-Ann, with a shudder.

'This is a most peculiar cave,' said Dinah. 'No roof – no floor – only a deep pool! And no sign of where the others went yesterday.'

'There must be *some* way out,' said Jack, quite determined to search until he found it. He began to walk all round the cave, flashing his torch on it, inch by inch. But there was no opening anywhere, not even a tiny hole. The walls were absolutely solid.

'Well, there's no passage leading out of *this* cave!' said Jack, giving it up. He glanced up to the roofless top of the cave. 'The only way is up there! But there are no footholds to climb up – nothing! Nobody could possibly climb up these steep walls.'

'Well then – is there a way out through the pool?' said Dinah, half in fun.

Jack looked at the black pool. 'No, I don't see how that pool can possibly contain a way out of this cave. Still – it's the only thing I haven't examined. I'll have a swim in it – or wade across!'

But it was too deep to wade. Jack took two steps and the water came over his knees. He stripped off his clothes and plunged in. Lucy-Ann didn't like it much. She watched Jack anxiously as he swam across and back.

'Can't feel the bottom at all,' said Jack, kicking out with his legs. 'Must be awfully deep. A bottomless pool and a roofless cave – sounds odd, doesn't it? I'm coming out now. The water's icy cold.'

He found his footing almost at the edge of the pool, slipped and went in again. He reached out to grasp the edge and his hand found something else. It felt like a small steering-wheel under the water!

Jack got out and dressed. He was shivering too much to do any more investigation till he had some clothes on. Then he knelt down by the edge of the pool and put his hand in to feel the curious wheel-like thing again.

'Hold my torch, Lucy-Ann,' he commanded. 'There's something odd here!'

Lucy-Ann held the torch in trembling fingers. What was Jack going to find? 'It's a little wheel,' he said. 'Why is it here? Well, wheels are meant to turn, so I'll turn it! Here goes!'

He turned it to the right. It ran easily. And then he jumped violently because both the girls screamed loudly and clutched him hard!

16

Inside the mountain

'What's the matter?' shouted Jack, jumping up. 'What's happened!'

Lucy-Ann had dropped the torch in her fright. The light went out and they were in darkness. She clutched at Jack again and startled him.

'Something touched me!' she whispered. 'Something ran its fingers all down me. Oh, Jack, what was it?'

'Yes, and me too,' said Dinah, in a trembling voice. 'I felt them. They touched my shoulder softly and then ran all the way down to my feet. What is it, Jack? There's something here. Let's get out.'

'Where's the torch?' said Jack impatiently. 'Oh, Lucy-Ann, I hope it isn't broken. You idiot, dropping it like that.'

He groped about for it on the floor and found it. Luckily it hadn't rolled into the pool. He shook it and the light came on. Everyone was very thankful.

'Now, what touched you?' demanded Jack. 'Nothing touched *me*!'

'I don't know,' said Lucy-Ann. 'I want to get out of here, Jack. I'm frightened.'

Jack swung his torch round behind the girls. He saw something that made him cry out in surprise. The girls didn't dare to look. They clung to him, trembling.

'See what touched you? A rope-ladder falling down just behind you!' laughed Jack. 'Well, what a surprise! You'd never dream of that!'

Dinah pulled herself together at once, and forced herself to laugh. 'Well! Fancy that! I really did think it was somebody touching me. It felt just like it.'

'It must just have run down quietly behind you from somewhere up high,' said Jack, flashing his torch upwards, and following the ladder with the beam as far as he could. 'Well, you made *me* jump all right when you yelled. I almost went head-first into the pool!'

'It happened when you turned that wheel down there,' said Lucy-Ann, still shivering a little.

'Yes. A very clever little idea,' said Jack. 'I must say this is a jolly well-hidden entrance to the mountain – better even than Ali Baba's cave! First there's the green curtain. Then just a crack in the rock. Then you come in and see nothing but a black pool and a roofless cave. Most people would just say, "How odd!" and go out again!'

'Yes. They would never, never guess about the ladder

that comes tumbling down when you turn the wheel hidden so cleverly in the water,' agreed Dinah. 'Most ingenious, all of it. Somebody with brains lives in this mountain!'

'Yes,' said Jack thoughtfully. 'Brains that work and produce minor earthquakes and crimson smoke, and plan for landing-grounds for helicopters on mountain-tops – and keep packs of Alsatians that would terrorize anyone roaming too near the mountain. Very remarkable brains! I wonder exactly what those brains are after!'

The girls stared at him in the dimly lit cave, with the black pool glinting up at them. Jack sounded very serious. He felt serious too. There was something very strange about all this. Something very clever. Much too clever. What *could* be going on?

He stared up the ladder. He felt very much inclined to go up it. He longed to see what was inside the mountain – and he wanted to find Philip again too. Then a hollow voice made them all jump violently.

'Naughty boy! Pifflebunk!'

'It's Kiki,' said Jack, relieved. 'You wretched bird, you made me jump! What do you think of this cave, Kiki?'

'Pifflebunk,' repeated Kiki, and made a noise like a mowing-machine. It sounded terrible in that roofless cave. The noise seemed to go up and up endlessly. Kiki enjoyed the sound. She began all over again.

'Be quiet,' said Jack. 'Goodness knows what will

happen if your noises arrive at the top of this ladder, and somebody hears them!'

'You're not going up, are you, Jack?' asked Lucy-Ann, afraid, as she saw Jack place a foot on the lowest rung of the rope-ladder.

'Yes. I'll just go up to the top and see what's there and come down again,' said Jack. 'I don't expect there'll be anyone on guard, because nobody would ever dream of us guessing the secret of getting the ladder down. You two go out into the sunshine and wait for me.'

'No. We're coming too,' said Lucy-Ann. They had lost Philip. She wasn't going to lose Jack! So she and Dinah began to climb up behind him.

The ladder was well made and strong. It swung to and fro a little as the three of them climbed it. Up they went, and up and up. There seemed no end to it!

'I'm stopping for a rest,' whispered Jack. 'You stop too. It's frightfully tiring, this.'

They clung to the rungs and rested, panting a little with their long climb. Lucy-Ann didn't like to think how far away the foot of the cave was. Nor did she like to think how far away the top of the ladder was!

They went on again. It was pitch dark, for Jack had put away his torch, needing both hands to climb with. Lucy-Ann began to feel that she was in a peculiarly horrid nightmare – one in which she would have to climb ladders in the dark until she awoke in the morning!

'I say – I can see a dim sort of light now,' whispered

Jack. 'I believe we must be coming to the top. Don't make any noise.'

They got to the top just as Lucy-Ann felt that her arms would not hold on to the ladder any longer. As Jack said, there was a dim light there. He climbed off on to a rocky floor, and the girls followed. They all lay panting for a few minutes, unable even to look round and see where they were.

Jack recovered first. He sat up and gazed round him. He was in a little chamber, lighted by a dim lamp. Big stone jugs full of what looked like water stood at the back, with mugs near by. Jack's eyes gleamed. Just what they wanted after their terrible climb! He fetched a jug and three mugs and the three of them drank deeply of the ice-cold water.

'Now I feel better,' said Jack, with a sigh. He put back the jug and mugs. There was nothing else to see in the room at all. At the far end was an open passage-way, leading into the heart of the mountain.

Jack went to it. Lucy-Ann called softly to him. 'Jack! Aren't you coming back? You said you'd only go to the top and look!'

'Well, I'm looking,' said Jack. 'There's a narrow passage here. Come and see. I wonder where it leads to.'

The girls went to see. Jack wandered along a little way and the girls followed, not liking to be left alone. They came to another dim lamp, set on a rocky shelf in the passage wall. Jack went on and on, following the winding passage, coming to lamp after lamp that lighted the way.

'Come back now,' whispered Lucy-Ann, pulling at his sleeve. 'We've gone far enough.'

But Jack felt that he couldn't possibly go back now. Why, he might meet Philip round the next corner! So on he went.

They came to a forking of the passage, which suddenly divided into three. The children stopped, wondering where the three passages led to. They all looked exactly the same to them.

And then, out of one passage capered somebody they knew very well indeed. It was Snowy!

The kid was as delighted to see them as they were to see him. He butted them all, rubbed his nose into their hands, and bleated joyfully. Jack felt pleased.

'We'll follow Snowy,' he said to the girls. 'He'll lead us to Philip!'

So they let the little kid dance in front of them, leading the way. He led them down the passage, into a vast, hall-like cave, into another passage, and then, to their great surprise, they came to a most amazing place.

It was like a vast laboratory, a work-room set in the heart of the mountain. It lay below them, and they had to lean over a little gallery to look at it.

'What is it?' whispered Lucy-Ann, awed at the amount of curious things there. There was no enormous machinery – only a vast network of gleaming wires, great glass jars standing together, crystal boxes in which sparks and flames shot up and down, and rows upon rows of silently spinning wheels that shone strangely as they spun. The wires ran from these all over the place.

In the middle of the work-room shone a curious lamp. It had many sides, and it glowed first one colour and then another. Sometimes it was so dazzling that the children could hardly look at it. Sometimes it died down to a faint red, green or blue glow. It seemed alive – a monster eye that watched over everything in that secret laboratory.

The children gazed, fascinated. There was nobody there at all. Everything seemed to work on its own, never stopping. The wheels spun round, the wires gleamed, and nothing made any noise beyond a very quiet humming.

And then – and then there began that faint, far-off rumbling they knew so well. Far below the laboratory, deep deep down, came a stirring and a groaning, as something happened in the depths of the mountain. Then, as had happened before, the mountain quivered a little, and shook, as if something tremendous had happened deep underground.

The great lamp in the middle suddenly grew bright, so bright that the children crouched back, afraid. It grew crimson, the brightest crimson they had ever seen in their lives. It began to belch out tiny puffs of crimson smoke.

Jack began to choke. He pushed the girls back into the passage, and they breathed the fresher air there in relief. Snowy, frightened, crouched against them.

'That's the smoke we saw coming out of a hole in the side of the mountain,' whispered Jack. 'There must be a chimney-pipe built from that lamp, right away up the mountain to the hole, where the smoke can escape.'

'What's going on, do you think?' asked Dinah, in awe. 'What's all that wire for, and the crystal boxes and things?'

'I haven't the least idea,' said Jack. 'But it's plain that it's something very secret, or they'd never do all this here, in this lonely, inaccessible place.'

'Atom bombs or something, do you think?' asked Lucy-Ann, with a shiver.

'Oh, no – you want enormous buildings for that,' said Jack. 'No – it's something very odd and unusual, I should think. Let's go back and peep.'

They went back, but everything was just as it had been, the wheels spinning silently, the crystal boxes sparking and flaming up and down inside, the great lamp watching like an eye, now crimson, now blue, now green, now orange.

'Let's go round the gallery and see where it goes to,' whispered Jack. 'I feel as if I'm in some sort of Aladdin's cave now – the Slave of the Ring might appear at any moment!'

They wandered on and came to another extraordinary

place. It was really only a high-roofed cave – but it was made into a great, sumptuous hall, with flights of steps leading up to what looked like a throne. Beautiful hangings hung down the walls from the roof, which glittered with shining lamps shaped like stars.

The floor was laid with a golden carpet, and ranged on each side were beautiful chairs. The children stared in astonishment.

'Whatever's all this?' whispered Dinah. 'Does some king live here? The king of the mountain!'

17

Philip again

'It's peculiar there's nobody about at all,' said Jack, staring round at the silent hall. 'Not a soul to be seen! I wonder where everyone is. All those wheels and wires and things whirring away busily by themselves, with nobody to see to them – and now this great empty place, with its throne and gorgeous hangings!'

'Jack!' said Dinah, pulling at his sleeve. 'Can't we find Philip now and rescue him? We've only got to go back through those long passages and down the rope-ladder! Snowy will take us to Philip, and we can take him safely to the entrance of the mountain.'

'Yes. That's a good idea,' said Jack. He stroked the little white kid by his side. 'Where's Philip?' he whispered, and gave Snowy a push. 'You show us, Snowy.'

Snowy butted Jack gently. He didn't seem to know what the boy meant. Jack gave it up after a bit. 'We'll wait and see if Snowy goes off by himself,' he said. 'If he does, we'll follow him.'

So they waited. Snowy soon became restive and set off down the big hall past the great throne. The children followed cautiously, keeping by the walls, as far in the shadows as possible. Snowy disappeared through some deep red curtains. The children peeped through them. On the other side was what looked like a small library. Books lined the walls. The children looked at the titles curiously. They could not understand what any of them meant. Most of them were in foreign languages, and all of them looked very learned and difficult.

'Scientific books,' said Jack. 'Come on. Snowy has gone through that opening.'

They followed him. He saw that they were coming and waited for them. They hoped he was taking them to Philip!

He was! He led them upwards through a curiously rounded tunnel-like passage, lit at intervals by the same kind of dim lamps they had seen in the first passages. It was weird going along in the half-dark, not able to see very far in front or behind. Snowy trotted in front like a little white ghost.

They passed big openings filled with what looked like stores of some kind. Boxes, chests, packages of all kinds were there, flung in higgledy-piggledy.

Jack paused to examine some. There were foreign labels on most of them. One had been opened, showing tins of food.

'Look,' said Jack, 'it's what I said. They have their

food brought here – by the helicopter, I expect. I wonder what in the world they're up to.'

They came to some steps hewn out of the rock itself. These led upwards rather steeply in a spiral. Snowy bounded up lightly, but the others panted as they went up and up, twisting and turning with the spiral of the stairway.

They came to a door set fast in the side of the stone stairway. It was a stout wooden door, with great bolts on the outside. Snowy stopped beside this door and bleated loudly.

Then the children's hearts jumped as they heard a familiar voice. 'Snowy! I'm still here! I can't get to you, Snowy, but never mind!'

'That's Philip!' said Jack. He knocked gently on the door. 'Philip! It's us! We're going to undo the bolts of this door.'

There was an astonished exclamation, and the sound of feet running across to the door. Then Philip's excited voice came through the door, eager and thrilled.

'Gosh, Jack! Is it really you? Can you let me out?'

Jack shot the bolts back. They were well oiled and went back easily. Philip pulled him into the space beyond as soon as the door was open. The girls followed too, with Snowy.

'Jack! How did you get here? I've been shut in this strange place with that black man. Look, there he is, over there. He sleeps most of the time. He's the one the dogs were after.'

Sure enough, there was the man, lying against the side of the cave, fast asleep. Jack and the girls looked round Philip's prison in wonder.

It was nothing but a cave in the side of the top of the mountain. It opened on to the sky . . . or so it seemed! At first the children could see nothing but a vast expanse of blue when they gazed out of the opening opposite to the door.

'It's almost at the top, this cave,' said Jack. 'Isn't it a miraculous view? You can see right over the tops of the mountains yonder. I've never been so high in my life before. It makes me quite giddy to look out for long.'

Dinah stepped to the edge of the cave but Philip pulled her back. 'No, don't go too near. There's an almost sheer drop there. And if you look down it makes you feel very strange – as if you're on top of the world and might fall any minute!'

'Hold my hand then, whilst I look,' said Dinah, and Jack wanted to see too.

'Lie down on the floor of the cave and look out of it that way,' said Philip. 'You feel safer then.'

So all four lay down and peered over the edge of the cave that was almost at the top of the mountain. It certainly gave them a curious feeling. Far far down below were the slopes of the mountain, and far below that the valley. Lucy-Ann clutched Philip tightly. She felt as if she was toppling over downwards! But she wasn't, of course. She was safe on the floor of the cave. It was just the terrific feeling of height that made her think she must be falling down and down!

'I don't like it,' she said, and came away from the ledge. The others were awed. They gazed until they too felt that they were going to fall, and then they pushed themselves back and sat up.

'Come with us quickly,' said Jack to Philip. 'We know the way out – and Snowy will guide us if we don't! We must go whilst there's a good chance. The whole place seems deserted. It's most peculiar.'

'Well, the men live on the very top of the mountain,' said Philip. 'The American has been telling me quite a lot. This cave is very near the top – so near that I can sometimes hear men talking and laughing. There must be a plateau on the summit – or some kind of flat place – because the helicopters land there.'

'Oh! Well, I suppose everyone must be up on the mountain-top then!' said Jack. 'We didn't meet a soul coming up here. Come on, let's go, Philip. Don't let's waste a minute. We can tell each other everything when we're safely out of this extraordinary mountain.'

They all went to the door – and then Jack pushed the others back quickly. He shut the door quietly and put his finger to his lips.

'I can hear voices!'

So could the others. Loud voices that were coming

nearer their door. Would the owners of the voices spot that the bolts were undone?

The voices came nearer and nearer – and then passed! Evidently nobody had looked at the bolts of the door. The children breathed again.

'Thank goodness! They've gone past!' said Jack. 'Shall we wait for a few minutes and then run for it?'

'No. Wait till the men come back and go up to the roof,' said Philip. 'I think they are only the paratroopers gone to get some stores to take up to the top.'

Everyone stared at him. '*Para*-troopers!' said Jack, in amazement. 'What do you mean? Why should there be paratroopers here?'

'This chap told me. His name's Sam,' said Philip, nodding towards the sleeping man. 'Let's wait till those fellows come back with their stores, or whatever they've gone to fetch. I don't think they'll even look at this door. They don't know I'm here!'

'Well – for goodness' sake tell us all about everything then,' said Jack, filled with intense curiosity. 'Paratroopers! It sounds impossible.'

'Well, you know when I was caught, don't you?' began Philip. 'They took me to that steep wall, behind a thick screen of creeper, and in at an opening there. I was pushed up some kind of ladder in the dark – a rope-ladder, I should think – and we went up for ages and ages.'

The others nodded. They knew all about that.

'We went through long passages, and came to a jolly frightening place – with wheels and things . . . Did you see it too?'

'Yes. Most extraordinary. But there was no one there,' said Jack.

'I didn't have time to see much,' said Philip. 'Then we went round a gallery – the one that looks down on that place of wheels and wires and sparks and flames – and came into a most magnificent place – like a room out of a palace!'

'Yes – we saw it too. A room for a king, with a throne and all,' said Jack. 'But nobody there!'

'Well, then I was pushed up passages and steps to this cave,' said Philip. 'And I was bolted in, and here I've stayed ever since! This man was pushed in too – but poor little Snowy was bolted out! He's come and bleated outside my door dozens of times. I hated that. He sounded so lost and miserable.'

Snowy was very happy now, however! He was curled up on Philip's knee, occasionally butting him gently to get a little more attention.

'I've had food pushed in through the door – all tinned stuff,' said Philip. 'But nobody's said a word to me, not even that nasty foreign-looking fellow who caught me. You should see his eyes! You often read in books about people with piercing eyes. Well, he's *really* got them – they go right through you! I was glad he didn't question me much, because I felt as if he'd know everything by reading my very thoughts.'

The others had been listening intently. Jack nodded towards the sleeping man. 'What did he tell you?'

'Oh, a lot of peculiar things,' said Philip. 'He said he saw an advertisement in the paper asking for men who had been paratroopers – you know, men who are trained to jump out of planes high in the air, and parachute to earth.'

'Yes. Go on,' said Jack, impatiently.

'Well, the hawk-eyed man – the one who captured me – he goes by the name of Meier, by the way – interviewed him at some office in Mexico, and offered him a terrific sum of money if he'd come and try some new kind of parachute-jumping.'

'What kind?' asked Dinah.

'I don't exactly know. Sam sounded a bit muddled when he told me – or else I didn't understand him,' said Philip. 'It's something to do with flying through the air on *wings* – wings fixed to his arms. Apparently you can't possibly fall to earth when you've got these wings on, and you can guide yourself where and how you like – just as birds do.'

'That's impossible,' said Jack at once. 'Quite mad.'

'Yes. That's why I think Sam got hold of the wrong idea,' said Philip. 'Well – this fellow Meier engaged a whole lot of ex-paratroopers, paid them fabulous sums, and brought them here, in helicopters, to the top of this mountain. And their job is to try out these wings – or so Sam says.'

'Has he tried them?' asked Jack.

'No. But three of his mates have. They had these peculiar wings fitted to their arms and were given orders to jump from the helicopter at a given moment – or else be pushed out,' said Philip.

'What happened?' asked Jack.

'Sam doesn't know,' answered Philip. 'You see, none of his mates came back. He's pretty certain they fell to their deaths. *He* didn't want to do the same – so he got away.'

18

A little exploring

There was a long pause after this strange story. It was very hard to believe – and yet they had seen and heard such strange things the last few days that they felt anything might be true of this lonely mountain.

'But what's the idea?' asked Jack, after a while. 'And why all the wheels and wires and things? I just don't get the hang of it all.'

'Nor do I. But Sam reckons that if the experiment came off, and men could really fly with these wings, somebody would make a most colossal fortune!' said Philip. 'Everyone would want them. Everyone would fly.'

'It sounds lovely,' said Lucy-Ann. 'I should love to fly like the birds do – much, much better than going in an aeroplane!'

They all felt the same – but nobody could really believe in these 'wings' that Sam had talked of.

'How did he escape?' asked Jack, nodding at the black man.

'He did an absolutely mad thing – as dangerous as jumping off a helicopter to try the "wings",' said Philip. 'He got a parachute out of the stores, came in here, fitted it on – and jumped!'

Everyone shuddered. 'What! Jumped out of this cave, right from the top of the mountain?' said Jack. 'Gosh, he's a brave man!'

'He is. His parachute opened, and he floated down to earth, landing with an awful bump. But of course he'd learnt how to fall, and he soon recovered. The next thing was – to find safety somewhere.'

'He couldn't have found a lonelier, more deserted bit of country than in these mountains,' said Jack. 'I suppose he didn't even know where he was.'

'He hadn't the faintest idea,' said Philip. 'I told him we were in Wales – but he didn't know where that was.'

'And then the dogs got after him, I suppose?' said Jack. 'Poor Sam!'

'Yes. He knew about them, because they live up on the mountain-top with the men. He says they're used to scare any possible wanderer who comes near this mountain – and, of course, to hunt anyone who does escape – or find anyone who crashes if the wings don't work.'

'That's more likely,' said Jack. 'Gosh, what a horrible, callous lot of men there must be behind all this! I never heard of anything like it in my life.'

'Sam says there's a king,' said Philip. 'The king of the mountain! Isn't it incredible? That throne must be for him. Sam's never seen him. He must be the spider at work, catching all these fellows and making them try out his mad experiments.'

'We thought there was some colossal brain behind all this,' said Jack. 'I suppose that hawk-eyed man – Meier – isn't the king, is he?'

'Oh, no! I don't know what you'd call him – sort of organizer, I suppose. He sees to everything – the stores – all the arrangements – shuts up the men when the helicopters arrive – and so on. There are two men, apparently, who work together on these things. The king is somebody who only appears on state occasions – such as when another pair of wings is produced, and the men have to go down to that great stateroom, listen to some speech they don't understand, and watch one of their number being picked to try out the wings.'

'Picking out a victim for sacrifice, it sounds like!' said Jack grimly. 'I don't like this at all. It's so *mad*.'

'Sam was ill the last time the king picked out his victims,' said Philip. 'So he hasn't seen the king of the mountain, as I said. He must be a twisted sort of chap – really callous and cruel, to make these fellows try out wings that can't possibly be any good.'

'I agree with you!' said Jack. 'And I think the sooner we get out of here and get into touch with old Bill, the better. I don't feel safe in this mountain. No wonder

Lucy-Ann got "feelings" about it. I've got quite a lot of feelings about it myself now!'

'Look – Sam's waking up,' said Lucy-Ann. They all looked at the man. He sat up, and rubbed his eyes. He looked across the cave and seemed surprised to see so many children.

Then he recognized Lucy-Ann as the little girl who had seen him up in the tree. He smiled, and then shook his head.

'Didn't I tell you to git away,' said Sam, looking solemn. 'This here is a bad mountain. Those men are bad, too.'

'We're going now, Sam,' said Philip. 'As soon as we think it's safe. Will you come too? We know the way out.'

Sam looked frightened. 'I'm scared of those dogs,' he said. 'I reckon I'm safe right here.'

'You're not. I bet you'll be the very next one chosen to try out the "wings" you told me about,' said Philip.

'The wings're better than those dogs,' said Sam.

Voices came past the door. The children fell silent and listened till they had gone past. Sam listened too.

'That was Pete and Jo,' he said.

'Well, Pete and Jo have gone up to the mountain-top again,' said Jack. 'Come on. It seems a good time to go now. We didn't meet anyone coming here – and the chances are we shan't meet anyone going back. What a tale we'll have to tell Bill!'

They opened the door cautiously. Snowy bounded out at once. Kiki was on Jack's shoulder, having kept silent for a surprisingly long time. She did not seem to like this peculiar mountain!

They went quietly down the spiral stairway, following its many turns round and round. They came to the openings where the stores were kept. It made them feel very hungry to see all the tins of food; but there was no time to think of eating now. They had to escape as quickly as possible.

Snowy led them down the dimly lit passages. The children expected to see the curious library of books at the end of them, but Snowy had apparently taken them a different way. They stopped after a while in dismay.

'I say – this isn't right. We didn't see that cave there before – I'm sure we didn't!' said Jack. They hesitated, not knowing whether to go on or go back. It would be awful to get lost in the heart of the mountain!

'I can hear some kind of noises,' said Lucy-Ann, listening. 'Let's creep on and see what they are.'

They went on down a wide passage that at times ran very steeply downhill. The air suddenly grew hot.

'Phew!' said Philip, mopping his forehead. 'I can hardly breathe.'

They came out on a kind of balcony that overlooked a great deep pit, so vast that it took the children's breath away. Far down in the middle of it men were at work, though what they were doing the children couldn't possibly tell. They were as small as ants.

Great lamps lit up the pit. The children gazed in astonishment. What *could* be going on down there?

Suddenly Jack nudged Philip. 'Look – the men have slid aside the floor of the pit – do you see? What's that under it?'

Jack might well ask! Out of the hole in the pit floor shone a brilliant mass of colour – but a colour the children did not know! It was not blue or green, not red or yellow, not any colour they had ever seen before. They gaped at it in surprise.

Then, suddenly they felt a curious feeling – a feeling of lightness, as if they were in a dream, and not quite real. They clutched the balcony rail, afraid. At the same moment the men down below slid the great floor over the hole in the pit again, and shut out the brilliant mass of unknown colour. At once the strange feeling passed away from the children, and they were themselves once more.

They felt a little weak. 'Let's go,' said Jack, scared. 'I don't like this.'

But before they could go there began that now familiar rumbling noise from the very depths of the mountain! The children clung to one another. It was so much louder now that they were *inside* the mountain. It was louder than thunder, an angry, unearthly noise. Then the balcony they were on began to shake.

Jack took one last look down into the strange pit. The men had disappeared – probably hidden safely behind rocky walls. Jack caught Lucy-Ann's hand and fled! After him came Philip and Dinah. Kiki clung to Jack's shoulder, more scared than any of them. Snowy had disappeared completely.

The four children tore up the steep wide passage that had led them down to the pit. The floor of it shook beneath their feet as they ran. The children felt sure that the whole of the great mountain was shaking. What powers were being used by these men? Surely they must have discovered some scientific secret unknown to anyone before!

The children did not stop running until they came to the end of the uphill passage. They were streaming with perspiration, and panting loudly. Snowy suddenly joined them and pressed against Philip's legs. All four children sank down in a heap and Snowy walked over them, unheeded.

'For goodness' *sake* let's get out of here,' said Philip at last. 'I daresay if we were scientists we shouldn't be a bit scared, only intensely interested – but all I can say is – let's get out of here!'

Everyone agreed heartily. The only thing was – which was the way? They got up and walked along a twisty little passage. It forked into two after a bit, and the children, not knowing which to take, took the right-hand one. It led them to a cell-like cave with a narrow bed in it, a jug and basin, and a shelf. Nothing more.

'Funny!' said Jack. 'I expect it belongs to Meier, or one of the other men. Let's go back.'

They went back to where the passage forked, and took the left-hand way. To their great surprise they came to hanging curtains of purple silk, patterned with great red dragons!

They stopped. Philip put his hand on Snowy to prevent him from darting forward. Jack crept to the curtains on tiptoe.

Beyond was a cave so beautifully decorated, so profusely hung with curtains and spread with thick carpets that it didn't seem like a cave at all. A couch stood in one corner, covered with a purple silk quilt, worked with the same red dragons as on the curtains they had seen.

Jack stared. Perhaps this was where the king slept. It felt deliciously cool here. Where did the little cooling draught come from? He saw a narrow rod hanging on the wall near him, with slits in it all the way along. He put his hand up and felt a draught of air. How astonishing! It was only a rod fixed to the wall. How could fresh air come out of it? Again Jack felt that there were remarkably ingenious brains at work in this mountain.

He heard voices from a room further on whose opening was hidden by the same kind of purple curtains that hung in other places. He tiptoed back to the others.

'We'll wait for a bit. There's somebody talking in the

room beyond this one. This is the king's bedroom, I should think.'

They waited, peeping through the curtains every now and then. They all began to feel terribly hungry. They were very relieved when the voices stopped and there was silence. They tiptoed through the bedroom and into the room beyond.

They stopped in delight – not at the strange beauty of the room – but at the gorgeous food on the table!

19

The king of the mountain

'Look at that!' said Jack. 'Somebody's been having a meal here – three people – and look at what they've left!'

'Can't we have some?' said Lucy-Ann, eyeing a great bowl of fresh strawberries and a jug half full of cream. Near by was a plate of cooked lobsters, and two dishes of mixed salads.

It was clear that three people had been having a meal there, judging by the plates and glasses, all of which were really beautiful.

'I call this a feast – a royal feast!' said Dinah, and she picked up a cake with cream icing on the top in the shape of a rose, and dug her teeth into it. 'I don't know who this stuff belongs to – but there's nobody to ask permission to share it – and I'm too hungry to wait!'

'So am I! We'll get Bill to pay for it if anyone objects,' said Jack, and set to work on a lobster. There were dishes of things the children had never seen before. They tasted one or two, but they were spiced in a way they disliked.

There were peaches and nectarines, pineapples and plums of all kinds. 'The helicopter must be pretty busy bringing all these!' said Philip, biting into the sweetest peach he had ever tasted in his life. 'I must say the King of this mountain does himself proud!'

Nobody came to interrupt them at all. Kiki feasted well, enjoying the food as much as the children. Snowy ate all the salad offered him, and for a treat was allowed to be on Philip's knee, with his forefeet on the table. He badly wanted to get on the table itself, and could not understand why Kiki was allowed there when he wasn't.

'If you eat any more, Kiki, you'll get the hiccups properly!' said Jack. 'Stuffing yourself like that! Greedy!'

'Pop goes Polly,' agreed Kiki, and would have given a cackle of laughter if Jack hadn't shushed her.

'Well – what about trying to find our way out again?' said Jack at last. 'I don't know whether it's anything to do with that strange feeling we had when the floor of the big pit was pushed back, and we saw that extraordinary mass of brilliance below – but I feel rather don't-carish now – not scared any more. I don't even feel that it's terribly urgent to get out of here, though I know it is!'

'It was a very unusual feeling,' said Philip. 'I thought I was going to float up into the air the next minute! I hung on to that balcony for dear life!'

They had all felt the same – and now they felt as Jack did – very 'don't-carish'. But that wouldn't do at all – it was imperative that they should find their way out as soon as possible.

They left the curious dining-room, with its laden table. They went into a passage that was much more brightly lit than the others they had walked down. Hangings decorated the rocky walls, great curtains that swayed a little in the draught that ran through the passages.

'This must be the king's own quarters,' said Jack. 'Maybe we shall come to the throne-room soon.'

He was quite right. They did. But this time the throne-room was not empty. It was full!

Men stood there silently. There were all kinds, and a tough-looking lot they were! They were of many nationalities. Some had the maroon beret that paratroopers have when in uniform. The peeping children thought that probably they were all old paratroopers. There were about twenty of them. Sam was there too, and Philip gave a little start when he saw him. Now it would be known that he, Philip, had escaped! Whoever had gone to bring Sam down here would have seen the unbolted door and found that he was gone.

Blow! Now he would be carefully hunted for, and it would be very difficult to escape. He nudged Jack and pointed out Sam to him. Jack, peeping through the curtains that hung before them, nodded and frowned. The same thought occurred to him as had occurred to Philip.

He debated whether to go off straight away now and

try to find the way out. But either they would have to go back the way they had just come, which obviously would not take them to the entrance they knew – or else they would have to go into the throne-room – where they would certainly be seen. No – they would have to stop where they were till this meeting, or whatever it was, was over.

Besides the paratroopers there were guards, men who looked like soldiers standing in an elaborate uniform down each side of the great hall. The throne was empty. There was no sign of the man Meier.

But suddenly there came a whispering among the men gathered there. The great curtains near the throne were flung back by two soldiers and the king of the mountain entered!

He seemed very tall, for he had a great crown that stood up from his head, embroidered with glittering stones. His wore a rich suit and cloak, and looked more like an Indian prince at some splendid festival than anything else. His yellowish face looked out impassively from below his great crown, and a mass of black hair swung down on each side. He sat down on the throne.

Beside him stood two men. Philip was sure that one was Meier. He didn't know the other, but he didn't like the ape-like face and enormous, burly figure. Meier's hawk-like eyes swept the room. He began to speak in a penetrating, most incisive voice, in a language that the children did not know. Then he paused and spoke in English.

The children listened, spell-bound. Meier spoke of the king and the wonderful gift he was giving to mankind – the gift of flying. He spoke of the grand men who were helping them in their experiment – the paratroopers willing to try the 'wings'. He spoke of the great wealth the men would receive, the honours that would be piled on them. Then he said it all again in a third language and then in a fourth.

He seemed to hypnotize everyone as he spoke. Jack could not help feeling that a lot he said was sheer nonsense – but he couldn't do anything but believe it whilst he heard it, and it was obvious that all the men there drank every word in, whether it was spoken in their own language or not. What a spell binder, thought Jack!

Then volunteers were called for. All the men stepped forward at once. The king then rose and, apparently at random, picked out two or three. He spoke a few inaudible words in an unexpectedly thin, reedy voice that didn't seem to go at all with his kingly presence.

Then Meier took charge again. He said that these men, among the first to fly with wings, would be sent back to their own countries after the experiment, with wealth enough to last them for a lifetime. All the others who had tried out the wings were now safely back in their homes, and were rich and honoured men.

'I *don't* think!' muttered Jack to Philip, remembering what Sam had related.

The king then walked majestically out and Meier and the other man followed. The guards ushered the paratroopers away and soon the great throne-room was empty.

When everyone had gone and there was complete silence, Jack whispered to Philip, 'We know the way out from here. Come on!'

They went to the huge laboratory, where the wheels and wires were still at their secret work. The children stood in the gallery above the big work-room and looked down at the strange lamp in the middle. Dinah suddenly clutched Jack and made him jump. He looked at her.

She pointed to where there was a great cluster of glass jars, with tubes running from one to the other. Jack saw somebody there.

It was an old man with a very large forehead, larger and rounder than any forehead Jack had seen in his life. The man was quite bald, which made his head seem more curious than ever. He bent over the glass jars and looked searchingly into them.

'Come on before he sees us,' whispered Jack, and pulled the others towards the passages that would lead them to the entrance. They went along them and at last came to the little chamber where the pitchers of water and the mugs were. Now to get down the rope-ladder and escape!

'What about Snowy?' whispered Dinah. 'How can we get him down?'

'I wonder how he got up before?' said Philip. 'And the dogs too. I never thought of that. I was just pushed up in the dark, and I was so scared I didn't think of Snowy or the dogs. They couldn't have climbed that ladder!'

'There's probably some hole somewhere that they went into,' said Dinah. 'A hole outside, I mean – too small for us, but big enough for Snowy and the dogs.'

As it turned out afterwards, Dinah was right. There *was* a small hole near the crack, and it was through this and up a narrow little tunnel that Snowy had passed with the dogs, who knew the way very well. The dogs' tunnel led eventually into one of the passages, and that was how Snowy had got into the mountain but had not been imprisoned with Philip.

Snowy was still with them. He knew the way he had come in by, but he wasn't going to leave the others. Jack switched on his torch and felt above for the rope-ladder.

'Where is the wretched thing?' he said. 'Surely it was just here!'

Snowy came and pressed close to him, and nearly sent him headlong down to the black pool. 'Hold Snowy!' he said to Philip. 'I almost went over then. I can't seem to find the ladder. It should be hanging down somewhere about here.'

'Let *me* look,' said Philip, giving Snowy to Dinah. He felt about too, and Jack flashed his torch all round and about to see if he could spy the rope-ladder up which they had all come.

But it wasn't there – or if it was, nobody could see it! Jack flashed his torch down into the hole as far as he could. No ladder at all!

'What's happened to it?' he said, exasperated.

'Perhaps someone has turned that little wheel in the pond the *other* way – and the ladder rolled up and put itself away,' suggested Dinah.

This was a dreadful thought. Jack began to look round the little chamber to see if the rope-ladder had been pulled up by the machinery set in motion by the wheel – but he couldn't see it anywhere.

His hand touched a spike on the wall. He focused his torch on it. 'This may be a lever!' he said to the others. 'Look!'

He pulled and pressed at the spike, and it suddenly gave way, pulling downwards. A slab of rock was moved smoothly – and there behind was the rope-ladder! How it worked with the wheel below the children could not imagine.

It certainly wouldn't work with them. It was evidently coiled or folded neatly in the hollow behind the rock – but how to get it from there nobody could make out. It needed some machinery put in motion to set it free. Then, Jack supposed, it would come sliding smoothly out of the place it was in, fall over the edge of the rock, and uncoil all the way to the bottom – hanging ready for any climber to come up.

'How does it work from up here though?' said Jack, for the twentieth time. All of them had pulled and twisted and tugged at the ladder, lying so snugly in its hiding-place – but it was quite impossible to move it.

'Give it up!' said Jack gloomily at last. 'No good! We're done for. It's absolutely maddening, just when we are almost out of this beastly mountain.'

20

An amazing secret

They sat in the little room for some time, disappointed and puzzled. Time and again they tried to make the rope-ladder slide out of its secret place, but it wouldn't. In the end they got very thirsty and very hungry. They drank all the water left in the jugs, and wondered where they could get something to eat.

They could only think of the room where they had feasted before. 'Let's go back to it and see if the remains of that meal are still there,' said Jack. 'I could do with another lobster or two!'

'Poor Polly!' remarked Kiki, who always seemed to know when food was being talked about. 'Polly's got a cold. Send for the doctor.'

'Oh, you've found your tongue again, have you?' said Jack. 'I thought you'd lost it! Now don't start screaming or cackling, for goodness' sake, or you'll have us caught!'

They found their way back to the throne-room,

which was still empty, and then to the room where the meal had been.

There were still the remains of the meal there. The children's eyes gleamed. Good! They felt better at once.

They sat down and reached for the food. Then suddenly Jack put his hand on Philip's arm and frowned. A noise had come from the next room – the beautifully furnished bedroom! The children sat as still as mice. Was anybody there?

Kiki suddenly saw Snowy with his front hooves on the table, reaching for the salad. In anger she flew at the kid and screeched.

'That's done it!' said Jack. And as he spoke, the hangings at the entrance to the room opened, and a face peered through.

It was the face they had seen down in the big work room – the face with the enormous forehead. It had bulging eyes of a curious green-blue, a hooked nose, and sunken cheeks, yellowish in colour.

This face stared in silence at the four children, and they, in turn, stared back without a word. Who was this strange old man with the great forehead?

'Do I know who you are?' asked the face, a puzzled look coming over it. 'I forget, I forget.' The curtains were swung further apart and the old man came right through. He was dressed in a kind of loose tunic of blue silk, and the children thought he looked a pathetic old thing. He had a thin high voice that Kiki immediately copied.

The old man looked astonished, especially as he could not see Kiki, who was behind a great vase of flowers. The children didn't say anything. They were wondering if it was possible to make a dash and get away.

'What are children doing here?' said the old man, in a puzzled tone. 'Have I seen you before? Why are you here?'

'Er – we came to look for somebody who was lost,' said Jack. 'And now we can't get out again. Could you tell us the way?'

The old man seemed so lost and wandering that it seemed to Jack that he might quite well be foolish enough to show them the way out. But he was wrong.

'Oh no, oh no,' said the old fellow at once, a cunning look coming over his yellow face. 'There are secrets here, you know. My secrets. Nobody who comes in may go out – until my experiments are finished. I'm the king of this place – my brain runs it all!'

He finished up on a high shrill note that gave the children an odd feeling. Was the old fellow mad? Surely he couldn't be the 'king' they had seen in the throne-room?

'You don't look like the king,' said Lucy-Ann. 'We saw the king in the throne-room – he was tall and had a great crown, and black hair round his face.'

'Ah, yes. They make me appear like that,' said the old

man. 'I want to be king of the world, you know, the whole world – because of my great brain. I know more than anyone else. Meier says I shall be ruler of the world as soon as my experiments are done. And they are nearly finished, very very nearly!'

'Does Meier dress you up like a king then, when you appear in the throne-room?' asked Jack, astonished. He turned to the others and spoke in an undertone. 'That's to impress the paratroopers, I suppose! He wouldn't cut any ice with them if they saw him like this.'

'I *am* a king,' said the old man, with dignity. 'Because of my great brain, you know. I have a secret and I am using it. You have seen my great laboratory, have you? Ah, my little children, I know how to use all the great powers of the world – the tides, the metals, the winds – and gravitation!'

'What's "Gravitation"?' said Lucy-Ann.

'It is the power that keeps you on the earth – that makes you come back to it when you jump, that brings a ball back when you have thrown it,' said the old man. 'But I – I have conquered gravitation!'

This seemed a lot of nonsense to the children. They were quite sure the poor old man was mad. He might have had a marvellous brain at one time – but he couldn't be much good now.

'You don't believe me?' said the old fellow. 'Well, I have discovered some rays that repel the pull of the earth.

Do you understand that, my children? No, no, it is too difficult for you.'

'It's not,' said Jack, interested. 'What you mean is – you think you've got hold of some rays that, if we use them, will cancel out gravitation? So that if you used the rays, say, on a ball, it wouldn't feel the pull of the earth to bring it back here, but would speed through the air and not fall to earth?'

'Yes, yes – that is it – very very simply,' said the old man. 'And now, you see, I have invented these wings. I send the rays through them. I imprison them in the wings. And then, when a man jumps from an aeroplane, he presses a button to release the power of the rays – and he does not fall to earth! Instead he can glide and soar, flap his wings, and fly like a bird until he tires of it – then he can imprison the rays again and glide to earth!'

The children listened to all this in silence. It was the most extraordinary thing they had ever heard.

'But – is it really true?' asked Lucy-Ann at last. The idea of flying like that was very tempting!

'Do you think we would have come here to this lonely mountain for our experiments, do you think Meier and Erlick would have poured out their money if they had not known I could do this?' demanded the old man, looking rather angry.

'Well – it just sounds so extraordinary, that's all,' said Lucy-Ann. 'It sounds perfectly *lovely*, of course – I mean,

I'd give anything to be able to fly like that. How clever you must be!'

'I have the biggest brain in the world,' said the old man solemnly. 'I am the greatest scientist that ever lived. I can do anything, anything!'

'Could you show us the way out of here?' asked Jack, in an innocent voice. The old man looked uncomfortable.

'If you use my wings, then you can go,' he said at last. 'We are all prisoners here till then, even I! Meier has said this must be so. He says I must hurry, hurry to get my wings quite perfect – time is short. Then I shall be made king of the whole world, and everyone will honour me.'

'Poor old man,' thought Philip. 'He believes everything that rogue of a Meier says. Meier and Erlick are using his brains for their own purposes.'

As suddenly as he had appeared, the old man went. He seemed to forget they were there. He vanished through the curtains and left them alone. They looked at one another, feeling uneasy.

'I don't know how much to believe,' said Jack. 'Has he really got hold of the secret of how to cancel out the pull of gravitation? Do you remember how peculiar we felt when we were looking at that extraordinary brilliant mass down in that pit – we felt sort of light, as if we ought to cling on to the balcony, or we'd float off into the air? Well, I bet some of those rays he spoke of were flying loose then!'

'Gosh, yes – that was strange,' said Philip thoughtfully. 'And, of course, all this would have to be done underground – so that the rays couldn't go flying off everywhere! The heart of a mountain seems a jolly good place for a terrific experiment like this – walls of thick rock all round. No wonder we heard rumblings and felt the earth shaking! That old scientist knows a thing or two. I'd be scared stiff to meddle with all the powers that scientists use nowadays. This is more extraordinary than splitting the atom.'

'I don't understand about things like that,' said Lucy-Ann. 'I feel like the people of old must have felt towards their magicians – I don't understand what they're doing, but it all seems like magic, and I'm scared!'

'You wait till you put on a pair of non-gravitation wings or whatever he calls them,' said Philip, helping himself to a peach. 'That'll be magic if you like.'

'Meier and Erlick must believe in the ideas the old man has,' said Jack. 'Or they wouldn't go to all the terrific trouble they do – and try to keep everything such a secret. I suppose, if the idea really came to something, they'd make such a colossal fortune that they'd be the richest men the world has ever known – and the most powerful.'

'Yes. *They'd* be the rulers – not the old man,' said Philip. 'They're just using him, and stuffing him up with all kinds of stories. He's as simple as can be, though he's got such a brain. They would give out that *they* were the inventors, not the old man. Fancy keeping him a prisoner here like that – and everyone else too!'

'Us included,' said Dinah. 'Well, I'm beginning to see daylight a bit now – understanding what's going on here – but I just can't believe it. Nor will Bill!'

They finished a very good meal. Nobody came to interrupt them. There was no sound from the old man's room. The children thought perhaps he had gone to bed for a rest, or had returned to his weird underground pit. They all made up their minds that nothing would persuade them ever to go down there again!

'What shall we do now?' said Jack. 'Snowy, tell us! Kiki, you've had enough peaches.'

'Poor Polly,' said Kiki sorrowfully, and wiped her beak on the table-cloth.

'Someone's coming!' suddenly said Lucy-Ann. 'Quick, hide!'

'Behind the hangings on the wall,' whispered Dinah, and the four children fled to the loose hangings. They squeezed behind them and waited, holding their breath.

It was two of the soldiers, who had entered the room to clear away the meal. They talked to one another in surprised voices, and indeed, they were filled with astonishment to see so much of the food eaten.

The children heard their light feet pattering to and fro. Then one of them gave a sharp exclamation, which the children didn't understand. They stood behind the curtains, their hearts beating fast. Kiki was on Jack's shoulder, silent and puzzled.

Suddenly Lucy-Ann gave a loud scream, and the two boys leapt out from behind their curtains at once. One of the soldiers had seen her foot below the hangings, and had pounced on her.

'Jack! Philip! Quick, save me!' she cried, and they rushed to her rescue.

21

On the mountain-top

Both the soldiers had got hold of poor Lucy-Ann. She was screaming wildly, and the two boys flew at the men. But to their great surprise they were thrown back as easily as if they had been feather-weights. Just a twist of the men's arms, and back they went, falling headlong to the floor.

They were up again in a trice – but this time one of the soldiers caught Philip in a vicious grip, and the boy found himself turning over in the air, and flying right over the man's head! He landed with a crash on the table, and sent all the dishes into the air.

What with Lucy-Ann's screams, the boys' yells, and the crashes of the dishes there was a terrific commotion. Kiki added to it by screeching loudly. Then she flew down and attacked one of the men. He fended her off.

Four more soldiers suddenly appeared, and that was the end of the children's resistance. They were all captured.

Kiki flew off somewhere, still screeching. Snowy had disappeared completely.

The four children were marched out of the room and taken to a bigger room, well furnished, but not nearly so elaborate as the king's rooms. Hangings covered the walls, but they were plain and simple. The roof of the cave was not covered, and the children could see the rough rock above their heads.

Lucy-Ann was sobbing. Dinah looked very pale and the boys were angry and defiant. They were all stood in a row against the wall. Philip felt in his pocket to see if his slow-worm was hurt in the scuffle. Sally Slithery had not liked life in the mountain. She had become lethargic and dull. But she would not leave Philip.

She was still there, coiled up. Philip wondered where Kiki and Snowy were. It was not like Kiki to fly off like that. She must have been very scared – or perhaps one of the dishes had struck her as it flew off the table.

In a few minutes Meier and Erlick, the two men who were the real power behind the poor old 'king', came into the room. Meier was glowering, and his piercing eyes glanced from one child to another sharply.

'So! There are four of you! Three of you came to find this boy, I suppose – and let him out of the cave he was in. You thought you could all escape – you thought it would be easy, so easy. And it was not?'

He fired this question at them, with a twisted smile on his hawk-like face.

Nobody answered. 'How did you find the way to let down the rope-ladder?' The man fired this question at them so suddenly that they jumped. 'Who told you how to get it down?'

Nobody said a word. Meier's eyes began to narrow, and the girls felt uneasy. He was horrid!

'I asked you a question,' he said. 'You, boy, answer me!'

'I used my brains,' said Jack shortly, seeing Meier looking at him.

'Does anyone else know of that entrance?' said Erlick suddenly. The children looked at him with dislike. He was like an ape, they thought! Meier was bad enough – but Erlick was ten times worse.

'How do we know?' said Philip, beginning to boil at the way these two men spoke to them. 'What does it matter if they do? Is what you're doing here so shameful that you need to hide even the entrance to the mountain?'

Erlick stepped forward and slapped Philip across the face. Lucy-Ann stopped crying, in greater fright than ever. Philip did not flinch. He looked the man boldly in the face, and did not even rub his smarting cheek.

'Leave him alone, Erlick,' said Meier. 'There are better ways of bringing a boy like that to heel than by slapping his face. And now we will send out the dogs to scour the countryside. If these children have friends anywhere near, the dogs will find them, and bring them in.'

The children's hearts sank. Would the Alsatians capture Bill and David then – and bring them to the mountain to make them prisoners too? That would be dreadful.

From somewhere outside came a hollow cough. Meier and Erlick jumped. Meier went to the entrance to the cave and looked out. There was nobody there at all.

'Is there another of you?' asked Meier. 'Is it boy or girl?'

'Neither,' said Jack, who had recognized Kiki's cough, and was hoping she would keep out. It would be just like these men to wring her neck.

'Pooh! Gah!' came Kiki's voice, and then a cackle that was enough to make the men's blood curdle. They went to the entrance of the cave again, and had a good look round, but Kiki was safely perched on a shelf of rock above their heads, and they could not see her at all.

'Send for the doctor,' said Kiki, in a sepulchral voice, that sent shivers down the men's backs. 'Send for the doctor.'

'Good heavens! Who *is* it?' said Erlick. He looked threateningly at the four children. 'If that's another boy out there, being funny, I'll skin him alive!'

'There are only four of us, two boys and two girls,' said Jack.

'And here we all are,' said Philip, in an insolent voice. He knew it was foolish to talk like this to the two men, but he couldn't help it. Both he and Dinah were fool-hardy when their tempers were up.

'Oh! And here you'll all stay!' said Meier. 'And I'll think up something to take the spirit out of you, my boy. You may have gone through your life cheeking everyone and throwing your weight about – but you won't do it with me. Now – walk in front of us, and keep going!'

The children were forced to walk out of the cave in front of the two men. They soon found themselves stumbling up the stone spiral stairs, going up and up. They came to the openings where the stores were, and then went on past those till they came to the door of the cave in which Philip had been bolted.

'Hey, you, boy! You're to go into that cave again,' ordered Meier. 'A few days without much to eat will soon take the insolence out of you. You others go on up.'

Poor Philip! He was shut once more into the cave that looked out to the sky – but this time he had no Sam to keep him company. He sat down, wishing he hadn't been so foolish as to cheek the two grim men. Then he was glad he had. *He* wasn't going to kow-tow to two rogues like that. All the same it was a pity he wasn't with the others – especially as now there was only Jack to be with the girls.

The other three were forced to go on higher, climbing steadily. And then – what a surprise!

They came up a broad flight of steps hewn out of the rock, on to the very top of the mountain itself. They stood there, catching their breath at the sight of the amazing panoramic view all round them. The top of the world! Surely they must be touching the sky itself!

The three forgot their troubles for a moment as they gazed round in wonder. Everywhere they looked there were mountains, rising high. Valleys, deep in shadow, lay far far below. It was wonderful to be up there in the blazing sunshine and cool breeze, after being in the dark mountain for so long.

The top of the mountain was extraordinarily flat. On three sides rose steep rocks, like teeth. Jack knew in a flash what mountain it was – Fang Mountain, the one he had noticed when they had set out. He looked round the mountain-top. Nothing grew there at all. It was bare, flat rock, the size of a great courtyard. At one side, playing cards in the shade, were the paratroopers.

They stared in surprise at the children. Runaway Sam was with them and he pointed to Jack and was evidently telling his companions about him and the others. Jack was glad that Philip had told Sam so little about himself and the other three. He did not want Meier to know any more than he already did.

There was an awning rigged up on the side opposite the paratroopers. Meier pushed the children towards it.

'You will stay here,' he said. 'You will not talk to those men over there at all. You will not go near them. You are prisoners, you understand? You have forced your way in here, where you are not wanted, and now we shall keep you here as long as we wish.'

'Can't Philip come with us?' begged Lucy-Ann. 'He'll be so lonely away from us.'

'Is that the other boy? No. He needs a little punishment,' said Meier. 'A little starvation diet! Then we will see if he will talk civilly.'

Meier and Erlick then left the three and disappeared into the mountain again. Jack and the girls sat down, looking doleful. Things weren't too good! It was a thousand pities that poor Philip was apart from them.

Evidently the paratroopers had been warned that they were not to go near the children, for they made no attempt even to shout to them. It was obvious that Meier and Erlick were used to being obeyed.

There was a natural parapet of rock near where the children were, that ran round the edge of the mountain just there. Jack got up and went to it. He sat on it and put his field-glasses to his eyes. If only he could spot Bill! And yet he was afraid that if Bill was there anywhere, the dogs might set on him and find him. He wondered where all the dogs were.

Then he sat up a little straighter on the parapet and focused the glasses on a small spot on the slope of the mountain. He had seen a movement. Could it be Bill and David and the donkeys?

No, it wasn't. It was the dogs! They had evidently already been let loose and were ranging the countryside.

If Bill was anywhere about, they would soon find him! Blow! Then Bill would be captured too. Jack wished he knew some way of preventing this happening, but he couldn't think of anything.

He wondered about poor old Dapple. Thank goodness they had tied him up so very loosely. He had plenty of range, and there was grass and water for him. But how the donkey would wonder what had happened to everyone!

Something touched Jack's hand and he jumped and looked down. It was Snowy! The kid had found his way to them and was nuzzling Jack in a half-scared manner.

'Hallo, Snowy! Have you been looking for Philip?' said Jack, rubbing the kid's soft nose. 'He's in that cave again. You can't get to him.'

Snowy knew that very well. He had already been to bleat outside Philip's door. He looked so dismal that Jack took him to the girls and they all made a fuss of him.

'What do you suppose has happened to Kiki?' asked Lucy-Ann after a time.

'Oh, she'll turn up all right,' said Jack. 'She knows how to take care of herself. Trust Kiki for that! She's probably leading those two men a fine old dance, coughing and sneezing and cackling and making a noise like an express train screeching in a tunnel!'

Jack was perfectly right. Kiki had been playing a fine game with Meier and Erlick, and as they had no idea that the children had a parrot, they were two extremely puzzled men. A voice without a body to it – how very strange!

Nothing happened for some time. Then, when the sun was sinking, there came a clamour of howls and barks, and the pack of Alsatians was brought up to the top of the mountain by two of the soldiers. The children watched to see if Bill had been caught, but there was no sign of any prisoner with the dogs. They heaved a sigh of relief.

The dogs were taken to a big wire enclosure some way off the children. 'You be careful of dogs,' said one of the guards to the children. 'They bite hard. You be careful!'

22

The helicopter

The children, however, were not in the least afraid of the dogs, for had they not all slept together with them some nights before? They did not tell this to the soldiers, of course. They waited till the men had disappeared and then they went over to the dogs.

But Philip was not there this time, and the dogs did not feel the same towards the girls and Jack as they had done towards Philip. They growled when Jack came near to them, and one showed his enormous white teeth. Lucy-Ann and Dinah shrank back.

'Oh! How terribly fierce they look! They've quite forgotten us. Jack, be careful.'

Jack was not afraid, but he was cautious when he saw that the dogs did not want to be friendly. They were strong, fierce creatures, disappointed in their hunting that day, hungry, and suspicious of Jack. Now, if he had been Philip how different their behaviour would have been! Philip's magic touch with animals would have put everything right. He had an irresistible attraction for all live creatures.

'Come away from them,' said Lucy-Ann, when she heard the growling taken up by most of the pack. 'They're making a perfectly horrible noise – just like wolves would, I'm sure.'

They went back to their own part of the mountain. 'A corner for the dogs, a corner for us, a corner for the men!' said Jack. 'Well – I wonder how long we're going to be here!'

Nobody brought them anything to eat at all for the rest of that day. They thought it was a very good thing they had had such good meals in the king's room! Jack wondered if they were supposed to lie on the bare rock to sleep. What brutes those men were, if they meant to keep them without rugs or food!

But just as it was getting dark three of the soldiers appeared. They carried rugs with them, which they threw down at the children's feet. One had brought a pitcher of water and mugs.

'What about something to eat?' asked Jack.

'Not bring,' said one of the men. 'Master say not bring.'

'Your master not nice,' Jack told him. 'Your master very nasty.'

The men said nothing. He and the others went away, soft-footed as cats. The children curled up in their rugs, wondering how Philip was faring, alone in his cave.

The next morning was unbelievably beautiful when the sun rose and lighted up the mountain-tops one by one. The three children sat on the parapet and watched. They all felt very hungry indeed. Snowy was with them. Kiki had still not appeared and Jack was getting a little worried about her.

Snowy leapt up on to the parapet beside Jack. There was a very steep drop from there, with a tiny ledge of rock jutting out some way below. Nobody could escape by climbing down, that was certain. He would just go slipping and sliding down the mountain and break all his limbs in no time.

Snowy stood there, his little ears pricked up as if he was listening. He suddenly bleated very loudly. And then, very muffled, hardly to be heard, a voice answered. Jack leapt up from the parapet. Was it Philip's voice? Where was his cave then? Anywhere near where they were?

Lucy-Ann and Dinah joined Jack, seeing his sudden excitement. Then Snowy gave them a really terrible shock. He jumped right over the mountain-top, off his perch on the parapet of rock!

'Oh!' shouted Lucy-Ann. 'He'll be killed!'

She wouldn't look to see what happened, but Dinah and Jack watched in horror. The little kid had leapt to the tiny ledge of rock jutting out some way below the parapet. He landed on it with all four tiny hooves close together! There was only just room for them – not half an inch to spare!

He stood balanced there, and then, when it looked as if surely he must topple off, he leapt to a small ledge lower down, slithered down a rough bit, and disappeared completely.

'Goodness gracious! What a thing to do!' said Dinah, taking a deep breath. 'My heart almost stopped beating.'

'Is Snowy all right?' asked Lucy-Ann, still not daring to look.

'Apparently. Anyway he's disappeared – and I should think he's probably found the cave where Philip is,' said Jack. 'All I hope is he won't try to get back the same way – or he'll certainly break his neck.'

But Snowy did get back the same way and appeared on the parapet about half an hour later, looking as frisky as a squirrel.

And round his neck was a note! It was tied there with string. Jack took it off quickly and opened it. He read it to the others.

How are you getting on? I'm all right except that I've nothing to eat, and only water to drink. I believe those brutes are going to starve me out! Can you send Snowy with anything for me to eat when you get a meal? Cheerio!
Philip

At that moment the guards arrived with a meal for the children. It was all out of tins but there was plenty. With it was a loaf of fresh bread. Dinah said she thought perhaps the soldiers had an oven down in the pit somewhere to bake their bread.

They waited till the men had gone and then Jack debated how to send food to Philip. He made some sandwiches and wrapped them up firmly in the paper the soldiers had brought the bread in. He slipped a note inside the sandwiches to say they would send food by Snowy whenever they could. Then he tied the packet very firmly on to Snowy's back. Snowy smelt it and tried to reach it, but he couldn't.

'Now you go to Philip again,' said Jack and patted the parapet to show Snowy that he wanted him up there. As soon as he was up Snowy remembered Philip and down he went again on his clever little feet, landing on first one tiny ledge and then another.

The other three felt pleased to think that Philip was having a meal instead of being starved. Jack took a look round the countryside below with his field-glasses, as they sat and ate, wondering if Bill would come that day. Time was getting on now. Surely Bill would arrive soon!

The day passed very slowly. The paratroopers were taken off into the mountain by the soldiers and didn't come back. The dogs were also taken out and Jack was sure he could see them ranging the countryside again.

They sent food to Philip by Snowy each time they

had a meal. It was a help to exchange cheery notes with him even though nobody felt all that cheerful. Kiki hadn't yet returned and all the children were now very worried about her.

The evening came. The paratroopers had not come back and the children wondered why. The dogs came back, however, but this time the children did not go over to them. The Alsatians were fighting over their meat and sounded savage and fierce.

It was a cloudy, sultry evening. The children dragged their rugs out from under the awning to a place where the breeze blew more strongly. They lay down, trying to go to sleep. The two girls slept, but Jack lay wide awake, feeling worried about Kiki and Philip and the girls too.

He heard a noise far away in the distance and sat up. He knew what that was – it was a helicopter! There was no mistaking the noise now. Was it coming to the mountain?

He awoke the two girls. 'Dinah! Lucy-Ann! The helicopter's coming. Wake up and let's watch. Get back under the awning, in case it lands too near us.'

The girls dragged their rugs under the awning. They went to sit on the parapet and listened, wondering if Philip was awake and listening too. He was. He was lying on his tummy, looking out of his cave, watching and listening. It was too dark for him to see anything much, but he hoped he might share in the excitement.

The noise came nearer and at last sounded very loud.

'Look – there it is,' said Jack, excited. 'See – going round the mountain a bit above us. Aren't they going to flash a light here to show it where to land?'

As he spoke two of the soldiers appeared in a hurry on top of the mountain. They ran to the middle of the great rocky courtyard and did something the children could not see. Immediately a strong light flashed upwards into the sky, and in its beam the children saw the helicopter, its wheels poised almost above their heads.

'There it is! It's landing!' cried Jack. 'See how it's dropping down slowly, almost vertically! It's just the right sort of machine to land on a mountain-top!'

The helicopter came down to the courtyard and stopped. The vanes ceased to whirl above it. Voices hailed one another.

'It's a jolly *big* helicopter,' said Jack. 'I've never seen such a big one before. It must be able to carry quite a large cargo.'

The beam of light was now directed on the helicopter and the children could see what was going on quite clearly. Boxes and crates were being tumbled out of it on to the ground, and the hard-working men were all very busy handling them, dragging them about, opening some of them and taking the contents down the stone steps to the store-places.

A lean-faced young man with a scar right across his cheek was the pilot of the helicopter. With him was a swarthy fellow who limped badly. They spoke to the workers in curt tones, and then left their machine and disappeared into the mountain.

'Gone to report to Meier and Erlick, I should think,' said Jack. 'Come on – let's go and have a look at the helicopter. Wish I knew how to fly it! We could escape nicely in it now.'

'And hover outside Philip's cave and take him off too!' said Dinah. They all went over to the machine. Jack got into the pilot's seat and felt grand. How he wished he knew how to fly the helicopter!

He was still sitting there when Meier, Erlick, the pilot and his companion, and one of the paratroopers appeared. Jack tried to scramble out before he was seen but he was too late. Meier saw him and dragged him out so roughly that he fell to the ground.

'What are you doing? You keep away from this machine!' shouted Meier in a fury. Jack skipped off to the girls, rubbing his shoulder.

'Are you hurt, Jack?' asked Lucy-Ann anxiously. He whispered that he was all right. Then he said something that made the girls stare fearfully at the group of men in the centre of the courtyard.

'I believe that paratrooper is the next one to try those "wings". They've brought him up to show him the helicopter and where he's to jump from.'

Both the girls thought it would be dreadful to have to leap from a machine high up in the air – and trust to the king's extraordinary 'wings'. They wondered how many people had tried them and failed. Nobody would know if they were efficient or not until they had been tried.

The paratrooper looked the helicopter over thoroughly. He talked to the pilot, who answered him shortly. Jack thought that the pilot wasn't any too keen about the para-jumping part. He would probably have been content to fly the goods to the mountain and finish at that.

'Tomorrow night you leave,' said the voice of Meier, cutting through the night. 'Come and eat now.'

Leaving two soldiers to guard the helicopter from the curiosity of the children, the rest of them disappeared into the mountain. Tomorrow night! What would they see then?

23

The wonderful wings

The three children retired to their rugs. They were afraid to go near the helicopter again, because the obedient soldiers, they knew, would stand no nonsense. Snowy appeared from over the parapet, full of curiosity. He ran over to the helicopter, but the guards hit out at him.

'The beasts! How can they be cruel to a little kid?' said Jack. 'Snowy! Come here! These fellows would make you into soup as soon as look at you. You'd better be careful.'

'Oh, Jack – don't say things like that,' said tender-hearted Lucy-Ann. 'Would they really? Surely nobody would ever have the heart to hurt Snowy?'

Snowy retreated hastily to the children and skipped up and down the parapet, as sure-footed in the dark as in the daylight. The beam of the lamp showed up the helicopter, but the rest of the courtyard was in darkness.

The dogs howled in their enclosure. They had not liked the noise the helicopter made, and they were uneasy and restless. The soldiers shouted threateningly to them, but the dogs took no notice.

'I don't like this adventure at *all*,' said Lucy-Ann suddenly. 'In fact, I simply hate it. I want to get away. I want to go back to Bill and Aunt Allie and Effans and Mrs Evans. Why did we have to find another adventure in these nice, peaceful summer holidays?'

'It just happens to us,' said Jack. 'Something in us attracts them, I suppose – like animals are attracted to Philip! Some people attract good luck, some attract wealth, some attract animals, some attract adventures.'

'Well, I'd rather attract something harmless, like cats or dogs,' complained Lucy-Ann. 'Oh dear! I do wish Snowy wouldn't keep walking over us when we're lying down.'

They fell asleep at last. In the morning, when they sent some food to Philip by Snowy, they sent a note also, telling him all they had seen in the night. Snowy brought a note back.

I'm sorry for the paratrooper! I wonder how many they've used in trying out this mad experiment. I'm glad I'm not chosen for anything as crazy as that! Keep your chin up! I'm all right here. I've got Snowy most of the time and Sally Slithery is getting so tame she eats out of my fingers. She sleeps on a bit of warm rock at the edge of my cave. Tell Snowy not to tread on her when he comes bounding in!
So long!
Philip

The day seemed very long again. The dogs were not taken down into the mountain and let loose on the countryside, but were exercised round and round the courtyard by the diligent soldiers. The children were glad about that.

'If old Bill arrives today, the dogs won't be out on the mountain-side. He'll be safe. So let's hope he comes. Not that he can do much if he does. He won't know where the entrance is – and if he finds it, he won't know how to work the rope-ladder – and there's no other way of getting in.'

Lucy-Ann looked very dismal. 'Shall we have to stay here all our lives long?' she asked.

The others laughed at her. 'No!' said Jack. 'Bill will do *some*thing – but don't ask me what!'

The paratroopers had not appeared again that day, not even the one who was supposed to be going to use the 'wings' that night. The helicopter stood there in the middle of the courtyard, the sun glinting on its motion-less shape.

Evening came. The children grew restive. The soldiers had brought them food as usual, but had not said a word. What were all the paratroopers doing? Having a ceremonial feast of something to celebrate their comrade's experiment?

And where, oh where, was Kiki? Jack was feeling very miserable about her now. He turned over and over in his mind all the things that might have happened to her. She had never been away from him so long.

That night the beam shone out again in the courtyard. Meier, Erlick, three or four servants and the paratrooper appeared, followed by the lean-faced, scarred pilot and his companion.

Then up the opening, stepping out majestically, came the king!

He was dressed in his grand robes and crown and was hardly recognizable as the poor, bald old fellow who had talked to the children a day or two back. He held himself proudly as he walked to the centre of the courtyard.

Behind came four uniformed guards, carrying a box. They laid it down at the king's feet. In silence he stooped down and opened it.

He took out a pair of wings! They glittered like gold, and were shaped like a bird's outstretched wings, big and wide. Lucy-Ann gasped in delight.

'Oh! Look, Dinah! Real wings! Aren't they lovely?'

The king was speaking to the amazed paratrooper. 'These will hold you up when you jump. Press this button here as soon as you leap from the helicopter. Then you will find that you cannot fall. You will no longer feel the pull of the earth. You will be free and light as air. Then you may use the wings, for guiding yourself, for planing, for soaring, whatever you wish!'

'Doesn't it sound marvellous?' whispered Lucy-Ann, drinking in every word.

'The wings must be fitted to your arms,' said the king. 'Hold them out and I will fix them on.'

'Here – is this all I'm going to have to stop me falling?' said the paratrooper.

'You will not need anything else,' said the king. 'In these wings are imprisoned powerful rays. At the press of the button they are released, and shoot towards the earth, preventing its pull on you. You cannot fall! But when you want to come to earth, press the button once more – and you will glide down gently, as the earth exerts her pull on you once more.'

'Yes, but look here – I understood it was a new kind of parachute I was trying out,' said the paratrooper. 'See? I didn't think it was stuff and nonsense like this!'

'It is not nonsense, man,' said Meier's curt voice. 'It is a great invention by the greatest scientist in the world. You will find Erlick and me waiting for you to come to earth when you have flown a mile or two. We shall take the dogs and find you. Then – riches for you, and honour for the rest of your life! One of the pioneer flying-men!'

'Look here – I'm a heavy chap,' began the paratrooper again. 'See? Those flimsy wings won't hold *me* – rays or no rays! I don't know about any pull of the earth on me – all I know is I'll have to fall, once I jump out with only those things on my arms. Are you crazy?'

'Get him!' suddenly said Meier, in a furious voice. Erlick and the soldiers at once pinioned the paratrooper's arms. He had to stand whilst the king fixed on the 'wings'. The children watched with bated breath.

The paratrooper cried out and struggled, but the ape-like Erlick was far too strong for him. 'Put him in the helicopter and take off,' commanded Meier. 'Go too, Erlick. Push him out at the right moment. If he's a fool he'll not press the button. If he is wise he will press it – and then he will see how well he flies!'

But the pilot now had something to say. He spoke in a drawling voice, clear and contemptuous.

'I think this fellow's too heavy. The last one was too. You'd better think again, boss, and get those wings made twice the size. I'm game for an experiment where there's a chance for everybody – but I reckon there's not much chance for a big fellow trying out those wings of yours.'

'Do you mean you refuse to take this fellow?' said Meier, white with anger.

'You've got it right first time, boss,' said the pilot, getting angry too, so that his scar showed up very plainly. 'Try a little fellow! I guess the experiment worked all right last time – for a minute or two – and then it petered out. These paratroopers are hulking great chaps – the ones you try out with me, anyway – and I tell you plainly I'm not taking anyone who doesn't want to go. Got it?'

Meier went up to the pilot as if he meant to strike him. Erlick pulled him back. 'That's right,' said the pilot, who had not turned a hair. 'Don't try any funny business with me, boss. I know too much – and there's others will know too much too, if I don't get back on time!'

He got into his machine, and the swarthy man, his companion, who had not said a single word all this time, got in beside him. The paratrooper watched them dazedly. The engine of the helicopter started up.

The pilot leaned forward and spoke again to Meier, who looked as if he was on the point of bursting with rage.

'So long! I shan't be coming next time – I'm going for a holiday! I'll be sending somebody who's not so pernickety as I am – but I warn you – try a little guy!'

The machine rose vertically into the air, circled round the mountain-side slowly, and then made off to the west. In a few minutes it could not even be heard.

The children had watched all this, the girls only half understanding what was going on. Lucy-Ann felt sorry for the frightened paratrooper and very glad he had not been forced to go off in the helicopter.

The little group left in the courtyard paced up and down. A lot of talk and argument went on, though the paratrooper did not seem to be joining in at all. He had stripped off the wings and was held securely by the soldiers. The king carried his precious wings all the time, but at last replaced them in the box and locked it.

'Very well,' he said, 'I agree. It may be that the men we choose are too heavy – but who else could we have asked? Only paratroopers are used to jumping from heights! Try someone lighter if you wish. It will make no difference to my ideas.'

And then the children heard a few words that made them gasp in horror. 'One of those kids will do,' said Meier. 'That insolent boy, for instance. We'll put the wings on him and he shall jump from the helicopter!'

24

The helicopter comes again

When the courtyard was completely empty, and the beam had gone out, leaving the mountain-top in darkness, Lucy-Ann began to cry bitterly. Jack and Dinah put their arms round her. They felt like howling too.

'He doesn't mean it,' said Jack, trying to think of something really comforting. 'Don't worry! He only said that to scare us. They'd never make Philip do a thing like that.'

'They didn't say it to scare us. They meant it, you know they did!' sobbed Lucy-Ann. 'What are we going to do? We've got to do *some*thing.'

It was all very well to say that – but what in the world was there to do? The children got very little sleep that night. They debated whether to tell Philip or not what had happened – and what was proposed.

They decided not to. It would be dreadful for him to lie alone in his cave and worry. So, when morning came and they sent Snowy to Philip with the usual sandwiches made from their own breakfast rations, they said nothing in the daily note about what had happened.

But to their great surprise, who should be ushered up the steps by the soldiers that morning, but Philip himself! He bounded forward to greet them, grinning.

'Hallo! They've let me out! Tired of starving me, I suppose, and seeing me get fatter and fatter. I say, did you see the helicopter last night? I heard it.'

Lucy-Ann and Dinah hugged him and Jack slapped him heartily on the shoulder. They were delighted to see him again. Snowy had come with him and acted like a mad thing, careering up and down the parapet as if he was in a circus.

They told him very little about the night before. He was rather puzzled that they said so little, even in answer to his questions. But Jack, by means of heavy frowns, had let the girls know they had better not say too much. He thought it would be wise to postpone saying anything in case Meier really hadn't meant what he said.

But it looked a bit odd, Meier letting Philip come up to be with the others, all of a sudden – and bringing them very much better food and plenty of it. 'Like victims being fattened for the sacrifice!' thought Jack. 'I wonder when the next helicopter's due? How long have we got? Oh, Bill, do make haste!'

Lucy-Ann and Dinah, fearing that poor Philip really would have to jump from the helicopter, were most affectionate to him. Dinah even enquired after Sally the slow-worm and did not shrink away when Philip brought her out of his pocket.

'I say! What's up with Dinah?' asked Philip at last. 'She's gone all sweet and sugary. It's not like her. She'll be offering to nurse Sally Slithery for me next!'

Philip felt sure there was something up. He couldn't *imagine* what it was. He wondered if it was bad news about Kiki. No – if Jack had heard any, he would be much more upset than he was. Philip felt uncomfortable. It wasn't like the others to keep anything from him. He tackled Jack about it firmly.

'Look here, Jack – something's up. Don't say there isn't – I jolly well know there is. So come out with it – or I'll go back to my cave and sulk!'

Jack hesitated. Then he took the plunge. 'All right, Philip – I'll tell you. But it's not good.'

He told him all about it – how the helicopter had arrived – what had happened – about the frightened paratrooper and the angry pilot – and finally about Meier's wicked suggestion that one of the children should try the 'wings'.

'I see,' said Philip slowly. 'And I suppose the one they're going to try is me?'

'That's what they said,' said Jack. 'The brutes! That experiment is only half-way to perfection – the wings aren't a hundred per cent foolproof, nor even fifty per cent – though they may be one day!'

'Well, well – to think I'm going to fly with wings,'

said Philip, trying to pass the whole thing off as a joke. He saw Jack's troubled face. 'Don't worry, old son. It won't happen! Something will turn up – and if it doesn't, I'm no coward!'

'I know. You don't need to tell me that,' said Jack. 'The girls are awfully upset. That's why we've seemed a bit funny with you. We just didn't want to tell you.'

Philip pranced up to the girls, flapping his arms like wings. 'Cheer up!' he cried. 'As soon as I'm out of that helicopter I'll fly off to Bill and give him the shock of his life!'

But it wasn't much use trying to make a joke of it. It was too serious. None of the children felt like playing with Snowy, who was very hurt and gambolled down the stone steps into the mountain to look for somebody with a bit more fun in them.

Three days went by. The children had almost given up all hope of Bill coming now. Surely he would have been along before, if he had come looking for them? They would have seen a search-party on the mountain-side, if one had come. But they saw nothing at all. It was most disappointing. They felt quite sick with watching and waiting.

They pondered whether to make a dash for freedom again and try for the rope-ladder once more. But Jack shook his head. 'No, they'll be on the watch now. There's always one of those soft-footed soldiers about. Meier will have put somebody on guard.'

There was one good thing, orders had evidently been given to feed the children well, and they had plenty of good food. Even their sad hearts did not take away their appetites and they tucked in well, helped by Snowy, who would devour every scrap of greenstuff or vegetable if he could.

And then, one night as they slept together under the awning, their rugs pulled round them, they heard the familiar sound of the helicopter! All four sat up at once, their hearts beating. Tears came into Lucy-Ann's eyes.

The helicopter circled round the moutain-top slowly. Then the bright beam came on and the courtyard was lighted up. The helicopter came slowly down and at last its wheels rested on the rocky yard.

There were two men in the machine, but neither of them was the same as before. The pilot had on big goggles and a peaked cap. The other man was bare-headed. He looked stern and grim.

Meier soon came up with Erlick and the soldier guards. 'You the boss?' called the pilot. 'I've taken Kahn's place. He's on holiday. Had a job finding this place. This is Johns, my mate. We've got the goods you wanted.'

There was the same unpacking as before, and boxes and crates were piled on the ground. The pilot and his companion jumped down.

'There is a meal ready for you,' said Meier. 'You will start back tomorrow night?'

'No. Got to leave tonight,' said the pilot. 'They're

making enquiries about some of our doings. Got to be back at once.'

'You have been told that – er – that er . . .' began Meier.

'What – that some paratrooper wants a jump off the helicopter?' said the pilot. 'Oh, yes. That's okay by me. If a chap wants to do that, well, it's no business of mine.'

'You will be paid very very well,' said Meier's grim voice. 'This time it is double the price. We have a young jumper – it is necessary for our experiments, you understand.'

There was a pause. Then the pilot's voice came again, sharp and enquiring. 'What do you mean – a *young* jumper?'

'A boy,' said Meier. 'He is here.' Then he turned to one of the soldiers and said something to him in a foreign language. The soldier darted off down the steps into the mountain. 'I have sent to tell the inventor that you have arrived,' he said. 'Now will you come to have a meal?'

'No,' said the pilot. 'I must be off. Get this boy and make him ready.'

Lucy-Ann's knees were shaking so much that she couldn't stand. Philip felt calm but rather fierce. All right! Let them strap those wings on him then – let them take him in the helicopter! He'd jump out all right! And if those wings *did* act – *if* they did – but would they?

Philip just couldn't bring himself to believe that they would.

The pilot had not seen any of the children, but now Philip had to go forward, fetched by one of the soldiers. The others followed, though Lucy-Ann had to hold on to Jack. Before the pilot could say a word to them, the king appeared. The children thought he must have dressed himself up very quickly! His crown was a little crooked, but otherwise he looked as majestic as ever.

The box with the wings in was carried by one of the soldiers. The king undid it and took out the wings. They really did look beautiful – and what was more, they looked as if they *would* be able to fly! Lucy-Ann hoped fervently that they could.

Philip made no fuss at all as the wings were strapped to his arms. He was shown the two buttons and nodded. He flapped his arms a little and was surprised to feel the power in the wings, as they met the air. The others watched him in admiration. Jack warmed to him. What pluck he had! – he didn't in the least show that he was scared. Perhaps he wasn't.

But deep down inside Philip was a nasty little core of dread. He kept it clamped down. Not for worlds would he have let anyone know it was there.

Then Meier, the king, Erlick and the others got a surprise. Little Lucy-Ann stepped forward and laid her hand on the arm of the king.

'Your Majesty! I think *I* ought to try out your wings

for you. I am much lighter than Philip. It would be an honour for me to try them.'

Philip and Jack looked thunderstruck. The idea of it! Philip gave the little girl a hug, putting his winged arms all round her.

'You're a brave darling! But *I'm* going! And what's more I'll fly back to this old mountain-top and just show you how well I'm doing.'

Lucy-Ann gave a sob. This was too much for her altogether. The pilot said nothing but got into the helicopter with his companion.

The king showed no hesitation at all in letting Philip go. It was pathetic the way he believed whole-heartedly in his extraordinary wings. His head was in the clouds. The people who performed his experiments for him and tried out his clever ideas were nothing to him at all.

Meier watched grimly as Philip climbed into the helicopter, helped by one of the soldiers, for his arms were hampered by the beautiful wings. The man would have been better pleased if the boy had objected and made a scene. He did not admire Philip's pluck in the least. His piercing eyes looked into Philip's and the boy looked back at him mockingly.

'So long!' he said, and raised one of his winged arms. 'See you later! Look out for youself, Meier. You'll come to a bad end one of these days!'

Meier stepped forward angrily, but the helicopter's engine began to whirr. The rotors went slowly round, gathering speed. Lucy-Ann tried to stifle a sob. She felt sure she would never see Philip again.

The helicopter rose straight up into the air. The pilot leaned forward and shouted something loudly. 'Don't forget Bill Smugs!' he called, and his voice was no longer the same as it had sounded before. It was quite different. It was somebody else's.

In fact – it was BILL'S VOICE!

25

A thrilling night

Only Lucy-Ann, Jack and Dinah knew what the last shout meant. Meier and the others had no idea at all. They hardly heard what was shouted.

But the children had heard all right! They gasped. Jack's hand found Lucy-Ann's and Dinah squeezed Jack's arm. They didn't say a single word until Meier, Erlick, the king and the servants had all disappeared once more. Then they made their way to their awnings, linking hands to keep together.

'Jack! That was *Bill*! Bill himself!' said Lucy-Ann, her voice going all funny as she spoke.

'Yes. And he knew if he yelled out, "Don't forget Bill Smugs," that we'd know it was him,' said Dinah. 'He called himself Bill Smugs the very first adventure we had – do you remember? Gosh – I never had such a surprise in my life!'

'And Philip's safe,' said Jack, in intense satisfaction. 'That's one good thing. The other fellow with Bill must be one of his friends. Philip will just chuck those wings overboard and that'll be that.'

'I feel as if I simply must sit down at once,' said Lucy-Ann. 'My legs will hardly carry me. I feel so joyful!'

She sat down and the others followed suit. They all let out a terrific sigh of relief. A heavy load rolled away from them. Philip was safe! He didn't have to jump out of the helicopter to try out an experiment for a mad old scientist, or for Meier and Erlick. He was with Bill.

'What made Bill think of getting a helicopter?' wondered Jack. 'Landing on the mountain-top with it too – under the noses of Meier and Erlick.'

'Well, don't you remember, you put in your note something about the helicopter we thought was landing up here?' said Dinah. 'The note we left with Dapple.'

'Yes, so I did,' said Jack. 'Well, that looks rather as if old Bill did come along here then – and found Dapple. Good for him! Trust Bill to get going somehow!'

'What's he going to do next?' said Dinah. 'Do you think he'll come back for us?'

'You bet he will!' said Jack. 'He'll park Philip somewhere safe and he'll be back as soon as he can. Perhaps tonight!'

'Oh, how lovely!' sighed Lucy-Ann. 'I don't like this mountain. I like Mrs Evans' farmhouse best. I don't like anyone here – that horrid Meier, and that awful fat Erlick, and those nasty little pussy-footing soldiers – and the king.'

'Well – I feel sorry for him,' said Jack. 'He's just got into the hands of rogues. No doubt they've made plenty of money already from his inventions. Now they're going all out for this one. I do wonder if there's anything in it.'

'Well, I'm jolly glad Philip hasn't got to find out!' said Dinah. 'Good old Philip – he was as plucky as could be, wasn't he?'

'Yes. And Lucy-Ann was jolly brave too,' said Jack. 'Whatever made you think of trying to go in Philip's place, Lucy-Ann?'

'I don't know. It sort of came over me all at once,' Lucy-Ann tried to explain. 'But I wasn't brave. My legs were wobbling like jelly.'

'The only thing that worries me is Kiki,' said Jack. 'I hope those men haven't done anything to her. She's never been away from us so long. I haven't heard so much as a hiccup from her!'

The others were worried too. Dinah couldn't help feeling pretty certain that Kiki had come to some harm. If Meier caught her that would be the end of her. Dinah shivered when she thought of his cold, piercing eyes.

Suddenly she gave a small shriek. 'Oh! Something's wriggling over my leg! What is it, quick?'

'It's the slow-worm,' said Jack, making a grab at it. 'Sorry, Dinah. You see, Philip didn't want to make poor old Sally share his jump – so he slipped her into my pocket when he thought you weren't looking. I didn't know she'd got out. Don't yell, Dinah. With everybody being so frightfully brave tonight, you might as well show your pluck too!'

And, surprisingly, Dinah did. After all, what was a slow-worm compared to Philip's jump – if he had had to jump? Nothing at all. Dinah drew her leg away, but made no fuss at all. Sally slithered round them for a little while and then went into Jack's pocket again.

'I just simply can't get over knowing it was Bill in that helicopter!' said Lucy-Ann for the twentieth time. 'My heart jumped nearly out of my body when he suddenly changed his voice to his own and yelled out, "Don't forget Bill Smugs!"'

'We'll have to be on the look-out for when he comes back,' said Jack. 'I'm sure it will be tonight. Perhaps no one will hear him but us, because we'll be the only ones expecting him. You can't hear a thing down in that mountain.'

'Oooh – wouldn't that be super, if Bill came back without being heard, and took us off?' said Lucy-Ann. 'What *would* Meier and the others think! They'd hunt all over the place for us!'

'And send the dogs out too,' said Jack.

'Shall we keep awake to look out for him?' said Dinah.

'No, you girls have a nap. I'll keep watch,' said Jack. 'I'm much too wide awake to go to sleep. I'll wake you as soon as ever I hear anything.'

'What about that beam of light that shows the

helicopter where to land at night?' said Dinah suddenly. 'Can you turn it on when you hear it coming, Jack?'

'I expect so,' said Jack, and went into the middle of the courtyard to find the switch that turned on the powerful beam.

But he couldn't find it anywhere. He hunted all over the place and gave it up at last. 'Can't find where the wretched thing turns on,' he said. 'Sickening!'

'Well, I daresay Bill can land all right,' said Lucy-Ann, who had the utmost faith in Bill's ability to do anything, no matter how impossible. 'You keep watch, Jack. I'm going to have a nap.'

She and Dinah shut their eyes, and in spite of all the terrific excitement of that night, they were both asleep in half a minute. Jack sat up, keeping watch. It was a cloudy night, and only occasionally did he see a star peeping out from between the clouds.

Good old Bill! How had he got that helicopter? How did he know how to fly one? Jack felt very thankful indeed that they had had the sense to leave a note behind with Dapple, telling everything they knew. Otherwise Bill wouldn't have known a thing about the mountain or its secret, and certainly wouldn't have guessed that helicopters landed on the top!

From far away a noise came through the night. Jack strained his ears. Yes – it was the helicopter coming back. It hadn't been long then – just long enough to drop Philip somewhere, hear his story and come back for the others. What a sell for Meier to find them all gone – and not to know what had happened to the wonderful wings!

The boy went to try and put on the lamp again, but could not find the switch at all. This was not surprising, because it was set in a tiny trap-door, let into the yard.

The helicopter came nearer. It circled the mountain. It rose vertically to land on the courtyard. Jack shook the two girls.

'It's here! Bill's back!'

The girls woke up at once. Snowy, who was asleep by then, woke up and leapt to his feet. He could feel the terrific excitement of the others, and sprang about madly.

'Look – it's landing!' said Jack, and the three of them strained their eyes to see the helicopter, a big dark shadow in the blackness of the night.

There came a slight crashing sound, and then the helicopter suddenly swung over to where Jack and the girls were. They had to dodge out of the way.

Bill's voice came on the air. 'Jack! Are you there?'

Jack ran to the helicopter as Bill switched on a powerful torch. 'I'm here, Bill. The coast's clear. Nobody's up here. Gosh, it's good to have you! Is Philip all right?'

'Quite all right. He's down on the mountain-side with Johns, the fellow who came with me, waiting for us. Get into the helicopter, all of you, and we'll go while the going's good.' Bill switched his torch round to see where the girls were, and in a moment all three were being helped up into the machine.

'I couldn't quite see where to land,' said Bill. 'I must have hit something coming down. I felt a good old jolt, and the helicopter swung round like mad. I hope she's all right!'

'You went into part of the rocky parapet, I think,' said Jack, helping the girls in. 'Oh *Bill*! This is grand! How did you . . .'

'All explanations later!' said Bill, and began to fiddle about with something in front of him. 'Now – here we go!'

The helicopter rose a foot or two in the air and then swung round in a peculiar way. Bill put her back to earth again at once. 'Now what's wrong? She shouldn't do that.'

Lucy-Ann was so longing to be off that she could hardly bear this. 'Let's go, let's go,' she kept saying, till Dinah nudged her to stop. Snowy was on Lucy-Ann's knee, as good as gold. She held on to him tightly, tense with excitement.

Bill tried again. Once more the machine rose into the air, and then did its peculiar swing-round. 'Something's wrong with the steering,' said Bill, in an exasperated voice. 'Why did I leave Johns down there? He might have been able to put it right. But I didn't think this machine would hold him as well as you three!'

In deepening dismay the children sat whilst poor Bill

tried his best to get the helicopter to rise and fly properly. But each time it swung round violently, and Bill could do nothing with it. He was secretly rather afraid that it would get completely out of control and swing right off the mountain-top. He could not risk an accident with the three children on board.

For at least an hour Bill experimented with the steering of the helicopter, but it would not answer to the controls at all. He made the children get out to see if lightening the load made any difference, but it didn't.

'It must have got damaged when you struck the parapet,' said Jack. 'Oh, Bill – what are we going to do now?'

'What about the way out by the wall?' said Bill. 'Philip told me all about it – something about a rope-ladder and so on. As a matter of fact, I did go to find the entrance there, when I came to look for you the other day – you spoke of it in your note, you remember – and I went behind the green curtain, found the crack in the rock and went in. But I couldn't go any further than that curious cave with no roof and the black pool at the bottom.'

'No. Nobody would find how to get out of that cave except by accident,' said Jack. 'We discovered how to get the rope-ladder down from above – by turning a wheel under the water in the pool. Down came the ladder!'

'Well – it seems to me we'll have to try to get out that way,' said Bill. 'This pest of a helicopter won't answer to her controls now. I daren't try and take off. We'd crash – and we haven't any wonderful wings to save us, either!'

'Oh, Bill – can't we really fly off in the helicopter?' said Lucy-Ann, her heart sinking like lead. 'Oh, I don't want to go down into that horrid mountain again! We might lose our way. We might get caught!'

'We'll have to try, I'm afraid, Lucy-Ann,' said Bill. 'Never mind – I'm here to protect you now. And, after all, it's the middle of the night, and nobody is likely to be about.'

'If only that helicopter would go properly!' said Jack. 'It's a piece of real bad luck that it won't. It's such a giveaway too. As soon as anyone sees it, they'll know something's up and will come to look for us.'

'All the more reason why we should get a move on now,' said Bill. 'Come on. Gosh, what's this banging against me? Oh, it's you, Snowy. Well, if you come too, you'll have to keep at our heels or you'll give the game away! By the way – where's Kiki? I haven't seen or heard her tonight.'

'We don't know *where* she is,' said Jack miserably. 'We haven't seen her for days – not since we were captured. She may be caged somewhere – or hiding in the mountain – or even killed!'

'Oh, *no*!' said Lucy-Ann. 'Don't say that. Kiki's too clever to let herself be captured. Perhaps we'll find her tonight!'

'Where's the way out of this place?' asked Bill, switching on his torch. 'Over there? Are there steps that go down into the mountain? Well, come on then. Every minute is precious now.'

They left the damaged helicopter in the yard and went towards the stone steps that led down into the mountain. Lucy-Ann shivered.

'I hoped I'd not go down there again! Take my hand, Bill, I don't like this!'

26

Flight through the mountain

Soon they were right down inside the mountain. They had passed Philip's cave, passed by the stores, and gone down the steep spiral stairway, cut in the rock.

It was very difficult to choose the right way to go, because all the dim lamps that lighted the passages were out. It was quite dark everywhere. Bill's powerful torch sent a bright ray in front of them, but he had to use it cautiously in case someone saw the light, and was warned of their coming.

There was a lot of standing still and listening, a good deal of argument on Jack's part and Dinah's about the right way to go. Bill was very patient, but his voice was urgent as he told them to think hard and choose the right way.

'If we followed Snowy, we'd probably go right,' said Lucy-Ann at last. 'He would know the way.'

'Well – but he doesn't know where we want to go,' said Jack. 'I mean, if he knew we wanted to go to the rope-ladder cave, he could lead us there all right – but we can't make him understand that.'

They ended up being completely lost. They found themselves in a dark tunnel, with a very high roof that none of the children recognized at all.

Bill began to feel desperate. If only he had been able to land without damage, this long trek through dark, unknown passages wouldn't have been necessary.

They went down very deep, and, quite suddenly, came out on to the high gallery that overlooked the pit. Bill drew in his breath sharply when he saw the mass of brilliance suddenly showing when the curious floor slid back for a moment. He and the children felt the strange feeling of lightness at once, but it passed immediately the floor slid over the glowing mass again.

There was nobody in the pit. Apparently the floor worked automatically by machinery of some kind, though there was none to be seen. That was the curious thing about the works in the mountain – there was no heavy machinery anywhere. Whatever power was used was not conveyed by iron or steel machines, and there was little noise except for the heavy rumbling that sounded before the shaking of the earth.

'There's obviously some metal in this mountain that can be used for that fellow's experiments,' said Bill. 'Some rare metal or other – like uranium, which is used for splitting the atom. There are a few mountains in the world which contain various rare metals – but usually they are mined for it and the stuff is taken out. In this case they haven't mined it – they are using it where it is! It's possible that they have to do that – in order to use the enormous thickness of the rocks in the mountain to protect the outer world from whatever rays they are experimenting with. Very ingenious!'

'I think we know the way back now,' said Jack, quite thankful at having found some place they recognized, even though it was the frightening pit!

He pointed behind them, up the wide, uphill passage that he knew went up and up for a long way. Bill switched his torch on it. 'Is that the way?' he said. 'Well, come along then.'

They went up the wide, steep passage. They came to the narrow, twisty little tunnel they had been in before and walked along till they came to the fork.

'Left-hand fork,' said Jack, and they took that. Bill was amazed to see the beautiful silken hangings that decorated the walls further on, and hung across the entrance to a cave.

Jack put his hand on Bill's arm. 'That's the king's bed-room, beyond,' he whispered. 'Dinah, have you got Snowy? Don't let him rush on in front.'

Bill tiptoed to the curtains and parted them. A dim light shone beyond. Bill looked with interest into the king's bedroom – and then closed the curtains quickly. He tiptoed back to the children.

'There's somebody lying on the couch there,' he whispered. 'An old fellow with a colossal forehead.'

'That's the king of the mountain!' whispered back Jack. 'The Great Brain behind all these inventions. I think he is an absolute genius, but quite mad.'

'He seems to be asleep,' said Bill. 'Is there any way we can go round this cave without waking him up?'

'No. I don't know of any,' said Jack. 'We've got to go through it, and then through a cave where he eats his meals, and then into the throne-room.'

Bill thought for a moment. 'We'll have to risk it then,' he said. 'We'll go through the room one by one, but for heaven's sake don't make a sound!'

They went through the king's bedroom one at a time, hardly daring to breathe. Dinah had tight hold of Snowy, praying that he wouldn't bleat when he went through the room!

Fortunately there were very thick carpets on the floor, so it was easy to make no sound. Lucy-Ann's heart beat so loudly as she tiptoed across that she thought it must surely wake the king with a jump.

Then they were in the room where the long table had held so much lovely food. But now it was empty and there was not so much as a dish of fruit on it.

Then on to the throne-room – and outside this, behind the lovely hangings patterned with the red dragons, the little company paused. A curious noise came to their ears – was it snoring? What was it?

Bill peeped through the hangings very cautiously. He grinned. In the throne-room, sitting or lying, were the paratroopers. A very long table had been set down the middle, and on it were the remains of a lavish supply of food and drink. Not a single man was awake!

'So that's where those fellows have been the last day or two!' whispered Jack. 'I wondered where they were. Gosh, they've fallen asleep where they are – what a pretty sight!'

Bill fumbled about in the hangings they were looking through. He was looking for a switch. He found one and whispered to the children. 'Now listen – I'm going to switch off the light so that we can get through the hall without being seen. Keep close to one side of it and get through as quietly as possible. Even if we do make a noise and some of those fellows wake up it won't matter – because they won't be able to see who it is!'

This was a good idea. The light went out with a slight click and the great hall was in darkness. The children, led by Bill, moved quietly along one side, their feet making no noise on the soft mats.

When they came to the immense laboratory Bill stood still in amazement. He knew a great deal more about these things than the children did, of course, and he could see what a brilliant, ingenious mind must be at the back of all the things at work there.

They stood in the gallery and looked down at the

wires and wheels, the glass jars and the crystal boxes, and heard the quiet, purposeful humming going on.

'What is it all doing, Bill?' whispered Lucy-Ann.

'It's transmuting, or changing, one power or energy into another,' said Bill soberly. 'Making it into usable form, so that . . .'

'So that it can be imprisoned in those "wings", for instance?' said Jack.

'Something like that,' said Bill. 'It's an amazing set-up altogether.'

There was nobody there. It did seem extraordinary that all these humming, spinning, whirring things should go on and on seemingly of their own accord, with just the king wandering round them occasionally.

Bill was so fascinated that for a few moments he forgot the urgency of finding the way out of the mountain. There was something dream-like about all this – it didn't seem real.

He was brought back to reality again by feeling Snowy butting against him. He jumped a little. Then he took Lucy-Ann's arm. 'Come along! What am I thinking of, stopping like this!'

Jack had found the passage that led out of the laboratory. He led them down it and they came to the great cave they had seen before. Bill's torch swept round it but there was nothing to see. Then they went into the passage that led to the roofless cave! The children felt they really were getting near freedom again – if only, only,

only they could find out how to get that rope-ladder out of its place in the wall!

They passed the dim lamps, which, for some reason or other, were lighted here. They came to the roofless cave, and Bill's torch picked out the pitchers of ice-cold water standing at the back to refresh those who had had the long and exhausting climb up the rope-ladder.

'This is the place where the ladder's kept,' said Jack, and he took Bill's torch and swung it to find the place in the rocky wall where they had seen it last.

But before he could spot it, Lucy-Ann tripped over something and fell with a thud. Bill picked her up. She had hurt her knees but she didn't make a sound. Bill told Jack to flash his torch on Lucy-Ann to see what she had fallen over.

She had stumbled over the rope-ladder itself! There it lay, stretching from its place in the wall, over the floor and then disappearing downwards over the edge of the cave – down, down, down to the cave with the pool far below!

'Look! The ladder's out!' cried Jack, forgetting to whisper in his excitement. 'Oh, Bill – let's come on down at once!'

'Somebody must have gone out of the mountain tonight,' said Dinah, 'and left the ladder down to come back by. I wonder who it was. We'd better be careful we don't meet them!'

'Jack, you go down first,' said Bill, who had been

examining with great interest the way the ladder was attached to the hole in the wall. It was extremely ingenious. Bill could see how wires must be run up from the wheel in the pool to a lever which released the ladder – whose weight then compelled it to run out over the floor to the edge of the cave, where it fell and then pulled itself undone until it had come to its last rung. What made it able to roll itself up again Bill could not imagine – but the brain that could devise all the amazing things inside that mountain would find that a very simple problem!

Jack went to the place where the ladder hung over the edge. He knelt down and put his feet one after another on a rung a little way down. The ladder felt as firm as before. It was very well made and strong.

'Well, here I go,' said Jack. 'Send the girls next, Bill, and then you come. Snowy's gone already, down whatever little hole he and the dogs use! I don't know where that is. I only wish I knew where poor old Kiki was. I don't like leaving her all alone in this beastly mountain.'

Bill shone his torch on him. The girls watched his head disappear as he climbed down.

'You go now, Lucy-Ann,' said Bill. 'Jack must be a good way down. You won't tread on his head. Then Dinah can go, and I'll follow last of all. Don't attempt to leave the cave below till I am down with you.'

Jack was going steadily down. What a long long way it was! And then a very peculiar thing happened. The ladder began to shake below him! Jack stopped climbing at once.

'Gracious! Somebody's climbing *up*! And I'm climbing down! Whoever can it be!'

27

Escape at last

No sooner had he felt certain that somebody was climbing up very steadily below him than Jack immediately stopped climbing down and began climbing back again at top speed. He didn't want to meet Meier or Erlick on that ladder.

Some way up he bumped into Lucy-Ann's feet. She gave a small squeal of surprise. 'It's all right, Lucy-Ann. It's only me,' said Jack in a low voice. 'There's somebody coming *up* the ladder. Go back again as quickly as you can!'

Lucy-Ann at once began to climb up as fast as possible, in a great fright. Gracious! How awful to feel that somebody was coming up the ladder just as they were going down! She felt certain it was that horrid Meier!

She in turn bumped into Dinah's feet and passed the urgent message on to the surprised girl. Dinah began to climb back again up to the cave at the top very quickly indeed. Lucy-Ann and Jack were immediately below her.

Jack felt as if somebody might catch his ankles at any moment.

And, of course, the next thing was that Dinah nearly got her head trodden on by Bill's big feet. He was descending at top speed to join the others, and was most amazed to find Dinah just below him.

'What's the matter? Didn't I tell you to buck up?' he said, and then caught Dinah's agonized whisper.

'Somebody's coming up! Quick, before they get Jack. Quick, Bill!'

Muttering something under his breath, Bill climbed back quickly. He pulled Dinah up, then Lucy-Ann, then Jack. The ladder still shook. The climber, or climbers, were coming up steadily.

'Back into the passages!' commanded Bill. 'We can't afford to be caught now. We'll wait till whoever it is has gone and then we'll try again.'

They came to where the passage forked into three, and Bill pushed them all up into the darkest one – but coming towards them were footsteps, and somebody's shadow at the far end! They all rushed back again.

But now the climber had reached the top of the ladder and was behind them. They tried the second passage and found themselves in a maze of funny little caves, all leading one out of another.

'Wait here!' said Bill. But they had been seen, and challenging voices now began to echo along the dark passages.

'Who's there? Come out at once!'

They didn't stir. They were all crouched in a dark corner, overhung by a rocky ledge. Bill wondered if the beam of a torch would find them. He was afraid it would.

The feet passed by in another cave. Then came more voices. The hunt was on! Bill groaned. It sounded as if four or five searchers were about now. They would separate and search until they had found them. And they had been so near freedom!

'Come,' said Bill after a moment. 'We'll try a better cave than this.'

But, before they could move, the flash of a torch shone into their cave. They all stiffened and stood absolutely still. The beam came nearer and nearer. Lucy-Ann forgot to breathe, and stood with her hand firmly clasped in Bill's.

Just as the beam of the torch was picking out Jack's feet – or so it seemed to Jack – a surprising interruption came. A voice came from somewhere near by, a hollow, mournful voice, full of misery and despair.

'Poor Kiki! Ding dong bell! Peepbo!'

Jack's heart leapt. *Kiki!* She wasn't dead, then! She must have been wandering, completely lost, all about the passages and caves for days. She didn't know they were close to her. She had seen the light of the torch and heard voices, and as usual she had joined in the conversation.

Bill's hand squeezed Jack's arm warningly. He was

afraid the boy might call Kiki, or exclaim out loud in delight. But Jack held his tongue. Kiki went on talking in the most melancholy voice imaginable.

'Send for the doctor! Musty, fusty, dusty, pooh, gah!'

Jack had never heard her so miserable before. Poor Kiki! She must have thought herself quite deserted.

A sharp voice rang through the cave. 'What in the world was that? Somebody's in this cave! Erlick, come here! Did you hear that?'

'What?' asked Erlick, coming in with another torch.

'A voice,' said Meier. 'Somebody's in here. Two people, probably. One talking to another. Stand there with your torch whilst I walk all round with mine.'

Meier began to walk round, examining all the walls carefully for hiding-places. Bill groaned silently. Now they had no chance to get to another cave at all.

Kiki gave a realistic sneeze and then a cough. Meier stopped his search and swung his torch in the direction of the sound.

'We can hear you! Come out or it will be the worse for you!' he shouted, in a furious tone.

Kiki was frightened. She had been without food for some time, and was hungry and unhappy. The man's angry voice filled her with panic and she flew off into the next cave, having no idea that her beloved Jack was so near her. It was just as well that she didn't know, for if she had known she would certainly have flown to Jack's shoulder and given their hiding-place away at once!

Her voice came from the cave further on.

'Polly put the kettle on! Send for the doctor!' Then came a loud hiccup, and an apologetic 'Pardon!'

'Good heavens! What's going on?' cried Meier, completely puzzled. 'It's that voice again that we've been hearing at intervals. Well, where there's a voice there's a body and I'm going to find it this time, if I have to shoot the caves to pieces!'

A loud report made Bill and the children jump in fright. Meier had drawn his revolver and fired wildly in the direction of Kiki's voice. Jack didn't like that a bit. He was afraid Kiki might be hit.

Meier and Erlick went into the next cave after Kiki's voice. It came to them from further away.

'Upsadaisy! Wipe your feet, you naughty boy.'

The children couldn't help smiling, scared though they were. Kiki always managed to say such ridiculous things in moments of urgency. There came another shot, which echoed all round the caves.

Kiki gave a cackle of scornful laughter, and then made a noise like a car changing gear. She came back to the next cave again, and the men followed. They still had not caught sight of Kiki because they were looking for a human being, running away in front of them, whereas Kiki flew high in the roof of the caves, and perched on small ledges, well hidden.

Somebody else ran through the cave where the children were, calling to Meier.

'Mr Meier, sir, sir! All children run away! Helicopter come back. All alone on mountain-top. No one there. Children run away!'

It was one of the numerous soldiers, who had evidently discovered the returned helicopter, and the disappearance of the pilot and the children. There was an amazed silence.

Meier raised his voice and let forth a stream of furious foreign words, none of which Bill or the children could understand. Then came Erlick's voice.

'No good going on like that, Meier. Get out the dogs. The children must have gone down the ladder. You left it down when you went out tonight, didn't you? The dogs will soon round them all up.'

'What's happened to the pilot, though?' raged Meier, and lapsed into some foreign language again. The soldier came pattering back through the cave again, presumably on his way to get the dogs.

'Send for the doctor,' called Kiki mournfully. She screeched like an engine and made Meier flash his torch in and out of the caves again, almost beside himself with rage.

Erlick, Meier and one or two others with them then began a loud argument in many languages. Bill didn't wait to hear what it was all about. He pushed the children out of their hiding-place and towards the nearest passage. Very quietly and quickly they all fled back towards the cave with the ladder. Maybe there was a chance now of escape. Jack wished with all his heart that he could take Kiki too.

They went down the ladder in the same order as before, Jack wondering fearfully if he would find anyone coming up this time, ready to catch him by the ankles. But he didn't. He reached the bottom safely, his legs shaking with the effort, panting and exhausted.

Lucy-Ann almost fell off the last rung, weak with relief to find she was at last at the bottom. It had seemed an endless climb down to her. She sank to the ground beside the pool, her heart beating painfully.

Dinah followed and threw herself on the ground too. Then came Bill, not so distressed as the others, but very glad indeed to be at the bottom of the ladder.

'Phew! The bottom at last!' he said. 'What a climb! Now come on – out we go on the mountain-side. We'll join up with Philip and Johns. If only those wretched dogs don't find us! Philip's told me about them and how you thought they were wolves. I don't fancy a pack of Alsatians on my trail, somehow, with Meier and Erlick urging them on!'

The dawn was beginning to come over the mountains. The sun was not yet above them, but a golden light was spreading upwards from the east. The children were very glad indeed to feel the fresh wind on their faces when they went out through the crack in the rock, and swung aside the big green curtain of creeper and bramble. They took deep breaths and gazed around them in the silvery light of dawn.

'Come on,' said Bill. 'I left Philip and Johns by a stream – where you left Dapple. We took Dapple back with us by the way, when David, Effans and I came with the rest of the donkeys to look for you. Philip said you'd know where the place was, even if we landed a little way from it in the helicopter – he thinks we're all coming through the air of course, to land on a good flat place where we left a light burning to guide me. It was a bit tricky landing in the dark with Philip and Johns! The helicopter nearly overbalanced. Still, we managed it.'

'Philip will be looking out for us by that light then?' said Lucy-Ann. 'Not by the stream.'

'No. I told him not to, in case anyone was roaming about there, saw the light and spotted him and Johns,' explained Bill. 'I thought Meier and Co. might possibly be on the look-out for Philip, if they thought he had jumped. I was supposed to radio back to them what had happened – but I didn't, of course!'

It was easy to find their way to the meeting-place, now that dawn was coming. But before they got there, a bit of good luck came to Jack – in the shape of Kiki!

She suddenly sailed down on him from the air with a cackle of delight, and a screech that nearly deafened them all. She flew to his shoulder and rubbed her head into his ear, giving it little pecks and pulls of love. Jack was so overjoyed that he couldn't say a word. He just scratched Kiki's head and made funny, loving noises, which Kiki immediately copied.

'Oh, *good*!' said Lucy-Ann in delight. 'Oh, Jack! Dear old Kiki, isn't it lovely to have her again. It's been awful without you, Kiki.'

Even Bill joined in the demonstrations of affection. 'You saved us, Kiki, old bird! You led those fellows such a song and dance that they let us escape. How did you know where we were? Did you fly out and follow us?'

Kiki didn't tell them, so they never knew, but Jack felt sure she had flown down into the roofless cave, and come out of the crack into the open air. Then she must have heard their voices and come to join them.

'God save the Queen,' said Kiki, in a happy voice, and gave a loud hiccup. 'Pardon! Pardon the queen pop goes Polly!'

'Oh, Kiki! We thought you were dead,' said Dinah. She looked round, missing Snowy. 'And now Snowy's gone! Where is he?'

'He hasn't been with us for some time,' said Bill. 'He'll turn up, I expect – just like Kiki!'

'Dithery Slithery,' said Kiki suddenly, cocking her head on one side and looking at Jack's pocket. Sally the slow-worm was half in and half out, enjoying being out in the fresh air again. Dinah didn't even squeal!

They went on their way, with Kiki firmly on Jack's shoulder – and suddenly they heard a yell.

'Hie! Here we are! Jack! Dinah! Lucy-Ann! Bill! And

oh, I say, there's Kiki too. Hurrah! You've escaped! But where's the helicopter? We've been waiting and waiting for it.'

It was Philip, of course, leaping up and down like a mad thing, with Johns standing stolidly behind him – and Snowy frisking about round them both. He had found Philip! So all the family were together again. They were full of delight – but wait – what was that howling noise in the distance?

'The dogs!' said Jack. 'They're after us!'

28

Trailed by the dogs

Lucy-Ann shrank back against Bill and Johns when she heard the savage howls and barks. She didn't at all like the idea of the dogs being after them!

Bill and Johns exchanged glances, and Bill said something under his breath and looked stubborn and angry. They had all been so pleased at their escape — and now here they were, about to be caught again! Nobody could do anything against ten man-hunting dogs!

'Bill! Get into the stream and wade up through the water,' said Jack suddenly. 'That's what the other man did when he wanted to break his scent. Dogs can't smell a trail through water. Let's all wade up the stream, and try and find a good hiding-place – a big tree, like Sam went up.'

'Well – it's a poor chance,' said Bill, 'but we'll try it! Blow that helicopter – behaving like that just when I wanted to take off to safety! We'd have been quite all right by now if it hadn't been for the damage to the steering.'

They all waded into the middle of the little stream. Up it they went, the water very cold to their feet. Lucy-Ann was between Bill and Johns. She felt very glad indeed that there were two grown-ups with them! In the distance the dogs barked again. They were certainly on the trail!

The little company went up the stream as quickly as they could, so that their scent was well broken. But they could easily be seen, and it was essential that they should get up into a tree, or find a cave as soon as they could.

And soon they found just exactly the thing! The stream disappeared into a large hole in the mountain. The clear water came bubbling out from there into the sunshine, swirling round the feet of the two men and the children – and of Snowy too!

'Look – it comes from that big hole,' said Bill, pleased. 'We'll go in there and hope it will take us all. We ought to be able to hide here till the dogs give up all hope of finding us.'

They crawled in one by one. Bill switched on his torch. There was only just room for them all, because a few yards back the hole narrowed down to a tiny tunnel, out of which the stream gushed madly.

They sat down where they could, squeezed up closely against one another. Jack and Philip had their feet in the stream. They sat there, listening to the distant yelping of the Alsatians.

Bill pulled some chocolate out of his pocket. 'I forgot about this,' he said, and handed it round. It was very comforting to have something to nibble. Johns had brought some too, so there was plenty.

'Do you think the dogs have lost the trail now?' asked Jack, not hearing the barking coming any closer.

'Yes. Sounds like it,' said Bill. 'They're at a loss, I should think. They must have come to the stream, jumped over it and found the trail was at an end. They probably won't have the sense to realize we've gone upstream.'

'But I should think the men with them would guess,' said big stolid Johns, who was taking this extraordinary adventure with the utmost calm, as if things like that happened to him every day. 'I know I would! If I were hunting a man with dogs, and we came to a stop by a stream, I'd order the dogs up- or downstream at once.'

'Oh dear!' said Lucy-Ann. 'Would you really? Well, I'm sure Meier will, then, when he catches up with the dogs, because he's terribly clever. He's got the most piercing eyes, Bill – honestly, they go right through you.'

'Well, he'd better not try looking right through *me*,' said Bill. 'He'd be sorry!'

'Pardon!' said Kiki. 'Sorry!'

'You forgot your hiccup, old thing,' said Jack, and Kiki solemnly produced one. Johns laughed suddenly.

He said he'd heard plenty of hiccups without birds, and seen plenty of birds without hiccups – but when you got the two together it was worth a lot!

'The dogs are coming nearer,' said Jack suddenly. They all listened, straining their ears. It was true. Their howls were distinctly louder.

'Meier's caught up with them, then,' said Dinah. 'And he's guessed our trick, and they're all coming upstream.'

'Yes. And they're sure to smell us here,' said Philip. 'Absolutely certain to. We can't diddle dogs like that!'

'Hey diddle diddle,' said Kiki, and screeched.

'Shut up,' said Jack, and tapped her on her beak. 'Do you want the dogs to hear you?'

'Pooh,' said Kiki, and nipped Jack's ear.

'Listen! I can hear the dogs splashing in the stream!' cried Philip. And so he could. The sound came to everyone's ears, and Lucy-Ann clutched Bill's hand even more tightly. Would this horrid adventure never end?

And then they saw the first dog, his red tongue hanging out, his breath coming in excited pants. He was half leaping in the water, not wading – in and out he leapt, in and out, coming nearer and nearer.

Then came Meier's hateful voice. 'Go on! Get them! Find them!'

The leading dog came right up to the hiding-place. He could smell everyone in there, as he stood in the stream outside the hole. He did not attempt to go in. He had found what he had been told to find – he had not been told to capture and hold.

He lifted his head and howled like a wolf. Kiki was very surprised. She attempted an imitation but an Alsatian's howl was beyond her. She only produced a curious whirring noise that made the dog cock his big head on one side and listen.

Then the other dogs came up, panting too, their tongues all hanging out. They stood beside and behind their leader, sniffing. They looked very fierce indeed!

'Not a nice sight,' murmured Bill to Johns, who was staring stolidly at the dogs as if he was perfectly used to being hunted by a pack of Alsatians and didn't mind it at all.

'Keep still,' Bill commanded everyone. 'As long as we don't attempt to move or get away, the dogs won't do anything more than stand there and stare.'

There came the sound of shouts and Meier and Erlick appeared, very red in the face with running. Meier stopped dead when he saw the pack of dogs standing looking in the hole where the stream poured out.

He pushed Erlick behind a tree quickly. It was plain that he feared Bill might have a gun. He shouted out loudly.

'Come on out! The dogs have found you. If you don't want them to set on you, come on out – and throw any gun you've got down on the ground, and put your hands up. We've got you covered.'

'Pleasant fellow, isn't he?' said Johns to Bill. 'It'll be nice to get hold of him. Do we go out, boss, or don't we?'

'We don't,' said Bill shortly. 'I doubt if he'll dare to set the dogs on us. He knows the children are here.'

'Meier wouldn't stick at anything,' said Jack. And he was right. When there was no answer, and not even a movement from the hole in the hill, Meier began to lose his temper as usual. He shouted out something in a foreign language, then changed to English.

'You heard what I said. You have one more chance. The dogs are ready to pounce. They'll round you up all right, and I warn you, their teeth are sharp, so don't resist!'

Still nobody moved. Lucy-Ann shut her eyes. She really couldn't look at the eager, panting dogs any more. She could see that they were just awaiting the word to rush into the cave and drag them all out.

And then Philip suddenly moved, and before anyone could stop him, he was outside the cave.

'Put your hands up!' called Meier, and Philip put them up. The dogs sniffed at him, and under his breath Philip talked to them.

'Don't you remember me? I'm Philip. You slept with me up on the rock. Fine dogs you are. We're friends, don't you remember?'

The dogs did not understand one word, but they understood his tone of voice. They remembered this boy. They felt his friendliness and his attraction. The leader began to whine a little. He longed to have this boy pat his head. But Philip had his hands above his head, and had only his voice to charm the dogs with.

He went on talking to them in a low voice, whilst the other children, and Bill and Johns, watched spellbound. They all thought the same. Philip, Philip, what is there in you that makes all creatures your friends? What gift have you got, so rare, so irresistible? 'Lucky boy!' thought Bill. 'And lucky for every one of us that you can charm these dogs!'

Meier called out angrily. 'Where are the others? Tell them to come too, or I'll give the order for them to be dragged out!'

The leader dog stood up and put his paws on Philip's shoulders. He licked the boy's face. It was a very wet lick, but Philip did not even turn away his face. That was the signal for all the other dogs to come round too. Quite forgetting Meier, they milled round Philip, trying to get near him, sniffing at him, giving him a lick when they got near enough.

He put down his hands. Meier would not dare to take a shot at him now in case he killed a dog! He ran his hands over their backs, patted their heads, rubbed their noses, and all the time he talked to them in the special voice he kept for animals.

Meier snapped out an order to the dogs. 'Fetch them out! Get them! Bring them here!'

The dogs turned their heads automatically at his commanding voice. They hesitated. The leader looked at Philip. 'Come with me,' said Philip. 'Come. You will find more friends in here.'

And, to Meier's everlasting astonishment, the boy actually led all the dogs to the cave, where at least four of them squeezed in to lick Lucy-Ann, Jack and Dinah! They sniffed doubtfully at Bill and Johns, growled at Snowy and Kiki, and then, when Philip laid a hand on Bill's arm and then on Johns', they accepted them as friends too.

'Philip! You're a marvel!' said Bill, in heartfelt admiration. 'It's magic you use — can't be anything else!'

'What a boy!' said the stolid Johns, allowing his face to change its expression for once in a while, and show great admiration.

'Meier's shortly going to have a fit, I think,' said Jack. 'He just can't understand all this!'

'Fetch them out, I say! I'll shoot the lot of you dogs, if you don't obey orders!' stormed Meier. 'What's come over you? Fetch them out!'

The dogs took absolutely no notice at all. Their leader had accepted Philip as master now, and they all followed his decision. What Philip said they would obey. They feared Meier, but they loved Philip.

Meier suddenly fired his revolver in a fury. He did not fire at the dogs, but over their heads. They jumped and growled, turning their heads towards him. Bill judged it was time to do something.

'Philip! Will the dogs obey you? Will they go for Meier and Erlick? If they will – order them to! We'll give that couple a taste of their own medicine!'

29

The tables are turned!

'Right!' said Philip. He pointed to the tree where Meier and Erlick were hiding behind its big trunk. 'See, boys! Fetch them out! Bring them here! Fetch them for me, then!'

Before Meier or Erlick knew what was happening the pack of Alsatians was speeding joyfully to obey. The whole pack flung themselves on the two rogues, and bore them to the ground. There was no chance to use a revolver. In fact Meier's gun rolled on the ground and was completely lost under the scrambling crowd of dogs.

'Don't hurt them! Bring them here!' ordered Philip in excitement, proud of his power to give commands to the pack of dogs.

Bill and Johns were now out of the cave, and Jack followed. The girls did not come out yet. They didn't want to! Lucy-Ann clutched Dinah's arm till she squealed. Both girls watched what was happening, breathless with intense excitement.

The dogs began to drag the two men over to Philip. Erlick, the great ape-like fellow, a real bully if ever there was one, was screaming for mercy, a coward, like all bullies. 'Call them off! I'll surrender! Call them off, boy!'

Meier fought savagely, not seeming to care whether he was bitten or not. He could not find his revolver and was beside himself with amazement, anger and fear.

The dogs were trained not to bite unless commanded, but one or two of them gave him a well-deserved nip – a little repayment for his callousness in dealing with them in their training. The leader got hold of him by the slack of his trousers, and, looking rather ridiculous, Meier was brought to where the boys and the two men were standing watching.

Then Erlick was brought too, trying to stand, almost weeping with panic. He remembered a gun he had in his pocket, and he reached to get it, thinking it was his last chance of escape.

But Johns was on the spot. 'Hands up,' he said. 'Any funny business on your part, Erlick, and the dogs can have you for all I care. Stand up, Meier, and put your hands up too.'

White with rage Meier put up his hands when the dogs allowed him to find his feet. He glared at the boys and Bill.

'What did you do to the dogs?' he snapped at Philip. 'They've never turned on me before!' He lapsed into a foreign language again and poured out streams of abuse.

'Shut up,' said Bill, who was now holding his own revolver in his hand. 'You talk too much.'

'Wipe your feet,' said Kiki's voice and she flew out of the hole and on to Jack's shoulder. 'Pooh! Gah!'

Meier glared at the parrot, recognizing the voice that had puzzled him for so long. If looks could have killed, certainly Kiki would have fallen dead at that moment. As it was she went off into one of her dreadful cackles, and Meier clenched the fists he was holding above his head, wishing that for one moment he could get hold of Kiki.

'What do we do now?' enquired Jack. 'It's a long way from home, Bill – and we've got no food to keep us going if we have to walk back.'

'Effans and Trefor and David are not far off,' said Bill. 'I told them to stand by somewhere near this mountain with plenty of donkeys, in case we needed them. I wasn't sure if the helicopter would fly very far with such a lot of you on board!'

'*Oh!* Will they really be near here?' said Lucy-Ann, gladly. 'Oh, Bill – you think of everything! Oh, *good*!'

'Can we take the dogs back with us?' asked Philip, who was still surrounded by furry bodies and wagging tails. 'I could look after them till we get them away somewhere. I daresay you'd like them for the police force, Bill. They're jolly well trained.'

'Thanks for the offer,' said Bill, with a grin. 'I'll accept it. And now – quick march! We'll leave this surprising mountain behind, and I and a few others will come back to it later. I feel it wants a little cleaning up. And we'll take that mad genius in charge before he does something dangerous. I wouldn't put it past him to blow up the mountain.'

'Good gracious!' said Lucy-Ann, in alarm. 'Well, let's get away before he does!'

They set off at a smart walk. Meier and Erlick walked in sullen silence. They had their hands by their sides now, for Johns had searched them both, and they were now weaponless. Jack and the others began to feel a familiar feeling of emptiness under their belts.

'I'm jolly hungry,' announced Dinah. 'Has Effans brought any food with him, do you think?'

'Well, Mrs Evans was so upset to hear that you were lost, that she immediately did an enormous baking,' said Bill, 'and I believe two of the donkeys are laden with the results. So let's hurry!'

'Where are they?' asked Jack.

'In the Vale of Butterflies, waiting for us patiently,' said Bill, with a grin. This was a most surprising thing to hear.

'The Vale of Butterflies!' cried Jack. 'Why, we couldn't find it! We began to think it was all Trefor's make-up!'

'Oh, no. It was really quite easy to find, if only David had known how to read a map,' said Bill. 'The name was on it in Welsh, so you wouldn't have understood it. But I don't believe David has ever learned to read a map properly! I shouldn't have let him go off with you as guide.'

'Did *you* find it then?' asked Lucy-Ann.

'Oh, yes. It's on the way here, actually,' said Bill. 'David took a wrong road, that's all – accidentally left the track. Anyway I told him to wait there with the donkeys, because I thought you'd rather like to see the butterfly valley, after having missed it and found a very strange mountain instead!'

'Oh! Everything's coming right!' said Lucy-Ann joyfully. 'The adventure is over, isn't it, Bill? Well – it doesn't seem nearly so bad now as it did!'

'Poor Lucy-Ann!' said Bill. 'You do have adventures thrust upon you, don't you? Never mind, you'll soon be back at the farm, enjoying Mrs Evans' wonderful cooking!'

'As soon as you came, things were all right,' said Lucy-Ann happily. 'It was super hearing you yell out, "Don't forget Bill Smugs!" last night. Gosh, was it only last night? It seems years ago!'

They went through a narrow pass between two mountains, feeling hungrier and hungrier – and there below them was the Vale of Butterflies!

They stopped in delight. The valley was a froth of coloured butterflies, red, yellow, white, pink, blue, copper, brown! There were thousands there, fluttering in the sunlight, darting erratically to and fro, hovering, dropping down to the millions of flowers. These made a carpet of brilliant colour, and the children thought they had never seen such a lovely sight before.

'Why are there so many butterflies, I wonder!' marvelled Dinah.

'I suppose because there are so many varieties of food-plants,' said Bill. 'This valley is apparently as famous for flowers as for butterflies, but because it is so much off the beaten track, it is rarely visited. I've no doubt the pack of dogs would have kept trippers away, anyhow!'

'There's Effans – and the donkeys!' cried Philip. 'Hey, Effans! Hallo, Trefor – and David!'

Dapple moved to greet Snowy, who ran in delight to his friend. Effans beamed. Trefor's blue eyes shone. Only David did not greet them eagerly. He kept his eyes on the ground and seemed ashamed.

'He got it hot and strong from Mrs Evans when he arrived back alone with the donkeys chasing after him,' explained Bill. 'I also had a few words to say to him, as you can imagine! So he now feels he can't look anyone in the face. It won't do him any harm to feel like that for a while. He behaved foolishly!'

'Poor David!' said Lucy-Ann. 'I expect he's sorry now,' and she spoke to the old man kindly. He looked at her gratefully.

'It's good to see you again, indeed to gootness it is, whateffer!' said Effans in his singing voice.

'Whateffer, whateffer!' shouted Kiki in delight. 'Look you, look you, whateffer!'

'That bird!' said Effans in great admiration. 'Look you, it iss a marvel, that bird. I would give ten pounds for a bird like that, whateffer!'

'She's not for sale,' said Jack, stroking Kiki. 'No, not for a million pounds. Where's the food, Effans? We're starving!'

'All explanations after the meal!' said Bill to Effans. 'We'll have a talk then, Effans, whilst the children go mad over the butterflies! Meier, Erlick, keep over there. Philip, tell the dogs to look after them.'

Effans stared in surprise at the two sullen men. Meier glared back. Erlick was full of self-pity, and had even begun to reproach Meier for his carelessness in letting them be captured. Meier looked at Erlick as if he could snap at him like the dogs.

'A pretty couple,' said Bill. 'I think we'll turn our backs on them. They spoil the view.'

Joyfully the children settled down to the finest picnic they had ever had. Mrs Evans had indeed surpassed herself. There was roast chicken, tender tongue, spiced ham, hard-boiled eggs, cucumbers, tomatoes, potted meat, fresh fruit, home-made lemonade which Effans had cleverly left cooling in a near-by stream, and so many other eatables that the boys despaired of even being able to taste them all!

They sat there on the hillside, the carpet of bright flowers spread at their feet – unbelievably brilliant in colour! And the butterflies!

'They're like flying flowers!' cried Lucy-Ann in joy. 'Hundreds of them! Thousands of them! What are they, Philip?'

'Fritillaries, painted ladies, commas, peacocks, ringlets, coppers, skippers, heaths . . .' reeled off Philip. 'My word, what a paradise of butterflies! I really will never forget this all my life long!'

It was a wonderful picnic – wonderful food, gorgeous butterflies, brilliant flowers – and plenty of laughter and jokes! Kiki was quite mad, and when she saw how Johns and Effans admired her, she showed off tremendously. She gave them her whole repertoire of noises, and Effans laughed till he choked.

The stolid Johns munched away, keeping his eyes on Kiki, and occasionally giving a slight smile at her more outrageous sayings.

'Indeed to gootness, whatetfer! Wipe your feet and blow your nose. Pifflebunk! Pardon!'

Snowy wandered round, taking titbits from everyone. The dogs watched from a distance, feeling certain that their friend Philip would not forget them. It was a very good thing that Mrs Evans had provided so much, because with two prisoners and ten dogs every scrap of food would be needed!

Bill, Johns and Effans exchanged news when the children had gone to wander through the clouds of butterflies. Effans listened gravely. Trefor and David tried to understand, but most of what Bill said was beyond their English. Effans told them the story in Welsh later.

'They are brave children, look you,' said Effans. 'Very brave children, whateffer!'

30

The end of it all!

They had to sleep out in the open that night. Effans gave the children the rugs he had brought, because all their sleeping things had been left behind in the cave, on the mountain-side. The prisoners slept apart, guarded by the dogs. It was very warm, and Snowy got pushed off by everyone when he tried to cuddle down first on top of Philip, then on Jack, and then on the girls.

They had had a very long talk with Bill and told him all their adventures down to the last detail. Bill had marvelled at their accidental discovery of the strange mountain and its even stranger secret. He had examined the 'wings' which Philip had given to Johns to take care of for him.

'I shall take those back to school with me next term!' Philip said. 'Won't the boys stare! I bet some of them will want to try them!'

'Well, all I can say is I should discourage anyone from jumping off the school roof or anything like that, and trusting to these wings,' said Bill drily. 'I have a feeling that the ingenious brain behind these things is failing a little – the old "king" will never discover how to make the wings he so much wants to make. But he certainly has invented some remarkable things. I have had a talk with Meier, and he has told me why he believed in Monally – that's the "king's" real name.'

'Why did he believe in him?' asked the children curiously.

'Well, apparently he has, at one time or another, produced the most remarkable inventions,' said Bill, 'and Meier has backed him and made a great deal of money out of them. How he came to find this mountain, and the rare metal in its heart, which the "king" wanted for his latest idea of conquering the pull of the earth, I haven't been able to find out yet. Some dirty work of some sort, I expect.'

'What are you going to do about everything?' asked Jack.

'Well – the paratroopers will be sent back home. The soldiers will be questioned and also sent back. I have a feeling there's something strange about them too. The "king" will be taken into safety,' said Bill. 'I shall send two or three scientists to the mountain to let them report on what they find there. I shouldn't be surprised if they advise us to destroy everything in it. The "king" has been meddling with dangerous things. With no one there to keep a guiding hand on them there might be a vast explosion.'

'It's a good thing we discovered it, isn't it?' said Lucy-Ann.

'A very good thing,' said Bill. 'And it's an even better thing you left that note with Dapple. If it hadn't been for that I'd never have found you.'

'What happened?' asked Jack.

'I came along to find you, complete with donkeys, after David's rush home,' said Bill. 'Instead I found only Dapple – and the note, which talked of very peculiar things indeed, and made me smell a very large rat.'

'Go on,' said Philip, interested.

'Well, I snooped round but couldn't find my way in through the roofless cave,' said Bill. 'So the only thing to do was to start finding out about helicopters. If somebody could land on that mountain-top, then so could I!'

'Good old Bill!' said Jack.

'And then,' said Bill, 'I found when I began making enquiries about all the helicopters in this country, who owned them and so on, that other people were also making enquiries about a few of them! Some of the helicopters had been flying off in suspicious circumstances, nobody knew where. So the police were even then enquiring into the matter – and I joined them, hotfoot!'

'And what did you find?' asked Dinah.

'I found a young pilot, with a terrific scar across his face!' said Bill. 'Ah – you know him, I see. And he spilt the beans, as we say! Told us he was worried about para-troopers jumping without proper parachutes and so on. And so, when he went on holiday, I took his place on the next helicopter trip – and hey presto, there I was on the top of the mountain!'

'Oh, Bill – it was heavenly to see you!' said Lucy-Ann.

Bill had told them all about Mrs Mannering too – how anxious she had been – how her hand had healed very well – and how she had begged in vain to be allowed to come with Effans and the others to meet the children, with the donkeys.

It was a long time before the children could go to sleep that night, for the day had been so exciting. The dogs lay and snoozed, one eye on the prisoners. The donkeys lay peacefully together. Snowy, sent off by each of the children, wandered off to Dapple and lay down beside him. Dapple was very pleased.

They got back to the farmhouse by dinner-time the next day, for Bill had got them all up very early the next morning. Mrs Mannering ran out in joy. She had been very worried indeed.

Mrs Evans followed. 'Indeed to gootness, it's grand to see you, whateffer! To think what you have been through, look you – as much danger as in war-time! It's glad we are to see you back!'

'It's well they are looking, too,' said Effans, in his up-and-down voice, beaming. 'And that bird, indeed, she is funnier than ever!'

'Whateffer, look you!' mimicked Kiki, also in a sing-song voice, and Effans went off into guffaws, imitated by Kiki. The two of them sounded so jolly that everyone else began to laugh too!

Mrs Evans, of course, had got another lovely meal ready for them all. And *what* a lot there were to feed that day too! She even found a fine supply of bones for the dogs, and Philip had to take them a good way off because Mrs Mannering said she really couldn't bear to hear such a munching and crunching as the ten dogs made short work of the bones.

What a lot there was to tell! Mrs Evans' eyes nearly fell out of her head as she listened, and handed out food of all kinds to everyone.

'To think of the children doing such things, look you!' she kept saying. 'Inside that mountain, indeed! Down in that pit too, look you!'

'Pardon, look you!' said Kiki, and gave a loud sneeze. Effans choked and Kiki copied him, making such a dreadful noise that Mrs Mannering said she was to go out of the room if she couldn't behave herself.

'Oh, Aunt Allie – she's just so glad she's back again,' said Jack, tapping Kiki on the beak.

'Send for the doctor,' said Kiki, fixing her wicked little eyes on Effans, who was still choking with laughter. 'Send for the weasel! Send for the look-you!'

Nobody could help laughing. Jack gave Kiki a very large plum, hoping to keep her quiet. Holding it in one clawed foot, Kiki dug her beak into it, making juice squirt all over poor Effans.

'Pardon!' said Kiki in delight, and did it again. Effans felt that he would exchange every one of his sheep for a bird like that. He watched Kiki and quite forgot to eat.

Johns was to take the prisoners down to the town, with David, escorted by two of the dogs. Mrs Evans said she would keep the rest of them at the farmhouse until the police had decided what to do with them.

'Mother – I suppose we couldn't possibly keep two or three of the dogs, could we?' asked Philip longingly.

'Good gracious, no!' said his mother. 'It's bad enough being landed with so many of your pets when you go back to school – but to have three great hungry Alsatians to look after would just kill me! No, they will be happier as police dogs.'

Bill was to stay until two or three scientists arrived to go with him to the mountain. Some police officers were to accompany them too, to round up the soldiers – though Bill did not expect any trouble from them at all. They probably had bad records, and had signed on with Meier to keep out of the way of the police for a while and to earn money.

'Can we go to the mountain too?' asked Jack hopefully. 'You might lose your way inside, Bill.'

'Oh, no I shan't,' said Bill. 'I found a nice little map of the inside of the mountain in Meier's pocket. I shan't lose my way – and you may as well give up all hope of coming with me, because you've been in quite enough danger these holidays. I'm afraid if I took you with me, another adventure might blow up – I never saw such children for smelling out adventures! I believe if I took you to visit my dear old aunt, we should find she had suddenly been kidnapped in a submarine, and you were forced to go to the other end of the world to rescue her!'

The boys were very disappointed not to go with Bill back to the mountain. Neither of the girls wanted to. Lucy-Ann was quite certain about that.

'I don't mind the adventure a bit, now it's all over and we can talk about it,' she said. 'But I didn't like it at the time. I hated that rumbling old mountain. Bill, Philip's going to let me wear his wings this afternoon in return for when I offered to jump from the helicopter instead of him. I shall fly from that high rock up there down to the farmhouse!'

'Indeed you won't!' said Bill promptly. Lucy-Ann laughed at Bill's shocked face.

'It's all right. I was only pulling your leg,' she said. 'But I'm going to wear them for a little while, and jump about, flapping them. Won't the hens be surprised?'

'Very,' said Bill. 'You'll stop them laying eggs, I should think! Look after her, Philip. See she doesn't do anything mad.'

Philip grinned. 'Lucy-Ann's all right,' he said. 'She's the most sensible one of us all.'

He put his hand into his pocket to feel if Sally the

slow-worm was there. An astonished expression came over his face. He gave a yell.

'Oh! Whatever's the matter!' said Lucy-Ann, jumping in fright.

'The most *wonder*ful thing has happened!' said Philip. 'Honestly, I never thought it of Sally.'

'What? What?' cried the others. Philip brought out his hand and opened it. It was full of what looked like little silvery darning needles, all wriggling about.

'Sally's babies! Mother, look! My slow-worm has got a whole lot of baby ones in my pocket. Oh, Mother, I don't believe any slow-worm has ever done that before to anyone! It's absolutely unique! Aren't they *lovely*?'

'Ugh!' said Dinah.

'Perfect!' said Jack.

'Do give me one for myself,' said Lucy-Ann. 'Oh, Philip! This is much, much more exciting than our adventure!'

'Much,' agreed Philip. 'Good old Sally! I've never had baby slow-worms for pets before – now I've got heaps.'

'You're not to keep them in your pocket, Philip,' said his mother. 'It's not good for them or for you.'

'But Sally will be so disappointed,' said Philip, in dismay.

The adventure was forgotten. All four heads bent over the silvery little creatures in Philip's palm. Snowy came to look. Kiki bent down from Jack's shoulders.

'Look you, whateffer!' she said, with her head on one

side, and opened her beak to hiccup. She caught Mrs
Mannering's eye and changed her mind.

'Pardon!' she screeched and went off into a cackle of
laughter. 'Bad Kiki! Send for the doctor, look you! Wipe
your feet and blow your pardon!'

The *Ship*

of adventure

Contents

1. A grand holiday plan   1
2. On the Viking Star   10
3. Everyone settles in   19
4. Philip collects a pet   27
5. Lucian arrives   39
6 The tale of Andra's treasure   48
7. Lucian is very helpful   57
8. The ship in the bottle   67
9. The secret of the Ship of Adventure   86
10. Hiding places   94
11. Lucian in trouble   103
12. The second piece of the map   111
13. Goodbye, Mr Eppy!   120
14. Things begin to happen!   129
15. Bill hears the tale   138
16. Bill makes a few enquiries   147
17. To Thamis at last!   156
18. A few surprises   166

19. All kinds of shocks   175
20. Exploring the treasure route   185
21. Kiki is very tiresome   193
22. Mr Eppy again   202
23. Treasure – and trickery!   210
24. Prisoners!   220
25. What happened in the night 227
26. Next morning   235
27. Unexpected visitors   243
28. Escape!   251
29. Happy ending after all!   259

1

A grand holiday plan

'Mother's got something up her sleeve,' said Philip Mannering. 'I know she has. She's gone all mysterious.'

'Yes,' said his sister, Dinah. 'And whenever I ask what we're going to do these hols she just says "Wait and see!" As if we were about ten years old!'

'Where's Jack?' said Philip. 'We'll see if he knows what's up with Mother.'

'He's gone out with Lucy-Ann,' said Dinah. 'Ah – I can hear old Kiki screeching. They're coming!'

Jack and Lucy-Ann Trent came in together, looking very much alike with their red hair, green eyes and dozens of freckles. Jack grinned.

'Hallo! You ought to have been with us just now. A dog barked at Kiki, and she sat on a fence and mewed like a cat at him. You never saw such a surprised dog in your life!'

'He put his tail down and ran for his life,' said Lucy-Ann, scratching Kiki on the head. The parrot began to mew again, knowing that the children were talking about her. Then she hissed and spat like an angry cat. The children laughed.

'If you'd done that to the dog he'd have died of astonishment,' said Jack. 'Good old Kiki. Nobody can be dull when you're about.'

Kiki began to sway herself from side to side, and made a crooning noise. Then she went off into one of her tremendous cackles.

'Now you're showing off,' said Philip. 'Don't let's take any notice of her. She'll get noisy and Mother will come rushing in.'

'That reminds me – what's Mother gone all mysterious about?' said Dinah. 'Lucy-Ann, haven't you noticed it?'

'Well – Aunt Alison *does* act rather as if she's got something up her sleeve,' said Lucy-Ann, considering the matter. 'Rather like she does before somebody's birthday. *I* think she's got a plan for the summer holidays.'

Jack groaned. 'Blow! I've got a perfectly good plan too. Simply wizard. I'd better get mine in before Aunt Allie gets hers.'

'What's yours?' asked Dinah, with interest. Jack always had wonderful plans, though not many of them came to anything.

'Well – I thought we could all go off together on our bikes, taking a tent with us – and camp out in a different place each night,' said Jack. 'It would be super.'

The others looked at him scornfully. 'You suggested that *last* hols and the hols before,' said Dinah. 'Mother said "No" then, and she's not likely to say "Yes" now. It *is* a good plan, going off absolutely on our own like that – but ever since we've had so many adventures Mother simply won't hear of it.'

'Couldn't your mother come with us?' suggested Lucy-Ann hopefully.

'Now *you're* being silly,' said Dinah. 'Mother's a dear – but grown-ups are so frightfully particular about things. We'd have to put our macs on at the first spot of rain, and coats if the sun went in, and I wouldn't be surprised if we didn't each have to have an umbrella strapped to our bike-handles.'

The others laughed. 'I suppose it *wouldn't* do to ask Aunt Allie too, then,' said Lucy-Ann. 'What a pity!'

'What a pity, what a pity,' agreed Kiki at once. 'Wipe your feet and shut the door, where's your hanky, naughty boy!'

'Kiki's got the idea, all right!' said Philip. 'That's the kind of thing that even the nicest grown-ups say, isn't it, Kiki, old bird?'

'Bill isn't like that,' said Lucy-Ann at once. 'Bill's fine.'

Everyone agreed at once. Bill Cunningham, or Bill Smugs as he had first called himself to them, was their very firm friend, and had shared all their adventures with them. Sometimes they had dragged him into them, and sometimes it was the other way round – he had got into one and they had followed. It really did seem, sometimes, as Mrs Mannering said, that adventures cropped up wherever Bill and the children were.

'*I* had an idea for these hols too,' said Philip. 'I thought it would be pretty good fun to camp down by the river, and look for otters. I've never had an otter for a pet. Lovely things they are. I thought—'

'You *would* think of a thing like that,' said Dinah, half crossly. 'Just because you're mad on all kinds of creatures from fleas to – to . . .'

'Elephants,' said Jack obligingly.

'From fleas to elephants, you think everyone else is,' said Dinah. 'What a frightful holiday – looking for wet, slimy otters – and having them in the tent at night, I suppose – and all kinds of other horrible things too.'

'Shut up, Dinah,' said Philip. 'Otters aren't horrible. They're lovely. You should just see them swimming under the water. And by the way, I'm *not* mad on fleas. *Or* mosquitoes. *Or* horse-flies. I think they're interesting, but you can't say I've ever had things like that for pets.'

'What about those earwigs you had once – that escaped out of the silly cage you made for them? Ugh! And that stag beetle that did tricks? And that—'

'Oh, gosh! Now we're off!' said Jack, seeing one of the familiar quarrels breaking out between Philip and hot-headed Dinah. 'I suppose we're going to listen to a long list of Philip's pets now! Anyway, here comes Aunt Allie.

We can ask her what she thinks of our holiday ideas. Get yours in first, Philip.'

Mrs Mannering came in, with a booklet in her hand. She smiled round at the four children, and Kiki put up her crest in delighted welcome.

'Wipe your feet and shut the door,' she said, in a friendly tone. 'One, two, three, GO!' She made a noise like a pistol shot after the word 'go', and Mrs Mannering jumped in fright.

'It's all right, Mother – she keeps doing that ever since she came to our school sports, and heard the starter yelling to us, and letting off his pistol,' grinned Philip. 'Once she made the pistol-shot noise just when we were all in a line, ready to start – and off we went long before time! You should have heard her cackle. Bad bird!'

'Naughty Polly, poor Polly, what a pity, what a pity,' said Kiki. Jack tapped her on the beak

'Be quiet. Parrots should be seen and not heard. Aunt Allie, we've just been talking about holiday plans. I thought it would be a super idea if you'd let us all go off on our bikes – ride where we liked and camp out each night. I know you've said we couldn't when I asked you before, but—'

'I say "No" again,' said Mrs Mannering very firmly.

'Well, Mother, could we go off to the river and camp there, because I want to find out more about the otters?' said Philip, not taking any notice of Dinah's scowl. 'You see—'

'*No*, Philip,' said his mother, just as firmly as before. 'And you know why I won't let you go on expeditions like that. I should have thought you would have given up asking me by now.'

'But *why* won't you let us go?' wailed Lucy-Ann. 'We shall be quite safe.'

'Now, Lucy-Ann, you know perfectly well that as soon as I let you four out of my sight when holidays come, you *immediately* – yes, *immediately* – fall into the most frightful adventures imaginable.' Mrs Mannering sounded quite fierce. 'And I am quite determined that these holidays you are not going off *any*where on your own, so it's just no good your asking me.'

'But, Mother, that's just silly,' said Philip in dismay. 'You speak as if we go out *looking* for adventures. We don't. And I ask you – what possible adventure could we fall into if we just went down to the river to camp? Why, you could come and see us for yourself every evening if you wanted to.'

'Yes – and the very first evening I came I should find you all spirited away somewhere, and mixed up with robbers and spies or rogues of some kind,' said his mother. 'Think of some of your holidays – first you get lost down an old copper mine on a deserted island, then another time you get shut up in the dungeons of an old castle, mixed up with spies—'

'Oooh yes – and another time we got into the wrong aeroplane and were whisked off to the Valley of

Adventure,' said Lucy-Ann, remembering. 'That was when we found all those amazing stolen statues hidden in caves – how their eyes gleamed when we saw them! I thought they were alive, but they weren't.'

'And the next time we went off with Bill to the bird-islands,' said Jack. 'That was grand. We had two tame puffins – do you remember, Philip?'

'Huffin and Puffin,' put in Kiki at once.

'Quite right, old bird,' said Philip. 'Huffin and Puffin they were. I loved them.'

'You may have gone to look for birds – but you found a whole nest of rogues,' said his mother. 'Gun-runners! Terribly dangerous.'

'Well, Mother, what about last summer hols?' said Dinah. '*You* nearly got caught up in *that* adventure!'

'Horrible!' said Mrs Mannering with a shiver. 'That awful mountain with its weird secrets – and the mad King of the Mountain – you nearly didn't escape from there. No – I tell you quite definitely that you can never again go off anywhere by yourselves. I'm always coming with you!'

There was a silence at this. All four children were very fond of Mrs Mannering – but they did like being on their own for some part of each holidays.

'Well – Aunt Allie – suppose Bill came with us – wouldn't that be all right?' asked Lucy-Ann. 'I do always feel safe with Bill.'

'Bill can't be trusted to keep out of adventures either,'

said Mrs Mannering. 'He's grand, I know, and I'd trust him more than anyone else in the world. But when you and he get together there's just no knowing what will happen. So, these holidays, I've made a very safe plan – and dear old Bill isn't in it, so perhaps we shall keep away from danger and extraordinary happenings.'

'What's your plan, Mother?' said Dinah nervously. '*Don't* say we're going to a seaside hotel or anything like that. They'd never take Kiki.'

'I'm taking you all for a cruise on a big ship,' said Mrs Mannering, and she smiled. 'I know you'll like that. It's tremendous fun. We shall call at all sorts of places, and see all kinds of strange and exciting things. And I shall have you under my eye, in one place all the time – the ship will be our home for some time, and if we get off at various ports we shall all go in a party together. There won't be a chance of any strange adventure.'

The four children looked at one another. Kiki watched them. Philip spoke first.

'It does sound rather exciting, Mother! Yes, it really does. We've never been on a really big ship before. Of course, I shall miss having any *animals* . . .'

'Oh, Philip – surely you can go without your everlasting menagerie of creatures!' cried Dinah. 'I must say it'll be a great relief to *me* to know you haven't got mice somewhere about you, or lizards, or slow-worms! Mother, it sounds super, I think. Thanks awfully for thinking up something so exciting.'

'Yes – it sounds smashing,' said Jack. 'We'll see no end of birds I've never seen before.'

'Jack's happy so long as he's somewhere that will provide him with birds,' said Lucy-Ann with a laugh. 'What with Philip with his craze for all kinds of creatures, and Jack with his passion for birds, it's a good thing we two girls haven't got crazes for anything as well. Aunt Allie, it's a wizard plan of yours. When do we go?'

'Next week,' said Mrs Mannering. 'That will give us plenty of time to get our things ready and packed. It will be very warm on the cruise, so we must get plenty of thin clothes to wear. White's the best thing – it doesn't hold the heat so much. And you must all have sun-hats the whole time, so don't begin to moan about wearing hats.'

'Isn't Bill coming?' asked Philip.

'No,' said his mother firmly. 'I feel rather mean about it, because he's just finished the job he's on, and he wants a holiday. But this time he's *not* coming with us. I want a nice peaceful holiday with no adventure at all.'

'Poor Bill,' said Lucy-Ann. 'Still – I daresay he'll be glad to have a holiday without us, for a change. I say – it's going to be fun, isn't it?'

'Fun!' said Kiki, joining in, and letting off a screech of excitement. 'Fun, fun, fun!'

2

On the Viking Star

It certainly was fun getting everything ready – buying flimsy clothes and enormous hats, masses of films for the cameras, guidebooks and maps. It was to be quite a long cruise, and the ship was to go to Portugal, Madeira, French Morocco, Spain, Italy and the Aegean Islands. What a wonderful trip!

At last everything was ready. The trunks were packed and strapped. The tickets had arrived. Passports had been got, and everyone had screamed in dismay to see how hideous they looked in their passport photographs.

Kiki screamed too, just for company. She loved screeching and screaming, but she wasn't encouraged in this, so it was a fine change to scream when everyone was doing the same.

'Shut up, Kiki,' said Jack, pushing her off his shoulder. 'Fancy screaming right in my ear like that! It's enough to make me stone deaf. Aunt Allie, will Kiki want a passport?'

'Of course not,' said Mrs Mannering. 'I'm not even sure she will be allowed to go with us.'

Jack stared at her in the greatest dismay. 'But – *I* can't go if Kiki doesn't. I couldn't leave her behind. She'd be miserable.'

'Well, I'll write and ask if you can take her,' said Mrs Mannering. 'But if the answer is no, you are *not* to make a fuss, Jack. I've gone to a lot of trouble to arrange this trip, and I can't have you upsetting it just because of Kiki. I can't imagine that she will be allowed to go – I'm sure passengers would object to a noisy bird like that.'

'She can be awfully quiet if she wants to,' said poor Jack. Kiki chose that moment to have a fit of hiccups. She hiccuped very well, and it always annoyed Mrs Mannering.

'Stop that, Kiki,' she ordered. Kiki stopped and looked reproachfully at Mrs Mannering. She began to cough, a small but hollow cough, copied from the gardener.

Mrs Mannering tried not to laugh. 'The bird is so *idiotic*,' she said. 'Quite crazy. Now, where did I put that list of things that I've got to do before we go?'

'One, two, three, GO!' shouted Kiki, and Jack just stopped her making a noise like a pistol shot. Mrs Mannering went out of the room, and Jack spoke solemnly to Kiki.

'Kiki, I may have to go without you, old bird. I can't

upset all the arrangements at the last minute because of you. But I'll do what I can, so cheer up.'

'God save the Queen,' said Kiki, feeling that it must be a solemn moment by the look on Jack's face. 'Poor Polly, naughty Polly!'

The last few days went by slowly. Lucy-Ann complained about it. 'Why is it that time always goes so slowly when you're wanting something to happen quickly? It's sickening. Thursday will never come!'

Jack was not so excited as the others, because a letter had come saying that parrots could not be taken on board. All four children were very sorry about it, and Jack looked really worried. But he did not grumble about it, or worry Mrs Mannering. She was sorry for him and offered to arrange with a woman in the village to look after Kiki for him.

'She used to have a parrot of her own,' she said. 'I expect she'd enjoy having Kiki.'

'No, thanks, Aunt Allie. I'll arrange something,' said Jack. 'Don't let's talk about it!'

So Mrs Mannering said no more, and even when Kiki sat on the tea table and picked all the currants out of the cake before anyone noticed, she did not say a word.

On Wednesday all five went off in Mrs Mannering's car to Southampton, followed by another with the baggage. They were in a great state of excitement. Everyone was in charge of something to carry, and Lucy-Ann kept looking at her package anxiously to make sure she still had it.

They were to stay at a hotel for the night and embark on the ship at half past eight in the morning, to catch the tide. They would be away at eleven o'clock, steaming steadily towards France – what an excitement!

They all had a very good dinner at the hotel, and then Mrs Mannering suggested going to the cinema. She felt sure that not one of the children would go to sleep if she sent them to bed at the usual time.

'Do you mind if I go and hunt up a school friend of mine, Aunt Allie?' said Jack. 'He lives in Southampton, and I'd like to spring a surprise on him and go and call.'

'All right,' said Mrs Mannering. 'But you're not to be late back. Do you want to go and see him too, Philip?'

'Who's this chappy, Jack?' asked Philip, but Jack was halfway out of the room. A mumble came through the door.

'What's he say?' said Philip.

'Sounded like "Porky" to me,' said Dinah.

'Porky? Who does he mean, I wonder,' said Philip. 'Somebody mad on birds, I expect. I'll come to the cinema. I'd like to see the picture – it's got wild animals in it.'

They went off to the cinema without seeing Jack again. He was home when they came back, reading one of the guidebooks Mrs Mannering had bought.

'Hello! See Porky?' said Philip. He got a frown from

Jack, and was puzzled. What was Jack up to? He changed the subject quickly, and began to talk about the picture they had seen.

'Now, to bed,' said Mrs Mannering. 'Stop talking, Philip. Off you all go – and remember, up at seven o'clock sharp in the morning.'

Everyone was awake long before seven. The girls talked together, and Philip and Jack chattered away too. Philip asked Jack about the night before.

'Why did you shut me up when I asked you if you'd seen Porky?' he said. 'And anyway – who *is* Porky?'

'He's that fellow called Hogsney,' said Jack. 'We called him Porky. He left ages ago. He was always wanting to borrow Kiki, don't you remember?'

'Oh, *yes*, Porky, of course,' said Philip. 'I'd almost forgotten him. Jack, what's up? You look sort of secretive!'

'Don't ask me any questions, because I don't want to answer them,' said Jack.

'You're being jolly mysterious,' said Philip. '*I* believe it's something to do with Kiki. You kept putting us all off when we asked you what you'd done with her. We thought you were feeling upset about it, so we didn't press you.'

'Well, don't press me now,' said Jack. 'I don't want to say anything at the moment.'

'All right,' said Philip, giving it up. 'I know you're up to something, though. Come on – let's get up. It's not seven yet, but we can't lie in bed on a morning as fine as this.'

They were all on the boat at just after half past eight. Mrs Mannering found their cabins. There were three in a row – a single one for her, and two double ones for the others.

Lucy-Ann was delighted with them. 'Why, they are just like proper little rooms,' she said. 'Jack, is your cabin like ours? Look, we've even got hot and cold water taps.'

'We've got an electric fan going in our cabin,' said Philip appearing at the door. 'It's wizard – lovely and cool. You've got one too.'

'The water is only just below our porthole,' said Dinah, looking out. 'If the sea got at all rough it would slop into the hole!'

'It would be well and truly screwed up before that happened!' said Philip. 'I'm glad we're at the waterline – it will be cooler in this warm weather. I say, isn't this super! I'm longing to sail off.'

They all went to see Mrs Mannering's cabin, which was the same as theirs but smaller. Then they went to explore the ship. She was quite big, but not tremendous, and was white from top to bottom – white funnels, white rails, white sides.

Her name was on each of the white lifeboats slung at the sides of the deck – *Viking Star*. Lucy-Ann read it a dozen times over.

'We shall have lifeboat drill tomorrow, I expect,' said Mrs Mannering, joining them on their exploration.

'There are big lifebelt jackets in our cabin cupboards,' said Lucy-Ann. 'I suppose you tie them round you.'

'You slip them over your head, so that half the jacket is at your front and half behind – and then you tie it firmly round you with the tapes,' said Mrs Mannering. 'You'll have to put it on tomorrow for lifeboat drill.'

It all sounded very exciting. They went round the ship, thrilled with everything. There was the sports deck, where someone was already playing quoits with thick rings of rope, and two others were playing deck tennis. 'Fancy being able to play games like this on board ship!' said Dinah.

'There's a cinema down below,' said Mrs Mannering, 'and a writing room, and library and lounge, and an enormous dining room!'

'And gosh, look – here's a swimming pool on the ship itself!' cried Jack in amazement as they came to a beautiful pool at one end of the ship, shimmering blue with water.

The ship's siren suddenly hooted twice very loudly. Lucy-Ann almost fell into the swimming pool with surprise. Mrs Mannering laughed.

'Oh, Lucy-Ann – did it make you jump? It made me jump too.'

'What a terrific noise!' said Lucy-Ann. 'My goodness,

it's a good thing Kiki isn't here. If she began to hoot like that siren she'd be impossible.'

'Shut up, idiot,' said Dinah in a low voice. 'Don't remind Jack we're going off without her.'

Lucy-Ann glanced round for Jack, but he wasn't there. 'Where's he gone?' she asked Dinah. But nobody had seen him go.

'He's somewhere about,' said Philip. 'I say, we must be sailing soon. Look – they're taking up the gangways. We'll soon be off!'

'Let's stand at this side and wave to all the people,' said Lucy-Ann. She leaned over the rail and watched the people crowded together on the dockside below. They were shouting and waving. Suddenly Lucy-Ann gave a squeal.

'Look! *Look!* There's somebody with a parrot *just* like Kiki! Honestly, it is. Where's Jack? I *must* tell him. Blow, he's nowhere to be seen!'

The engines of the ship had now started up, and the children felt a vibration under their feet. Lucy-Ann strained her eyes to look at the parrot that was so very like Kiki.

'It *is* Kiki!' she cried. 'Kiki! Kiki! Goodbye! I'm sure it's you!'

The parrot was chained to a young man's wrist. Whether it was making a noise or not the children could not tell because of the hullabaloo going on. It certainly was remarkably like Kiki.

'We're off! We've moved away from the quay!' cried Philip. 'Hurrah, we're off!' He waved madly to everyone. Lucy-Ann waved too, and watched the parrot. It was getting smaller as the ship moved away towards the open water. Its owner seemed to be having trouble with it. It was flapping its wings, and pecking at him.

Then it suddenly rose into the air – the chain parted – and the parrot sailed right over the stretch of water between quay and ship, screeching madly.

'It *is* Kiki, it is, it is!' yelled Lucy-Ann. 'Jack, where are you? JACK!'

3

Everyone settles in

Dinah, Lucy-Ann and Philip rushed to find Jack. The parrot had reached the ship, and they had lost sight of it. They were all certain it was Kiki, and Philip had a shrewd idea that Jack would not be quite so surprised about it as they themselves were.

Jack was nowhere to be found. It was most exasperating. They hunted for him everywhere, and at last Lucy-Ann thought of his cabin. 'He might be there,' she said. 'Though why he wants to go and shut himself up there just at the exciting moment when the ship is leaving Southampton, I really can't imagine! And where's the parrot? She seems to have disappeared too.'

They went down the stairs to the cabins and found their way to the passage where theirs were. They flung open Jack's door and crowded in. 'Jack! Are you here? What do you think we've just seen?'

They stopped in surprise at what they saw. Jack was sitting on his bed in the cabin, and Kiki was on his shoulder, making a curious crooning noise into his ear, pulling at it gently.

'Gosh!' said Philip. 'So she found you. I suppose it *is* Kiki?'

'Of course, idiot,' said Jack. 'What a bit of luck, wasn't it? Old Porky brough her down to the quay to see me off, chained to his wrist – and she broke the chain and flew over to me! Came into my porthole too – brainy old bird!'

'*Porky?* The boy you used to know at school! Did you give Kiki to *him* to mind for you?' said Lucy-Ann, amazed. 'But – how did she get down here?'

'I brought her in the car yesterday,' said Jack, putting one hand over his ear so that Kiki could not nibble it. 'She was in the picnic basket I was carrying, as quiet as a mouse. I was terrified one of you would ask me to open the basket and get you out something to eat!'

'But I say – won't Porky be upset to have her escape like that?' said Dinah.

'And *how* did she know you were here, if you were down in your cabin?' wondered Lucy-Ann. 'Perhaps she heard me call her. That must have been it – she heard me yelling "Kiki! Kiki!", broke her chain in her excitement and flew over – and by a lucky chance she chose your very porthole!'

'You'd better tell Aunt Allie all that,' said Jack, with a grin. 'It makes a very fine story – better than mine!'

The three stared at him in silence. 'You're a determined old fraud, Jack,' said Philip at last. 'You arranged it all; I bet you did! Yes, even arranged for the chain to snap and for Kiki to see or hear you at your porthole.'

Jack grinned again. 'Well, I think Lucy-Ann's idea is very good – shouting to Kiki like that and making her so excited that she flew across to the ship. Anyway, she's here, and here she stays. I'd better keep her down in the cabin, I think.'

They all made a fuss of old Kiki, who enjoyed it very much indeed. She couldn't understand the noise the vibration of the engines made, and kept cocking her head on one side to listen. She tried an imitation, but not a very good one.

'Now don't you do any funny noises,' Jack warned her. 'You don't want to be hauled up before the Captain, do you?'

'Pop goes the weasel,' said Kiki, and pecked his ear. Then she suddenly gave a most realistic sneeze.

'Don't,' said Jack. 'Use your handkerchief! Gosh, Kiki, I couldn't have gone without you.'

Everyone was pleased to know that Kiki was safely with them. They broke the news as gently as possible to Mrs Mannering. She listened in annoyance, but it did not seem to occur to her for one moment that Kiki's arrival was anything but an unfortunate accident. She sighed.

'All right. If she's here, she's here. But for goodness' sake, Jack, keep her locked up in the cabin. You really will get into trouble if the passengers complain about her, and she may be sent to the crew's deck and put in a cage if you don't keep a firm hand on her.'

So Kiki was locked into the cabin, and passed the first day wondering whether *she* was giddy, or whether there was a slight earthquake going on all the time. She had no idea she was in a big ship, and could not understand its movements, though she had many a time been in small boats.

The first day seemed lovely and long. The *Viking Star* slid easily through the calm, blue water, her engines purring sweetly, leaving behind her a creamy wake that seemed to have no end, but to stretch right back to the horizon itself. England was soon left behind. The first stop was to be Lisbon in Portugal.

It was fun to go down to meals in the big dining room and choose what they liked from the long menu. It was fun to go up on the sports deck and play deck tennis and try to keep their balance as they ran for the rubber ring. It was even fun to go to bed – because it meant snuggling down into a narrow, bunk-like bed, turning out the light, feeling the breeze from the electric fan cooling their hot bodies and hearing the plish-plish-plash of the water just below their portholes.

'Lovely!' said Lucy-Ann before she fell asleep. 'I hope this trip doesn't turn into an adventure. I like it as it is. It's quite exciting enough without having an adventure.'

It wasn't quite so nice in the Bay of Biscay! The sea

was rough and choppy there, and the boat pitched and tossed and rolled. Mrs Mannering didn't like it at all. She stayed in her cabin, but the four children were as right as rain. They turned up to every meal in the dining room, and ate steadily right down the menu. They would even have gone up to try and play deck tennis on the sports deck if one of the stewards had not firmly forbidden them to.

And then, quite suddenly as it seemed, everything changed. The sea grew blue and calm, the sun shone out very hotly indeed, the sky was brilliant, and every officer and man appeared in spotless white.

Mrs Mannering felt all right again – and Kiki grew very, very impatient at being kept in the cabin. She was already great friends with the steward and stewardess who looked after the cabins. They had soon got over their astonishment at finding her in Jack's cabin

They had not seen her at first. She was sitting behind the little curtain that hung at the side of the porthole, which Jack had to keep shut in case Kiki flew out. It was the stewardess who heard her first. She had come in to make the beds.

Kiki watched her slyly from behind the curtain. Then she spoke in a firm and decided voice.

'Put the kettle on.'

The stewardess was startled. She looked round at the door, thinking that someone must be there speaking to her. But nobody was.

Kiki gave a loud hiccup. 'Pardon,' she said. The stewardess felt alarmed. She looked all round. She opened the cupboard door.

'What a pity, what a pity!' said Kiki, in such a mournful voice that the stewardess could bear it no longer and flew to find the steward. He was a dour and determined Scot with very little patience.

He came into the cabin and looked round. 'What's to do, wumman?' he said to the stewardess. 'What's scairt ye? There's naught here.'

Kiki gave a loud cough, and then sneezed violently. 'Pardon,' she said. 'Where's your hanky?'

Now it was the steward's turn to look amazed. He stared all round the cabin. Kiki gave a loud and realistic yawn. She had a wonderful collection of noises. She couldn't resist looking round the curtain to see how her performance was going.

The steward saw her and strode over to the porthole. 'Now look ye here – it's a parrot!' he said. 'Did ever ye hear the like? A fine and clever bird it must be to do all that! Well, Polly – you're a clever wee bird, that's what you are!'

Kiki flew to the top of the cupboard and looked at the steward and stewardess, first out of one eye and then out of the other. Then she made a noise like the dinner-gong being beaten for the ship's meals. At the end she went off into one of her cackles of laughter.

'It fair beats ye, doesn't it?' said the Scots steward,

amazed. 'A rare, bonny bird it is. The laddie that owns it should think shame on himself to keep it shut up here.'

'It scared me, right enough,' said the stewardess. 'I wonder if it would like a grape. My great-aunt's parrot loved grapes. I'll go and get some.'

Pretty soon Kiki was enjoying some black grapes, and when Jack came along to see her, he found the cabin floor scattered with grape pips, and two admiring people gaping at Kiki in delight.

'Dirty bird!' said Jack sternly, looking down at the pips. 'You come down off that cupboard and pick up these pips.'

'Pips,' said Kiki. 'Pops. Pip goes the weasel.'

'I hope she hasn't been annoying you,' said Jack to the stewardess.

'Oh, she's wonderful,' said the woman. 'I never saw such a clever bird. You ought to take her up and show her off.'

It wasn't very long before Jack did take her up to the deck above on his shoulder, much to the surprise and amusement of all the passengers. Kiki had a wonderful time showing off. The only thing she couldn't bear was the hoot of the ship's siren, which always startled her so much that she fell off Jack's shoulder in fright every time she heard it. She didn't know what it was or where it came from, and usually flew off to hide herself somewhere whenever she heard it.

She came to the lifeboat drill, and Lucy-Ann was

certain she was upset because she had not a small life-jacket to wear. They all put theirs on, went to their right lifeboat and listened to a short talk from one of the officers about what they were to do if danger arose. Lucy-Ann hoped fervently that it wouldn't.

'We're going to land in Lisbon tomorrow,' said Mrs Mannering. 'But none of you is to wander off alone. I'm not going to have any adventure starting up. You'll all keep close to me – please understand *that*!'

4

Philip collects a pet

Soon the days began to slip by quickly. After Lisbon Lucy-Ann and Dinah lost count of them. They did not even know if the day was Monday, Tuesday or any other. They knew Sunday because everyone went into the big lounge then and listened to the captain taking a short church service.

For days they saw no land. Philip grew very excited when a shoal of flying fish flew out of the sea and stayed up in the air for some time. They were lovely little things.

'What makes them do that?' wondered Lucy-Ann.

'Just being chased by some hungry big fish,' said Philip. 'Wouldn't you leap out of the water and try and fly through the air if an enormous fish was after you, Lucy-Ann? Gosh, I wish one of the fish would fly on deck. I'd just love to see it close to.'

'Well, you couldn't possibly make it a pet, thank goodness, because it would die in your pocket,' said

Dinah. 'It seems unusual for you to be without any pets at all, Philip. Very nice!'

But she spoke too soon, because Philip collected a pet two days later! They had called at Madeira, left that island, and gone on to French Morocco. It was there that Philip collected his strange little pet.

The children liked French Morocco. They especially liked the bazaars, although the air was so strongly scented that Mrs Mannering said it made her feel faint, and she walked along with smelling salts pressed to her nose. The children soon got used to the air, though Kiki didn't, judging by the number of 'Poohs' she said. 'Pooh! Gah! Pooh!'

Dinah tried out her French on the black-eyed traders, and was pleased when they understood. She bought a tiny brooch, and Lucy-Ann bought a blue vase.

'Don't you see anything *you* like?' she asked Philip. He shook his head.

'I don't want things like that. Now if I could see something really exciting – say an old dagger – or, I tell you what! Something I've always wanted and never had.'

'What's that?' asked Lucy-Ann, determined to buy it for him if only she could see it.

'You'll laugh – but I've always wanted a ship in a bottle,' said Philip.

'I've never even seen one,' said Lucy-Ann, astonished. 'A ship *inside* a bottle, do you mean? What a peculiar thing? How is it put there?'

'I don't know,' said Philip. 'It's daft of me to want it, really – it's just one of those ideas you get, you know.'

'I'll be sure to look out for one for you wherever we go,' promised Lucy-Ann. 'Oh, do look at Kiki. She's taking sweets from those little children there. She'll make herself sick again!'

Mrs Mannering insisted that they should all stay close to her, and keep with the ship's party. The four children wished they could explore by themselves, for they liked the people and their strange, dark, narrow little shops.

'Certainly not,' said Mrs Mannering. 'Why, didn't you hear what happened to the man at the next table to ours on the ship? He and his wife went off by themselves in a taxi to visit some place or other – and the driver took them to a deserted hill, and wouldn't take them back to the ship till they had given him all the money they had!'

'Gracious,' said Lucy-Ann, surprised.

'He brought them back just as the gangway was being drawn up,' went on Mrs Mannering, 'so they had no time to make any complaint. *Now* you know why I want you to keep with the ship's party. No more adventures for you, if I can help it! It would be just like you all to disappear somewhere, get into awful danger and put a few more grey hairs into my head!'

'You haven't *really* got very many,' said Lucy-Ann. 'Just about one for each of our adventures, that's all! I *will* keep near to you, Aunt Allie. I don't want an adventure either.'

The next day there was to be a trip by motor coach to a famous place inland – an old town on the edge of the desert. 'The motor coaches will be here on the quay at half past ten,' Mrs Mannering told the four. 'Be sure to wear your sun-hats. It will be terribly hot.'

It was on that trip that Philip collected his new pet. The motor coaches duly arrived and everyone crowded into them, feeling extremely hot. Off they went at top speed down a sandy road that for a time seemed to run through what looked like a bare desert. Large cactus plants grew by the roadside. Lucy-Ann thought they looked ugly and spiteful with their numerous prickles and fat bulging bodies.

After two hours they came to the old town. Its ancient arches and towers seemed to spring up suddenly out of the sand. Little dark-eyed children, with hardly anything on, ran to meet them, their hands held out.

'Penn-ee, penn-ee,' they said, and Kiki echoed them at once. 'Penn-ee, penn-ee!'

They all went into the narrow street of the old town. The guide took them to an ancient building and began to drone on about its history. Then one by one the party climbed steep, winding steps up an enormous tower.

Halfway up Philip looked out of a great stone window. It had no glass, of course. The wall was so thick that he could sit on the window sill with his legs stretched right out. He hung on to the side of the window and slid forward to look down.

Far below he could see a little crowd of excited children. They were pointing upwards and chattering. Some of them were throwing stones.

'Now what are those little scamps throwing stones at?' thought Philip. 'If it's something alive I'll knock their heads together!'

He slid down from the enormous window sill and ran down the great winding stairs. A stone flew through a window opening not far from the bottom, and he stopped.

He heard a small whimpering noise and, hidden in a corner of the window opening, he saw a little heap of brown fur. He went over to it. What could it be?

Click! A stone flew near him. Blow those kids! He stepped to the window and looked down sternly. 'You stop that!' he shouted. 'Do you hear me? Stop it!'

The small children looked in consternation at this sudden apparition. They disappeared in a hurry. Philip reached over to the brown bundle. A small wizened face peeped out at him with mournful brown eyes. Then it was covered by tiny hands.

'Why – it's a monkey – a tiny monkey!' thought Philip. He knew how scared the small creatures were, and he was afraid of frightening this poor little mistreated animal. He had seen plenty of monkeys in that part of the country already, but not near – they always kept well out of the way.

Philip spoke to the small creature in what Lucy-Ann

called his 'special animal voice.' It uncovered its funny little face again, and then, with one bound, was cuddling into the boy's shoulder, nestling against his neck, trembling. He put up a cautious hand and rubbed its soft fur.

No animal had ever been able to resist Philip's magic. Horses, dogs, cats, snakes, insects, birds – they came to him at once trustingly and confidingly. Not one could resist him. It was a gift that everyone marvelled at and envied him for.

Philip sat down on the broad window sill and talked to the scared and miserable little monkey. It chattered back in a high, cheeping little voice. It looked at him shyly out of childlike brown eyes. Its tiny brown fingers wound themselves round one of his. It was Philip's devoted slave from that moment.

When the others came pattering down the stairs in front of the rest of the party, they were astonished to see the small monkey cuddling up to Philip.

'There – I knew he'd get hold of something sooner or later!' said Dinah. 'Ugh! A nasty, dirty, smelly little monkey, full of fleas too, I expect.'

'Well, it *is* dirty and smelly, and I'm sure it's got fleas,' said Philip. 'But it isn't nasty. It's been stoned by those wretched children down below. Both its legs are hurt.'

'Poor little thing,' said Lucy-Ann, almost in tears. Jack stroked the tiny thing's head, but that only made it shrink closer to Philip.

'You're not to take it back to the ship with you,' began

Dinah. 'I shall tell Mother if you do. I won't have a monkey in our party.'

'He's coming with me,' said Philip sternly.

Dinah began to lose her temper. 'Then I shall tell Mother I won't have it. I shall—'

'Dinah, it's so *small*, and it's *hurt*,' said Lucy-Ann, in a shaky voice. 'Don't talk like that. It's so unkind.'

Dinah flushed, and turned away. She was cross, and horrified at the thought of having a monkey 'tagging along' with them, as she put it – but she did not want to go against the other three. She said no more, though she was unhappy for the rest of the day.

How Philip hid the monkey till he got back to the ship only he knew. The fact is that no one even noticed it. Jack and Lucy-Ann helped him valiantly by standing in front of him whenever they thought anyone might see the monkey. Dinah would not help, but on the other hand she did nothing to give the secret away.

Back in the cabin, the three children pored over the tiny creature. 'It's not even a grown monkey,' said Philip. 'How those children could stone a little thing like this beats me. But I suppose in every country there are cruel and unkind people – after all, we've seen boys back at home throwing stones at a cat. Look – its legs are bruised and cut, but they're not broken. I can soon get those right. I wonder if it would let me wash it – it's so dirty.'

The little thing would let Philip do anything in the world he wanted to. The children spent two hours washing and drying it gently. Jack brought a small shoe-brush to brush its fluffy fur. It let Philip put iodine on its cuts and gave only a tiny whimper.

'There!' said the boy. 'You look fine. What's your name?'

The monkey chattered something, and the children listened. 'It sounds as if he's saying "Micky-micky-mick",' said Lucy-Ann.

'Right. If he thinks his name is Micky, Micky it is,' said Philip. 'I wonder what Kiki will think of him.'

'She won't like him much,' said Jack. 'She'll be jealous. Good thing we left her in the girls' cabin. She'd screech the place down if she saw us washing and brushing Micky.'

Kiki certainly was most amazed to see Micky on Philip's shoulder that night. She stared, and then, just as Jack had said, she screeched – one of her very best express-train screeches. Mrs Mannering put her head in at the cabin door to protest.

She suddenly caught sight of the monkey and stepped forward in surprise, wondering if she had seen aright. 'Oh, Philip! You oughtn't to have brought it back to the ship. What a tiny thing!'

'Mother, some children were stoning it. I had to bring it away,' said Philip. His mother looked at him. It was just exactly the kind of thing Philip's father had done when he was alive. How could she scold him for something that was in his very blood?

'Well – I don't know if a fuss will be made if you keep him on the ship,' she said, stroking the monkey's head. 'What does Dinah say about it?'

'She was very cross at first, but she didn't say much,' said Lucy-Ann. 'She's still in our cabin, I think. She'll get over Micky. She'll have to.'

'Micky – Kiki – Micky – Kiki – Micky – Kiki,' said Kiki triumphantly, as if she had suddenly discovered something very clever. She loved words that sounded the same. 'Micky – Kiki, Micky – Kiki—'

'Shut up, Kiki,' said Philip. 'I say, what a pity he's called Micky – we'll never stop Kiki saying those two words now. But he *is* Micky. We can't alter his name now.'

So Micky he was, and in a day or two he was everyone's friend – yes, even Dinah's! He had such a dear, comical face that it was impossible not to like him when he looked at you out of mournful brown eyes.

'He's such a baby and yet he's got such a wise, wizened little face,' said Lucy-Ann. 'And I do like his tiny fingers – just like ours! Don't you, Dinah?'

'Well – he's not as awful as I thought he was at first,' admitted Dinah. 'I can't say I want him sitting on my shoulder all day long, like Philip – and I'm sure he's still got fleas – but he's really not bad.'

'He *hasn't* got fleas,' said Philip, annoyed. 'Don't keep saying that.'

Micky soon recovered his spirits, and from being a

gentle, confiding little thing, he became a mischievous, chattering madcap. He leapt about the cabin as lightly as a squirrel, and Dinah was always scared he would take a flying jump on to her shoulder. But he didn't. He was wise enough not to do that!

Kiki was alarmed to see these acrobatics, and when the two were together in the same cabin she always turned to face Micky, so that she could jab him with her beak if he leapt at her. But he left her alone, and took very little notice. She didn't like that at all!

She took to calling his name in Philip's voice, which she could imitate perfectly. 'Micky! Micky!'

The monkey would look round at once, but would see no Philip. 'Micky!' Kiki would say again, and the monkey would begin to leap all over the place, trying to find Philip.

Then Kiki would cackle with laughter, and Micky would go off in disgust and sit on the porthole sill with his back to Kiki, looking through the thick glass out to sea.

Kiki certainly had the best of it because she soon found that she could make noises that terrified Micky. If she barked like a dog the little creature went nearly frantic with fright. He was puzzled too. He watched Kiki closely, and soon realised that no dog barked unless Kiki was in the cabin. Then was Kiki some kind of bird-dog?

The next time she barked she followed it with a fierce

growl. This was too much for Micky. He picked up a tablet of soap from the basin and flung it at the surprised Kiki. It hit her full on the beak and she gave a squawk of alarm and nearly fell off her perch.

Micky sent a toothbrush after the soap, and then the tooth-mug. He was a very fine shot, and soon Kiki was flying round the cabin trying to find a place to shelter from the volley of articles that Micky was sending after her – hairbrushes, combs, a roll of film, anything he could get hold of!

Philip stopped the battle when he came in. 'Micky! Pick them all up!' he said sternly. 'What did Kiki do to you to make you lose your temper like that? Bad Micky!'

'Naughty Micky, bad boy!' said Kiki at once, and went off into one of her cackles of laughter. Micky picked everything up humbly. Then he went to sit on Philip's shoulder as usual. Kiki was jealous. She flew to his other shoulder.

The monkey chattered at her. Kiki chattered back, in exactly the same monkey voice as Micky used. He stared in amazement, and answered excitedly. Philip listened, amused.

'Well, I don't really know if you understand one another or not,' he said. 'But it's just as well you should. I don't want to find my cabin strewn with all my belongings each time I come into it. So just be friends! Do you hear, Kiki and Micky?'

'Pooh,' said Kiki, in a friendly voice, and nibbled at him.

'Pooh to you!' said Philip. 'And kindly stop nibbling my ear!'

5

Lucian arrives

The children soon felt that the *Viking Star* was their home – a floating home, containing everything they wanted except the open countryside. They got to know every nook and cranny on the ship, they explored the engine room under the eye of Mac, the chief engineer, and they were even allowed up on the bridge by the first officer, a very great honour.

Mrs Mannering made friends on the ship with two or three people she liked. There were only a few children on board besides Jack and the others, and they were much younger and so spoilt that nobody wanted to have much to do with them.

'I rather wish there were more children of your own age,' Mrs Mannering said to her four. 'It might be more fun for you.'

'Well – *we* don't want anyone else, thanks,' said Philip. 'We're all right on our own. It's bad enough having those other spoilt kids around – always wanting to mess about with Micky, and trying to get Kiki to talk to them.'

'She's too sensible,' said Jack. 'Kiki just looks at them and says "Shut up!" whenever she sees them.'

'How rude of her!' said Mrs Mannering. 'I do hope you stop her when she talks like that to the other children.'

'Well, actually I don't,' said Jack. 'She only says what I jolly well would like to say myself. Spoilt little brats! I'm going to push that nasty little yellow-haired girl into the swimming pool one of these days – coming whining round me asking me if she can hold Kiki. *Hold* Kiki! What does she think Kiki is – one of her frightful dolls?'

'You mustn't push the child into the pool,' said Mrs Mannering, horrified. 'I do agree she wants slapping – but she's only a little girl, Jack.'

'She's a human mosquito,' said Jack. 'I just wish I had a fly-swatter when she comes near.'

'Well, all the kids are getting off at the next stop,' said Philip, fondling Micky who, as usual, was on his shoulder. The boys looked a curious pair, one with a parrot on his shoulder, the other with a monkey. The passengers smiled whenever they saw them.

'I'm glad to hear those tiresome children will soon be gone,' said Dinah, who was not very fond of youngsters. 'But I expect some equally dreadful ones will embark in their place.'

She was wrong, as it happened. Only one boy embarked; no girls at all. All the spoilt youngsters left, stumbling down the gangway at Naples, screaming and complaining to the last, certainly a most unpleasant collection of small children. Jack and the others watched them go with pleasure, and Kiki screeched after them. 'Goodbye, good riddance, goodbye, good riddance!'

'Jack! She's never said that before,' said Mrs Mannering reproachfully. 'You must just have taught her!'

'Kiki only reads my thoughts, Aunt Allie,' laughed Jack. 'I say – look here – here comes Brer Rabbit!'

The children giggled as they watched a tall, gangling boy come up the gangway. His mouth certainly was exactly like a rabbit's. The front teeth stuck out, and his chin sloped backwards. He was about as old as Jack and Philip. He wore large, round glasses that magnified his eyes and made them look rather staring. He had a very amiable grin on his face as he came up the gangway.

He seemed very excited, and was talking in a mixture of English and some foreign language to a rather languid-looking lady behind him and a short, burly man who wore dark sunglasses that completely hid his eyes.

'Uncle, Aunt, we're off at last! Oh, I say, what a magnificent ship! I'm sure I shan't be seasick in her.' Then he went off into what sounded like a string of gibberish but was really a foreign language. Kiki cocked her head when she heard this string of what sounded to her like complete nonsense.

As the boy passed she spoke to him in a conversational tone, pouring out the same kind of gibberish that she had heard. The boy looked at her in amazement.

'Oh, I say! A talking parrot. Oh, I *say!*'

'Oh, I say!' repeated Kiki immediately. 'Oh, I *say!* Oh, I SAY!'

'Shut up, Kiki. Don't be rude,' said Jack.

Micky leaned forward on Philip's shoulder and sent out a stream of excited chattering to Kiki. The boy stared in delight.

'Oh, I say! A talking monkey too! What's he saying?'

'He says he thinks he's seen you somewhere before, but he can't remember where, and he wants to know if Kiki the parrot remembers,' said Philip solemnly. Lucy-Ann gave a delighted giggle. The boy stared openmouthed, then he laughed, showing all his big teeth.

'Oh, you're pulling my leg, aren't you? But I say – what fun – a parrot that talks, and a tame monkey! Aren't you lucky!'

'Get on, Lucian, get on,' said the burly man behind him, and gave the boy a push. Lucian went forward at a run, turning round to give the four children an apologetic grin for leaving them so abruptly. The man said something in an annoyed voice to the woman with him, but as he said it in a foreign language the children didn't understand a word. They guessed at once, however, that Lucian was not very popular with his uncle!

'Well – if Rabbit is the only boy to come on board here, I suppose he'll pin himself on to us all day long,' said Philip. 'What a weed!'

'Oh, I say!' said Kiki. Jack groaned.

'Now we shall have Kiki saying that day and night. It's a good thing Micky can't talk properly – we'd never get a word in edgeways!'

The ship sailed off again into waters bluer than ever. It was pleasant to go to the bow of the ship and feel the breeze. Both Kiki and Micky liked this too.

Just as Jack and Philip had feared, the new boy tagged himself on to them whenever he could. The children always knew when he was coming because Kiki invariably gave them warning.

'Oh, I say!' she would squawk, and the four would sigh. Lucian again! He would come up grinning amiably, and settle himself beside them.

He told them all about himself immediately. He had no father or mother. His father had been English, but his mother was Greek, so he had plenty of Greek relations. He went to school in England, but spent most of his holidays with his relations. He was fourteen, nearly fifteen, he didn't like games, he loved history, and he wished his name wasn't Lucian.

'Why?' asked Dinah.

'Well – because the boys at my school change it to

Lucy-Ann,' explained Lucian. 'I mean – fancy having a name that's as girlish as that.'

'It's *my* name,' said Lucy-Ann. 'I like it.'

'Well – it's very nice for *you*,' said Lucian. 'But awful for me. Especially when they shorten it and call me Lucy.'

'Juicy Lucy!' said Kiki at once in delight. 'Juicy Lucy! Oh, I say!'

Everybody roared, even Lucian. Kiki cackled too.

'Juicy Lucy, goosey-Lucy, oh, I say!' carolled Kiki.

'Oh, I say, really – that bird of yours is a regular comic, isn't she?' said Lucian in admiration. 'Gosh, I wish I could borrow her to take back to school. I say, do *you* take her to school with you?'

'I used to,' said Jack regretfully. 'But she kept telling our form-master to wipe his feet and shut the door, and when she yelled out "Don't sniff, use your hanky" to the Head, well, that was about the end.'

'Do you remember how you put her in a cupboard once, to hide her in class – and she went off like fireworks, fizzling and popping and exploding?' said Philip with a grin. 'It was just after Guy Fawkes Day – she remembered the noises.'

Lucian listened in the greatest admiration, his wide mouth open as if he listened with that as well as with his ears.

'Oh, I say! What happened?'

'Well – we exploded too!' said Philip. 'And after that,

the master did – in a different way, of course. We had to put Kiki out to live with someone in the village. We go to see her every day, naturally, and have her on half-holidays and weekends.'

'And she always goes to every school match and cheers like anything – doesn't she, Jack?' said Lucy-Ann.

'She's a wonder,' said Lucian. 'Let me have her for a minute.'

'Look out – she won't go to strangers,' warned Jack. But Lucian was already trying to get hold of the wonderful parrot. He soon let her go. She gave him a vicious nip with her curved beak, and he yelled. To Lucy-Ann's amazement she saw tears in his eyes!

He turned and went off without a word, sucking his bleeding thumb. The others looked at one another.

'He was crying,' said Lucy-Ann, in sheer amazement that a boy of fourteen should do such a thing.

'He's a nitwit,' said Jack, trying to calm down Kiki, who had put up her crest tremendously, and was dancing angrily from one foot to another.

'Nit-wit,' said Kiki, pouncing on the word at once, 'Nit-wit, wit-nit, tit-bit, bit-nit, oh, I say!'

'You're a bad bird, nipping people like that,' scolded Jack. 'That was a nasty nip.'

'Nip-wit,' announced Kiki.

'Yes, that's about what you are – a nip-wit!' said Jack with a chuckle. 'Now don't you start, Micky! We've had enough rudery from Kiki.'

Micky had started off on one of his long strings of excited gibberish. It was comical to see how seriously and solemnly Kiki listened to this, with her head on one side.

She answered the little monkey gravely when he had finished his excited announcement, whatever it was.

'Rikky-likky-acky, icky, pop-pop-pop!' she said. The children roared. 'She thinks she's talking his language. Good old Kiki! You can't get the better of *her*,' said Philip. 'I'm glad she's more friendly with Micky now. He's such a dear.'

'He's getting awfully mischievous, though,' said Dinah, who now thought of the monkey much more kindly. 'He went into a dozen cabins yesterday, and collected all the soaps out of the basins and put them in one of the armchairs in the lounge.'

'Gracious!' said Jack. 'He'll be getting into trouble soon.'

'You mean *we* shall,' said Philip. 'I wish we could teach Kiki to keep an eye on Micky for us – but she encourages him. I'm sure it was Kiki who told the monkey to climb up the mast to the man in the crow's-nest there and give him an awful fright.'

'Micky's a dear,' said Lucy-Ann, and she tickled him under his furry chin. He looked at her with wise, sad eyes. Lucy-Ann knew he was very happy now, but she was always worried because he looked at her sorrowfully.

She only half believed Philip when he told her that all monkeys looked sad.

'There's the gong for lunch,' said Dinah thankfully. 'I feel as if it's about an hour late today, I'm so hungry. Come on, everybody!'

6

The tale of Andra's treasure

The *Viking Star* was now going off to cruise among the islands of the Aegean Sea. The water was a beautiful dark blue, and the children thought it was the nicest part of the trip, seeing the islands loom up out of the purple-blue sea.

Lucian proved himself quite useful here, because he knew that part of the sea very well. He was able to tell them about the different islands, and he was full of exciting stories of old pirates and robberies at sea, and the taking of treasure.

'See that island we're coming to,' he said. 'That's Oupos. It's only small, but it's got an old castle on it with one of the biggest dungeons in the world. The old sailors used to take prisoners at sea, and sail to Oupos, and dump their prisoners in the dungeons. Sometimes they left them there for years – till they were old men.'

'How horrible!' said Lucy-Ann. 'Have you been on Oupos?'

'Yes, once,' said Lucian. 'I saw the holes for the dungeons too. Nearly fell down one myself.'

'What do you mean – holes for the dungeons?' asked Philip.

'Well – the yard of the old castle was pitted with holes – deep, very deep holes,' explained Lucian. 'And when a prisoner was landed on the island he was dragged to the great yard and popped down the nearest hole. He fell down, down into the dungeons below, and joined the other prisoners there.'

'How awful! Couldn't he get out again?' asked Jack in horror.

'No. The only way out was up the steep, deep holes,' said Lucian. 'No one could climb up those.'

'But how were the prisoners fed?' asked Philip.

'Easy,' said Lucian. 'The guards just went to the holes each day and tipped food down.'

'I don't know whether to believe that or not,' said Jack.

'I tell you I've been on the island and seen the holes,' insisted Lucian. 'Of course, the dungeons aren't used *now* – the yard is all overgrown, and you can hardly see the dungeon holes. That's how I nearly fell down one.'

'Would you have been there till you were old?' asked Lucy-Ann.

'Of course not. My uncle would have got a rope and hauled me up,' said Lucian. 'I should probably have broken my leg, though.'

'Tell us some more tales about these old islands,' said Jack. 'I wouldn't mind visiting one or two!'

'Well, I dare say we could, if I asked my uncle,' said Lucian surprisingly.

'What do you mean? What's your uncle got to do with it?' demanded Philip. 'You talk as if he owned the islands.'

'He does own quite a few,' said Lucian. 'Didn't I tell you? It's a craze of his, I think. He buys this one and that one, explores it thoroughly – and then maybe he gets tired of it and sells it again.'

The four children looked at Lucian to see if he was telling the truth. It seemed extraordinary to them that anyone should buy and sell islands as if they were cakes or something.

'But – what does he do it for?' asked Jack. 'I mean – is he interested in old things – is he looking for antiques or something?'

'He's very interested in history,' said Lucian. 'Yes, and in old things generally. You should see his house in Athens. He's got the most marvellous collection of things from these old islands. He's crazy about them.'

The children thought about Lucian's uncle. They could not tell if he was crazy or not. He seemed an ordinary, rather cross grown-up to them, hard to size up because he always wore dark glasses and they could not see his eyes.

'You don't know what people are *thinking* if you can't see their eyes,' Lucy-Ann said, and it was true.

'I expect I get my liking for history from my uncle,' said Lucian. 'I'm always top in that. Bottom in everything else, of course. And I *loathe* games.'

'Yes, you've told us that before,' said Jack.

'But only about fifteen times,' put in Dinah.

'Oh, I say!' said Lucian. 'Sorry! It's just that I do detest them so much.'

'Sixteen times,' said Lucy-Ann.

'Goosey-Lucy,' remarked Kiki – very aptly, the children thought. They grinned at one another, Lucian *was* a goose – a silly, credulous, aggravating, tiresome goose, a nitwit and a rabbit – but he was quite harmless and sometimes really amusing.

'To come back to your uncle,' said Jack. 'Do you honestly mean he owns some of these exciting islands?'

'Oh, yes. He doesn't own Oupos now. But he owns the one we'll soon be passing. That'll be Helios. He's about finished with it now, though. He sent his men there to dig and explore, but they didn't find much.'

'What *did* they find?' asked Lucy-Ann with interest.

'Let me see – they found three magnificent vases, but that was about all,' said Lucian. 'They were cracked, of course – they nearly always are, it seems to me. He found a pair of daggers too – frightfully old I think those were. And he got a lot of rubbish too – you know, bits of broken crockery, pieces of jewellery not worth anything

– oh, yes, and he got a little carving of a goose. He gave it to me.'

'Goosey-Lucy,' put in Kiki again. She appeared to be listening hard to all Lucian's rigmarole.

'Shut up, Kiki. Don't interrupt,' said Jack. 'Go on, Lucy – I mean Lucian.'

'Oh, I say! Don't you start calling me that, Jack,' said Lucian, looking hurt.

'Don't be an ass. Get on with your story,' said Jack. He had no patience with Lucian when he began getting hurt, which happened quite a lot.

'Do you know any more stories about the islands?' asked Lucy-Ann, seeing that Lucian still looked upset.

'Well – there's the story of the Andra treasure ships,' said Lucian. 'That's supposed to be absolutely true. I've heard my uncle tell it many a time.'

'Go on – tell us,' said Philip, scratching Micky's back for him as he lay cuddled in the boy's arms, fast asleep.

'Well, it happened hundreds of years ago,' began Lucian. 'I can't remember the exact date. There was a king called Panlostes who had a kingdom on one of these islands, a large one. I expect you know that most of them had rulers of their own. Well, Panlostes had a son.'

'What was he called?' asked Lucy-Ann.

'I don't know,' said Lucian. 'Anyway this son had an accident when he was small, and he lost one eye and hurt his foot so that he limped. He wanted to marry the daughter of a king on the mainland of Greece, a girl called Andra.'

'But she wouldn't have him because he was one-eyed and limped, I suppose,' said Jack. 'And there was someone else she liked and wanted to marry.'

'Well – if you know the story . . .' began Lucian, half annoyed.

'I don't. But I know lots like it!' said Jack. 'Go on.'

'Andra's father said the girl should marry the one-eyed prince if King Panlostes would send him gold and arms and treasure worth half his kingdom,' went on Lucian, warming up again. 'So the King got ready a fleet of ships and stuffed them with riches of all kinds, and one morning they set sail from the island to go to the mainland.'

Lucy-Ann gazed out over the dark-blue sea, imagining the fleet of small ships, their sails filled with the wind, their holds packed with rich treasure. She heard the sharp commands, the creaking of the old wooden ships, the billowing, flapping noise of the sails. Lucian took another breath and continued.

'Well – the girl Andra sent word to the man she really wanted to marry to tell him about the ships. And he got ready some ships himself and set out to intercept the treasure fleet.'

'Did he find them?' asked Lucy-Ann.

'Yes, he did. But when he attacked them and finally defeated the fleet – he found no treasure!'

'Gracious! Where had it gone?' asked Dinah. 'Had they dumped it into the sea, or something?'

'No. The captain of the fleet had never meant to deliver the treasure safely. He had made up his mind to take it to an island he knew of, land it there, hide it safely and come back for it when he could. He meant to tell both Kings that he had been attacked and robbed on the way to the mainland.'

'And he *was* attacked – but he had hidden the treasure!' said Jack. 'What happened next?'

'The captain was killed and so were half the men. The rest of them made off in their ships and scattered far and wide. A search was made for the hidden treasure, but it couldn't be found.'

'Golly – was nothing more ever heard of it?' said Philip.

'Oh, yes. Some of the men thought they remembered where the island was where they had landed the treasure one night. They made up an expedition secretly and went to look for it. They quarrelled and fought – and in the end only two or three men were left. One of them had made a rough map.'

'A map of the island? Was it ever found?' asked Dinah in excitement.

'Yes. Years later. A Greek merchantman got hold of it somehow and pored over the old map till he had made some sense out of it. He made up his mind that it could refer to only five out of all the islands in the Aegean Sea – and there are heaps and heaps, you know. So he began to explore them one by one.'

'Did he find the right one?' asked Lucy-Ann, her eyes shining. 'This is a lovely story, *I* think.'

'Yes – the old story says he did find the island – and found out where the treasure was too. But before he could do anything about it, he died.'

There was a disappointed silence. 'But who got the treasure then?' asked Jack.

'Nobody,' said Lucian. 'The old merchantman never told a soul. But it's said that *some*where there's a copy of the map and plan he made. Goodness knows where! He hid it before he died, or so people say. He lived about a hundred years ago.'

'What a thrilling story!' said Dinah. 'I wish *we* could find the map. Where did the old man live? Surely the map would be hidden in the house he had?'

'I should think it's been searched from top to bottom,' said Lucian. 'I know the island he lived on. We shall come to it in a day's time. It's called Amulis.'

'Oh! Are we going to land on it?' cried Lucy-Ann. 'I'd like to!'

'Yes. We usually do call there,' said Lucian. 'It's quite a big island, with towns and villages, and some good shops that sell antiques and things. Visitors often go in parties from the ships and buy things.'

'We'll go together!' said Dinah. 'I want to buy some things – I haven't nearly enough. Come with us, Lucian, you'll really be a very great help!'

7

Lucian is very helpful

Mrs Mannering was pleased to hear that the ship was to call at the romantic island of Amulis. She, like the children, had been fascinated by all the misty-purple islands that kept looming up in the dark-blue sea. She had been dipping into Greek history, and somehow it seemed as if the Aegean Sea belonged to the past, not to the present.

The children borrowed her books and read them too. How old these islands were, and what stories they held! Lucy-Ann was fascinated by them. She stood at the deck rail and watched all day long.

'Why are there so many?' she said. 'What do you call a collection of so many islands? It's a long name, I know.'

'Archipelago,' said Mrs Mannering. 'You know, Lucy-Ann, it's said that once all these islands were joined together, making a great mainland. Then something happened, and the sea rushed into what is now the Mediterranean basin, filled it up, and drowned a lot of this mainland. Only the highest parts, the hills and mountains, were left – and they show above the water as islands – the Aegean islands we are cruising among!'

'My goodness,' said Lucy-Ann, her quick imagination showing her a great sweep of water rushing relentlessly over a land where towns and villages stood – swallowing them up one by one, drowning them – and at last leaving only the highest parts showing above the surface of the waters. 'Oh, Aunt Allie – do you mean that far below us, on the ocean bed, are the ruined remains of cities and villages? Did it happen long ago?'

'Thousands and thousands of years ago,' said Mrs Mannering. 'There wouldn't be a trace of them left now. But it explains the myriads of little islands in this sea. I'm glad we are to visit one of them.'

'You're not afraid of us falling into some exciting adventure now, are you?' said Lucy-Ann slyly. 'You think it will be safe to visit this romantic little island?'

'Quite safe,' said Mrs Mannering, laughing. 'For one thing I shall be with you.'

'We've asked Lucian to come too,' said Dinah. 'I know he's a nitwit – but he really does know about these islands, Mother. He's told us all sorts of stories about them. His uncle owns some of them.'

'Yes, I heard that he did,' said Mrs Mannering. 'I've talked to his wife – quite a nice woman. I can't say I'd like a husband who did nothing but buy up islands and dig frantically for months, then sell them and start somewhere else. He's got a bee in his bonnet, I think. Still, he certainly seems to have made some interesting finds – finds that have made him a wealthy man!'

The *Viking Star* sailed into a small port the next day. The children were hanging over the deck rail and were surprised when their ship came to a stop and anchored where she was without steaming to the jetty.

'We can't get any closer in – the jetty isn't suitable for us. We're too big,' explained one of the officers to the children. 'You'll go ashore in a motor launch.'

Sure enough a launch came out to the ship, and a score or so of passengers climbed down the ladder to the deck of the launch. The four children went, of course, and Lucian, also Mrs Mannering and some of the other interested passengers. Lucian's people did not go. They knew so much about the island that they had no desire to visit Amulis.

But to the children it was all very thrilling indeed. The motor launch sped off to the jetty where they all landed. Lucian was quite at home on the island, which he had visited before with his uncle.

'You keep with me. I can show you all the interesting things,' he said. 'And I can talk to the people too, and bargain for you if you want to buy anything.'

Lucian was certainly very, very useful. He pushed off the flock of little children who came crowding round begging for money, and sent out such a fierce stream of odd-sounding words that even Kiki was most impressed.

He knew his way about and was quite good at explaining things.

'Here's the market. The people from the hills up there bring their goods down here – look at them on the stalls – then they spend the money they get at the shops in the town. Or they go to the cinema.'

The people were a picturesque lot. They wore big hats because of the sun, and a collection of nondescript white garments that might have been anything, but which suited them quite well. The children were beautiful, Lucy-Ann thought, with their dark eyes, beautifully shaped faces and thick curling hair.

Lucian took them to an old ruined castle, but the boys were disappointed because there were no dungeons to be seen. The girls were amazed to see people apparently living in parts of the castle, together with their goats and hens.

'They're very poor islanders,' explained Lucian. 'They've got nowhere else to live. Further inland, if I'd time to take you, you'd see people living in caves in the mountainsides. They used to do that thousands of years ago too. It's strange to think those caves have sheltered people century after century.'

'Do those cave-people go to the cinema in the town?' asked Dinah.

'Oh, yes. They love it, though they can't read anything in English on the screen. The speech is translated, of course,' said Lucian. 'They live in two worlds, really –

the world of long ago, when people used caves as shelter and scraped along with their goats and hens and geese, and in the world of today, where there are motorcars and cinemas and so on.'

'A weird mixture,' said Jack. 'I shouldn't know where I was!'

'Oh, they know, all right,' said Lucian, and he paused to shout angrily at a small child who was trying slyly to pull at a ribbon Lucy-Ann was wearing in her dress. Kiki also began to scream excitedly, and Micky jumped up and down on Philip's shoulder, chattering. The child fled in terror. Lucy-Ann felt quite sorry for it.

Lucian took them to the shops. Some of them were small, secret shops, dark and full of strange goods. One shop, which was full of antiques to attract visitors, was quite big.

'You can go in here if you want to look round and buy something,' said Lucian. 'Oh, I say! Where's Micky gone?'

'Just to have a little exercise on the canopy over the shop,' said Philip. Micky was amusing, the way he often leapt off Philip's shoulder and hung on to all kinds of things nearby, scampering here and there, flinging himself through the air to some fresh place, never once falling or missing his hold. He was now galloping over the sun canopy, running from side to side, occasionally stopping to fling himself up to a window ledge overhead and then drop back. But when he saw that Philip was going into the shop below he threw himself down from the canopy and with a flying leap was back on the boy's shoulder.

'Can't get rid of you, can I?' said Philip. 'You're a bad penny, always turning up – and you do make my neck so hot!'

The shop was fascinating to the four children. They had no idea which things were genuinely old and which were not. Lucian, with the knowledge he had picked up from his uncle, pointed out a few really old things, but they were far too expensive to buy. Lucy-Ann looked at her money and asked Lucian if there was anything at all she could afford to buy.

He counted it up. It was Greek money, and Lucy-Ann had no idea of its value.

'Yes, you might buy one or two things,' he said. 'There's this blue carved stone, for instance.'

'No, I don't want that,' said Lucy-Ann. 'I really want to buy something for Philip. It's his birthday soon. Is there anything he would like? Don't let him see it – it's to keep for his birthday.'

'Well – what about this tiny carved ship?' said Lucian, holding out a miniature ship, exactly like some of the ships in the harbour. 'It isn't old, of course.'

Seeing the ship reminded Lucy-Ann of something. 'Oh! *I* know what I'd like to buy for him, Lucian. I've just thought. Something he badly wants.'

'What's that?' said Lucian.

'He wants a ship in a bottle,' said Lucy-Ann. 'I know it sounds a funny thing to ask for, but Philip says he always *has* wanted a ship in a bottle.'

'Well – I don't think I've ever seen one *here*,' said Lucian. 'It's not the kind of thing they sell. Wait a minute. I'll ask the johnny who's at the back of the shop. He'll know.'

He made his way through the masses of curious goods and disappeared behind a screen, where he could be heard talking to someone. He appeared again a minute later.

'No, they don't sell things like that here,' he said. 'But he says he knows where there is one, though it's rather a dirty old thing, and he thinks it's cracked.'

'Where is it?' asked Lucy-Ann. 'I could clean it up, if it isn't *too* badly cracked.'

'He says he saw it on a shelf in a house belonging to an old fisherman, not far from here,' said Lucian. 'I'll take you, if you like. Would Mrs Mannering mind?'

Mrs Mannering was with the ship's party, but she was keeping an eye on Lucian and his little company. Lucy-Ann thought she had better go and ask permission. They went out of the shop and found Mrs Mannering with the rest of the party having a cool fruit drink in a curious little courtyard overshadowed by an enormous tree.

'Aunt Allie – I want to give Philip a ship in a bottle for his birthday, and I've heard of one. Lucian says he'll take me to get it. May I go?' asked the little girl.

'Yes, but don't be long, Lucian,' said Mrs Mannering. 'It's not far, is it?'

'Oh no – just behind the market, that's all,' said Lucian, and set off with Lucy-Ann. They crossed the noisy market, falling over stray hens and getting in the way of a herd of goats. They came to a tall blank wall and went round it. On the other side was a sloping court-yard, and round it were set several quaint little cottages made of stone.

Lucian went to one of them and shouted in at the open door. A croaking voice answered him. 'Want to come in?' he asked Lucy-Ann. 'It will be a bit gloomy, I expect.'

Lucy-Ann didn't really want to go in, but she thought it would be rude to refuse, so she stepped over a hen that was squatting on the step, and went into a small dark room that seemed to the girl to be full of laundry and the scents of smoke and cooking.

'There's the ship in a bottle. Look,' said Lucian, and he pointed to a stone shelf at the end of the room. There was a broken pot on it, an old bone – and the bottle! Lucy-Ann peered at the bottle to see if there was a ship inside. It was so sooty and dirty that she could not see through the glass.

Lucian said something to the old woman sitting on a stool, picked up the bottle and carried it to the door. He wiped it with his handkerchief, and held up the bottle for Lucy-Ann to see.

'There you are. You can *just* see the ship now. We'd have to wash the bottle in soapy water before we got the dirt off. It's quite a good ship – nicely carved. And I should think Philip would like it if he really wants one, though I can't imagine why anyone should long for a ship in a bottle.'

'Oh, I can!' said Lucy-Ann, peering at the ship. 'I've often longed for things like this – you know, quite useless, but nice and unusual. I had a friend once who had a glass ball, and inside was a little snowman – and when you shook the ball a whole lot of snow rose up inside the ball and showered itself down over the snowman. I loved that. So I know why Philip wants this.'

'Well – shall I ask the old woman if she'll sell it?' asked Lucian. 'The bottle is dirty and cracked, so it's not worth much.'

'Yes ask her. You know how much money I've got. I can spend all that,' said Lucy-Ann. Lucian went back into the cottage with the bottle, nearly falling over two clucking hens on the way. A loud argument could be heard from inside. Lucy-Ann stayed out in the open air, listening but not understanding a word. She felt she could not bear to brave the dark inside the cottage again.

Lucian came out triumphant. He carried the bottle. 'Well, there you are. I've spent half your money. The old woman wanted the money badly, but she said she didn't know what her old grandad would think if he knew she'd sold a ship that had been in that bottle and in that family for years and years. However, as her grandad must have died long ago I don't expect he'll mind. Here you are.'

'Oh, thank you, Lucian,' said Lucy-Ann gratefully. 'I'll get a bit of paper and wrap it up. I do, do hope Philip will like it. It's an exciting present, isn't it?'

But it was going to be much, much more exciting than Lucy-Ann imagined!

8

The ship in the bottle

Lucy-Ann managed to get some paper and wrap up the bottle and ship before Philip saw it. The others were curious to know what she had got, but she would not tell them.

'It's something breakable, because you're carrying it so carefully!' said Jack. When they got back to the ship and she and Dinah got into their cabin, Lucy-Ann unwrapped the bottle and showed it to her.

'What a dirty old thing!' said Dinah. 'What is it? You haven't spent your money on that, surely!'

'Half of it,' said Lucy-Ann. 'It's for Philip's birthday. He said he wanted one. It's a ship in a bottle.'

'Is it really? Gosh, so it is!' said Dinah, interested. 'Let's clean it up and see it properly. Isn't it a big one?'

They rubbed soap on a flannel and proceeded to clean up the bottle. Once the glass was clean the ship inside could be plainly seen. It was a beauty, quite big, intricately carved, with carefully made sails. In contrast to the bottle, it was clean and free from dust. The colours it had been painted with were still bright.

'Look at that!' said Lucy-Ann in delight. 'It must be a model of one of the old Greek ships. How did it get into the bottle, Dinah? Look, the neck of the bottle is small and narrow – nobody could possibly push that lovely little ship through the neck. It would be quite impossible.'

'I can't *imagine* how it got into the bottle,' said Dinah, puzzled too. 'But it's certainly inside. Won't Philip be pleased? I rather like it myself.'

'Oh, so do I. It's wizard,' said Lucy-Ann. She stood it on a shelf. The bottle had a flat side, and stood on this, the lovely little ship sailing along, as it seemed, in the middle of the bottle, all its sails set.

'What's the ship called?' said Dinah, peering at it. 'I can't tell, can you? The letters on it aren't like ours. They must be Greek.'

The ship in the bottle was duly given to Philip two days later on his birthday. He was thrilled. Lucy-Ann glowed with delight when she saw how pleased he was.

'But *where* did you get it? Why, it's the nicest one I've ever seen!' he said. 'Quite the nicest. Really beautifully made. I wonder how old it is. I'm glad it's such a nice big one too. Most of the ships in bottles I've seen are much smaller than this.'

Micky and Kiki came to look at the ship in the bottle. Micky saw the ship through the glass and tried to get hold of it. He couldn't, of course, because of the glass, and it puzzled him.

'Happy Christmas,' said Kiki to Philip every now and again. She had been taught to say 'Happy returns' but she kept mixing it with 'Happy Christmas,' which she said every few minutes.

'Thanks, old thing,' Philip said. 'Happy New Year to *you*!'

'Oh, don't muddle her any more,' said Dinah. 'Let's go and show Mother the ship in the bottle.'

They went up on deck and found Mrs Mannering. Her deckchair was next to Lucian's aunt's chair, which she found rather trying sometimes, as she didn't very much like the uncle.

'Look, Mother – see what Lucy-Ann's given me for my birthday – something I've always wanted,' said Philip.

It was admired, and then passed on to Lucian's aunt and uncle to see. Mr Eppy looked at it carefully. He seemed puzzled.

'The ship is very old – really old,' he said. 'But the bottle is modern. The idea of a ship in a bottle is a comparatively recent one, of course. But the ship inside is far older – almost an antique! Very interesting.'

'It's got a name carved on it, very small,' said Lucy-Ann. 'I can't read it. Can you, Mr Eppy?'

He peered at it and spelt it out. 'Yes – A-N-D-R-A –

queer name for a ship! Never heard of one called that in Greek.'

'I've heard the name before,' said Lucy-Ann, and she tried to remember. 'Oh, yes – wasn't it the name of the girl in that lovely treasure story of Lucian's – the girl who didn't want to marry a one-eyed man? Well, we often call our ships by the names of girls or women – look at our big liners, *Queen Mary* and *Queen Elizabeth*. I don't see why a Greek ship shouldn't be called after a princess too.'

Mr Eppy wasn't listening. He wasn't at all interested in any of the children, not even in Lucian, his own nephew. He yawned and settled himself to sleep. Mrs Mannering nodded to the children to go. Micky and Kiki were rather tiresome when anyone wanted to sleep. Kiki's squawks and Micky's chatter and tricks didn't appeal to the grown-ups as much as they did to the children.

They took the ship in the bottle back to the cabin – this time to the boys' cabin. Philip decided to put it on the shelf opposite his bed, where he could see it. He was very pleased with it indeed. It was quaint and strange, and beautiful, and he had always wanted it. Now he had it.

'Be careful that monkey of yours doesn't tamper with it,' Jack warned him. 'He's very curious about the ship inside – keeps trying to touch it through the glass, and he gets quite annoyed when he can't.'

The *Viking Star* cruised from island to island. Time

did not seem to exist, and not one of the children had any idea of the days. It was all like a pleasant dream where, fortunately, the food tasted very real and very nice. In fact, as Jack said, if the food had not tasted jolly real he might honestly have thought that he *was* dreaming.

And then a squabble blew up between Micky and Kiki that broke up the dream in a strange way, and made things very real and earnest indeed from that time onwards.

It happened one evening. The boys had gone up to play deck tennis with the girls, and for once had left Micky and Kiki down below in their cabin. Micky was such a nuisance when they played deck tennis because he *would* fling himself after the rubber ring and, if he got it, tear up to the top of the nearest pole and sit there, chattering in glee.

So he had been relegated to the cabin that sunny evening with Kiki as company. Kiki was cross. She did not like being left behind. She sat on the porthole sill and sulked, making a horrible moaning noise that distressed Micky very much.

The monkey went to sit beside her, looking at her enquiringly, and putting out a sympathetic paw to stroke Kiki's feathers. Kiki growled like a dog and Micky retreated to the shelf, where he sat looking puzzled and sad.

He tried once more to comfort Kiki, by taking Jack's

toothbrush over to her and trying to brush her feathers with it, chuckling with delight. Kiki turned her back on him and finally put her head under her wing, which always puzzled and frightened Micky. He did not like her to have no head. He began to look for it cautiously, parting the parrot's feathers carefully and gently. Where had the head gone?

Kiki spoke from the depth of her feathers. 'Nit-wit, nit-wit, nit-wit, oh, I say! Grrrrrrr! Wipe the door and shut your feet! God save the Queen.'

Micky left her in despair. He would wait till she grew her head again, and became the jolly parrot he knew. He put the toothbrush back into its mug and considered the sponge nearby. He picked it up and sucked some moisture out of it. He sponged his little face with it as he had seen Philip do. Then he got tired of that and darted back to the shelf again.

What could he do? He looked down at the shelf. On it was the ship in the bottle. Micky cautiously put his hand down to the bottle. Why couldn't he get that little thing inside? Why couldn't he get it and play with it? He put his head on one side and considered the ship inside.

He picked up the bottle and nursed it like a doll, crooning in his monkey language. Kiki took her head out of her wing and looked round at him. When she saw him nursing the bottle she was jealous and cross.

'Shut the door, shut the door, naughty boy,' she scolded. 'Where's your hanky, pop goes the weasel!'

Micky did not understand a word, and it would not have made any difference if he had. He shook the bottle hard. Kiki raised her crest and scolded again.

'Naughty, naughty! Bad boy! Pop-pop-pop!'

Micky chattered at her, and would not put the bottle down. Kiki flew across to the shelf and gave the surprised monkey a hard peck. He gave an anguished howl and flung the bottle away from him, nursing his bleeding arm.

The bottle fell to the floor with a crash, and broke in half. The little ship inside was shaken loose from its base and fell over on its side. Micky saw it and leapt down to it. Here was that thing inside the bottle at last! He picked it up and retired under the bed in silence.

Kiki was shocked by the noise of the bottle falling and breaking. She knew it was a bad thing to happen. She made a noise like a motor mower, and then relapsed into silence. What would Philip say?

Five minutes later the two boys came clattering into the cabin to wash and put on clean things for dinner. The first thing they saw was the broken bottle on the floor. Philip looked at it in horror.

'Look! It's smashed! Either Kiki or Micky must have done it!'

'Where's the ship?' said Jack, looking all round. It was nowhere to be seen. It was not till they hauled Micky out from underneath the bed that they got the ship. He had not harmed it at all. He got three hard smacks, and Kiki got three hard taps on her beak.

'My beautiful present!' groaned Philip, looking at the little carved ship. 'Look, isn't it a beauty, Jack? You can see it better now it's out of the bottle.'

Jack looked at it and pulled at a tiny knob in one side. 'What's this?' he said. To his great surprise the knob came out and he could look inside the ship.

'It's hollow inside,' he said. 'And there's something there, Philip – looks like paper or parchment. I say – what can it be?'

Philip suddenly felt excited. 'Parchment? Then it must be an old document! And why should it be hidden inside the ship? Only because it contains a secret! I say, this is super. Goodness knows what the document is!'

'Let's probe it out and see,' said Jack. 'Look – this little section of the ship can be moved, now we've taken that knob out – and we'll just about have room to get out the parchment.'

'Be careful! It may fall to pieces if it's very old,' Philip warned him. Jack removed the loose section of the ship and put it beside the knob. Then, very carefully, he began to try and probe out the parchment. But he was excited and his hands trembled too much.

Then the gong went to say that dinner was ready. 'We can't go,' groaned Jack. 'We *must* find out what this is!'

'Look out – you're tearing it,' said Philip. 'Let's wait

till after dinner, Jack. We won't have time now. And I think the girls ought to be here to see all this.'

'Yes. You're right. We'll wait till after dinner,' said Jack with a sigh. 'Lock the whole thing up, Philip. We can't risk anything happening to the ship and its secret!'

So they locked the little ship up in a cupboard, and then, hot with excitement, went up to have their dinner. What a thrill! They could hardly wait to tell the girls!

The two girls could not imagine what was the matter with the boys that dinner time. Jack kept grinning quite idiotically at them, and Philip did his best to do a little whispering, to give the news.

Mrs Mannering frowned at him in surprise. 'Philip! You forget yourself. Say what you have to say out loud, please.'

That was just what Philip could not do, of course. 'Er – who won at deck tennis?' he said feebly.

'Well, really – I can't imagine why you had to say that in a *whisper*,' said Mrs Mannering. 'Don't be silly, Philip.'

'Sorry, Mother,' said Philip, not looking in the least sorry, but extraordinarily pleased. He simply could not help it. He kept thinking of the ship and its secret parchment. It was something really exciting, he was sure of it.

As soon as dinner was over the four children slipped away. When they got to a safe corner Jack clutched at the girls. 'Lucy-Ann! Dinah!'

'What *is* it?' said Dinah. 'You both acted like lunatics at dinner. What's up with you?'

'Shh! Listen! You know that ship in a bottle,' began Jack, but Philip interrupted him.

'No. Let me tell. Well, Micky and Kiki broke the bottle between them, the wretches, and when we got down into the cabin, there it was, smashed on the floor – and the ship was gone!'

'Where?' said Lucy-Ann, upset.

'Micky had it, under the bed. We got it and looked at it – and will you believe it, there was a knob that came out, and then we could remove another section of the ship – and inside there's a parchment document of some sort!'

'*No!*' cried the girls both together, thrilled to hear the news.

'It's true. You come down and see. Don't tell anyone though, especially Lucian. It's our own secret.'

They all tore down to the boys' cabin and nearly knocked over the steward, who had been turning down the beds.

'Sorry!' said Jack. 'Have you finished, steward?'

'Yes, I've finished – but what's all your hurry?' said the astonished steward. He got no answer. The door closed in his face, and he heard the latch being put across to lock it. Now what were those children up to?

Inside the cabin the light was switched on and the

cupboard unlocked. Philip took out the little carved ship. The others crowded round to look at it.

'See – you take out this knob – and that loosens this section of the side – and it comes right out,' said Philip. 'And now look – can you see the document neatly crammed inside? I'm sure it's parchment.'

The girls took a deep breath. 'Gosh – it's a thrill,' said Dinah. 'Get it out, quick!'

'We'll have to be careful not to tear it,' said Jack. 'Stand back a bit, you girls. You keep jogging my arm.'

How the boys managed to wheedle the closely folded paper out of the inside of the wooden ship was a miracle. Little by little they edged it out, until at last it was completely out, and the inside of the ship was empty.

'There we are!' said Jack triumphantly as he laid the yellow parchment carefully on the dressing table. 'Now to see what it is.'

With gentle, careful fingers Philip unfolded the parchment. It spread out into quite a big sheet. The children pored over it, thrilled.

'It's a map!'

'A plan of some kind!'

'I can't read the words. Blow, they must be in Greek or something!'

'What *is* it? It looks like some island or something!'

'Look at these marks – they must be the bearings of the compass – look, would that be north, south, east, west?'

'It's *two* maps, that's what it is. Look, this bit must show an island, I think – surely that's meant to be sea round it. And that bit is a plan – a plan of some building, I should think, with passages and things.'

The excited talk went on and on, each of the four children trying to press closer still to the map. Philip remembered that he had a magnifying glass and went to get it. Then they could see even better, and could make out a few strange words and marks too faded to see before.

'See this faint word here, at the left-hand side, right at the top,' said Lucy-Ann suddenly. 'Well, it looks exactly like the name on the ship, doesn't it? Let's compare them and see.'

They looked at both the words, first on the ship and then on the map. They certainly were the same.

'Well – Mr Eppy said the ship's name was *Andra* – and if the name on the map is the same, it must have something to do with an island or a person called Andra,' said Dinah.

There was a silence. Everyone was digesting this, and wondering if they dared to say what they thought it meant. No – it wasn't possible. It simply wasn't possible.

Lucy-Ann voiced their feelings first. She spoke in rather a breathless voice.

'Andra – the name of the girl who wouldn't marry the one-eyed prince. Do you suppose that one of the ships of treasure sent out and lost was called Andra in her honour? And do you suppose Andra was the name given to the search for the treasure – and that's why this ship and this map are marked Andra?'

'It can't be!' said Jack under his breath. 'It isn't possible that we have hit on the old plan that was lost – the copy of the older plan made hundreds of years ago! It just isn't possible.'

'It's probably a hoax,' said Philip, feeling perfectly certain that it wasn't.

'No – it can't be,' said Dinah. 'Mr Eppy, who knows about old things, told us the ship was old, didn't he? He was puzzled about it, because he said the ship was far older than the bottle.'

'Well, I'll tell you what *I* think,' said Jack slowly. 'I think this may be the plan – and I think probably that old Greek merchantman who copied the original one and died, hid it in this ship – which he may have carved himself.'

'Yes – and after he died his family may have kept it as a curio, not knowing what was inside it – and later on somebody else got the ship and thought it would be a very suitable one for putting inside a bottle,' finished Philip.

'But *how* did it get inside?' wondered Lucy-Ann. 'That's a real puzzle to me.'

'It's quite easy, really,' said Jack. 'The masts are hinged – they lie flat on the hull with threads tied to them. The ship's hull is slipped through the neck of the bottle –

then the threads tied to the mast are pulled, and up come mast and sails! The threads are drawn away and the bottle sealed with the fully rigged ship inside!'

'Gosh – how clever!' said Lucy-Ann. She looked at the ship again, and at the map lying beside it, old and yellowed.

'To think we are looking at a plan that was first drawn ages ago by a Greek admiral in charge of a fleet of treasure ships! And on this very map is shown where that treasure is still hidden – and we're the only people in the world that know the secret!'

It certainly was rather a tremendous thought. Silence fell on the four children. They looked at one another. Lucy-Ann spoke again, timidly.

'Jack! Philip! This won't be another adventure, will it?'

Nobody answered her. They were all thinking about the strange map. Jack voiced their thoughts.

'The thing is, as Lucy-Ann says – we may be the only ones in the *world* that know this secret – but it's all Greek to us! We can't read a word on the map; we don't even know the name of the island that's marked here. It's maddening.'

'We shall have to find out,' said Dinah.

'Oh yes – run round to various Greek people – Mr Eppy, for instance – and say, "Please will you decipher this strange document for us?" That's not a very bright idea, Dinah. Anyone who knows anything would see there was something worthwhile in this map – and it would disappear like a shot!'

'Oh dear – would it?' said Lucy-Ann. 'Do let's be careful of it, then.'

'I know what we could do to make sure nobody could possibly steal it and use it,' said Jack. 'We could cut it carefully into four pieces, and each one of us could have a bit – then if anyone tried to grab our bits he wouldn't be any better off – he'd only have a quarter of the plan, which wouldn't help him much!'

'Yes – that's a good idea,' said Philip. 'Though why we are imagining thieves and robbers like this I don't know!'

'Only because we've had a bit of experience in our other adventures,' said Dinah. 'We're getting to know how to handle them now!'

'And you know,' said Jack, still thinking of his plan, 'if we cut the map into four pieces, we could quite well go to *four* different people to ask them to decipher each quarter – without their seeing the other bits at all – so *they* wouldn't be any wiser, but *we* could fit their explanations together and get a complete picture of what the map means.'

'That's really a very clever idea, Jack,' said Philip, considering it. 'All the same – I vote we don't go to Mr Eppy about one of the bits.'

'I don't see why not,' said Jack. 'He won't be able to tell anything from one bit, and we certainly shan't say we've got the rest. In fact, it wouldn't be a bad idea to go to him first – he'd be able to tell all right if it was a genuine document. If it isn't we shan't need to waste our time trailing round to find three other people to decipher the other bits.'

'Do you think he might guess what *we* guess – that this map is a plan of the Andra treasure hiding place?' asked Philip, still doubtful of the wisdom of asking Mr Eppy about the map.

'We won't give him the bit with the name "Andra" on,' said Jack. 'And we won't say a word about the other bits, or even where we found them. We'll just say we came across his bit in our explorations, but we don't know where. Lucy-Ann doesn't need to say a word. She's the only one who knows where the ship was bought – *we* don't. So we can truthfully look him in the eye, and say "No, sir – we haven't any idea where this bit of paper originally came from. It just – er – kind of appeared." '

'I hope he believes you,' said Dinah. 'He never seems to believe a word that Lucian says.'

'Oh, well – that nitwit,' said Jack.

'Lucian's really nicer than you think,' said Lucy-Ann. 'It was all because of him, don't forget, that I got this ship – I'd never have found the ship in the bottle if it hadn't been for him.'

'Well, he shall have a small share in the treasure if we find it,' said Jack generously.

'Oh – are we going to look for it, then?' said Lucy-

Ann. 'What about Aunt Allie? What will she say? And will the *Viking Star* mind us going to hunt for a treasure island?'

'Don't jump ahead, Lucy-Ann,' said Jack. 'How can we possibly settle anything in the way of future plans till we know what the map says? I imagine Aunt Allie will be as thrilled as we are when she hears about this.'

'Well, I don't,' said Lucy-Ann. 'I think she'll hate it. She'll take us all straight back home! She won't have us rushing about looking for islands and treasure, *I* know. She's had enough of that kind of thing with us.'

'We shan't tell her, then, till everything is settled – and, when it is, we'll send for old Bill,' declared Jack.

Lucy-Ann cheered up immediately. As long as Bill Cunningham was there, nothing would matter. The four sat down on the two beds, quite tired out with their exciting talk. They wished the electric fan would go twice as fast because they felt so hot. It whirred away, turning this way and that, a real blessing in the warm cabin.

A terrible noise, far louder than the electric fan made, came to their ears. They jumped.

'That's Kiki – making her express-engine screech,' said Jack. 'Come on – we'd better get her or we shall have the captain himself down to see what's up. My gracious, there she goes again. We've left her too long in the girls' cabin. Little wretch!'

The children hurried to the cabin next door, anxious

to stop Kiki before other passengers complained. Kiki was standing on the dressing table in front of the mirror, screeching at herself. Although she knew mirrors very well indeed, there were still times when she flew into a rage at seeing another parrot there, one that she could not peck.

'Stop it, Kiki, bad bird!' cried Jack. 'I'll tie your beak up, I will! Bad bird, naughty Polly!'

'Happy returns,' said Kiki, speaking to Philip and ignoring Jack. She made a sound like a cork being popped out of a bottle, and then another noise like the gurgling of a liquid being poured out.

'She wants a drink,' said Jack. 'Sorry, old thing. I forgot you'd be hot in here.' He filled a tooth-glass with water and Kiki sipped it thirstily. Micky came out for a drink too.

'We are awful,' said Philip. 'We forgot all about these two in our excitement. There's always water for them in our cabin, but there isn't any in the girls'. Poor Kiki, poor Micky!'

'Nit-wit,' said Kiki politely. She gave a realistic hiccup. 'Pardon! Micky, Kiki, Micky, Kiki, Micky, Ki—'

'That's enough,' said Jack. 'We don't think that's funny. Come along for a walk on deck. We'll all get some fresh air, and then sleep on our plans.'

They went up on deck with the parrot and the monkey. The other passengers smiled to see them. They liked the four children and their amusing pets. Kiki gave a hiccup every time she passed anyone, and immediately said 'Oh, I say! Pardon!' She knew that made people laugh, and she loved showing off.

It was cool on deck in the evening air. The children said very little because they were thinking such a lot. The bottle – the ship – the old map – quartering it – deciphering it – hunting, hunting, hunting for – Andra's treasure!

Down in their cabins that night they all found it very difficult to go to sleep. They tossed and turned, wishing they could get cool. Micky and Kiki were on the porthole sill for coolness. The boys had it open always now, because neither of the pets showed any sign of wanting to go out of the big round opening.

Lucy-Ann lay thinking in her bed. She had the old familiar feeling of growing excitement and anticipation, mixed with a little dread. She knew that feeling! It was the one she got when an adventure was beginning. She called softly to Dinah.

'Dinah! Are you asleep? Listen – do you think we're beginning one of our adventures again? Do, do say we're not!'

'Well, if we are, whose fault will it be?' came back Dinah's voice, very wide awake. 'Who bought that ship?'

'I did,' said Lucy-Ann. 'Yes – if we plunge headlong into an adventure this time, it'll be all because *I* bought the little ship – the Ship of Adventure!'

9

The secret of the Ship of Adventure

When the morning came, the boys began to realize the difficulties in front of them concerning the strange document they had got hold of. The matter did not seem half so easy to tackle or a quarter so straightforward as they had imagined the night before.

Things the boys had pooh-poohed, such as Mrs Mannering's objections, suddenly seemed very awkward indeed. In fact the whole idea lost its rosy glow and seemed to recede into the realm of the impossible. It was very disappointing.

But when they got out the map again, which Philip had carefully put into an envelope and kept under his pillow all night long, the excitement of the night before swept over them once more. *Somehow* they must get the map deciphered, they must find out for certain if it was genuine – and then, who knew what might happen?

They made their plans. The map must be carefully cut into quarters. Each quarter must be placed in a small envelope, which in turn should be put into one a little larger. Each child must secrete his bit of the map either about his or her person or in the cabin.

That was the first thing to do. Then one of them must take his quarter to Mr Eppy and see what he said. Not the bit with the name of the island on, of course, but one of the other pieces.

'And Lucy-Ann mustn't come with us when we ask him,' said Philip. 'Because if he asks us straight out where we originally got the paper we can all say truthfully we don't know – but Lucy-Ann can't say that – and she'd blush or something and give the game away.'

'I should *not*,' said Lucy-Ann, who did not want to miss any of the excitement.

'You would. You're such a truthful person,' said Philip. 'Don't look like that, Lucy-Ann – it's a very nice thing to be, and we wouldn't have you any different. It's only that this is important, and it just might spoil things if you show there's something up.'

'All right,' said Lucy-Ann with a sigh. 'Perhaps you're right. I do wish Mr Eppy would take off his sunglasses sometimes – I just don't know what he's really like if I can't see his eyes.'

'I should think he's all right, except that he's a bit short-tempered,' said Jack. 'He's nice to his wife, and he's always very polite to Aunt Allie. Of course, he's pretty awful to Lucian – but then if *we* had poor old Rabbit for a nephew we'd be pretty awful to him too.'

'We are now, sometimes,' said Lucy-Ann. 'Like when we go on and on and on at him to have a swim in the ship's pool when we know he's scared stiff of the water.'

'It's only to see what excuse he'll think up each time,' said Jack. 'He's a marvel at excuses.'

'Well – what about this map – when shall we take it to Mr Eppy?' asked Philip. 'And if he says it's genuine, what do we do next? Is there anyone else on the ship we can ask about the next bit of the map?'

'Yes – there's the deck steward,' said Dinah. 'He's Greek. He could decipher it all right, I should think. And there's that little Greek woman who keeps the shop on the promenade deck – she'd be able to do a bit too, I expect.'

'Yes. We're getting on!' said Philip, pleased. 'Well – what about doing a bit of snipping?'

'I've got some very, very sharp scissors,' said Lucy-Ann. 'They're in my cabin. I'll go and get them. And I'll see what Micky and Kiki are doing there at the same time – up to some mischief, I expect!'

'Well, we couldn't have them here while we get out the map,' said Jack. 'Micky might quite well make a grab at it and throw it out of the porthole, like he did yesterday with the postcard I'd just written!'

'What a horrible thought!' said Dinah. She visualized their precious map sailing away out of the porthole and she got up to shut it. 'Just in *case*,' she said, and the boys laughed.

Lucy-Ann went to get her scissors. She was a long time coming back, and the others got impatient. 'What *is* she doing? She's been ages.'

When Lucy-Ann came back she had Kiki with her. 'I had to bring her,' she said. 'She had got Micky into a corner, and she was dancing in front of him from one leg to another – you know how she does when she's cross – and she was growling terrifically just like a dog. Poor Micky was scared stiff. I just had to stay and comfort him a bit.'

'What you mean is, you stayed and had a good game with them both,' grumbled Jack. 'Keeping us waiting all this time. Where are the scissors?'

'Blow! I left them behind after all!' said Lucy-Ann, and departed again in a hurry, looking rather red. She came back immediately, with the scissors in her hand. Kiki was now contentedly perched on her beloved Jack's shoulder, singing something that sounded like 'Humpty-Dumpty, three blind mice' over and over again in a very quiet little voice. She knew she had been naughty.

Jack took the scissors and, very carefully and solemnly, cut the precious document in half. The parchment crackled as he cut it. The others held their breath and watched.

Then Jack cut the halves into half again, and there, on the boys' dressing table, lay the four pieces – four exciting parts of a rare and unique document – if it was what the children imagined it to be!

'Now for small envelopes and then a bit larger ones,' said Dinah. She rummaged in the boys' writing cases and produced four fairly strong little envelopes. Each bit of the map was carefully slipped into one. Then four bigger envelopes were found, and the small envelopes were slipped into those. Good! The first step was taken.

'We can easily paste the four bits together once we have got all the pieces deciphered,' said Philip. 'Now – what's the best time to interview Mr Eppy – and exactly how shall we set about it?'

'It would be quite a good time now,' said Jack. 'He's usually up in his deckchair – and he'll probably be awake because it's not long after breakfast!'

'I say – are we to tell Lucian anything about this?' said Lucy-Ann.

'Don't be silly! Of *course* not!' said Jack. 'I wouldn't trust old Lucian with anything. His uncle has only got to bark a few words at him and he'd tell him everything he knew – and a lot more that he didn't, besides.'

It was decided that Jack's bit should be the one presented to Mr Eppy. It had not the name 'Andra' on it, neither had it the name of the island, so far as they could tell. It had one part of the island, with a few obscure hieroglyphics.

'What are hiero-something-or-other?' asked Lucy-Ann when Jack used the word. 'It sounds like a medicine or something!'

'Hieroglyphics? Well – these squiggly marks that we

don't understand,' said Jack. 'Marks that stand for words. Secret symbols, perhaps.'

'Secret symbols – it sounds thrilling,' said Lucy-Ann. 'Now – where shall I hide my bit?'

'*Not* in your writing case or anywhere obvious like that, Lucy-Ann,' said Philip. 'I know where I'm going to hide *mine*.'

'Where?' asked the others, and watched as Philip rose and went to his dressing table. It was fixed to the wall, of course – every bit of furniture in the cabins was fixed either to the wall or to the floor, so that it would not move if the ship rolled. Between the wall and the dressing table was a thin space, no more than a crack. Philip bent down and slid his envelope into this crack.

'There!' he said. 'No one will dust there – it's absolutely hidden between the bottom of the dressing table and the wall. Where will you put yours, Jack?'

'I'll keep it on me,' said Jack. 'My shorts have got a thin lining. I'll take out a few stitches so that I can slip my bit in. I'll pin it up afterwards. But I shan't hide mine yet, because I've got to show it to Mr Eppy.'

Dinah had thought of a really excellent place. She took the others to the cabin. Behind the electric fan was a panel of wood to which it was fixed. She slid her envelope neatly into the crack between the panel and the wall of the cabin. It hid it completely. She had had to turn off the fan to use the hiding place, of course – now she turned it on again, and the others voted her hiding place as first class – no one would ever think there was any-thing hidden behind an electric fan that whirred round and round all day and night!

'Good for you!' said Jack. 'Now what about Lucy-Ann?'

'Think of somewhere that Micky can't get at,' warned Philip. 'He's watching you. He can't get Dinah's piece because he's afraid of the fan. He'd never dare to explore behind it!'

'Could I slip it under the carpet?' said Lucy-Ann.

'No,' said Jack. 'The stewardess might feel it there when she was doing the carpet and get it out.'

'Well – I know – what about at the back of a drawer space?' said Lucy-Ann. She pulled out one of the draw-ers in her dressing table and set it on the floor. She got a drawing pin from her pencil box and pinned the pre-cious envelope to the very back of the drawer-space.

'There!' she said. 'No one can possibly see it's there unless they pull the drawer right out – and why should they do that?'

'Yes. That's fine,' said Jack, and the others approved too. 'Micky's not strong enough to pull the drawer out, even if he wants to. Now, what about going and tackling Mr Eppy?'

'Right. Lucy-Ann, you go up to the deck-tennis place with Lucian whilst we talk to his uncle,' said Philip. 'Then you'll both be out of the way.'

Lucy-Ann went off to find Lucian. He was mooning

about by himself, wondering where they all were. He was delighted to see Lucy-Ann, and agreed at once to have a game with her. He liked her the best of the four – probably because he felt she didn't make fun of him as much as the others.

'Well, *they're* disposed of all right,' said Jack, watching them go up the steps to the sports deck. 'Come on. We'll make for the deckchairs. Kiki, do decide which of my shoulders you want to sit on – this flapping to and fro is most uncomfortable!'

'I wish you'd have Micky for an hour or two,' groaned Philip. 'He's like a hot-water bottle by my right ear this morning.'

The passengers watched the three children with their parrot and monkey as they passed by. They had got used to them by now, and enjoyed the antics of the two pets. Mrs Mannering was on the watch for them.

'I wondered where you'd got to,' she said. 'Where's Lucy-Ann?'

'Playing with Lucian,' said Jack. He sat down by Mrs Mannering. Mrs Eppy and her husband were the other side of her. Jack spoke loudly so that his voice would carry well.

'I've got an unusual thing here,' he said. 'An old, old document, I should think. Do you suppose Mr Eppy would be kind enough to look at it for me, Aunt Allie?'

'Well, ask him!' said Mrs Mannering. 'He's here.'

10

Hiding places

Philip and Dinah were sitting on the edge of the same deck chair together, next to Mrs Mannering's. Jack was on the foot-end of her chair, with his bit of paper. They all looked very innocent and unconcerned.

'I don't really like to bother Mr Eppy now,' said Jack. 'He's reading.'

Mrs Eppy heard. She tapped her husband on the arm. 'Paul,' she said. 'Jack wants to ask you something.'

Mr Eppy knew that perfectly well, but he had pretended not to hear. He looked up.

'Very well,' he said grudgingly. 'What is it?'

'Just some old bit of paper we found,' said Philip, joining in. 'Probably quite uninteresting. We can't understand anything on it, of course.'

'It mayn't be old at all,' said Jack, flipping his bit with his thumb.

'It *looks* old,' said Mrs Mannering, getting interested. 'Where did you get it?'

'I don't really know – picked it up somewhere on one of the islands we visited,' said Jack. 'Do you know exactly where, Dinah?'

'No,' said Dinah truthfully. 'I've no idea.'

'Nor have I,' said Philip.

'Pass it over,' said Mr Eppy, sounding rather bored. His wife passed him the piece of parchment. He took it and glanced at it, meaning to pass it back with a scornful remark. What did these children know about old things? Nothing! It was probably a bit of an old letter, blown about by the wind, that they had picked up in the street. Or maybe they had bought something and this was part of the paper it was wrapped in. Mr Eppy looked at it and opened his mouth to say something contemptuous.

But he did not say a word. He went on looking and looking at the paper. Finally he took his dark glasses off and looked at it without them.

'Er – is it genuinely old, sir?' asked Jack at last, not able to wait any longer.

Mr Eppy did not answer. He was feeling in his pocket for something. He took out a little black case and undid it. Inside was a strong magnifying glass set in an eyepiece that could be screwed into the eye – something like watch repairers wear when repairing watches. Mr Eppy screwed the glass into his eye like an enormous monocle, and once more bent over Jack's piece of parchment.

He looked for a very long time. The children waited,

almost breathless. Why didn't he speak? Why was he such ages? It was mean of him!

At last Mr Eppy took the eyepiece out of his eye and looked at the children. They got a shock because they had never seen his eyes without dark glasses before. He had not nice eyes at all! They were decidedly cold. One was blue and the other was dark brown. Dinah felt a little shiver down her back. How very, very peculiar! She couldn't help staring at him, looking first at one dark-blue eye and then at the other dark-brown one. Was one false? No – how silly! – he would have eyes that matched if one was false.

'Well,' said Mr Eppy, and paused as if he was thinking what was best to say. 'It's – er – quite interesting. Er . . .'

'But is it genuinely *old*, Mr Eppy?' insisted Jack. 'That's what we want to know.'

'The parchment isn't all here,' said Mr Eppy, and his eyes glanced from one to the other of the children. 'This is only a piece of it. And judging by the *edges* of the parchment it has been recently cut. Rather odd that, don't you think so?'

This was most unexpected. Jack answered at once, feeling that there must be no pause which might give them away.

'Gosh – how very strange! Well, I suppose we've just got hold of *one* bit, sir. Er – I wonder who's got the rest of it.'

'So do I,' said Mr Eppy, looking at Jack and swinging his eyepiece to and fro on his finger. 'I should be very, very interested to know.'

'Why, sir?' asked Philip, looking perfectly innocent, much to Dinah's admiration.

'Well – I can't tell much from this one piece,' said Mr Eppy. 'It would be a help to have the rest.'

'What *can* you tell, Mr Eppy?' asked Dinah.

He looked at her with his odd eyes. 'I can tell that it shows part of an island,' he said. 'An interesting island – with some secret on it. I could perhaps tell what the *whole* secret is if I had the other bit of the parchment.'

'What a pity you haven't got it, sir,' said Jack, holding out his hand for his piece.

'*Where* did you say you found this?' said Mr Eppy, snapping out the question so suddenly that the children jumped.

'We didn't say – because we don't know,' said Jack, at once.

Mr Eppy frowned. He put his dark glasses on again, and became the familiar, rather puzzling man they knew, with his peculiar eyes completely hidden.

'I'll keep this parchment for a while,' he said, and actually took out a wallet to place it there.

'I'd rather you didn't, sir, if you don't mind,' said Jack. 'I'm going to take it home – er – for the school museum – if it's genuinely old and all that.'

373

'Yes, it's genuine,' said Mr Eppy dryly. 'I'll buy it off you. I'm interested in old things, as you know.'

'We don't want to sell it, Mr Eppy,' said Jack, getting alarmed. 'It can't be worth anything, anyway. We want it as a curio.'

'Very well. But I should like to borrow it for a while,' said Mr Eppy, and he calmly slipped the parchment into his wallet, and put the wallet into his pocket. Then he picked up his book and began to read.

Jack looked at the others in dismay. He was angry and crestfallen – but what was he to do? He could not snatch Mr Eppy's wallet and grab his piece of parchment from it. And if he kicked up a terrific fuss, Mrs Mannering would be angry, and Mr Eppy would get suspicious – if he was not suspicious already!

Philip and Dinah were dumbfounded. The cheek of it – taking their parchment like that! Would he give it back? They wished they had taken a tracing of it. If only they had! Now they might never get back their treasured bit of parchment.

They got up and went, feeling that they must talk about it. Mr Eppy took no notice of their going. Jack did not dare to say anything more to him, but he glowered at Lucian's uncle as if he could tear his wallet out of him.

They went to their cabin. 'Beast!' said Jack. 'Surly fellow! What sauce to pocket our parchment like that!'

'Hope we get it back,' said Dinah gloomily.

'There's one thing – we jolly well know it's old – and

genuine – and holds something most interesting to Mr Eppy,' said Philip, cheering up a little. 'We do know that. He was quite knocked out when he first looked at it – even had to get that eyepiece arrangement out. I bet he knows it may be part of a treasure plan.'

'I don't think, somehow, it was a very good idea to take it to Mr Eppy,' said Dinah. 'There may be markings on it that tell a man like that – who knows about old things – far more than they would tell anyone else.'

'I hope he doesn't guess we've got the other bits,' said Jack.

'He does,' said Philip. 'I bet he does.'

Lucy-Ann came bursting into the cabin. 'Hello!' she said. 'How did you get on? I had to stop playing with Lucian because that uncle of his came up and called him. He took him off somewhere.'

'He did, did he?' said Jack. 'I suppose he's going to ask him what *he* knows, then. Good thing he knows nothing!'

'What happened?' said Lucy-Ann. 'You all look rather down in the mouth. Wasn't it genuinely old?'

'Yes. But Mr Eppy has taken it and put it into his wallet,' said Jack. 'And I bet we don't get it back!'

Lucy-Ann was horrified. 'But why did you let him take it, you *idiot!*'

'Well, what would *you* have done? Knocked him off his deckchair, grabbed his wallet and run off with it?' demanded Jack, going through a performance of knocking somebody down and grabbing something. Kiki was astonished and rose into the air in fright, squawking. She settled on top of the cupboard in alarm. Jack took no notice of her. He was really crestfallen at what had happened – after all their wonderful, careful, clever plans too!

'We'll just have to hope he gives it back, that's all,' said Philip. 'And if he does, it will probably mean he's got a very nice copy of it!'

'We'll have to find out what he has said to Lucian,' said Jack. 'He'll probably tell him to try and pump us about this bit of parchment – and find out if we have the other bits – and where we got the thing from – and when – and where the rest of the plan is.'

'Yes. And we'll make up a perfectly marvellous tale and stuff him up like anything!' said Dinah, her eyes sparkling. 'Come on – let's think of one! If Mr Eppy's up to some game, we'll be up to one too. Now – what shall we say if Lucian pumps us?'

'Well, we said *we* didn't know much about it, so perhaps we'd better pretend that Lucy-Ann knows *all* about it,' said Jack, looking more cheerful as he considered the idea of pulling Lucian's leg, and perhaps Mr Eppy's as well.

'Oh dear,' said Lucy-Ann in alarm. 'Have I got to tell a whole lot of fairy tales to Lucian?'

'No. We'll do that for you,' said Jack with a grin.

'Now then – let's think. How shall we say that Lucy-Ann got hold of that parchment?'

'She was standing on the sports deck one day,' began Dinah, 'and she was feeding the gulls that live round about these islands.'

'And a great big gull came up with something in his beak,' went on Philip. 'He flew round Lucy-Ann's head, and . . .'

'Dropped a paper at her feet when he swooped down for bread,' said Jack. 'She picked it up and showed it to us – and we thought, aha, only a very clever man like dear Mr Eppy could decipher this strange document handed over by a generous gull . . .'

'And so we took it to show him,' finished Dinah. She giggled. 'It's too silly for words. Lucian will never swallow that.'

'He will. But his uncle won't!' grinned Philip, 'Serve him right. He'll expect to get the goods from Lucian when he's pumped us – and he'll find he's got rubbish!'

'Well, don't make *me* say it,' said Lucy-Ann. 'I'd go scarlet the whole time.'

'Listen – isn't that Lucian now?' said Jack. 'You go off, Lucy-Ann. Look, take this book, and say you're taking it to Aunt Allie. Go on. That will get you out of the way. It *is* Lucian. I know his idiotic humming.'

Lucy-Ann snatched a book and went to the door. It opened as she got there, and Lucian's rabbit face came round it.

'Hello, hello!' he said. 'Can I come in?'

'Yes, do,' said Lucy-Ann, squeezing by him. 'I'm taking this book to Aunt Allie. But the others are here. They'll *love* to see you.'

11

Lucian in trouble

'Hello, Lucian,' said Jack. 'Come in. Have a sweet.'

'Oh, thanks,' said Lucian, and sat himself down on the bed. He took a large piece of peanut crunch out of the tin Jack offered him. 'I say – this is jolly good stuff.'

'Like a game of deck tennis?' asked Philip.

'Er – well – actually I only like playing with Lucy-Ann,' said Lucian, who was so very bad at the game that even little Lucy-Ann sometimes beat him hollow. 'Can't give you others much of a game, you know. I say – my uncle's been telling me about that bit of parchment you showed him.'

'Has he? What did he say?'said Jack.

'Well, he thinks it may be the genuine goods, all right – but he can't tell without the other piece or pieces,' said Lucian, munching away. 'Oh, I say – look at that monkey. He's taken an enormous piece of nut crunch!'

'Yes – almost as big as your bit!' said Dinah, who

noticed that Lucian invariably took the largest piece of crunch from the tin.

'Oh, I say – did I really take a big bit?' said Lucian. 'Have to watch myself! You never told me about that bit of parchment. Why didn't you? I'd have liked to see it.'

'Well – it isn't very important, is it?' said Philip. 'I mean – we never thought you'd be interested.'

'Oh, but I *am* – like anything!' said Lucian, crunching hard. Micky was crunching too, and Kiki was watching him balefully. She didn't like nut crunch, but she couldn't bear to see Micky enjoying his. 'You might tell me all about it, you really might. Where you got it, and – er – everything.'

'Didn't your uncle tell you where we got it?' asked Dinah innocently. Lucian looked surprised.

'Gosh, no,' he said. 'Did you tell him? Well, why on earth did he ask me to find out?'

He had given himself away properly. The others winked at one another. 'Well, perhaps we *didn't* tell him,' said Jack solemnly. 'Did we, or didn't we?'

'Didn't, did, didn't, did,' remarked Kiki, thinking it was time that someone took notice of her. But nobody did.

'It's a shame not to tell old Lucian,' said Dinah in a kind voice. Lucian beamed.

'Yes. After all, he's a friend of ours,' said Philip.

Lucian was so overcome by this remark that he swallowed a bit of nut crunch and choked. Kiki immediately had a choking fit too. She did that kind of thing remarkably well. Jack thumped Lucian on the back, whereupon Micky actually went to Kiki and thumped her too. The children roared with laughter, but Kiki was furious with Micky and chased him all over the cabin.

'Oh dear,' said Dinah, wiping tears of laughter away. 'Those creatures will be the death of me. Now – what were we talking about?'

'About me being a friend of yours, and so you'd tell me about that bit of parchment,' said Lucian promptly. 'Oh – may I really have another bit of crunch? I say, thanks awfully.'

He took a bit, remembering not to take the largest there this time.

'Oh yes,' said Jack. 'We were saying it was a shame not to tell old Lucian. Well, old chap, it happened to Lucy Ann, actually. Let's see . . . er . . .'

'She was standing on the deck, ready to feed the gulls that fly over from the islands,' said Jack. Lucian nodded. He had often seen Lucy-Ann feeding them.

'And suddenly a very large gull flew round her head holding something in its beak,' went on Philip. 'That's right, isn't it, Jack?'

'Absolutely,' said Jack with a solemn face.

'And lo and behold – when the gull came down for its bread, it dropped the parchment at Lucy-Ann's feet!' said Dinah. 'What do you think of that, Lucian? That's right isn't it, Jack?'

'Oh, definitely,' said Jack in a firm voice.

Lucian stared. His mouth dropped open. 'Oh, I say!' he said. 'Isn't that amazing! I mean to say – whoever would have thought of that?'

As the three of them had thought of it quite easily, they did not answer. Dinah felt a dreadful urge to giggle and turned her face away. Lucian seemed quite overcome with the story.

'I mean – honestly, it's like a fairy tale or something, isn't it?' he said. 'That gull dropping it at Lucy-Ann's feet.'

The others agreed that it *was* exactly like a fairy tale. 'Most extraordinary,' said Lucian, getting up and swallowing the last of his nut crunch. 'Well, I must be off. Thanks awfully for telling me all this. Oh, I say – what's happened to the bottle that the ship was in? You've got the ship without the bottle now!'

'Yes. Micky and Kiki broke it between them,' said Jack. 'Little wretches! Still, it's a nice ship and doesn't need its bottle.'

Lucian went out. The others grinned at one another. What a leg his was to pull! Poor old Lucian – he just *asked* for his leg to be well and truly pulled!

'I can just see him spouting that all out to his disbelieving uncle,' said Jack. 'Come on – if I don't get up into the fresh air and have some exercise I shall expire. Let's find Lucy-Ann and have a game of quoits or something. It's too hot now for deck-tennis.'

They played games all the morning, and then went

down to lunch, feeling very hungry indeed. To their surprise Lucian did not appear at lunch. They wondered if he was ill. Mrs Mannering asked his aunt about him.

'No, he's not ill – just a touch of the sun I think,' said Lucian's aunt. 'He's lying down and keeping quiet.'

'I vote we go down to Lucian's cabin and see if he's all right,' said Jack. 'He's never minded the sun before.'

Down they went, and knocked quietly. There was no answer. Jack turned the handle and went in. Lucian was lying on his bed, his face in his pillow.

'Are you asleep, Lucian?' said Jack softly.

Lucian turned over abruptly. 'Oh – it's you,' he said. Jack saw that the boy's face was blotched and tear-stained.

'What's up?' he said. 'I say, can the others come in? They're outside.'

'Well – if they want to,' said Lucian, who obviously was not welcoming visitors but did not like to say so. All four children were soon in the cabin. Lucy-Ann was distressed when she saw Lucian's blotched face.

'What's the matter?' she said. 'Is your sunstroke very bad?'

'It isn't sunstroke,' said Lucian and, to the children's horror, his eyes began to fill with tears. 'It's my beastly, horrible uncle!' He buried his face in the pillow again to hide his tears.

'What's he been up to?' said Jack, not very sympathetically, because he thought it was too feeble for words for a boy of Lucian's age to behave like that.

'He called me all kinds of names,' said Lucian, sitting up again. 'He – he called me a nitwit – and a nincompoop—'

'Poop!' said Kiki. 'Nit-wit!'

'Now don't *you* start,' said poor Lucian to the parrot. 'He said I was a born idiot and a fool and—'

'But *why*?' asked Lucy-Ann astonished.

'Well, I told him how Lucy-Ann got that silly bit of parchment,' Lucian told them. 'You know – just how you told me. I thought he'd be so pleased to think I'd found out what he wanted to know. But he wasn't.'

'Wasn't he? That was too bad,' said Philip, thinking that Lucian deserved his scolding for running straight to his uncle with the fairy tale they had made up – they had meant him to, of course, but what a tittle-tattler he was!

'I said to him, "A gull brought the parchment down to Lucy-Ann and laid it at her feet,"' related Lucian in a dramatic manner. 'And Uncle said "WHAT?" So I told him again.'

'And what did he say the next time?' asked Jack trying not to laugh.

'All the things I told you. He was very insulting and offensive,' said Lucian. 'After all, he believed all the other things I told him. I can't think why he didn't believe *that*.'

'What other things did you tell him?' asked Jack at once.

'Oh, nothing much. He just wanted to know if I'd

been shopping with any of you – and where – and all that. I told him I'd been shopping with Lucy-Ann – and how we'd found that old ship in a bottle for her. And he said, "Ah – of course – the *Andra*! The *Andra*!". Just like that. I tell you he was most peculiar altogether.'

The others listened to this in silence. Mr Eppy had certainly pumped Lucian to some purpose. He knew they had bought the ship and where – he remembered seeing the name when they asked him what it was – the *Andra*. He was putting two and two together. Probably he already guessed that the parchment had been found in the ship because that ass Lucian would be sure to have told him that the bottle was broken and the ship free of it.

'Did you tell your uncle the bottle was broken, that the ship was in?' asked Jack.

'Er – yes, I think I did,' said Lucian. 'I say – I haven't done anything wrong, have I? I mean – you don't mind my telling my uncle all this?'

'We didn't mind your telling him about the gull and the bit of paper in the least,' said Philip truthfully. 'I'm sorry your uncle is so disbelieving. It was wrong of him to call you names like that.'

'It was, wasn't it?' said Lucian plaintively. 'He's got no right to. He called *you* a few names too.'

'Well, don't repeat them,' said Jack. 'You really ought to learn to respect people's confidences, Lucian. I mean

– it just isn't *done* to go round repeating to somebody else the things you've been told, possibly in confidence.'

'Now *you're* angry with me too!' wailed Lucian. Jack got up in disgust. This kind of behaviour was too much for him altogether. He did not even feel sorry for Lucian for getting into trouble because of a cock-and-bull story that they had made up specially for him. Lucian just walked into trouble as fast as he could!

The others got up too. Only Lucy-Ann was sorry about Lucian. Still, even she was disgusted at his tears and self-pity – really, he ought to pull himself together.

They went out without a word, leaving Lucian feeling miserable, upset, angry – and very, very hungry!

'Come to our cabin for a minute,' said Jack. 'We ought to have a few words about all this. Mr Eppy is putting two and two together a bit too fast. What an idiot Lucian is! Why did he have to blab about that ship so much? We'd better put it in a safe place in case Mr Eppy borrows it as he did our parchment.'

They went into the boys' cabin, and Philip gave a cry that made them all jump. 'Look – he's borrowed it already! It's gone!'

12

The second piece of the map

It was true – the beautiful little carved ship was no longer in its place of honour on the shelf. It was gone.

The four children stared at one another in exasperation. Blow Mr Eppy! What right had he to 'borrow' things like this? Would he give it back?

'What's he borrowed it for, anyway?' wondered Dinah. 'If he goes so far as to suspect that we found the parchment there I still don't see why he should borrow it. He's got the parchment, anyway!'

'A *bit* of it, only – and he knows it,' corrected Jack. 'He probably thinks the rest of it is still in the little carved ship – either that we haven't noticed it, or that we have kept it there. And he's borrowed it to see.'

'Stolen it, you mean,' said Lucy-Ann scornfully. 'Horrid man! I think he's awful.'

'Shall I go and ask him if he's got it?' said Philip. He was feeling very angry – quite ready to beard any lion in its den!

The others considered this. 'Suppose he *didn't* take it?' said Jack. 'It would be jolly awkward, accusing him of it.'

'Who else would have taken it?' demanded Philip. 'Nobody!'

'Look – let's go and have a swim in the pool and forget it for a bit,' said Dinah. 'If you still feel like bearding the lion afterwards, you can go. It's so awfully hot. I'd love a swim.'

'All right,' said Philip reluctantly. 'But I might not feel so keen on going after Mr Eppy afterwards.'

However, he was still of the same mind after his swim. The others couldn't help admiring him – they really thought it was a brave thing to do, to go and tackle Mr Eppy and accuse him of 'borrowing' their ship!

He went off to find Mr Eppy. He was not in his cabin. He was not in his deckchair. Where could he be? Philip began to hunt over the ship for him, determined to find him. He saw him at last coming out of the radio office.

'Mr Eppy,' said Philip, marching boldly up to him. 'What have you done with our ship?'

Mr Eppy stopped. Philip wished to goodness he did not wear those dark glasses. He had no idea if Mr Eppy was surprised, angry or what.

He soon knew. Mr Eppy spoke in a very snappy voice indeed. 'What do you mean, boy? What ship do you speak of?'

'The little carved ship we showed you – the one in the bottle – called *Andra*,' said Philip, wishing more than ever that he could see Mr Eppy's eyes and read what was in them. 'What have you done with it?'

'I think you are mad,' said Mr Eppy coldly. 'Quite mad. As mad as Lucian, who comes to me with a fairy tale about a little girl, a gull and a piece of parchment. What nonsense, what fiddlesticks! And now you come to me with a question about a toy ship! You think I have taken it to float in my bath, perhaps?'

'*Did* you take it, Mr Eppy?' persisted Philip.

'No! And do not dare to insult me with your fairy tales and your crazy questions any more!' thundered Mr Eppy.

He strode off, his mouth very grim. Philip was a little shaken. Well – he had not got much change out of Mr Eppy, that was certain. Blow the man! Philip felt absolutely certain he had got the ship. He went down to meet the others in his cabin. They would be waiting for him there.

He opened the cabin door and went in. 'Well,' he said, 'it's no go. He says he hasn't got the ship – but I bet he has. I feel it in my bones!'

'Then your bones tell you wrong,' said Jack, and he pointed across the room to the shelf on the wall. 'Look there.'

Philip looked, and gasped. The little carved Ship of Adventure was back in its place again!

'Where was it?' he asked. 'Gosh, what an idiot I've made of myself, accusing Mr Eppy of having it! Where on earth *was* it?'

'We don't know,' answered Dinah. 'We all came in here a few minutes ago after we left you on your way to tackle Mr Eppy – and the first thing we saw was the ship!'

'There it was, on the shelf – just where we left it this morning,' said Lucy-Ann.

'Who put it back?' asked Philip.

'Aha – if we knew that, we'd know who took it,' said Jack. 'I still think it was Mr Eppy. If you remember, he came in to lunch *after* we did – he could easily have slipped down here and taken the ship then. And he could just as easily have put it back whilst we were having our swim. If he saw us in the pool, which is quite likely, he'd know that he had plenty of time to slip down here and replace it.'

'The knob's a bit loose,' said Dinah. 'We think he found how it worked all right, and removed that wooden section and examined the inside of the ship thoroughly.'

'I see. And when he found there was nothing there he generously brought it back!' said Philip. 'I don't like that man. He'll be hunting round all our cabins looking for our other bits of parchment, if we don't look out.'

Lucy-Ann felt alarmed. 'Oh, dear – will he find them, do you think?'

'He might,' admitted Philip. 'They seem jolly good

hiding places to us, but they probably would be easy enough for him to discover.'

'I say – are we going to get the other bits deciphered now?' said Dinah suddenly. 'You know, we thought we'd ask the little Greek woman who keeps the shop on the ship, and the deck steward. Suppose Mr Eppy gets to hear we've been showing other people more bits of parchment. He'll soon be after them.'

'Yes, that's a point,' said Jack. 'But if we don't get them deciphered, we're no better off than we were. Hidden treasure is no use to anyone if they don't know in the least where it is. Anyway, we don't even know if the plan *does* show hidden treasure – all we know is that it is a genuine old document, and that Mr Eppy is distinctly interested.'

'I think we could trust the little shopwoman not to say a word,' said Lucy-Ann. 'She's nice, and she likes us. If we told her it was a secret, wouldn't she keep it? After all, we've got to ask *some*body!'

They debated whether the shopwoman was trustable or not. They decided that on the whole she was.

'She said she'd show me some photographs of her children,' said Lucy-Ann. 'She's got three on some little island or other. She leaves them with her grandmother when she goes on the ship. Couldn't we all go and see the photographs, and then ask her about the parchment?'

'Trust Lucy-Ann to know everyone's life history,' grinned Philip. 'It beats me how she does it! She already knows the names of the second officer's children, and she knows everything about the stewardess's old mother and what illnesses she suffers from, and she even knows how many dogs the captain himself has kept during his whole life!'

'I *don't*,' said Lucy-Ann indignantly. 'I simply wouldn't *dare* to ask him about dogs. Anyway, he can't have had any on board ship.'

'I'm only pulling your leg, Lucy-Ann,' said Philip. 'Actually I think your idea of looking at the shopwoman's photos and then springing our parchment on her – or a bit of it – is a good one.'

'Let's go now, then,' said Lucy-Ann, looking at the clock. 'Everyone always has a sleep in the afternoon at this time – no one is ever in the shop. She'll be alone.'

They went off together. Philip had the idea of first finding out where Mr Eppy was – just in *case* he should be snooping round!

He came back and reported. 'He's asleep in his deck-chair on the promenade deck. His head's well back, and he's not reading or anything.'

'How do you know he's asleep?' demanded Jack. 'You can't tell if his eyes are open or shut behind those awful dark sunglasses.'

'Well – he *looked* asleep,' said Philip. 'Sort of limp and relaxed. Come on – we'll go to the shop now.'

They went to the little shop. The Greek woman who

kept it showed all her white teeth in a pleased smile when she saw the children with Kiki and Micky.

'Ah, Kiki, Micky, and what mischief have you done?' she asked, tickling the little monkey and poking Kiki in the chest. 'One, two, three, GO!'

Kiki immediately made a noise like a pistol shot, which was just what the little Greek woman meant her to do. She was quite familiar with Kiki's ways, and always roared with laughter when the parrot hiccuped, coughed or sneezed.

'Tell him to snizz,' she begged. 'I like when he snizzes.'

So Kiki obliged with a fine variety of 'snizzes', much to Micky's amazement. Then out came the photographs and the children were treated to a life history of each of her three little girls. Dinah thought that surely never in this world had there lived such children before – so sweet, so good, so loving, so religious, so incredibly beautiful – and so extraordinarily boring!

Then Jack thought it was *their* turn to talk. He nudged Philip, who at once brought out his piece of the map. 'Look,' he said to the shopwoman. 'Can you make head or tail of this for us? It's an old, old document we found. What does it say – and what does it show?'

The Greek woman looked at it sharply with her bright black eyes. 'It is a plan of some sort,' she said. 'But you have not got the whole of it here – what a pity! It shows part of an island called Thamis or Themis, I cannot tell which. See, here is its name in Greek – but you will not understand the letters, of course. Your alphabet is different. Yes, it is part of an island, but where it is I do not know.'

'Can't you tell anything else from the map?' asked Dinah.

'There is something of importance on the island,' said the woman. 'Perhaps a temple? I do not know. There is a building marked here – or maybe it is meant to be a city. Again I do not know. I could tell you more if I had the whole of the map.'

The children had been so engrossed in all this that they had not heard the soft footsteps of someone coming. A shadow fell across them. They looked up and Lucy-Ann gave a gasp. It was Mr Eppy, his dark glasses hiding his eyes as usual.

'Ah – something interesting. Let me see,' said Mr Eppy coolly, and before anyone could stop him he had twisted the parchment out of the Greek woman's fingers and was looking at it himself!

Philip tried to twist it out of *his* fingers, but Mr Eppy was on his guard. He held it aloft and pretended to joke.

'He won't let Mr Eppy see! Bad boy!'

'Bad, naughty boy!' echoed Kiki at once. Micky, thinking it was a game of snatch, suddenly leapt up in the air and lunged out at the paper. He got it in his little paw, fell back to Philip's shoulder, and then, still with the parchment in his hand, leapt to the top of the shop and sat there, out of reach, chattering excitedly.

Mr Eppy knew when he was beaten. 'What a funny little creature!' he said in an amiable voice that managed to sound quite angry too. 'Well, well – we'll have a look at the parchment another time!'

And with that he left the dumbfounded children, walking off rapidly back to his deckchair.

13

Goodbye, Mr Eppy!

'*Well!*' said Dinah, finding her voice first. 'Of all the cheek! Philip, he *couldn't* have been asleep when you saw him in his chair! He must have seen you looking at him and guessed you were up to something – and looked about till he found us.'

'Blow him,' muttered Philip. 'Now he's seen *two* of the bits. He knows what the island is too because the name was on that second bit. That's an awful bit of bad luck.'

They left the surprised little shopwoman and went moodily up to the bow of the ship, glad to feel the wind in their faces. Micky had come down as soon as Mr Eppy had left them, and Philip had his bit of parchment back safe. But the damage was done – Mr Eppy had seen it!

'If there *is* anything in our idea, Mr Eppy has seen enough to cotton on to already,' said Jack gloomily. 'I can't say that we have been at all clever over this. Anything but.'

'Simply *given* our secret away,' said Dinah. 'We're losing our grip!'

'Anyway – I don't really see what we could have *done* about the treasure,' said Lucy-Ann suddenly. 'I mean – we can't possibly go hunting for it, even if we knew exactly where it was. So we might as well give it up, and if Mr Eppy wants to go hunting after it, let him!'

'Well, I must say you're very generous, giving up what might have been *our* treasure – and just saying Mr Eppy can have it!' said Jack, exasperated. 'All because you don't want an adventure again!'

'Oh, I say!' cried Kiki, and the children stopped talking at once. Kiki had given her usual signal for the approach of Lucian. Up he came, grinning amiably. He appeared to have completely forgotten his last meeting with them in his cabin, when he had been in tears. His face still looked a bit blotched, but otherwise he seemed very cheery.

'Hello!' he cried. 'Where on earth have you been the last half-hour? I've been looking for you everywhere. I say, look what Uncle's given me!'

He showed the children some pieces of Greek money. 'I expect he was sorry for going for me like that, don't you?' he chattered on. 'Anyway, he's in a very good temper now. Aunt can't understand it!'

The children could understand Mr Eppy's sudden good spirits very well indeed. They grinned wryly at one another. Mr Eppy had got what he wanted – or some part of what he wanted – and he was pleased. It struck Jack that Mr Eppy probably always got what he wanted, in one way or another. He wouldn't much care *which* way. He thought uneasily that they ought to find safer hiding places than the ones in the cabins for the remaining pieces of parchment.

He felt very gloomy. What was the use of bothering? *They* would never be able to do much about the treasure! How could they? Aunt Allie would not hear of it, he knew. And there would *have* to be some grown-up in charge. If only Bill had come on the trip with them!

An idea came into his head. 'I'm going off by myself for a little while,' he announced. 'See you later.' Off he went with Kiki, thinking about his idea. What about looking up the island Thamis or Themis, whichever it was, on a modern map and seeing if it was shown there? It would be interesting to see whereabouts it was. Why, it might be quite near where they were cruising!

He went down to the ship's little library with Kiki and asked for a good map of the islands. The librarian gave him one and looked disapprovingly at Kiki. He did not like parrots in his quiet library.

'Blow your nose,' Kiki advised him. 'Wipe your feet! How many times have I told you to shut the door? Pooh! Gah!'

The librarian said nothing at all, but looked down his nose. He had never in his life been spoken to like that – and by a parrot too! He was most irritated.

'One, two, three, GO!' said Kiki, and made the noise of a pistol going off. The librarian almost jumped out of his seat.

'Sorry about that,' said Jack hastily, afraid that the librarian would turn him out. He tapped Kiki on the beak. 'Manners, Kiki, manners. Shocking!'

'Shocking,' repeated Kiki in a mournful voice, and began to sniff in exactly the same way that the librarian did.

Jack pored over the map of the islands, forgetting all about Kiki in his interest. For a long time he could not see Thamis – and then there it was, before his eyes! It was not a large island, and was marked with what seemed to be a city or town just on the coast. One or two small marks seemed to indicate villages – but there was only the one town.

So that was where the legendary fleet of treasure ships went years and years ago! They put in at that city by the sea, sailing into the port at dead of night. How did they unload the treasure? Were the people there in on the secret? Where was it put? It must have been hidden remarkably well if no one had ever found it in all the years that had gone by.

Jack pored over the map, his imagination giving him picture after picture, and making him stirred up and excited. He gave a deep sigh, which Kiki immediately echoed. If only he could go to Thamis – to that city by the sea – if only he could just have a *look* at it!

But it would be Mr Eppy who would do that – Mr Eppy who knew all the islands by heart, and who could afford to hire ships to go from one to the other, exploring each one as he pleased. Jack folded up the map with another sigh. He put the whole idea away from him once and for all. You couldn't go on treasure hunts unless you were grown-up – his common sense told him that all the plans he and the others had made were just crazy dreams – lovely dreams, but quite impossible.

Jack strolled out of the library and up on deck. They were heading for another island. They were to go close by it so that the passengers might see the romantic coastline, but they were not calling there.

At least, so Jack had thought. As they came near he saw that he must have been wrong. The ship was either going into the port there, or people were going off in a motor boat that had come out to meet the ship. The ship's engines stopped at that moment, and Jack leaned over the side to watch the motor boat nose its way near.

It soon lay alongside the big ship, rising and falling gently on the waves. A ladder was shaken down the side of the *Viking Star*. Someone began to climb down, someone who waved back to others on the ship and called out in a foreign language.

And then Jack got a shock. The someone was *Mr Eppy*! He was calling goodbye to his wife and nephew. He climbed right down to the motor boat and jumped deftly to the deck. His big suitcase was lowered on a rope and swung down on the deck beside him. He looked up and waved again, his dark glasses showing clearly.

Jack scowled down angrily and miserably. Blow Mr Eppy, blow him! Jack felt sure he knew why he was leaving the boat. Mr Eppy knew enough to set things in motion for the grand Andra treasure hunt. He was going to Thamis. He would smell out the treasure that Jack and the others had happened on in that old map. It would be his.

And probably Jack would never even know what happened about it – never know if it was found, or what it was, or anything. It was like reading a tremendously exciting book halfway through, and then having the book taken away and not knowing the end of the story.

The motor boat chugged away from the ship. Mr Eppy and his sunglasses disappeared. Jack turned from the deck rail and went to find the others. He wondered if they knew about Mr Eppy.

He found them in the cabin. Micky had eaten something that disagreed with him and had been sick. They were looking after him anxiously. They had not even noticed that the engines of the ship had stopped and were now starting again.

'There!' Dinah was saying as Jack came into the cabin. 'He's all right now – aren't you, Micky? You shouldn't be so greedy.'

Jack came in looking so gloomy that everyone was startled. 'What's up?' said Philip at once.

'It's *all* up,' said Jack, sitting down on the nearest bed. 'Who do you think's gone off in a motor boat – suitcase and all?'

'Who?' asked everyone.

'Mr Eppy!' said Jack. 'Hotfoot after our treasure! He knows the island, he's guessed the Andra treasure may be there – and he's gone to set things going. At least, that's how *I* see it!'

'That's a blow,' said Philip. 'We've messed everything up properly. He certainly doesn't let grass grow under his feet,'

'We may as well give up all our grand ideas,' said Dinah. 'What a shame! I did feel so terribly thrilled.'

'I bet he had just been sending a radio message for a motor boat to take him off here when I met him coming out of the radio office,' said Philip, remembering. 'Just that first bit of parchment must have got him going. Now he's seen the second and he's certain!'

'It's bad luck,' said Lucy-Ann. 'We don't usually mess up things like this. Hello – who's that?'

'Oh, I say!' said Kiki at once – and sure enough the door opened, and in came Lucian with his everlasting cry. 'Oh, I say! What do you think's happened?'

'You've got rid of your uncle,' said Dinah at once. Lucian grinned.

'Yes. He's gone. Said he had had an urgent business

message and couldn't fool about cruising around with Auntie and me any longer. Gosh, I'm glad he's gone.'

'Yes, he's not a pleasant person,' said Jack. 'I'm glad he's not *my* uncle. Some of his little ways are not what you might call attractive.'

'They're *not*,' said Lucian, who felt he was quite free now to speak his mind about his uncle. 'Do you know – he wanted me to take your little carved ship to him and not say a word to you about it? What do you think of that?'

'Not much,' said Jack. '*Did* you take it?'

'Of course not!' said Lucian with such indignation that everyone felt he was telling the truth. 'What do you take me for?'

Nobody said what they took him for. They felt that it would be a pity to spoil his pleasure. Lucian beamed round at them.

'Now we can have a jolly good time, without my uncle, can't we?' he said.

'I can't say your uncle makes any difference to us one way or another,' said Jack. 'I don't want to talk about him any more. He's an unpleasant subject for discussion. There's the gong to dress for dinner, Lucian. You'd better go. You had no lunch and you must be ravenous.'

'I jolly well am,' said Lucian and went, looking quite delighted with life. The others, however, looked anything but delighted. In fact, they looked distinctly gloomy.

'Well – that's the end of what looked like a most promising adventure,' said Philip.

But he was wrong. It was not the end. It was really only the beginning!

14

Things begin to happen!

Things began to happen the very next day. The ship was cruising along as usual in a purple-blue sea, and the sun shone down from a sky spread with dazzling white clouds and patches of brilliant blue.

Gulls glided by, and all kinds of other seabirds bobbed on the water, or soared high above the ship. Everyone was peaceful in their deckchairs, reading or snoozing, waiting for the mid-morning drink of iced lemonade brought by the stewards. Even the children were lazing in their chairs, tired after their strenuous morning game at deck tennis.

Kiki sat on the back of Jack's chair, snoozing too. She had been chasing gulls, calling to them in a voice so like theirs that the poor things were completely bewildered. Now she was tired out. Micky was curled up in the shade of a lifeboat, fast asleep.

A small page-boy appeared, the one who ran messages

and fetched odds and ends for the passengers. He carried a long envelope on a salver.

He called out loudly as he went. 'Radiotelegram for Mrs Mannering, please. Radio for Mrs Mannering, please.'

Philip nudged his mother, and beckoned to the call-boy. Mrs Mannering looked up, startled to hear her name shouted out. The boy came up to her and presented the radiotelegram.

She tore it open, wondering who it was from. She read it out loud to the listening children.

Your aunt seriously ill and calling for you. Fly back if you can, and I'll take over the kids. Radio me, please.
Bill

There was a silence. 'Oh dear,' said Mrs Mannering. 'This *would* happen on a cruise. What shall I do? It's all very well for Bill to say "Fly back". But where from? And how can I leave you all?'

'Don't upset yourself, Mother,' said Philip. 'I'll see to things for you. I know the second officer very well and he'll tell me what you're to do.'

'As for us, you needn't worry at *all*,' said Jack. 'You know we're all right on the boat. You wouldn't want us all to fly back with you, surely!'

'Oh no. Of course not. Especially after I've paid such high fares for you all on this cruise,' said Mrs

Mannering, still looking worried. 'Oh dear – I do hate sudden things like this. I really do.'

'Mother dear, it's all right,' said Dinah. 'You can get a plane from the very next place we stop at if there is an airfield. You'll be in England tomorrow. And Bill will take over, as he said. He'll probably meet you at the airport when the plane lands there, see you safely on to your train, and then catch a plane to join us. He'll enjoy the rest of the trip. Maybe you'll be back too.'

'Oh no, I shan't – not if Aunt Polly has got one of her really bad turns,' said Mrs Mannering. 'She's been so good to me – and to you too – that I *must* stay with her till she's quite herself again. Oh, I do hate leaving you four by yourselves.'

Mrs Eppy could not help overhearing all this. She spoke to Mrs Mannering. 'I can keep an eye on the four for you till your friend comes, you know. After all, I have to look after Lucian, and he's much the same age. I shall be pleased to do what I can.'

'Well, that's good of you,' said Mrs Mannering, getting out of her deckchair, helped by Philip. 'I suppose it's idiotic of me to worry about them – they're all quite big now – but they do seem to get into such awful scrapes sometimes!'

She went off with Philip. He was very useful indeed. He found the second officer, and very soon he had worked out all the details with him. The ship would go out of her way a little and call at an island that had an airport. A radio message would be sent immediately so that a plane would be waiting. In no time at all Mrs Mannering would be back in England.

'We could wait at the island till your friend comes on *his* plane,' said the second officer after consulting with the captain. 'It would only mean altering our programme a very little – it is a very free-and-easy one, as you know. Now – do you want to radio instructions to Mr Cunningham so that he will know what time to meet your plane at the airport?'

It was amazing how easily everything was arranged after all. 'I was silly to get upset and flustered,' said Mrs Mannering to the children. 'Thanks to Philip it's all been arranged beautifully. I'll be away tomorrow, and Bill will arrive later – probably that evening. It's wonderful!'

The girls helped her to pack. The *Viking Star* steamed to a large island where there was a good airport. The children saw aeroplanes taking off as they came near, for the airport was on the coast.

A motor boat came out to take Mrs Mannering off. She kissed all the children goodbye. 'Now don't get into any scrapes,' she begged them. 'Be good. Keep away from danger and trouble. Give Bill my love and tell him if he leads you into anything I'll never, never forgive him!'

They waved goodbye as the motor boat chuffed away to the port. They watched it through their binoculars and saw Mrs Mannering getting out on to the jetty with a porter carrying her cases.

'She's got into a taxi,' announced Jack. 'Now she's off to the airport. She'll soon be away!'

Half an hour later an aeroplane took off from the airport on the coast and rose into the air. It flew towards the ship, circled it twice and made off to the west.

'That was Mother's plane,' said Philip. 'I think I even saw her waving. Well – safe journey to her! And now we must look out for old Bill.'

A curious silence fell on the children. They were all thinking the same thing, but nobody quite liked to say it. Jack cleared his throat.

'Er – you know – now that this has happened – er . . .' He stopped.

Everyone waited politely. 'Well, go on,' said Dinah.

'Er – I was just thinking,' said Jack, 'just thinking that now – well – with old Bill coming and all. Er . . .'

He stopped again. Dinah gave a little giggle. '*I'll* say it for you,' she said. 'It's what we've all been thinking, I know. Dear old Bill is coming – and we can tell him all about the map and the Andra treasure – and Mr Eppy. And maybe – *maybe*, he'll do something about it!'

'Gosh, yes,' said Jack. 'I didn't know how to put it without seeming a bit heartless, as Aunt Allie has only just gone. But things are a bit different now. Bill may think we *ought* to do something.'

'How – simply – super!' said Philip, drawing a deep breath. 'Just as we'd given up hope!'

'We couldn't *possibly* drag Mother into an adventure,' said Dinah. 'But Bill's different. I mean – he won't want us to plunge into an adventure, I know – but he may quite well think *he* ought to do something about it.'

'And we shall at least know what's happening,' said Jack. 'Won't it be grand to show him the little carved ship – and the map – and tell him everything! Good old Bill!'

Lucian came up with rather a solemn expression on his face. 'I say! I'm awfully sorry about all this. I do hope your mother arrives safely, Philip, and that her aunt will get better. I hope all this won't spoil the rest of the cruise for you. I am most awfully sorry.'

'Thanks,' said Philip. 'We shall get over it.'

'Oh, I say, I quite forgot to give you this,' went on Lucian. 'I'm so sorry. My uncle gave it to me before he left and said I was to hand it to you. I can't imagine what it is.'

Jack took it. He guessed what it was, and he was right. It was the piece of the plan that Mr Eppy had 'borrowed'. He had put it into a sealed envelope with a little note.

Thanks. Not very interesting after all.
P. Eppy

Jack laughed. 'Not very interesting, says he! I bet he's got a careful tracing of it. Much good may it do him!'

He went off to put it into its safe place – in the lining of his shorts. He was glad that Mr Eppy hadn't seen all the other pieces of the plan. Still, he probably did not need to. He might guess where the treasure was, if he knew the island. If so, it wouldn't be there long!

The day went by rather slowly. Mrs Eppy was rather annoying because she took very seriously her promise to look after the children. She hunted them out at mealtimes, and even told the table steward to seat them at her table.

But Jack was not having that. 'No, Mrs Eppy,' he said firmly but politely. 'We expect our friend, Bill Cunningham, tonight – or at the latest, tomorrow morning. We will keep our own table and eat with him. Thank you all the same.'

Lucian was disappointed and sulked. He did not even smile when Kiki and Micky had a fight over a banana and ended by pulling it in half.

After the evening meal the children went up on deck, hoping against hope that Bill would arrive that night. The second officer had had no message, so thought he probably *would* arrive.

'He would surely have radioed me if he was coming tomorrow,' he said. 'He knows we're holding the ship here for him. All the same, I'd go to bed if I were you kids – he may come in the middle of the night!'

They would not hear of going to bed! They sat up on deck and watched the sun go down in a blaze of gold. They saw the clouds turn rosy-pink. Then they watched night creeping over the sea from the east, and saw the water turn more and more purple, till at last they could hardly tell it from the sky. Then the stars came out brilliantly, and the water sparkled again.

Lucy-Ann was almost asleep in her deckchair when Jack nudged her. 'Wake up! There's a plane. It may be Bill's!' She was awake at once, and went to the deck rail with the others.

The plane went down to the airport landing ground. It must be Bill's! After about half an hour they heard a motor boat starting up its engine in the port.

'It's Bill coming out now!' cried Lucy-Ann in excitement. 'Dear old Bill!'

The motor boat came nearer and nearer. It stopped by the ship, and a ladder was thrown down. Someone began to climb up. Lucy-Ann could contain herself no longer.

'Bill!' she cried. 'Is it you, Bill? BILL!'

Up came a familiar voice. 'Ahoy, there! Bill it is!'

And Bill it was. He came climbing on to the deck, and the four children ran to him at once. They smothered him, hugged him, and were bear-hugged back.

'Dear Bill! Good old Bill! It's grand to see you. *Now* everything's fine.'

'Yes, everything's fine!' said Bill, swinging Lucy-Ann right off her feet. 'Gosh, it's good to see you all! *Now* we'll have some fun!'

15

Bill hears the tale

Bill was hungry and thirsty. The children, excited and happy, took him down to the lounge, where he ordered chicken-and-ham sandwiches and a drink for himself, and, for a treat, some sandwiches for the children.

'Though, let me tell you, you'll have awful dreams tonight, having a meal so late,' he warned them. 'So if you are chased by bears, fall out of aeroplanes or get shipwrecked in your sleep, don't blame *me!*'

'We shan't,' said Lucy-Ann. 'Anyway, now I know you're here, I shan't even *mind* having nightmares – you'll turn up in them to rescue me!'

The steward brought the meal, smiling. He had also brought a banana each for Micky and Kiki, on two separate plates. Kiki was very much impressed with the plates – it wasn't often *she* had a plate! She insisted on putting her banana back on her plate each time she had taken a bite, which amused the children immensely.

'Kiki's gone all polite, I see,' said Bill, taking an enormous bite of his sandwich. 'Gosh, this is good. I haven't had anything to eat for hours. Well, kids, how's things?'

'We've a lot to tell you, Bill,' said Jack. 'Jolly interesting too. We've happened on something very exciting.'

'You would, of course,' said Bill. 'But don't think you're dragging me into any hare-brained escapade this time! I've had enough of you and your adventures! I've come out for a nice, quiet, restful trip.'

Kiki gave a tremendous squawk and made him jump.

'Micky! You've taken Kiki's banana!' said Jack. 'Philip, smack him. There'll be a fight soon, if you don't. All right, Kiki, I'll get you another. Poor old thing, that's what your good manners brought you – you put your banana down politely on your plate after each bite – and Micky goes and takes it!'

'Nice little monkey,' said Bill, tickling Micky under the chin. 'Yours, I suppose, Philip. It beats me how you collect pets wherever you go. Let's see – you've had a fox cub, a lizard, a slow-worm, a snowy-white kid, two puffins, white rats, and now a monkey. Well, well – so long as you don't collect a hippopotamus or a flock of lions I don't mind!'

The children were bursting to tell him about the treasure plan, but they felt they ought to let him eat his sandwiches first. He told them how he had met Mrs Mannering at the airport in England, and had seen her safely off to her aunt. Then he had taken his own private aeroplane and set off.

'Alone?' asked Jack.

'No. With a friend of mine – Tim Curling – don't think you've met him,' said Bill. 'Don't you want all your sandwiches, Lucy-Ann? Right, I'll help myself. Yes, Tim came too, and I've left him with the plane. He's going to hire a motor boat and do a bit of cruising.'

'Oh! I wish we could too,' said Dinah.

'*Do* you?' said Bill in surprise. 'But I thought you liked being on this big, comfortable ship. You're used to rowing boats and sailing ships and motor boats – this big ship must be a real change.'

'Yes, it is. But – well, shall we tell you our news, Bill?' asked Jack eagerly.

Bill ate the last vestige of the sandwiches and finished his drink. He yawned a vast yawn and Kiki immediately did the same. 'I suppose it can't wait till morning, can it?' he said. Then he saw the disappointed faces of the children and laughed. 'Oh, all right. Out with it.'

'Fetch the little carved ship, Lucy-Ann,' said Jack. 'I've got the four bits of the map. Hurry. We'll wait till you come back before we begin.'

Lucy-Ann sped off. She came back very quickly, panting, with the little ship in her hands. Bill took it. 'What a beauty! This is valuable, you know. Where did you get it?'

Then out came the story of how Lucy-Ann had discovered the ship in the bottle, with Lucian, and had bought it for Philip's birthday. In low, excited tones, so that no one else could hear, the children told of the breaking of the bottle and the unexpected finding of the parchment inside the ship. Then Jack produced the parchment, still in its four quarters. Bill glanced at it with great interest. Then he stood up.

'Come on down to my cabin,' he said. 'I think it would be wiser to talk there. This is all rather extraordinary.'

Very pleased with Bill's reception of their tale, the children trooped down the stairs to the cabins. They all crowded into Bill's. They knew it well because it had been their mother's. They managed to squash themselves on to the bed, with Bill in the middle.

'Move Micky up a bit, will you?' said Bill. 'He keeps breathing down my neck. Now then – what's this map? It's very old, I can see that. Why is it in four pieces?'

They told him. They told him the old legend of the lost Andra treasure. They told him of Mr Eppy's strange behaviour. They told him of his departure and all that they feared.

Bill listened intently, asking one or two curt questions now and again. When they had finished he took out his pipe and began to stuff it very slowly with tobacco. The children waited. They knew that Bill was thinking hard. Their hearts beat fast. What did Bill think of their tale? Would he take it seriously? *Would he do something about it?*

'Well,' said Bill, putting his pipe into his mouth and

speaking out of one side whilst he hunted in his pocket for matches. 'Well – I think you've got something there – but I'm basing my feelings on Mr Eppy's behaviour, not on your map, which I don't know enough about to decipher. You've been very ingenious in trying to get it explained to you, and you've fitted various curious facts together very well – such as finding the name Andra on the little ship, and noticing it again on the map.'

'Yes – that was a bit of luck,' said Jack. 'You really *do* think the map is genuine, Bill? I mean – do you think there's any hope of its really showing where the old treasure is?'

'I can't say,' said Bill, puffing away at his pipe. 'Can't possibly say. I'd have to take the map to an expert, get it deciphered properly, find out all I can about the old Andra legend – it may be just a tale, you know – and see if there really is an island called Thamis, and what it's like.'

'There *is*,' said Jack triumphantly. 'I found it on a map.'

Bill began to laugh. 'I don't know how it is that you children always seem to happen on something extraordinary,' he said. 'Just when I thought we were in for a lovely, peaceful trip I shall have to go hunting about for an expert on old documents, and get him to translate Greek so old that it's probably impossible to read correctly. And if there's anything in it I suppose we'll have to see this island called Thamis.'

'Bill! Will you really?' cried Jack in delight, and Philip bounced up and down on the bed, nearly upsetting everybody. Dinah clutched Lucy-Ann, her eyes shining. They were all so pleased because Bill had not pooh-poohed the whole idea.

'We'd better get to bed now,' said Bill. 'It's very late. We'll talk about all this in the morning – but don't get excited! We can't possibly do more than give this map to an expert, and then maybe run over to Thamis and back if it's near enough, just to give it a look over. After all – we're on a cruise, you know.'

The children got up reluctantly. Bill went with them to their cabins. 'I'm going up on deck to smoke my pipe,' he said. 'Happy dreams!'

In the early morning Jack and Philip woke up with a jump. They sat up in bed. Light was just filtering through their porthole, and a curious noise was coming from far below them.

'It's the engines of the ship,' said Jack in relief. 'I wondered whatever in the world it was. What a weird noise they're making! What's happening?'

'They've stopped,' said Philip, after listening for a minute or two. 'No – there they go again – clank-clank-clank. They don't sound a bit right. They don't purr like they usually do. I hope nothing's wrong.'

'Now they've stopped again,' said Jack. 'Well – if there's any danger we shall hear the ship's siren hooting and hooting and the steward will come along and bang on our door.'

'Yes. And our life jackets are ready in the cupboard, so we've nothing to worry about,' said Philip, feeling sleepy again. 'It's nothing. Let's go to sleep.'

But in the morning they found that the ship was still not using her engines. She lay there on the purple-blue sea, rocking a little, with the airport island lying not more than a mile or two off.

'Funny!' said Jack, and dressed quickly. He banged on the girls' door as he went by with Philip. The two boys tore up on deck and found their friend, the second officer.

'What's up?' they asked him. 'Why have we stopped?'

'Mac's got trouble with his engines,' said the officer. 'Soon be all right, I expect.'

They saw Bill coming along. He had been up for some time, walking round the deck for exercise. They rushed to him, and he grinned. 'Hello! Ready for breakfast? I'm ravenous. Hello, Micky, hello, Kiki.'

'Micky-Kiki-Micky-Kiki, Micky-Ki . . .' began Kiki. Jack tapped her on the beak.

'That's enough. Take a bit of exercise. Go and chase the gulls!' But Kiki did not want to. She was bored with the gulls now. Besides, she wanted breakfast. Breakfast was nice on board ship because there was always grapefruit, and Kiki liked that. She loved the cherries on top of the grapefruit halves, and the children took it in turn to give her one.

When breakfast was over they took Bill all over the ship. They were not allowed down in the engine room because of the trouble with the engines. Mac was in a fearful temper, and had been up all night long working on them.

A message was put up on the ship's noticeboard that morning.

Owing to engine trouble, the *Viking Star* is putting back to port. Passengers will be notified further at six o'clock this evening.

With a curious clanking and labouring the *Viking Star* made her way slowly to the island with the airport. Motor boats came roaring out to meet her and find out what was wrong. In one of them was Bill's friend Tim. He was soon on board, and Bill introduced him to the children.

'Tim, here are the four children I've told you about. Be careful of them, or they'll pull you into a perilous adventure. That's the kind of children they are. Put them in the middle of an iceberg and they'll find an adventure somehow!'

The children liked Tim. He was younger than Bill, had a mop of unruly curly hair which the wind did what it liked with, and eyes as green as Lucy-Ann's. He had as many freckles as she and Jack had, and a most infectious laugh.

'You'd better come off in the motor boat with me, hadn't you?' he said to Bill. 'Come back to the island. It's interesting.'

'Right,' said Bill. 'We'll have the day together. Come on, you four – down the ladder with you!'

16

Bill makes a few enquiries

They had a wonderful day on the island. Tim hired a car and away they went to explore. They had lunch in a big town set in the centre of the island, a proper town with shops and buses and cinemas.

After lunch Bill disappeared. 'I've heard of an old chap who's a real expert at old documents,' he told the children. 'One of the greatest experts there are. It's a bit of luck. I'll go and see him. You've got the four bits of the map with you, haven't you, Jack?'

Jack nodded. The children had decided that it would be safer to bring them than leave them behind. He gave them to Bill in an envelope. 'I *do* hope the expert will say it's genuine,' he said earnestly. 'I say – shall we tell Tim?'

'You'd be quite safe to,' said Bill. 'Tim is all right! Whether he'll believe you or not is another matter!'

So, while Bill was gone, the children told Tim their secret. He was inclined to grin at first and laugh it all off as a tale. But they were so serious that he saw that they, at least, believed in it all. He tried to be serious too.

'Well, it's marvellous,' he said. '*I* believed in all these treasure tales when I was a kid too. Jolly nice of Bill to take it seriously and go off to have your map explained.'

The children saw that he did not really take their tale seriously, and they dropped the subject, polite but disappointed. A little doubt crept into Lucy-Ann's mind. *Was* it all a tale? No – surely Mr Eppy wouldn't have behaved so oddly if there had been nothing in it.

Bill was a long time gone. The children were tired of waiting, and Tim was just suggesting they should take a run in the car to a strange-shaped hill in the distance when he came back.

'Sorry to have been so long,' he said. 'I found the old boy – looks as if he'd come out of the fifteenth century, he's so old and dusty – and so slow I could have screamed. But he knew his stuff all right.'

'What did he say?' asked Jack, crimson with anticipation.

'It's genuine. No doubt of that at all,' said Bill, and everyone breathed loudly in relief. 'He doesn't know if it's a copy of any older map, or a fresh one made by a Greek sailor a hundred or so years ago – probably a mixture, he says. The island is Thamis. It is shown clearly on the map, and even if the name had not been there it could have been recognized by its shape – it's curiously formed at one end.'

'Yes. I noticed that,' said Philip. 'Go on, Bill!'

'The map is in two distinct parts,' went on Bill. 'One shows the island, and on it is marked a city or a port. He doesn't know the island himself so he can't tell. The other part shows this same city or port, and is apparently a guide or directions to some spot in the city where something valuable is placed. He says it isn't clear if this valuable thing is treasure or a temple or even a tomb – he only knows it was something of value to the person who first drew the map.'

The children were listening, all eyes and ears. This was marvellous!

'But – doesn't he think it's the Andra treasure?' asked Jack.

'He apparently doesn't know that tale very well – he says there are hundreds of old legends of pirates and treasure ships and kidnapping and so on – most of them untrue. He hadn't much to say about that. He is inclined to think it's a temple.'

'*I* think it's the Andra treasure,' said Lucy-Ann, her eyes shining. 'I really do!'

'I got him to re-draw the whole map for us with the Greek words in English – he speaks English extraordinarily well,' said Bill, and he spread out a nice new sheet of paper on his lap, drawn with fine lines and marked with words. The children pored over it, too thrilled to speak.

Yes – there was the old map re-drawn – put into English – the faded marks shown clearly. How simply wonderful! Even Tim was intensely interested, and almost began to believe in it.

Jack read some of the words out in a whisper. 'Labyrinth – Catacombs – Two-Fingers – Goddess – Bird – Bell – gosh, what does it all mean? Are the labyrinths and catacombs in this city or port? Was the treasure taken down them?'

'We don't know. All we know is that a way is shown here to a certain place in the city where a certain valuable thing can be found – if it hasn't already been found and taken away or destroyed,' said Bill. 'But you must remember that the original of this map is probably hundreds of years old – the way shown on this map possibly no longer exists. In fact, the probabilities are that it doesn't.'

'Oh, Bill – do you really believe that?' asked Dinah reproachfully.

'Well – to be perfectly honest, I do,' said Bill disappointingly. 'I think the map is genuine – no doubt about that at all – but I also think that as all this happened so long ago there's no hope of finding the secret way shown here. It would either have been built over, or destroyed, or even completely forgotten, so that there may not even be an entrance to the labyrinths or catacombs, whatever they are.'

'But Mr Eppy obviously thinks there's some hope,' said Philip.

'Oh, that reminds me – this old chap, the one I've been to see, knows Mr Eppy. He says he's a real crank about these things – quite dippy about them – and goes off on all sorts of hare-brained schemes,' said Bill. 'Buys and sells islands as if they were books or carpets or pictures! He admits that Mr Eppy knows a lot about the islands, and about the antiques that can be found in them – but he doesn't think that because he believes in the map, for instance, that necessarily means there is anything to get excited about. Rather the other way about, I gathered.'

'Blow!' said Jack. 'So there may be nothing in it after all. In fact, probably not.'

'In fact, probably not, as you say,' agreed Bill. 'All the same, if we had the chance, which we shan't have, of course, I wouldn't mind hiring a motor boat and chugging off to have a look at Thamis, wherever it is.'

'Oh, I do wish we *could*,' said Lucy-Ann. 'It would be lovely just to *see* it.'

'I could run you over there,' said Tim unexpectedly. 'That is, if it's not too far away.'

'No time,' said Bill, folding up the map. 'We've got to be back by six, as you know. Thanks all the same, Tim. Now, we'd better be off, I think.'

By the time they got to the port it was half-past five. The *Viking Star* had been piloted right in to the pier, and was lying there looking very white and beautiful, but with no sign of the bustle about her that usually meant she was soon sailing.

The gangway was down, and passengers were trooping along it. Lucian was among them with his aunt. They had not seen him all day, except in the distance, and then they had taken no notice of him, not wanting him to tag himself on to them now they had Bill. He waved to them and shouted.

'Oh, I say! Where have you been all day? My aunt wanted you to come with us and have lunch with one of my relations on the island.'

'Sorry! We had other plans!' called back Jack. 'See you some time.'

'Who's the boy?' enquired Bill. 'Oh – it's Lucian, I suppose, the nephew of your Mr Eppy. He must be a bit of a nuisance to you!'

'We can manage him all right,' said Philip. 'Look – here's the noticeboard. There's a big notice up. What does it say?'

The notice was printed in chalk on the big black noticeboard.

Passengers are regretfully informed that the *Viking Star* will have to remain in port for a day or two until damage to her engines is repaired. Passengers may remain on

428

board if they wish, or stay in a hotel provided by the Company, or may use the motor boats which the said Company will provide for the use of any passengers wishing to explore this romantic part of the Aegean Sea. (Signed) L. Petersen, *Captain*

The same thought struck all four children at once. They turned to one another, their eyes shining.

'We could, couldn't we?' said Lucy-Ann, and the others understood at once. Jack nodded, his eyes bright. He slipped his arm through Bill's.

Bill looked round at the children. He smiled broadly, and then laughed out loud to see the four eager faces looking at him, all with the same question in them.

'Can we go to Thamis, after all – that's what you want to know, isn't it?' he said. 'Well, I don't see why not. It looks as if we'll be here a few days, and if the Company provides us with a motor boat, well, we'll agree to their kind proposal and off we'll go in one!'

'*Bill!* BILL! How marvellous!' cried everyone, and Jack and Philip began to thump one another on the back, and the girls squeezed Bill's arms till he yelled. Kiki and Micky flew off the boys' shoulders in a hurry and retired in surprised annoyance to the top of the noticeboard.

'Come on – stop this pantomime,' said Bill, still laughing to see the children's excitement. 'Let's get up on deck and make a few plans before we change into clean things for dinner. Get Micky, look – he's beginning to rub out the top part of the notice with his tail.'

They went up to a favourite corner on the promenade deck and sat down. 'It's too good to be true,' said Jack, delighted. 'We keep on thinking things are no good, we'll have to give them up – and then something happens and everything's all right.'

'Yes. We knew we couldn't do anything without Bill, and he wasn't here – and then he suddenly came,' said Lucy-Ann.

'And then we knew we still couldn't do anything because we'd have to go with the ship on her cruise,' said Dinah. 'And now she's held up, and we can go off by ourselves!'

'Extraordinary how you children get what you want,' said Bill. 'Now about this motor boat tomorrow. I rather think we'll hire one on our own. If we take one that the Company provides we'll have to go with some of the other passengers – and they certainly won't want to go to Thamis, wherever it is.'

'And we wouldn't want them to, either,' said Jack. 'No – let's have a boat of our own. Can Tim come too?'

'He's got other plans,' said Bill. 'But we'll tell him, just in case he'd like to come. Well – it certainly will be a thrill. I must find out this evening exactly where this Thamis is. I'll get hold of the second officer and ask him if there's a sailor on board who can tell me anything.

We'll have to find out the precise route or we might go cruising among these islands for weeks!'

'Oh, Bill – isn't it grand?' said Lucy-Ann. 'I can't wait for tomorrow. Jack, Philip – we're really going to see the treasure island after all! We really are!'

17

To Thamis at last!

Bill soon got all the information he wanted. 'That's the best of being grown-up,' said Dinah. 'Grown-ups always seem to be able to find out anything, and get things cut and dried in no time.'

'Yes – Bill's found out where Thamis is, has ferreted out a map of the route, and has even got the name of a Greek sailor who owns a motor boat and knows the way!' said Jack, in admiration.

'How did he find all that out?' asked Lucy-Ann.

'Got hold of a Greek sailor below decks, and found he had a brother who runs one of the motor boats,' said Philip.

It was the following morning. The children had had a big breakfast, and had been provided with enormous packets of food to take with them by the steward who looked after them so well at table.

'I've packed a whole grapefruit, two cherries and four

bananas for Master Micky and Miss Kiki,' he said with a twinkle in his eye. Lucy-Ann went off into giggles.

'Oh – it does sound funny to call them that! Miss Kiki! Kiki, did you hear that? Miss Kiki!'

'Misskiki, kickmissy, missmicky,' said Kiki and cackled loudly.

They all walked down the gangway to the pier. They found Tim waiting for them. He had heard the news.

'Hello, sir,' he said to Bill. 'Can I do anything for you today?'

'Well, we're going off to have a look at Thamis,' said Bill. 'I've hired a motor boat from a Greek who apparently knows the route. Like to come with us?'

'Well, if you've made your own plans, sir, I won't come today,' said Tim. 'I've got a chappy here who wants a spot of flying. Can I take the plane up?'

'Yes, of course,' said Bill.

'And if you fly over Thamis, wave to us,' said Jack.

'Right,' said Tim with a grin. 'I'll look it up and see where it is. Look out for us!'

He went off, and Bill turned to find the boat he had hired. A small, dark Greek came up, with brilliant eyes and a shy smile. He saluted, and spoke in broken English.

'I'm Andros, sir, please. My brother, he say Mister want my boat. Mister, sir, she here.'

'Right. Thanks, Andros,' said Bill, and he looked at

the spick-and-span little boat lying alongside. 'Very nice boat. Now, you know the way to Thamis, don't you?'

'Thamis. Yes, Mister. But Thamis poor place. Andros take you find islands.'

'No, thanks. We want to go to Thamis,' said Bill firmly.

Andros seemed surprised at their wanting to go to Thamis. 'Poor island,' he said again. 'Visitors not go there, Mister, sir. I take you fine place.'

'Look here – don't you know the way to Thamis?' said Bill. 'Sounds as if you don't. Oh, you do. Then to Thamis, please, and let's get on with it.'

'Thamis, Mister, sir,' agreed little Andros. 'Yes, yes, Thamis. Old, old island, but nothing there now, Mister, sir.' He glanced with interest at the parrot and the monkey. 'They come too also?'

'Of course,' said Jack, stepping into the boat and helping the girls in. 'Come on, Bill, Mister, sir!'

'Mistersir, mistersir, mistersir,' screamed Kiki. 'Pop goes the weasel! Bang, pop, God save the Queen.'

Andros gaped at her open-mouthed. Micky leapt on to his shoulder and back to Philip's, chattering. He was excited. He even pulled Kiki's tail, a very silly thing to do because Kiki would now watch for a good chance to nip Micky's – and Micky had quite a long tail to nip!

Andros started up the engine. The motor boat nosed out of the little harbour, leaving behind the great *Viking Star*, beautiful but silent. Soon they were out on the open sea, skimming along, bobbing up and down on the white horses that reared themselves every now and again. The sun was hot but the wind was strong. The girls' hair streamed out straight, and they laughed in delight to feel so much wind in their faces. After the heat on the ship it was lovely.

'How far is Thamis?' asked Jack. Andros turned his curly head.

'Four hours, five hours,' he said.

'Do you go there much?' asked Bill.

'No, no, Mister, sir. Poor island. I go to Janos, the next one, where my sister lives,' said Andros. 'Thamis dead island, Mister, sir.'

'What does he mean?' wondered Jack. 'A poor dead island! Doesn't sound much of a place, does it?'

'Well, there must be some sort of port or town there,' said Philip. 'The one marked on the map. It looked quite a big one. There must be plenty of people living there, and that means shops and things. It can't be quite dead!'

It was a lovely journey to Thamis. The sea was choppy, and yet was full of glints and sparkles. The boat sped along like a live thing, the engine purring away. At twelve o'clock they all had a picnic lunch and blessed the steward who had packed them such a fine one.

'Five different sorts of sandwiches – four different kinds of cake, half a pound of sweet biscuits, rolls and butter and cheese and tomatoes – and the grapefruit, cherries and bananas for Kiki and Micky,' said Jack.

Lucy-Ann sat contentedly eating with the wind in her face. She looked very happy. The others looked at her and nudged one another. They waited. They knew exactly what she was going to say. She opened her mouth, and at once all the others chimed in together.

'You know, we always think food tastes *much* nicer when it's eaten out of doors!'

Lucy-Ann stared at them in surprise. 'How very peculiar! I was *just* about to say exactly the same thing,' she said.

The others chuckled. 'We knew you were,' said Philip. 'You always do say it, Lucy-Ann. We watched for you to open your mouth and begin, and we said it for you!'

'Idiots,' said Lucy-Ann and laughed. Andros laughed too. He liked these children and their funny pets. He had refused to share their food and was eating his own lunch. It was made up of black bread, some very strong-smelling cheese and a jug of some kind of drink.

Kiki and Micky ate their dinner solemnly together. Micky was not very pleased with the terrific breeze that blew every hair on his body backwards or forwards, depending on which way he sat. Nor was Kiki pleased when her feathers blew round her like an umbrella turning inside out. The two of them sat together in a little sheltered place sharing the grapefruit, the cherries and the bananas. Micky politely peeled a banana for Kiki and handed it to her.

'He skins it just like we do,' said Lucy-Ann. 'I always think he's so clever at that.'

'Clever,' said Andros, pointing to Micky. 'Good and clever.'

Micky unfortunately spoilt Andros's good opinion of him by throwing away the banana skin so carelessly that it landed on the sailor's head, hanging ridiculously over his right eye. Kiki gave one of her rich chuckles, and was just about to add her banana skin to Micky's when Jack took it away from her.

'Mistersir, mistersir, mister Pollysir,' squawked Kiki, trying to snatch it back.

The boat went on and on, occasionally passing other islands, one or two large ones, but most of them small. Finally Andros raised his hand and pointed to the east.

'Thamis,' he said. 'Mister, sir, Thamis.'

Everyone looked eagerly to where he pointed. They saw a small island, purple in the distance, rearing itself out of the waters as they sped nearer. Thamis! Was it really Thamis, the old island marked on the treasure map?

Eagerly the children leaned forward and watched it take shape as they raced nearer. Lucy-Ann's imagination began to work. Long, long ago, she thought, this is where the fleet of treasure ships stole up to in the night. Soon we shall see the city marked on the map – the treasure city!

'Perhaps,' she thought, 'one of the ships was called the

Andra like our own little Ship of Adventure. Perhaps it sailed into the very spot we're making for now. We're getting quite near. We shall see the city soon – the one marked on the map.'

'Is there a good harbour?' asked Bill, turning to Andros. The man looked surprised.

'Oh, no, Mister, sir. No harbour now. Only two places to land. I, Andros, know them both. I take you to old city port.'

'Good,' thought Jack. 'Now we shall soon be there – in the old city marked on the map. I hope it won't be *too* modern, like the towns we've seen on some of the islands. Ah – now we're getting in close.'

They were. They could see rocky beaches. The waves pounded on them. They looked for the town, and saw buildings coming down to the water's edge. It seemed strange that there was no proper harbour. City ports always had a harbour.

The boat ran in gently, Andros looking out for rocks and taking a course he seemed to know. He was making for a little channel that led inland.

The children fell silent as they neared the island. Their eyes were fixed on the city. It did not look right, somehow. Something was the matter with it. It looked – well – *dead*, Lucy-Ann thought.

Jack remembered his binoculars and put them to his eyes. He gave an exclamation. 'Gosh! Would you believe it!'

'*What?*' said everyone at once impatiently.

'It's all ruins,' said Jack, and he lowered the glasses and looked at the others. 'It's a *ruined* city! I never thought of that!'

'I, Andros, told that,' said the sailor. 'I tell you poor island, dead island. One farm, two farms, perhaps. City gone. Nobody there. All gone to other islands now.'

They nosed into the little channel. It was deep and calm. 'You get out and I wait?' enquired Andros. 'Not see much. All dead and poor this island. Yes, Mister, sir. I take you better places.'

'We'll get out, Andros,' said Bill. 'Bring the rest of the food, Jack. We may as well explore now we're here, and we'll picnic in the old ruins. They will be quite interesting, I expect.'

Not knowing quite what to think, the children leapt off the boat on to a ledge. They climbed up some old worn steps, and came into what must have been the main street of the ruined city. It was overgrown now and difficult to walk in. There were ruins everywhere. Bill looked at a few of them closely.

'These are hundreds of years old,' he said. 'I wonder what made the people leave Thamis and go elsewhere. I suppose the island couldn't keep them in food. What a place!'

'It's got such a weird deserted feeling about it that I feel I'm living hundreds of years ago,' said Lucy-Ann. 'I wish the city would come alive – be full of the long-ago people, walking and running here along the street, looking out of the old broken window-openings, going down to whatever harbour there was to see the ships!'

'Well, I hope the city *doesn't* come alive,' said Dinah. 'I'd be scared stiff. I don't like it much as it is.'

It was built on a steep hill, and the ruined buildings rose one above another, some just a wall or two, others a hollow shell, and still others looking fairly habitable until the children peeped inside and saw the holes in the roofs and the walls.

Almost at the top was an old ruined temple, one or two graceful arches still remaining. Its massive columns stood in a broken row, with one or two gulls perched on the jagged tops. Bill scraped aside some of the grass that grew on the floor of the temple, and pointed out lovely mosaic stones to the children.

'Bill, is there anything here at all that's on the map?' asked Jack. Somehow it was all so different from what he had imagined that the idea of hidden treasure now seemed ridiculous. Bill got out the re-drawn map.

'Look – this is where we came in with our boat, surely,' said Philip, pointing. 'It says "CREEK". Well, wouldn't you call that channel a creek? And look – the entrance or beginning of the way to the treasure is some-where near the creek.'

'Oh, Bill – let's go back and explore along there!' said Dinah.

Bill laughed. 'We've certainly got a bee in our bonnet about this! All right. Come on. It'll be on the way to the boat, anyway.'

'Just let's get to the top of the hill,' said Jack. 'We could see over the rest of the island then. It's not very large.'

'Right,' said Bill, and they climbed to the very top. They could see away over to the other side of the island, where the dark-blue sea was tipped with white horses. It was a bare, rocky place, but here and there were green patches, and small buildings could be seen.

'The farms Andros spoke of, I suppose,' said Bill. 'My word – he was certainly right when he called it poor and dead! It's not quite my idea of a treasure island!'

They turned to go down the hill on which the ruined city was built. They made their way carefully. Halfway down Lucy-Ann stopped and listened. 'I can hear something,' she said.

'So can I,' said Dinah. 'It's a bell ringing! Whatever can it be?'

18

A few surprises

It seemed so very unusual to hear a bell ringing in that
dead and silent city that the little company felt really
startled. The sound came nearer.

'Dong-dong-dong.' Kiki didn't like it either and
crouched against Jack's cheek. Micky chattered quietly.

'Dong-dong-dong!'

'Something's coming round that corner,' said Jack
suddenly. And something did.

It was a donkey, a little grey donkey with a big bell
hanging from his neck! With him was a small boy, an
imp of a boy, riding astride, with panniers each side of
the donkey, great baskets that were full of something
covered with white cloths.

'Good gracious!' said Dinah, and she sat down on a
big stone, most relieved to see that it was just a donkey
bell that had startled them all. 'I don't know *what* I
thought was coming!'

'I suppose the boy's from one of the farms,' said Bill,

looking puzzled. 'But why has he come here? There is nobody living here.'

Then an even more surprising thing happened. The boy caught sight of the five people watching him and grinned a welcome. He leapt off the donkey, pointed to the pannier baskets and shouted out something that sounded unlike anything they had heard before, but which the children imagined must be Greek spoken in the local accent of Thamis. Then he brought the donkey right up to them and began to throw back the cloths that covered whatever was in the panniers.

'It's food,' said Bill in amazement. 'Bread – cheeses – meat. Gosh, he's unpacking the lot.'

The boy unpacked everything, chattering all the time. He evidently could not understand why nobody helped him, and addressed quite a few cutting remarks to the two boys, who, of course, could not make head or tail of them.

'Here, boy,' said Bill. 'What's all this?'

He pointed to the pile of food. The boy sent out another explanation, pointing to Bill and then pointing to the food.

'Anyone would think he had brought all this for *us*,' said Bill, exasperated. 'I can't understand it at all.'

The boy mounted his donkey again. He held out his hand to Bill, palm upwards. That was plain enough. He wanted money!

'Well, well – it beats me,' said Bill astounded. 'A very

fine welcome to Thamis, I must say – but most unexpected. We don't want the food, sonny. WE DON'T WANT IT. TAKE IT BACK!'

No amount of shouting could make the boy understand. He got very angry, and tapped his palm smartly to make Bill understand he wanted money. In the end Bill tipped a handful of coins into his hand. He counted them carefully, nodded his head, grinned brilliantly, and then very unexpectedly spat at Micky. Micky spat back, and Kiki growled like a dog.

The donkey backed away from Kiki and began to bray. 'Eee-yore! Eee-eee-yore!'

Kiki was extremely startled, but she soon recovered, and produced a very good bray herself. The boy gave a yelp of surprise, kicked his donkey hard with both his bare heels and galloped away round the corner, the donkey's bell ringing hard. 'Dong-dong-dong-dong-dong!'

Bill sat down and scratched his head. 'Well, what do you make of *that*?' he said. 'A present of some very fine country food, sent by somebody we don't know, who can't possibly have known we were here.'

'It's a puzzle,' said Jack. 'I wouldn't mind one of those rolls.'

They all had one. They were very good. They sat and munched them, wondering about the boy. They could not make head or tail of his appearance.

'What are we going to do with this food?' said Philip.

'It won't keep if it's left out in the sun. It seems an awful waste of good food to leave it mouldering here.'

'It does,' said Bill. 'Well – the only thing we can do is to carry it into a cool place somewhere and hope that boy will come back!'

They picked up the food and went into a nearby building. There was a hole in the floor, shaded by a half-ruined wall. They packed all the food there, wondering what would happen to it.

'Now we'd better go down to the creek and see if we can find the entrance, or whatever it is, shown on the map,' said Bill. He pulled it out of his pocket and looked at it. The children looked too. 'We shan't find it, so don't think it!' said Bill, who was secretly of the opinion that there was nothing to be discovered in this poor, 'dead' island.

They went down the overgrown, stone-strewn street and came to the rocky creek. The motor boat was there, rocking gently. Andros was fast asleep on the shady side of the boat.

The little party walked down the rocky ledge to the boat. Then they looked up the creek. Bill gave an exclamation. 'Of course! That's it!'

'*What*, Bill?' said the children at once.

'Well, "Two-Fingers" is marked on the map, apparently for no reason at all. The expert swore that's what the old Greek word meant. I just thought it might be an old name for someone – but now I see what it meant. Look up there.'

The children looked where Bill pointed, and above their heads some way away to the left they saw a peculiar rock. It was like a clenched hand with two fingers raised! Yes – two fingers. There they were. And 'Two-Fingers' was marked on the map!

'Come on. That's a guide of some sort,' said Bill, and they climbed along till they came to the queer two-fingered rock. They found a hole behind it, a hole that would quite easily allow a person to step into it. Bill fumbled for a torch. He switched it on.

'There may be a passage of some kind,' he said. 'Yes – there is! This is really extraordinary! I think, Jack, you'd better go back to the boat and get a lantern or two if you can find them. My torch isn't too good.'

Jack sped down to the boat. Andros was still asleep. Jack spotted two lanterns and brought them carefully up to the two-fingered rock, handing them at awkward places to Philip, who had come to meet him.

'Good,' said Bill. 'We'll light these. I'll take one and you can take the other, Jack. I'll save my torch.'

They lit the oil lanterns inside the hole. It wasn't big enough for a cave. It really was just a large hole behind the strange-looking rock – but at the back was what looked like an entry into the hill. Could it possibly be the entrance shown in the map?

'Do you think it is, Bill?' asked Lucy-Ann eagerly,

when the lanterns were lit, and Bill held one up to peer into the narrow rocky passage behind the hole.

'No. I can't believe it is,' said Bill. 'It must have been known for years by everyone in the city, when it was alive with people. It's just a coincidence, I expect.'

The children, of course, didn't think it was. They felt very thrilled indeed as they made their way along the dark little passage. It went for a hundred yards and then came out into a wide space. Bill held up his lantern. It shone on to rocky walls – but what was that at the back? The wall looked different there.

He took his lantern over to it. The beam shone on to large blocks of stone built like a great irregular door. 'I wonder why that was built here,' said Bill, surprised. He swung the lantern round to light up the rest of the cave. The walls were of smooth, shiny rock. There was not the smallest opening there at all. The only opening was the one they had come in by from the narrow passage.

He swung the light on to the built-in stones again. Then he put the lantern down.

'This was built to block up some other opening,' he said at last. The children's hearts sank. 'It is immensely strong, as you can see for yourselves – a door of great blocks of stone, a door that can't possibly be opened, or got through in any way.'

'Bill – do you think it's blocking up the entrance shown on the map?' asked Jack, dismayed.

'Well, yes – I do,' said Bill. 'It's been built many,

many years – it's old, as you can see. Why it was built, goodness knows! Anyway, there it is – and we're stopped right at the very outset! If this is the way shown on the map, the way that one must follow to get to wherever the treasure was hidden, it's impossible to follow it. Quite impossible!'

'Oh, Bill!' said Lucy-Ann almost in tears. 'It's too bad. Isn't there *any* way through?'

'Well – send Micky to see,' said Bill. 'If there's even a small hole Micky will find it. You know what monkeys are. Send him, Philip.'

'Go, Micky – go and hunt about,' said Philip. Micky looked at him enquiringly. He did not like this business of exploring dark passages, but he leapt off Philip's shoulder and obediently went off on an exploration of his own. Kiki watched him and then flew to a ledge at the top of the immense stone doorway.

'Send for the doctor,' she said in a hollow voice. 'Polly's got a cold. Send for the doctor.'

Micky bounded up to join her. He scurried about, putting his paw here and there, into crannies and crevices. But obviously there was nothing to find, for he soon came back and leapt on to Philip's shoulder, nestling closely into his neck.

'No go,' said Bill. He set the lantern down on the floor, meaning to put the map away. Just as he was folding it up Lucy-Ann gave an astonished cry.

'What's the matter?' said Jack, startled.

'Look – what's that over there – on the floor? Surely, it's – it's – a *torch battery*!'

Philip saw the thing she meant and went to pick it up. He brought it to the light of the lamp. 'Yes – that's just what it is – an old worn-out battery from a torch rather like Bill's. Bill – you haven't dropped a battery, have you?'

'Of course not,' said Bill. 'Yes, this is certainly an old battery – somebody must have thrown it down and put a new battery into his torch – whoever he may be! We are obviously not the only ones to know this place!'

Lucy-Ann shivered. She was sorry she had spotted that battery now. It made her feel uneasy. Who had been in this walled-up cave, and why?

'Let's go, Bill,' she said. 'We can't do any good here – it's all walled up. Let's go back to Andros. I don't like this.'

'Right. We'll go back,' said Bill. 'In any case, we ought to go now. We've been here ages, and we've got to get back to the ship tonight. Come along.'

They made their way out of the cave, down the narrow passage in the rocky hill and came to the hole. They climbed round the two-fingered rock and made their way to the creek.

And then they got a terrible shock. The motor boat was gone! They stared as if they could not believe their eyes.

'Where's the boat?' said Dinah feebly.

They looked up the creek and down. No sign of the boat at all. How very extraordinary! And then Jack gave a cry and pointed out to sea.

'Isn't that it? Look – right out there?'

They all strained their eyes, and Bill nodded his head grimly. 'Yes – that looks like it. What on earth made Andros go off without us? What an astounding thing to do!'

'He was fast asleep in the boat when I got the lantern,' said Jack. 'Never stirred. Everything seemed all right then.'

'Blessed if I understand it,' said Bill, looking bewildered. 'He seemed a good trustworthy chap – and I haven't even paid him. What in the world has possessed him to act like that?'

'That boat's going pretty fast,' said Philip. 'Almost out of sight now. Well, well, well – here we are marooned on our treasure island, sure as eggs are eggs!'

Lucy-Ann was very much alarmed. She took Bill's arm. 'What are we going to do?' she said. 'Are we to stay here, Bill?'

'Lucy-Ann, of course we are,' said Jack before Bill could answer. 'Where are we to go if we don't stay here? Have you got an aeroplane stowed away somewhere, ready for this emergency?'

'Shut up, Jack,' said Bill, putting his arm round Lucy-Ann. 'We shall be all right, don't fret, Lucy-Ann. It's only one of our adventures!'

19

All kinds of shocks

They stood there for a little while, not certain what to do. It was all so very unexpected. Then Bill shook himself and grinned round at the others.

'Well – it looks as if we've got to spend the night here, doesn't it? – and get our supper ourselves. Thank goodness we've got the food that extraordinary boy brought on his donkey! And Jack's got the rest of our picnic lunch as well.'

'Oh, *yes* – I'd forgotten that!' said Dinah, pleased. She had been thinking they would have nothing to eat.

'We can go and tuck in straight away,' said Bill. 'We'll find somewhere to sleep all right – it's very warm, and we shan't come to any harm. I don't particularly want to go and find one of those farms we saw, in case Andros takes it into his head to call back for us. He must have gone crazy.'

It was a curious evening that they all spent on Thamis. They went to find the store of food and had a very good meal indeed. They put the rest of it safely back in the cool place they had stored it in at first. Then they went wandering round the silent, ruined old city again. Lucy-Ann found an old pot with a broken neck, which she was very pleased with. Jack found some kind of metal fork – at least that is what he took it to be – with two of its prongs gone.

Bill had been hunting about for some place to sleep in. He had not been very successful. At last he chose a room not far from the ruined temple, one that had three walls and a little roof left. It was overgrown with thick grass but would have to do for a bedroom.

The sun was going down. It would soon be gone. Bill decided to put the food in the 'bedroom' too – it would be handy if they wanted any. He and the boys removed it from the place it was in and put it carefully in some thick, cool grass. They were glad there was such a lot!

When the sun disappeared everyone felt tired. Lucy-Ann was yawning her head off, and so was Kiki. Micky explored the ruined little room thoroughly, approved of it and settled down on Philip as soon as the boy had made himself a fairly soft bed in the thickly growing grass.

The four children fell asleep at once. Kiki perched herself quietly on Jack's middle as soon as she knew he was asleep. He had pushed her off two or three times, but this time he did not wake, and she remained where she was, her head tucked under her wing.

Bill lay and looked up at the stars he could see through the holes in the roof. He was angry with himself for bringing the children to Thamis. Now they had landed in difficulties again – all because of a legendary and most elusive treasure, one that certainly had not existed for years – if it had ever existed at all!

He puzzled over the boy on the donkey who had brought the food. He puzzled over the blocked-up entrance and the battery Lucy-Ann had found. But more than anything he puzzled over the sudden disappearance of Andros.

He was just about to fall off to sleep when he heard a noise. Micky must have heard it too, because he stirred and his small head looked round the 'bedroom'. Bill lay and listened, holding his breath. *Was* it a noise he had heard?

Then he heard the unmistakable sound of a voice! Then another voice, deep and complaining. Where did they come from?

He sat up cautiously and listened again. The voices came once more, and then Bill heard footsteps – footsteps coming down the ruined city street! He did not like it at all. Who on earth was walking through the old dead city in the middle of the night?

Kiki had heard the voices too. She flew out of the room she was in and hid herself under the ledge of an arch, waiting. The footsteps came nearer. The voices came too, talking together. Bill silently posted himself beside a broken window opening and watched. There was only starlight to see by, but he might be able to make out something.

Two dark figures came up the street. They stopped every now and again. It seemed to Bill as if they were looking in the ruined buildings to find something. Would they look into this one and find the children? Bill debated whether he should go out and accost these people. Who were they, anyway?

Then he decided that people who walk the streets of a ruined city at dead of night are not perhaps the best people to ask help from, and he remained where he was.

The two dark figures arrived nearby. He heard their voices again, but they spoke in a foreign language – Greek, probably – and he could not understand a word. They were obviously looking for something, Bill thought – and then he suddenly guessed what it was.

The food, perhaps! Maybe the boy had brought it for *them* – and they had not been there – but Bill had, and had got it instead. Now the men were looking for it, sure that the boy had dumped it somewhere.

'They'll look in here then, sure as anything,' thought Bill. But they didn't. Just as they got to the broken doorway, near where the parrot was perched, Kiki went off like a pistol shot.

CRACK!

The children all woke up at once and sat up. They

454

were too startled to make a sound, and as soon as they heard Bill's 'Shh!' they sat silently waiting.

The two men were most alarmed. Bill could see them clutching one another. They said something rapidly, obviously asking each other what that noise was.

Kiki considered them. She didn't like them. She began to cackle with laughter, and this horrified the men more than anything else could have done. Kiki's laughter was so completely idiotic that it froze them to the marrow.

Kiki stopped. She swelled out her throat and began to make her famous noise of an express train screeching through a tunnel, getting louder and louder and louder. It was a magnificent effort and had very satisfactory results.

The men yelled too, in panic, and set off as fast as they could, certain that something terrible was coming after them. Kiki sent another pistol shot after them and then relapsed into cackles.

'Well, really, Kiki,' said Bill, when the two men were completely gone. 'What a performance!'

'Who was it out there, Bill?' asked Dinah.

'I've no idea,' said Bill. 'But I have a feeling it was two hungry fellows come to look for the food the small boy presented us with today. Anyway, they've departed in a great hurry.'

'Kiki was marvellous, wasn't she?' said Jack. 'Good old Kiki! Clever bird!'

Kiki gave an outsize hiccup. 'Pardon! Send for the doctor! Pop goes the weasel.'

'Yes. Very nice. But that's enough now,' said Jack. 'Bill, who do you think those men were?'

'I've just told you – I've no idea,' said Bill. 'This place beats me. Come on, let's go to sleep again. I don't some-how think those fellows will come back – and if we have any other visitors I've no doubt Kiki will deal with them!'

They settled themselves off to sleep again. Bill lay awake wondering a little more, then he too fell asleep. He did not wake till morning.

The others were already awake. Jack had awakened very thirsty and had gone to look for water. He found a well beside a tumbledown house some way down the hill, and saw water in it. It was not long before he had rigged up a way of bringing up the water, which was crystal clear and cold. He tied string round the broken pot Lucy-Ann had found and lowered it down the well. It did not hold much water because the neck was broken, but it was enough for them all to quench their thirst. They had breakfast off the rolls and cheeses, and hoped the boy would come again that day!

'Go down and see if there's any sign of the boat, Jack,' said Bill when they had finished. So off he went, and soon came back to report that the creek was empty. No boat was anywhere to be seen.

'Well – we shall just have to wait about, that's all,'

said Bill. 'It will only be a question of time till we are taken off. Tim will wonder what's happened, for one thing. Or Andros will discover he's done a crazy thing, and come back for us!'

At about twelve o'clock they heard the dong-dong-dong of the donkey's bell again, and round the same corner came the imp of a boy. Bill knew what to do this time! He and the others unpacked the food, the boy was paid and, with the donkey's bell ringing loudly, he departed, much better pleased with his reception. Everyone stared after him.

'Really very extraordinary,' said Bill. 'Let's hide the food quickly, before the real recipients come along. We'll have a meal ourselves too. I'm hungry!'

They dragged the food to the room in which they had slept the night before, and had a good meal before they hid the rest. Bill wondered if he should find his way to one of the farms for help. But what help could they give? And what kind of a reception would he get? Anything might happen to him on this lonely island. He might be robbed and kept prisoner, or even killed.

Jack asked Bill to give him the map to study – the redrawn one. 'Not that it's going to be much use,' said Jack with a grin. 'Now that I'm on Thamis I don't think so much of it as I did. And it's difficult to believe in treasure when all you can see around you is a lot of ruins.'

Bill gave him the map. Jack took it into the space

once occupied by the temple, and sat down in a corner. Lucy-Ann came to sit with him. Kiki settled between them, murmuring companionably.

The two red heads bent over the map together. 'It's got so many things on it that I can't make anything out,' said Jack. '"Two-Fingers" – well, we know what that means, all right – and now look here – a lot further on it says "Bell". Well, what does that mean? Bell! What has a bell? A donkey, of course – and schools have bells – and—'

'Churches,' said Lucy-Ann. 'I expect this old temple had a bell once upon a time. I wonder where it was.'

She looked round and about but could see no place where a bell could have hung.

Jack looked at her suddenly. 'Lucy-Ann – of *course* – a temple *would* have a bell. The temple may be one of the clues, one of the guides to the treasure.'

'Do you think so?' said Lucy-Ann doubtfully. 'But – surely the treasure would have been hidden deep *underground* somewhere – not in the temple up here. We know the entrance to the secret passage was far *down* the hill, just above the creek.'

'Would it be hidden *under* the temple, perhaps?' said Jack. 'Or somewhere near? Maybe the temple had vaults. I say – that's an idea! If this one once had vaults, they must still be there. *Vaults* don't become ruins, like buildings. They're not exposed to wind and rain and sun. Vaults! Yes – going deep down into the hill – reached by an underground passage from the creek – a passage that could be approached easily enough from the sea – could be used by sailors who wanted to smuggle in goods. Lucy-Ann, there must be vaults! Come on – we'll look for them.'

Lucy-Ann, half excited, half disbelieving, got up and followed Jack. He began to hunt all over what must have once been the courtyard. It was too overgrown to tell if any way could be found underground.

They leaned against a great half-broken column to rest themselves. There was a large piece out of the column just above their heads, and Kiki flew up there to perch. At that moment Micky came bounding into the old courtyard of the temple, followed by the others. He saw Kiki and leapt up beside her.

She wasn't expecting him, and was startled and angry. She gave him such a violent nip that he lost his balance on the ledge – and fell backwards into the inside of the enormous column!

He shrieked with fright as he fell, and Kiki poked her head inside the hole to see what had happened to him.

'All gone,' she announced in a hollow voice. 'All gone. Ding-dong-bell.'

'You idiot, Kiki!' shouted Philip. 'Hey, Micky, Micky! Come on up!'

But there was no Micky. Only a little whimpering cry came up. 'He's hurt,' said Philip. 'Here, Jack, give me a leg-up. I'll go down into the column after him. He can't have fallen very far.'

Jack gave him a leg-up. He got on to the broken place, swung his legs in and was about to jump down when he stopped and looked in cautiously.

'Hey, Bill!' he called. 'Hand me your torch. I'd better look before I leap, I think. There's something odd here!'

Bill handed him up his torch. Philip switched it on and looked down into the hollow of the great column. He turned and looked back at the others.

'I say – it's amazing. It looks as if there's steps at the bottom of this column! What do you think of *that*?'

20

Exploring the treasure route

Everyone was amazed. Steps! Stone steps leading downward at the base of the hollow stone column! Jack gave a loud whoop.

'I bet they go to the vaults!'

'*What* vaults?' asked Dinah in astonishment. But Jack was too excited to tell her.

'Bill   let's go down. Come on. We're on the track of the treasure. Didn't the map say "Bell"? Well, the temple must have a bell. I bet the treasure's somewhere underneath!'

'You're talking double Dutch,' said Bill, not following this at all. 'Philip – come down. Don't attempt any scatterbrained exploration till we get the lanterns, and till I have a look myself. Do you hear me?'

'Yes, right, Bill,' said Philip reluctantly, and jumped down. 'Micky's down there somewhere – he must have fallen on the steps and gone bumping down. I can still hear him whimpering.'

'I expect he got a bit of a shock,' said Bill. 'Go and get the lanterns and also the food, you boys. If we are going underground, we'd better prepare ourselves!'

Before the boys returned Micky had come back – a Micky very frightened and sorry for himself indeed. He looked for his beloved Philip but he wasn't there, so he went to Lucy-Ann and let her nurse him like a baby. He whimpered all the time, and Lucy-Ann was very distressed.

'Now, now – you haven't really hurt yourself,' she consoled him. 'Just a bruise or two, I expect. It was very, very naughty of Kiki. Still, you've made a wonderful find, Micky. Really wonderful!'

Kiki was very ashamed of herself. She went into a corner and put her head under her wing. Nobody took any notice of her at all.

The boys came back. Bill had had a good look down the hollow column with his torch. It puzzled him how the ancient folk, who had used the column as a way of getting underground, had made an entry in it. He could see no way of entry at all – except, of course, through the great hole broken in the column.

'It's a narrow spiral stairway,' he told the girls. 'Probably Jack is right. It may lead down to the vaults of the temple – a very secret way to them, possibly known only to the head priest. Come on, boys – help the girls up. I'll go down first.'

He dropped down deftly to the head of the steps. He

shone his torch down. Yes, it was a spiral stairway, as he had thought. It would be very narrow here, but probably got wider lower down. He had almost to crawl down the first twelve steps, and two or three times he nearly slipped because the treads were so narrow and steep.

The girls followed, helped by the boys. Dinah took one lantern, finding it very difficult indeed to manage with it, and at last had to hand it down to Bill because she needed both her hands at the top of the stairway. Lucy-Ann went down by the light of the second lantern, held by Jack.

The food was dropped in behind them. 'Might as well leave it there,' called back Bill. 'We can fetch it if we need it – and it's as good a hiding place as anywhere else.'

So they left the food at the top of the stairway on a stone ledge, and pretty soon all five were a good way down. As Bill had thought, the stone steps grew very much wider and easier a little further on.

Micky was now on Philip's shoulder again. Kiki had followed Jack into the column, very quiet and subdued. Down they went and down.

They came to the end of the stairway. It finished in a vast cave or vault that stretched out endlessly in the rock of the hill. The lanterns only lit up a small part of it.

'Yes – here are the vaults all right,' said Jack. 'The way we've come to them must have been a very secret one, I should think. Look – there's another way up, Bill – over there – more stone steps – straight ones this time, not spiral – going quite steeply upward.'

'Yes. I should think that was the ordinary way used up and down to the vaults,' said Bill. 'The way we came is very well hidden. See, from here you can't even see it, hidden behind that enormous rock.'

He swung his torch up the wide sweep of steps to which they had now walked over. 'I'll go up and see where they lead to,' said Bill, and up he went. They heard his steps going up and up, and then they stopped. They heard them coming down again.

'Came up against a stone ceiling!' he reported. 'Probably there's an exit there, closed up by a great stone trapdoor overgrown now with weeds and grass. That was obviously the ordinary way in and out. Well, where do we go from here?'

'Bill, let's look at the map again,' said Jack. 'I'm sure we must now be at the place marked "Bell". "Bell" for temple, you know.'

By the light of Bill's torch they all pored over the map again. Bill traced the 'Treasure path' with his finger. '"Two-Finger Rock",' he said. 'We were there, and were stopped by the walled-in place.'

'Yes – then the next thing marked is "Goddess",' said Philip. 'Can't think what *that* means!'

'Something on the way from "Two-Finger Rock" to here, perhaps,' said Jack. 'We could go and see. Then

464

look – there comes "Tomb". I suppose that's where someone was buried.'

'Yes – in a stone cell, I should think,' said Bill. 'And then we come to "Bird", which seems rather strange.'

'Then to "Bell",' said Jack triumphantly. 'And that's where *we* are, I bet!'

'Yes – but not where the treasure is,' said Bill. 'Look – you go on to here – marked "Labyrinth". Not so good, that.'

'What's a labyrinth, exactly?' asked Lucy-Ann.

'A maze – a place where it's so winding and muddling that you can easily get lost,' said Dinah. Lucy-Ann did not like the sound of that at all!

'Labyrinth,' she said. 'Well, what's next?'

'"Catacomb",' said Bill. 'And that, apparently, is where the treasure was put! What a way to bring it!'

'Let's go and find it!' said Jack cheerfully. He folded up the map and put it into his pocket. 'Come on – we've got nothing else to do. I must say it's nice and cool down here after the heat up above in the sun!'

'The thing is – which way do we go?' said Bill. 'One way goes to the "Labyrinth," the other to the "Tomb". But although the points of the compass are marked on the map to make things easy, we're not able to see the sun, so we have no idea of direction. Anyone got a compass?'

Nobody had. 'Well – we'll have to guess,' said Bill.

'There's only two ways to go apparently – to the right or to the left. Let's go right.'

So they set off to the right of the vault – Bill with his torch, the two girls holding hands and each boy carrying a lantern. The shadows were weird, and the hollow echo of their feet strange and rather alarming. Kiki and Micky did not like it at all, and they sat silent on the boys' shoulders.

They went for some way and then came to a wide passage that led downward in a smooth slope. It went for a good way, and then stopped short at what appeared to be a door. It was a wooden door and had once been immensely stout and strong. Even now it was still good, but one of the hinges had given way and, as the children first pushed and then pulled it, the other hinges gave way too and the door fell inward, almost on top of Bill. He just leapt away in time.

He shone his torch on it. Carved right across the door was an enormous bird. 'There you are – "Bird",' said Jack, pleased. 'That was one of the clues, wasn't it, Bill? It's an eagle – beautifully carved too.'

'Now we know which way we're going – the wrong way!' said Bill. 'Still, we'll go on now – this is amazing!'

Leaving the fallen Bird-door behind, they went through the opening. Looking back, they saw that the passage they were now following forked into two by the door – evidently there were two ways to go there – and the right one was the Bird-door – hence the clue called "Bird".

They went down a very narrow passage indeed. It ran downward, as the other had done, until it opened out into a narrow chamber. There was a smooth stone ledge at one side. At each end were wooden slabs carved with intricate symbols. The little company stopped to look at them.

'This must have been a tomb,' said Bill. 'Possibly where a priest was buried. There are many old burial places like this.'

'The sailors who carried the treasure must have had to carry it through this tomb,' said Philip. 'Perhaps they knew this way because they robbed tombs.'

There was no door to the tomb, but the doorway was cut out smooth and level. Possibly there had once been a door. Beyond it the passage began again, sloping downward more steeply still.

'Now for "Goddess",' said Jack. 'I say – it's a pretty good guide, this map, isn't it, Bill? If we had been able to make our way through "Two-Finger Rock" – where the hole was, you know – we could have used the map as an absolutely accurate guide.'

'Look out – there are steps,' said Bill. 'Cut into the rock. It gets pretty steep here.'

They went carefully down the steps. At the bottom was a beautiful archway. It was made of some kind of marble, set into the natural archway of the rock. Beyond the arch was a marble floor, still smooth and shining, for there was no dust underground.

The walls were carved too, the solid rock itself chipped out into figures and symbols. Eagles, doves, foxes, wolves – curious designs and patterns decorated the whole of the strange little cave.

'This must be "Goddess",' said Bill. 'A place to worship some little-known goddess, I imagine – hidden under the ground, only to be visited in secret.'

'Yes – that must be it,' said Philip. 'Isn't it strange? I suppose those carvings are hundreds of years old!'

'And now for the last clue – or first, whichever you like to call it,' said Bill. '"Two-Fingers"! We know what that is, anyway. But we shall come up against the other side of the stone door, I've no doubt. Here we go. My word, it's steep now, isn't it? No steps either. Be careful, you girls!'

They made their way, stumbling, down a very steep passage – and, just as Bill had said, they came up against the other side of the walled-up doorway they had seen when they had gone into 'Two-Fingers' hole. They stopped and considered.

'Yes – we've found the treasure route all right,' said Bill. 'Now – we'll start from here again – "Two-Fingers" – and we'll work our way back – past "Goddess" and "Tomb" and "Bird", till we come to "Bell" – the temple vault.'

'And *then* we'll go on!' said Jack, almost trembling with excitement. 'On to "Labyrinth" and "Catacomb" – and "TREASURE"!'

21

Kiki is very tiresome

Back they all went, through the curious little cell that must once have been a marble temple underground dedicated to some strange goddess – through the old tomb, and over the fallen door carved with the bird – and soon they were back in the temple vault.

'Now we start off the other way – to the left,' said Bill, who was now almost as excited as the four children. 'Come along – down this passage here. Hold up your lantern, Philip. My torch isn't very strong.'

'Does this passage lead into the labyrinth – the maze where people get lost?' asked Lucy-Ann a little fearfully. 'Shall *we* get lost?'

'No. We'll find some way of keeping safe,' said Bill. He and Jack looked closely at the map. 'Although this part is marked "Labyrinth", it shows only one route or passage – but every now and again the letter "R" turns up – for "Right", I suppose. We seem to have to turn to the right six times. Well, if we come to a fork, we shall know what to do – right every time! Come along! Put the map back in your pocket, Jack.'

They went down the low-roofed winding passage for a little way, and then Jack called out to the others. 'I say – anyone got Kiki?'

They all stopped. 'I haven't,' yelled back Lucy-Ann. 'Nor has Dinah.' Bill said he certainly hadn't, and as for Philip, he only had Micky on his shoulder.

'She flew off my shoulder when we got into the vault,' said Jack, remembering. 'Kiki! KIKI! Where are you?'

There was no squawk or screech in reply. 'Blow!' said Jack. 'I'll have to go back and get her. I'll catch you up.'

He ran back. The others went on. Jack had a lantern and could easily catch them up.

They soon came to a fork. 'We take the right-hand one,' said Bill. 'This way!' The passage twisted and turned extraordinarily often, and it was impossible to know if they were going forward, or if by so much turning and twisting were going in the opposite direction.

'One right turn – two – and this is the third,' said Philip. 'Three more right turns and we'll be at the catacomb!'

'Ooooh,' said Lucy-Ann. 'I hope it won't be long! I'm tired of these dark passages. This one is stony – I keep hitting my toes against some stone or other.'

'I wish Jack would catch us up,' said Philip, who was last. 'I keep thinking I hear him behind me – and when I turn he isn't there. Ought we to wait for him, Bill?'

'Yes – perhaps we ought,' said Bill, and they stopped. But no Jack came. Gracious, what *could* he be doing? Lucy-Ann began to feel worried.

'Jack!' she called. 'JACK! Are you coming?'

'Better go back for him,' said Bill, puzzled. 'I hope to goodness he hasn't missed the way. He knew we had to turn right each time.'

They went back for some way – and then Bill stopped. 'I suppose *we're* right?' he said. 'I don't some-how remember this passage – it's got such a very, very low roof. I've just bumped my head against it, and I certainly didn't do that coming along!'

'Oh, dear – surely we haven't missed our way – it seemed so easy – turn to the left each time going back,' groaned Dinah. 'It *must* be right, Bill.'

Bill was uneasy. He certainly did not remember this low-roofed passage. He made up his mind. 'We'll go back,' he said. 'I think we missed the last left turn, some-how.'

So they went back – but soon they came to a dead stop! The passage grew narrower and narrower, and at last nobody could squeeze through. *That* couldn't be right, either!

'Wrong again,' said Bill much more cheerfully than he felt. Secretly he was scared and horrified. How big was this labyrinth? How far did it go into the hill? On the map it looked a short route – but the labyrinth itself might spread for miles, intersected by mazes of passages, criss-crossing, wandering round and round.

'It's a real maze,' thought Bill. 'And probably there are only one or two direct routes across it – and we've missed the one we ought to have taken. Goodness knows how long we'll be wandering about here!'

'I wonder where Jack is,' said Lucy-Ann anxiously as they wound in and out of the curious passages of the labyrinth. 'I do hope he's all right.'

Where *was* Jack? He had gone back to get Kiki, and had heard her talking mournfully to herself in the temple vault, perched on the spiral stone stairway that led up to the broken column. He called her.

'Kiki! What are you doing there? Why didn't you come with us, idiot? Now I've had to come all the way back for you!'

Kiki was tired of being underground. She wanted to go up into the sunshine. Also she wanted a drink and there seemed to be no water below the ground.

'Kiki! Come along! I want to get back to the others,' called Jack.

'Send for the doctor,' said Kiki, preening her wings. 'Polly's got a cold, send for the doctor.'

'Don't be so *tiresome*,' said Jack, exasperated, and he went over to where Kiki sat. She flew up a few steps and cocked her head at Jack. He could see her plainly in the light of his lantern, and he was cross.

'You're behaving very badly,' he scolded her. 'Come down and sit on my shoulder, bad bird.'

'Naughty Polly, send for the doctor,' said Kiki, who seemed to have got the doctor on her brain. She flew up a few more steps. Jack had to follow. Blow Kiki! She *would* behave like this just when he wanted to catch up the others.

He reached the parrot and she flew higher again. Finally she disappeared.

Jack yelled up the stone steps angrily. 'You wait till I get you, you bad bird! Playing me up like this! For the last time, come down!'

A mocking voice floated down to him. 'Wipe your feet, don't sniff, pop goes the doctor!'

That was really too much for poor Jack! He climbed the spiral stone stairs as fast as he could, finding it very difficult indeed at the top, where they came up at the bottom of the broken column. At last he stood inside the column. He could see very well now, for the sun shone in through the hole in the stone. Kiki was sitting on the broken edge of the hole, preening herself in the sun. She kept a lookout for Jack, knowing he was very cross.

'Oh, I say!' she said loudly. 'Oh, I say!' She flew off the edge of the hole and disappeared from Jack's view. He could still hear her calling out, though. 'Oh, I say! Oh, I say!'

Saying all kinds of rude things about Kiki under his

breath, Jack found a rough foothold in the inside of the column and heaved himself up to the hole. He swung himself through the hole and jumped down into the sunshine, looking round for Kiki.

There she sat, not far off, in a tree of some kind, peering down the hill. 'Oh, I say!' she cried in a shrill voice, and then went off into a cackle of laughter.

Jack ran to the tree angrily – and then he stopped. Someone was coming up the hill – someone quite familiar – astonishingly familiar! Someone with teeth that stuck out in front, and with a chin that was hardly there at all!

'*Lucian!*' said Jack, too astonished to move. And Lucian it was. No wonder Kiki had suddenly gone off into a stream of 'Oh, I says!' Lucian stopped and stared at Jack as if he really could not believe his eyes.

'Oh, I say!' he said. 'Oh, I SAY.'

'Hello,' said Jack feebly, and grinned. 'Er – what in the world are *you* doing here?'

'Well, I might say the same to you,' said Lucian. 'Of all the extraordinary things! Well, I never! I can't believe it!'

'How long have you been here?' asked Jack. 'Why are you here?'

'I only came today,' said Lucian. 'My uncle's here, you see – goodness knows why! I don't know when he came exactly. Anyway, he got here and then sent for another motor boat to come to him here on Thamis, bringing some men he wanted, and some goods – and I thought I'd come along too. The *Viking Star* is held up, as you know, and I was bored stiff. I suppose my uncle's going to get some antiques here or something.'

Jack digested all this in silence. Oho! So Mr Eppy was there too, was he? He was hot on the track after all. Jack thought quickly. What a pity he had met Lucian! Now the boy would tell Mr Eppy.

'Jack, what are *you* doing here? You really must tell me!' said Lucian insistently. 'It's *too* extraordinary. And Kiki too! Where are the others?'

'Why should they be here?' said Jack. He did not want to tell Lucian about them – or where they were – or how to get to them. That would never do. He thought hard, but he could not come up with a plan – except that if he could get rid of Lucian he would pop down the broken column, get down the spiral stairway to the vault, and warn Bill. Bill would know what to do.

How could he get rid of Lucian? Lucian wasn't likely to let him out of his sight at all. And blow, blow, blow! – there was Mr Eppy coming up the hillside now with three other men!

Mr Eppy was too surprised to speak when he suddenly caught sight of Jack and Kiki. He stopped dead and stared through his dark glasses. He took them off, rubbed them, and was about to put them on again when Lucian went off into one of his silly fits of giggling.

'Oh dear! Oh, I say! You can't believe your eyes, can you, Uncle? Nor could I. But it really *is* Jack – and Kiki the parrot too.'

For one wild moment Jack wondered if he should run for it – run from the surprised men and hide somewhere till he could manage to get back to Bill and warn him.

But there was no time. At a word from Mr Eppy the three men with him ran up and stationed themselves behind Jack. Then Mr Eppy came up and stood in front of him.

'And what exactly are *you* doing here?' he said, in such a peculiar, menacing tone that Jack was astonished and scared. 'Where are the others?'

'We came to explore a bit,' said Jack at last. 'That's all. Anyone can come and explore these islands. The *Viking Star*'s engines broke down and the passengers were told they could hire motor boats and cruise among these islands.'

'Why did you come to *this* one?' asked Mr Eppy, still in a fierce voice. Lucian answered unexpectedly for him.

'Oh, Uncle! I expect he came hunting for the treasure you told me about.'

'Hold your tongue, idiot of a boy,' said Mr Eppy, almost spitting at poor Lucian. 'And now *you*' – he turned to Jack again – 'how dare you come trespassing on *my* island!'

'It isn't yours,' said Jack.

'It is. I have just bought it!' said Mr Eppy. 'Ah – you didn't know that – but you know *why!*'

22

Mr Eppy again

Yes, Jack did know why Mr Eppy had bought the island. He stared at the man miserably, his heart sinking. If the island was Mr Eppy's, then the treasure would be his too. Once again it looked as if the adventure had come to a sudden end.

'You know *why* I have bought it?' repeated Mr Eppy. 'Tell me, boy.'

'Well – I suppose you wanted to look for treasure on it,' said Jack in a low tone. 'But you won't find it. You only saw two pieces of the map, remember!'

'Then you will tell me what was on the other pieces,' said Mr Eppy in a dangerous tone.

Lucian was by now looking distinctly frightened. 'Here, I say, Uncle,' he began. 'I don't think you ought to talk to old Jack like that, you know. I mean to say . . .'

Mr Eppy took a step backwards and slapped Lucian neatly across the mouth. His hand made a noise like a whip-crack and Kiki immediately imitated it. Then she scolded Mr Eppy. 'Naughty boy, naughty boy, nit-wit, mister-sir!'

Lucian burst into howls. He put his hand up to his mouth, and stumbled away to a corner. The three men did not turn a hair.

'That is how I treat foolish boys,' said Mr Eppy, turning back to Jack. 'Are you going to be foolish too?'

Jack said nothing. Mr Eppy put his face close to his, and hissed at him so startlingly that Jack took a sudden step back and trod on the foot of one of the three men.

'Where are the others?' demanded Mr Eppy with his face close to Jack's. 'They must be here too. I sent away your boat yesterday. I threatened the man with prison for daring to land people on my island!'

'Oh – so *that's* why Andros ran away,' said Jack in disgust. 'What a foolish thing to do, Mr Eppy! Don't you know he'll come back again, probably with help?'

'He won't,' said Mr Eppy. 'He knows I shall put him in prison if he opens his mouth. No, no – I knew what I was doing. When I saw the boat there I guessed you and that big friend of yours were interfering here. I have heard of him! This is *my* island! Everything on it is mine.'

'All right, all right,' said Jack. 'But why send the boat away without us? Why not send us off too? If you had told us it was yours – and I know you do buy and sell islands – we wouldn't have trespassed without permission.'

'I wanted you here,' said Mr Eppy. 'You have the

plan, have you not? You did not leave it behind you? Ah, no – you would bring such a precious thing with you!'

Jack was silent. Of course – that was why Mr Eppy had sent the boat away without them – he meant to get the plan! And as he thought of that, Jack also thought of something else – something absolutely maddening.

He had the plan on him – the re-drawn one. He had looked at it with Bill underground, and had not given it back! Suppose Mr Eppy searched him. He would most certainly find it. How could he destroy it before he was searched?

'It was you, I suppose, who met the farmboy yesterday, and today too, and took the food I had sent for,' said Mr Eppy. 'A most extraordinary thing to do! I am not pleased with things like that – they make trouble for me.'

'Well – goodness gracious – how in the world were we to know that the food was for *you*, when we didn't know you were here, and couldn't understand a word the boy said?' cried Jack. 'Your boat wasn't in the creek. We didn't know anyone else was visiting the island.'

'I came to the other creek,' said Mr Eppy. 'But I shall not tell you where it is. No – not till you tell me where the others are – and then, when I have the plan, maybe, I say *maybe*, I will set you free from this island – all of you who have come to interfere with my plans.'

'It's ridiculous,' said Jack in disgust. 'We haven't come to interfere. Bill would be the first to say we'd all go, if he knew you had bought the island.'

'Where are the others?' barked Mr Eppy suddenly.

'Somewhere about,' said Jack indifferently. 'Why don't you look for them? And don't shout at me like that. I'm not Lucian.'

'Has this Bill the plan?' asked Mr Eppy, his voice getting sharper.

'Why don't you find him and ask him?' said Jack. 'Call him! See if he answers! If I'm here why shouldn't he be?'

Mr Eppy gave Jack such a sudden box on the ears that the boy had no time to dodge it. Kiki almost got the slap too, but rose into the air in time. She pounced down on the angry man and gave his ear such a vicious nip that he yelled in agony.

Jack suppressed a smile. Serve him right! Good old Kiki! The parrot sailed to a high branch and perched there, scolding hard.

'Bad boy, naughty boy! Gr-r-r-r! Go to bed, go to the doctor, go to the weasel!'

Mr Eppy said something sharply to the three silent men behind Jack. In a trice they had him pinned by the arms, flat on the ground. Then, with a practised hand, one of the men searched him. He drew out the plan at once.

Mr Eppy took it. Jack could imagine how his eyes gleamed behind the dark glasses!

'And so! *You* had it,' said Mr Eppy. He unfolded it, and saw that it was not the original plan. He looked at it closely. 'What is this? It is drawn by someone who has seen the other one – it's been drawn for you. Has it been deciphered and translated?'

'Find out for yourself,' said Jack, still lying on the ground. He expected a kick or a blow, but Mr Eppy was so intent on the re-drawn plan that he did nothing. Jack remembered that the man had seen only two parts of the map before – enough to tell him which island to come to, and that there was treasure there. He must now be studying the other parts with eager interest.

'"Two-Fingers",' he muttered. Then he looked at Jack. '"Two-Fingers",' he said. 'That showed on the piece I saw before – and I found the two-fingered rock. But there is no way through.'

'Oh – so that was your old battery we found in the hole, I suppose,' said Jack, sitting up. 'We wondered whose it was.'

Mr Eppy did not answer, or seem even to hear him. He was studying the map again. He was muttering something to himself. '"Two-Fingers" – "Goddess" – "Tomb" – "Bird" – "Bell" – "Labyrinth" – "Catacomb" – that is the route they took. The whole of it!' Then he began to mutter in Greek, and Jack could no longer understand him.

Lucian was still holding his hand up to his mouth, and his face was tear-stained. Kiki was down by him, pecking at his shoelace. 'Oh, I say!' she was repeating. 'Oh, I say!'

'Have you found the way at all?' demanded Mr Eppy.

'What way?' said Jack innocently.

'Pah! The way to the treasure chamber!' spat Mr Eppy.

'Pah!' spat Kiki at once. 'Pah!'

'I'll wring that bird's neck,' threatened Mr Eppy. 'Answer my question, boy.'

'No, we haven't found the way,' said Jack truthfully, feeling quite glad that they had gone the wrong way and not the right one in their following of the route! All the same, he wondered if Bill and the others had managed to find the way by now without him. But surely they would have waited for him. They must be wondering what in the wide world had happened to him! Jack hoped fervently that they would not all come climbing out of the broken column. If they did they would be taken prisoner by Mr Eppy and his men, and Bill would find it extremely difficult to keep his secret. In fact, it would not be any good his trying, now Mr Eppy had the map.

'Once Mr Eppy knows the way down the broken column the treasure is as good as his!' thought Jack. 'What a good thing Lucian didn't spot me getting out of it! I only hope the others don't make a sudden appearance. I'm sure they will soon!'

But they did not, for the very simple reason that they had lost their way in the labyrinth! They were still wandering about the passages, getting more and more anxious. They had lost Jack, and had lost their way too.

'This awful maze!' said Dinah in despair. 'Look, Bill – I'm *sure* we've been in *this* passage before. I remember the way this horrid piece juts out – it knocked my elbow last time, and this time too. I'm sure it's the same.'

'We're going round and round and in and out, and goodness knows whether we're near the vault or near the catacomb!' groaned Philip.

Bill was very worried. He stood and thought for a moment, trying in vain to get a sense of direction. It was so difficult underground! He set off again, and soon came to a fork.

'Well,' he said, 'I vote we go right here. It may be one of the places where we're supposed to go right. So we'll hope for the best! Come on!'

They trailed after him, Lucy-Ann getting very weary of it all. They reached another fork and turned right once more. Then they came to where the passages branched into four. Again they took the right-hand fork. Bill was feeling a little more cheerful. Perhaps they were on the right road now. They no longer came to blind ends where they had to turn back as they had been doing before. Ah – here was another fork. Well, to the right again!

The passage ended abruptly in a downward flight of steep steps. Bill swung the lantern up high and peered down the steps.

'We've come the right way at last!' he said. 'These must be the catacombs – underground caves and passages all joined together, that were once used as hiding places, burial places and goodness knows what!'

'Oh, Bill – have we really come right?' said Lucy-Ann joyfully. 'I thought we were lost for ever and ever! Do we go down the steps?'

'We do,' said Bill. 'I'll go first. Come on.'

Down he went and the others followed carefully. There were about thirty steps, and it seemed to the children as if they really were going down into the bowels of the earth. At the end was a strange place stretching out into the darkness. Lining its walls were stone shelves, rocky niches, hollowed-out places that looked as if they had been used for storing things in, or for people to hide in and sleep.

They came to a hole in the floor of this extraordinary place. Bill shone his torch down it. It was a shaft leading downward, and there were footholds in the rock. 'I'm going down,' said Bill. 'I've got a hunch this is the place!'

He disappeared down the shaft with his torch, and soon his voice came back, excited and loud.

'This is it! This is the treasure chamber – THE TREASURE'S STILL HERE!'

23

Treasure – and trickery!

The three children and Micky almost fell down the shaft, they were in such a hurry. They handed Bill the lantern and, by the light of that and of Bill's torch, they looked in wonder round the curious treasure chamber.

It was perfectly round, as if it had been hollowed by machinery from the rock – though actually, of course, it had been done by hand. Thrown higgledy-piggledy into this enormous round cave – perhaps flung down the shaft in a hurry – were mouldering barrels and boxes and brass-bound chests.

Bursting out of them was a perfect medley of strange and amazing goods – chains of some kind of metal, set with precious stones – brooches, armlets, anklets – combs for the hair made probably of gold, and set with tiny stones – beautiful vases of metal, perhaps gold, perhaps brass, but too tarnished to tell. Beautifully wrought daggers lay in one corner, and what looked like armour of some kind in another – all fallen from the mouldered chests and boxes, or possibly burst out of these when they were thrown down the shaft so long, long ago.

There were broken models of figures and articles that looked like drinking cups and bowls, and yet other things whose use the children simply could not guess.

'Well, well, well,' said Bill, as thrilled as the children. 'What a treasure hoard! Andra's treasure, maybe – we shall never really know. But whether it is or not, it is certainly worth half a small kingdom because of its age! Look at this dagger – it must be hundreds of years old – perfectly preserved down in this dry shaft. I should think only our museums can show things like this now.'

'Bill! It's super!' said Philip, his eyes shining in the lantern-light as he picked up treasure after treasure, everything beautifully modelled and carved.

'I suppose the things like robes and cloaks and shoes have all mouldered away,' said Dinah regretfully. 'I'd like to have dressed up in those. Oh, Bill – we've really found it!'

'I wish Jack was here,' said Lucy-Ann, with tears in her voice. 'He would have loved it so. Where *can* he be, Bill?'

'I should think he probably took a long time finding Kiki and decided he wouldn't risk coming after us by himself,' said Bill. 'I'll tell you what we'll do – we'll go back and find him, and then we'll bring him here to have a look at the greatest treasure in the world!'

'But shall we be able to find our way back?' said Philip doubtfully. Bill was very doubtful about this too. Also his torch was giving out and he was sure the oil in the lantern would not last much longer. It was very necessary to find their way back, pick up Jack, and also have something to eat! Excitement had kept them going, but now all of them were feeling very hungry indeed.

'If we manage to get back quickly and find Jack we'll all have a meal,' said Bill. 'Then if Jack's lantern is all right we'll use that to come here again – but this time we'll be sensible and mark the walls as we go along! Actually I think we could find our way here easily enough if we concentrated on going right, right, right all the time. We must have missed one of the right turns.'

They climbed back up the shaft, leaving the extraordinary hiding place behind them. What a strange treasure chamber! How old was it? Had anyone else seen it since it had been put there?

They found themselves in the catacombs again. It was easy to get back to the steep flight of steps. Up they went into the labyrinth and began to make their way through the passages. 'Now we must keep left, left, left,' said Bill, 'then we shall be quite all right.'

But no – once more they missed their way and began the everlasting wandering round and round and in and out of the maddening underground maze. Lucy-Ann was almost crying with weariness.

All this time Micky had been quietly on Philip's shoulder, clinging to his head in awkward places. He too was tired of the curious dark walk that everyone was taking. He wanted to be out in the open, he wanted something to eat and, even more, he wanted something to drink.

He suddenly leapt off Philip's shoulder and landed on the floor of the passage. He began to scud along by himself. Philip called out to him.

'Hey, Micky, Micky! Come here! We don't want to lose you too!'

Micky slowed down, but he still went on. Bill called to Philip. 'Leave him, Philip! I believe he knows the way out. Animals have a good sense of direction, you know – a kind of homing instinct. Maybe he can take us straight to the broken column!'

Micky did not know what Bill was saying, but if he had known he would most certainly have agreed. Of course he knew the way! Of course his instinct told him exactly the right way to go – left, left, left, without any silly mistake such as the humans had made. Why, he, Micky, could have taken them straight back to the vaults at any time if only they had told him they wanted to go!

'Well, here we are in the vault again!' said Philip thankfully when, in a very short space of time indeed, they came out into the enormous temple vault. Lucy-Ann was so thankful that she began to cry very quietly to herself. Nobody could see. She wiped away a few tears, then stopped her crying, feeling rather ashamed. She slipped her hand into Bill's. He squeezed it comfortingly.

'We're all right now,' he said. 'We've found the treasure and found our way back – now we'll find Jack! As we haven't heard or seen anything of him, I imagine he's out in the open, waiting for us!'

Jack was still in the courtyard with Mr Eppy, Lucian and the three men. It was some time later, and the boy had not been having at all a nice time. Mr Eppy had been on and on at him, trying to find out where the others were, and whether Jack knew the route to the treasure.

He had threatened Jack, had boxed his ears several times, and had boxed Lucian's too when he had tried to come to Jack's help. Jack had been surprised at Lucian for that. He had always thought him such a feeble boy. He looked at Lucian gratefully.

'Thanks, Lucian,' he said. 'But don't interfere, old chap – you'll only get hurt. I can look after myself. Your uncle will get into trouble for ill-treating me, don't you worry!'

Jack had begun to feel extremely hungry. So had the others, presumably, because Mr Eppy changed the subject suddenly and began asking Jack where they had put the food they had got from the farm-boy. Jack remembered perfectly well where it was – inside the broken column, on the stone ledge at the base of it, where the stone stairway began – but how could he say that? It would give the secret away completely!

So he sat silent, shaking his head to Mr Eppy's exasperated questions, getting more and more hungry – and getting really rather anxious about the others too. Where in the world could they be? The sun was going down already, and soon it would be night.

And then Kiki began to talk excitedly. She left Jack and flew to the broken edge of the hole in the column. She peered down it. Jack bit his lip. Oh, Kiki, Kiki, don't give the game away!

Kiki had heard the others coming. She had heard Bill's deep voice as he came up the spiral stairway; she had heard Lucy-Ann's high voice just behind. She had gone to welcome them.

'Kiki!' called Jack. 'Come here.'

'Shut the door, shut the door, wipe your feet, beg your pardon!' shouted Kiki excitedly, her head inside the column. And then an answering call came from inside too.

'Hallo, Kiki, old bird! So there you are! Where's Jack?' It was Bill's cheery deep voice.

Mr Eppy sprang to attention at once. He gave a short sharp order to his three men, and they ran to the column to wait. Jack gave a yell.

'Look out, Bill! Danger! Look out!'

There was silence from inside the column. Then Bill's voice came up again.

'What's up?'

'Mr Epp . . .' began Jack, and was silenced as Mr Eppy placed a heavy and very rough hand over his mouth.

Bill shouted again. 'What's up?' As he got no reply he appeared at the hole in the column and swung himself astride the edge. The men were at the other side, hidden, waiting to spring.

Bill saw Mr Eppy apparently holding down Jack, and he leapt off the broken edge of the hole in the column at once. The three men sprang on him and bore him to the ground.

One sat on his head so that he could not shout. Jack squirmed under Mr Eppy's hand, kicking and trying to bite, but the man was very strong indeed.

Then up the column came Philip, wondering what had happened to Bill, and when he saw him being well and truly sat on he sprang to his rescue. Mr Eppy shouted a few words and the men released Bill. He sat up at once, feeling his nose, and wondering if any of his teeth were loose!

'What on earth is all this?' he began. But before he could go on, a call from inside the column came to him. It was Lucy-Ann.

'Bill! Oh, Bill! What's happened? Can we come out?'

Bill considered. 'I'm going to help the girls out,' he said to Mr Eppy, who nodded, and very soon both girls, and a very scared Micky, were standing in the old court-yard with Philip, Jack and Bill.

'What's happened?' said Lucy-Ann. 'Oh, I'm so glad to see you, Jack. I was dreadfully worried about you. Gracious, there's *Lucian*!'

'Oh, I say!' said Lucian, trying to put a brave face on things. 'Fancy meeting *you* here!'

Mr Eppy said something snappish in Greek and poor Lucian collapsed again. Then Mr Eppy turned to Bill, who was now eyeing him with a very sinister look indeed. Bill was extremely angry, and his injured nose was swelling rapidly.

'Look here, Eppy, or whatever your name is,' he said, 'you're going to run into serious trouble. You can't roam round with a posse of shady fellows like these, acting like gangsters. What are you doing here, anyway?'

'It's *my* island,' said Mr Eppy with a note of triumph in his voice. 'I've bought it. You can clear off – *when* I've found the way to the treasure with your help. Otherwise I shall have you arrested for trespassing and for trying to steal what is mine.'

'You're mad,' said Bill, in scorn. 'Absolutely crazy. I don't believe a word of it! You only heard of the island a day or two ago – you haven't had time to buy it. That's a wonderful tale – but you won't get *me* to believe it. Now, you keep your hands off all of us, and behave yourself – or you're the one that's going to land in prison and pretty quick too!'

Mr Eppy gave an order – and Bill was pounced on again by the three men. He was down on the ground in no time, and one of the men was tying his wrists and ankles together. Bill was strong, but his strength was no use against the three. Mr Eppy had Jack by the wrists so that he could not go to Bill's help, and as soon as Philip ran to help, he was struck by one of the men and sent spinning. Lucy-Ann began to cry with fright.

Lucian did nothing. He was trembling in a corner. Kiki and Micky were high up in a tree, watching in amazement. What was all this to-do? Kiki swooped down and gave Mr Eppy a nip on the ear again, and he nearly let Jack go, the pain was so sharp.

After Bill was tied up, the boys were tied too. 'Don't touch the girls,' threatened Bill. 'If you do you'll get more than you bargained for when we get out of here!'

It was no use. Dinah and Lucy-Ann were also tied up. Dinah was angry and mutinous, and Lucy-Ann was very frightened.

'And now,' said Mr Eppy, 'now *we* go to find the Andra treasure. *My* treasure! You had only the plan – I have the island, and I shall soon own the treasure! Thank you for showing me the way down!'

He went inside the column, and the three men followed him. Lucian was beckoned over and made to go down just behind his uncle. He looked very frightened.

'Well!' said Bill. 'Of all the scoundrels! Can we possibly get free whilst they're down there? It's our only chance!'

24

Prisoners!

Everyone waited till the last man had disappeared down the column. Then Bill spoke.

'Well, I'm blessed if I'll ever look at a treasure map again, or listen to anything you kids have to tell me! It's fatal. We plunge into trouble immediately. Jack, Philip – can you possibly loosen your ropes?'

'I've been trying,' said Philip, and Jack said the same. 'Those beasts know how to tie knots all right. The rope is biting into my ankles like anything, and I can hardly move my hands.'

All of them had their hands tied behind their backs, and it was really impossible to get free. Bill rolled himself over and over to the girls. He was very sorry for poor Lucy-Ann. Dinah was as tough as a boy, but Lucy-Ann could not help being scared.

'Lucy-Ann, don't be upset,' said Bill, ending up just by her. 'We'll think of some wonderful way to get even with these rogues.'

'I hope they'll get lost in the labyrinth,' said Jack fiercely, still struggling with the rope that tied his wrists.

'They probably will,' said Bill. 'In any case, they'll be a long time gone. We must somehow get free before they come back.'

'The first thing *I'll* do when I get free is to hop inside the column and get some of the food we put down there,' said Jack. 'That's if the brutes have left us any! I bet they've taken most of it with them.'

Bill privately thought they probably would have taken it, but he didn't say so. He gave up trying to loosen the rope round his wrists. It only made it cut into his flesh unbearably.

He looked round to see if there was a sharp stone he could perhaps rub his ropes on. He saw one and rolled over to it. But as his hands were behind his back he could not see what he was doing, and cut his fingers on the stone till they bled. He gave it up.

Kiki was up in the tree, muttering to herself. All the shouting and struggling had frightened her. She cocked her head down at Jack and decided it was safe to go to him. She flew down and landed on his middle.

'Send for the doctor,' she said, her head on one side. 'Send for the doctor, mistersir.'

'Good idea, Kiki,' said Jack, with an attempt at a grin. 'Tell him to come quickly! Telephone him at once!'

Kiki at once gave an imitation of a telephone bell

ringing. It sounded queer in that old ruined courtyard! Even Lucy-Ann gave a little laugh.

'Hello, hello!' said Kiki, pleased at the attention she was getting. 'Hello!'

'She's telephoning now!' grinned Jack. 'Good old Kiki. Got the doctor yet? Tell him we're all suffering from a nasty attack of Eppy-itis!'

Micky leapt down from the tree to join in the fun. He too had been badly scared, but now that everyone was talking and laughing, and the noisy men had gone, he felt safer. He landed on Philip, and tried to cuddle on to his shoulder. Philip was sitting up, his hands tied behind him.

'Sorry I can't stroke you, old thing, and make a bit of fuss of you after your scare,' said the boy. 'But my hands are tied! Yes, that's right – go and look for them. I've still got them – but they're behind me!'

Micky badly wanted to be nursed, but he could not find any arms to cuddle into! He went behind Philip to investigate. What had the boy done with his hands and arms? Ah – there they were behind him! Micky pulled at Philip's hands with his tiny paws. He wanted to be stroked and petted.

'Sorry, Micky – nothing doing,' said Philip. He grinned round at the others. 'Micky can't understand why I don't use my hands to pet him! He's pulling at them!'

Micky had discovered the rope that bound Philip's

wrists together. He was puzzled. What had Philip done with this rope? Why was it so tightly round the boy's hands? Micky tugged at the rope, and pulled at the knot.

Philip sat very still. 'That's right, Micky,' he said, in a caressing voice. 'That's right! You tackle those knots. Then I can pet you all you like!'

Everyone pricked up their ears at once. They looked eagerly at Philip. 'I say, Philip – is Micky – can Micky – do anything?'

'Don't know,' said Philip. 'He's fiddling about like anything. Go it, Micky. Pull those knots undone!'

But Micky couldn't. His tiny paws were not strong enough to undo the tightly tied knots of the rope. He gave it up. But he thought of something else!

He put his mouth down to the rope, and tried to gnaw it with his teeth!

'What *are* you doing, Micky?' cried Philip, feeling the wet little mouth against his wrist. 'Gosh, Bill, the clever little thing is trying to *gnaw* through the rope now!'

Everyone watched Philip intently. His face showed clearly all he was thinking. 'That's it, Micky – bite away!' he said. 'Good little monkey! No, go away, Kiki – don't interfere with Micky!'

Kiki had gone to Philip and was now getting behind him to see what Micky was up to. She watched him.

'One, two, three, GO!' she said, for all the world as if she was encouraging him.

'Come here, Kiki. Leave Micky alone in his good work,' ordered Jack, and Kiki came obediently.

'How's Micky getting on?' asked Bill.

'Fine, I think,' answered Philip, trying his hands to see if they felt any looser. 'I think the rope doesn't feel quite so tight. Go it, Micky.'

It was a long job, but Micky was patient and perservering. Once he knew that he was doing what Philip wanted, he went on and on. Bill marvelled at the way Philip understood animals and animals understood him. Any creature would do anything in the world for Philip!

'They're getting loose!' exclaimed Philip. 'Go on, Micky – just a bite or two more!'

And, sure enough, after another bout of patient gnawing, the rope snapped when Philip pulled on it. He brought his freed hands round to the front of him, groaning.

'My word – they're painful! Thanks, Micky, old thing – you did a very good job of work. Wait till my hands feel a bit better and I'll pat you from head to tail!'

The rope was still dangling from one of his wrists, the knots in it tied as tightly as ever. Philip picked it off with the other hand. He opened and shut his numb fingers, and then proceeded to pet the little monkey, who, delighted to be fussed, snuggled into Philip's arms with contented little grunts.

Nobody hurried Philip. Nobody begged him to be

quick and undo *their* bonds. Everyone knew that it was right for Micky to have his reward.

'Now, that's enough, old fellow,' said Philip at last. 'I must see to the others. You come and help!'

Philip put Micky on to his usual place on his shoulder. He felt in his pocket for a knife. His hands still felt queer and stiff, but they were rapidly getting more life into them. He brought out his knife and clicked it open.

He cut the rope round his ankles, and then he tried to stand up. His feet felt numb, for his ankles had been tied very tightly. But he was soon able to walk steadily. He went straight over to the girls.

He cut their bonds with his knife and Lucy-Ann gave a groan of thankfulness. 'Oh, Philip – thank you! That's better. Dinah, are your hands all right?'

'Bit stiff and numb,' said Dinah, rubbing them together. 'Wouldn't I like to tie up Mr Eppy! And wouldn't I make the ropes tight! The brute! He must be mad.'

Soon everyone was free. Bill found it hardest to stand because his ankles had been tied very viciously, and so had his hands. It took him some time to get the blood flowing freely in them, and it was a very painful process at first.

Everyone made a fuss of Micky, and the little monkey enjoyed it all thoroughly, chattering softly. Jack kept an eye on Kiki. She was jealous, and was looking out for a chance to nip Micky's long tail.

'I'll tie *you* up if you try any tricks, Kiki,' warned Jack, and tapped her smartly on the beak. She put her head under her wing, muttering to herself. 'Poor Polly, poor Polly, don't sniff, use your hanky!'

'She's irrepressible!' said Bill, still massaging his wrists. 'Well, I feel better now. What about some food, lads? *If* it's still there, of course!'

Jack was halfway to the column already. He had to get Philip to give him a good leg-up because his ankles still felt weak. Up he went, and dropped down inside. He looked about for the food. It was dark inside the column now, for the sun had gone. He felt about and, to his delight, found some bread and what felt like cheese. He called to Philip.

'Look out, Philip, I'm throwing the food out.'

Philip waited. Out came bread, cheese and a packet of some kind of meat. 'Wait a bit – here's some more bread,' shouted Jack, and out it came.

Jack climbed out again, grinning. 'They must have been in such a hurry to get to the treasure that they didn't even stop for a snack!' he said. 'They *must* have seen the food there.'

'Bill, is it safe to sit and have a meal?' asked Lucy-Ann anxiously.

'Quite safe,' said Bill. 'I'm going to sit here by the column and I shall be very, very sorry for anyone who tries to get out whilst *I'm* here!'

25

What happened in the night

It was getting quite dark now. The sun had gone a long time ago, and the children could hardly see one another as they sat together in the courtyard, munching hungrily.

'I've never known bread and cheese to taste so lovely,' said Dinah. 'Actually I didn't think this cheese was terribly nice yesterday – sort of sweetish – but today it's heavenly.'

'Only because you're so hungry,' said Jack, giving Kiki some of his. 'It's goat-milk cheese, isn't it, Bill? I say, look at Micky stuffing himself.'

'Pop goes Micky,' remarked Kiki, coming in at the right moment as usual. 'One, two, three, POP!'

'Idiot,' said Jack. 'Well, Bill – what are you thinking about?'

'Quite a lot of things,' said Bill soberly. 'We've had an extraordinary day. And I'm just planning what to do about it.'

'Wasn't that treasure wonderful!' said Lucy-Ann, her eyes shining.

Jack had, of course, heard all about their adventures underground by now, and was very envious because he was the only one who had not seen the treasure chamber, with its remarkable collection of riches. He had listened with amazement, and had wished and wished he had been with the others.

'What are your plans, Bill?' asked Philip, feeling that he could think sensibly again now that he was free and had had a good meal. 'I suppose we can't do much tonight.'

'No, we can't,' said Bill. 'That's quite certain. We've been through enough today without taking on any more adventures. Besides, the girls are nearly asleep, poor things!'

So they were. Excitement and exercise had completely tired them out. Lucy-Ann lay cuddled against Dinah, her eyes closed.

'Well, I'm pretty sleepy myself,' said Jack. He yawned loudly. 'I wouldn't mind a nice long snooze!'

'Anyway, Bill – what *could* we do, even if we *wanted* to do anything tonight?' asked Philip, beginning to yawn too. 'We can't escape! Andros won't come back, that's obvious, if Mr Eppy has threatened him with prison. After all, he's only an ordinary boatman! I expect Mr Eppy gave him plenty of money too, to make up for us not having paid him.'

'Yes – money and threats combined would soon send Andros away,' said Bill. 'In any case, Andros would know, of course, that Mr Eppy had his own boat here – possibly two boats, as he sent for more men and goods. So we shouldn't be absolutely stranded as Mr Eppy could always bring us back.'

'Gosh, yes – his boats must be *some*where, mustn't they?' said Philip, waking up considerably. 'We've only got to find them, Bill, and we're all right! Hadn't we better snoop round now, before the others come back from underground?'

'No. Nothing more tonight,' said Bill firmly. 'I've already planned to do that tomorrow. When we find Mr Eppy's boat or boats, we'll be all right, I hope. Now listen – I'm going to be on guard for the first four hours, and, after that, you, Jack, and then you, Philip, will have a two-hour watch, and by that time it will be morning.'

'What are we going to watch for? Are we to wait for dear old Eppy to pop his head out and say "Hello, there"?' asked Jack, with a grin.

'Exactly,' said Bill. He had now lighted one of the lanterns, and it gave a weird light to the scene. 'You two boys are tired – you won't be any good at watching till you've had a sleep. You can have your turn when I wake you.'

'Right,' said Jack, settling himself against Philip. 'We'll let the big tough guy watch first. As a matter of fact, I believe I'm asleep already.'

'What will you do if the others appear?' asked Philip, with interest. 'Knock them on the head as they come out of the hole?'

'Probably,' said Bill, and he lit his pipe. 'You don't need to worry about that. Good night! I'll wake you in four hours' time.'

The two boys were asleep almost before he had finished his sentence. The smell of Bill's tobacco wafted round the courtyard. Micky smelt it in his sleep and cuddled closer to Philip. He did not like the smell of tobacco. Kiki was standing on Jack, her head under her wing. The girls were absolutely still, sleeping soundly although they had such an uncomfortable resting place.

Bill put out the lantern. Only the glow of his pipe shone in the courtyard now and again. He was thinking hard. He went over all the happenings of the last two days. He considered Mr Eppy's assertion that the island was his. He puzzled over the whereabouts of the other creek, where probably Mr Eppy's boat or boats were. He wondered how the little party underground was getting on. He hoped fervently they were well and truly lost in the labyrinth.

He made his plans for the next day. They would find the boats. That would be the first thing. Where on earth would the creek be – the second creek that Andros had spoken about? Perhaps it would . . .

A noise stopped his thoughts at once. He put down his pipe and stood up, a silent figure close to the broken column. He listened. The noise had come from underground, he was sure of that.

Well – if it was the company coming back, he was in for a wakeful night! Bill picked up a large piece of wood that he had had his eye on all evening. It had probably been part of a door or window frame – now it would make a very good weapon!

He stood by the column, listening intently. A scraping noise came up to him – someone was climbing up the last part of the stone spiral. The noise stopped. The someone was evidently in the column now. What was he doing? He appeared to be feeling about for something. 'The food!' thought Bill, with a grin. 'Well – it's gone!'

A little whimper came up to him, and then a shaky voice said, in a low tone, 'Jack! Philip! Are you there?'

'Why – it's Lucian!' thought Bill in astonishment. 'Well – he can't be alone!'

He listened again. The whimpering began once more, rather like a miserable dog's. There was no sound of any other voice, or of anyone else coming up the stairway. Bill made up his mind. He leapt up to the broken edge of the hole in the column, switched on his torch and looked down.

Lucian was standing below him, his terrified face looking up, dirt caked on his cheeks. He put up his hand as if he expected Bill to aim a blow down at him.

'Lucian!' said Bill. 'What are you doing here? Where are the others?'

'I don't know,' moaned poor Lucian. 'They only took me down as far as that vault place at the bottom of these steps. They wouldn't let me go any further with them. They told me to stay there till they came back, and not to stir. My uncle said he'd half kill me if he didn't find me waiting for them when they came back.'

'Didn't they come back, then?' said Bill, keeping his torch on Lucian's face.

'No. And they went hours ago,' cried Lucian. 'I don't know what's happened to them. And I'm so hungry and cold and tired – and I'm frightened down there, too. I didn't dare to have my torch on all the time in case the battery gave out.'

Bill believed the frightened boy. 'Come on up,' he said. 'Here – take my hand and jump. Go on, Lucian, *jump*! Surely you can leap up here.'

Poor Lucian couldn't. In the end Bill had to get into the column and shove him up to the hole. Even then Lucian looked about to fall off. He was in a terrible state of nerves.

At last he was safely down in the courtyard, and Bill gave him some bread and cheese. He fell on it as if he hadn't eaten for a month.

A thought suddenly struck him. 'I say – how did you get free? I mean – weren't you all tied up?'

'Yes,' said Bill grimly. 'We were. But fortunately for you, we got free – yes, all of us. The boys are asleep over there, and the girls are nearby. No, don't wake them –

they're tired out. If we'd all been tied up still, you would have stayed in that column all night. Not a nice thought, Lucian!'

'No,' said Lucian, and shivered. 'I wish I hadn't come to this horrible island. What's going to happen? Are you going down to look for my uncle? He must be completely lost, you know.'

'He can stay lost, as far as I'm concerned,' said Bill. 'In fact, it will do him good. Your uncle is not a man I've any kindly feelings for, at present.'

'No. He's horrible,' agreed Lucian. 'Once he'd found the treasure he'd planned to leave you stranded here, all of you, and go off by himself to get more men to come and remove it.'

'Nice, thoughtful fellow,' said Bill. 'Well, young man, you'd better get some sleep. And tomorrow you're going to help us, to make up for the misdeeds of your nasty-minded uncle.'

'Oh – I'd be very glad to help you,' said Lucian at once. 'I would really. I'm on your side, you know that.'

'Yes, I expect you are,' said Bill. 'You'll have to be from now on, anyway!'

'How can I help you tomorrow?' asked Lucian.

'By taking us to the creek where your uncle's boats are,' said Bill at once.

'Oh, of course – if only I can remember where it is,' said Lucian anxiously. 'I'm not awfully good at remembering routes, you know. But I daresay I'll remember that.'

'You'll have to,' said Bill grimly. 'And now, go to sleep. No – don't go over to the boys. Just stay where you are. And mind – if your precious uncle arrives during the night, there's to be no warning to him from *you*. Otherwise some unpleasant things will happen to you.'

'Oh, I tell you I'm on *your* side now,' protested Lucian, and settled himself as comfortably as he could. 'Good night, sir. See you in the morning!'

26

Next morning

Four hours later Bill woke Jack. In a few sentences he told the surprised boy about the arrival of Lucian. 'He keeps saying he's on our side now, but you never know with a nitwit like that,' he warned Jack. 'So keep your eye on him. And if you hear the *slightest* sound from underground, prod me awake at once, Jack!'

'Right, Bill,' said Jack, fresh from his sound sleep. 'I say – they've been a long time underground, haven't they? They *must* be lost!'

'I sincerely hope so,' said Bill. 'I don't imagine they will be lost for ever, however desirable that might be – that labyrinth isn't a frightfully big one. Well, I'm going to sleep, Jack. Keep your wits about you!'

Jack was still sleepy. He was afraid he might find it difficult to keep awake, so he lit the lantern, and walked round the courtyard. He shone the light on to Lucian. He was so fast asleep that he did not even stir. Philip was soundly off too, and as for the girls, not an inch of their faces was to be seen, they were cuddled up so closely to one another.

Kiki accompanied Jack on his rambles round the courtyard. She knew she had to be quiet, so she whispered all the time. She wasn't very good at whispering, and tickled Jack's ear till he could not bear it any longer. He took her off his shoulder, and made her perch on one of his arms.

His two hours went by without anything happening at all. He woke Philip. It took a long time because the boy was so very sound asleep. As fast as Jack rolled him over to wake him, he rolled back again, his eyes still shut.

Jack took off one of Philip's shoes and tickled the soles of his feet. That woke him up all right! Philip sat straight up and glared round at the lantern Jack held.

'What are you . . .' he began, in a loud voice, and Jack shushed him at once.

'Shh, idiot! You'll wake the rest! Sorry about tickling your feet, but I simply *couldn't* wake you! It's your turn to watch now.'

Philip put on his shoe, saying something uncomplimentary to Jack under his breath. Micky woke up too, and looked in astonishment round the yard. He had forgotten where he was.

Jack told Philip in whispers about Lucian's arrival. Philip was amused. 'So Lucian is on our side now!' he said. 'Well – he's not a bad sort really – only he's *such* a nitwit! Poor Lucian – I guess he was scared out of his life!

Right, I'll keep my eye on him – though honestly he wouldn't have the nerve to do anything he shouldn't. And if our dear Mr Eppy pops his head up out of the column, I shall have the greatest pleasure in conking him good and hard.'

Jack grinned. 'Well, I'm off to sleep again,' he said. 'Good hunting, Philip!'

Philip's eyes persisted in closing, as he sat there keeping watch. He got up and walked about, as Jack had done. It would be an unforgivable thing to sleep while he was on guard. Quite unthinkable. He wondered what the time was, and glanced at his watch. The hands were phosphorescent, and showed him the time. Five o'clock – or getting on that way. He looked at the eastern sky. It was already silvering with the dawn.

It was almost at the end of Philip's two hours that the noise came. By this time the sun was up and the sunlight was on everything, clean and new and beautiful. Philip was enjoying the warmth of the first slanting beams when he heard the noise.

He pricked up his ears, and Micky began to chatter softly. 'Shh!' said Philip. 'I want to listen.' Micky was silent at once.

The noise came again – the scraping of boots on stone. They're coming! thought Philip, and he ran to where Bill was sleeping face down in the grass that grew over the yard. 'Bill! Wake up! They're coming!'

Bill woke up at once. He sprang to his feet, all sleep

gone in an instant. Jack awoke too, and so did the girls. Only Lucian slept on, but nobody took any notice of him.

Bill ran to the column. He took the big wedge of wood from Philip. 'Stand back,' he said to the girls. 'I don't expect for a moment I'll have much trouble, but you never know. I'm not standing any nonsense from Eppy and Co.'

He stationed himself just under the broken edge of the hole in the column. He listened. Voices came up to him. Someone was evidently now standing inside the column, having come up to the top of the spiral stairway. Bill heard what was said, but couldn't understand it.

However, he recognized Mr Eppy's voice, and took a firm hold of his piece of wood! Mr Eppy stood still for a moment and listened to someone shouting up to him from the stairway below. Then he called up in a low voice.

'Lucian? Are you there, Lucian?'

Lucian *was* there – but he was fast asleep, so of course he didn't answer. Mr Eppy called again softly. 'Lucian!'

Bill answered, in a grim voice. '*I'm* here – Bill Cunningham – and I'm waiting for you, Mr Eppy! The moment you try to get out of there I shall knock you back – with this weapon!' Bill banged his wedge of wood down on the column with such a noise that everyone jumped violently, and Lucian woke up.

There was a dead silence inside the column. Then

there was a scraping noise, as if someone else was coming up the stairway. Voices spoke together, very low.

'How did you get free?' came Mr Eppy's voice again. 'Did Lucian free you? He's not here.'

'No, he didn't,' said Bill.

The voices spoke together again. Then Mr Eppy called up urgently.

'Mr Cunningham! My men tell me that they have just found poor Lucian down here – badly hurt. He needs help. Let us come up at once.'

This was a most astonishing piece of news, especially to Lucian, whose mouth fell open in amazement. He was about to speak when Jack nudged him to be quiet. Bill was handling this!

'Sorry to hear that, Mr Eppy,' said Bill. 'Hand him up and we'll look after him. But you remain below. That's definite.'

Another conference took place in low voices. Then Mr Eppy spoke again.

'I must ask you to allow us to come up with the boy. He is seriously hurt. I am very distressed about him.'

Lucian's face was a study. Dinah almost giggled as she watched him. Bill answered at once.

'Nothing doing. Nobody comes up except, er, Lucian. Hand him over.'

As Lucian was even then sitting on the grass in the courtyard it was quite impossible for Mr Eppy to hand him over. Lucy-Ann whispered to Dinah, 'Isn't he a terrible storyteller!'

Bill began banging idly on the column with his wedge. 'Well, you don't seem to want to part with Lucian,' he called. 'Now I warn you – if anyone appears at the hole in this column they're for it!'

Bang, bang! That was Bill's piece of wood on the column again. It couldn't have pleased Mr Eppy very much. He was not a brave man, and it was easy to imagine his feelings down in the column!

'Can we have some food?' he called at last.

'No,' Bill shouted back hard-heartedly. 'There is barely enough for our breakfast.'

Judging by the scraping noises that could then be heard, Mr Eppy and the others had decided to go back down the stairs and have a conference. Bill jerked his head at Jack.

'Give out the food that's left to everyone. I'm staying here in case any of these fellows tries something funny. I have a feeling there's a revolver or two among them, so whatever happens I can't let them appear at the top.'

Jack and Philip shared out the remaining food. Bill gulped down his share, keeping eyes and ears open for any movement or sound from the broken column. But there was none.

He beckoned the others over to him at the end of the rather unsatisfactory meal. 'Now listen,' he said in a low voice. 'I must stay here, you can see that. What you have to do is to go with Lucian and find the creek where the boat or boats are, belonging to Mr Eppy. Be careful there are no men left in them.'

'There are two men with two boats,' said Lucian. This was disappointing news. Bill considered again.

'Well – the thing to do first of all is to find the creek with the boats,' said Bill. 'Don't show yourselves. Just find the creek so that we know the way. Then come back here. We'll hope that farm-boy arrives with more food at twelve o'clock, as he usually does.'

'We could do with it,' said Jack.

'So could our dear Mr Eppy and his friends,' grinned Philip. 'Bill, what do we do after we've found the creek and the boats, and come back to report?'

'We send Lucian down with a message supposedly from his uncle, to tell the men to come along up here,' said Bill, 'and we pop down and go off in the boats!'

'But, I say – you'll go on the rocks!' protested Lucian at once. 'You can't come to these islands without a boat-man who knows them. You'll be wrecked!'

This was a problem to be faced. Bill considered again.

'Well – we'll have to make up our minds about that when the time comes. In the meantime, off you go. Lucian, lead the way.'

Lucian, looking rather doubtful, went to the sloping city street. He set off down it, and turned off to the left halfway down.

'You seem to know the way, all right,' said Jack approvingly. Lucian looked at him uneasily.

'I don't,' he said. 'I'm absolutely no good at this kind of thing. I can never can find my way anywhere. I've no sense of direction at all. I shall *never* find the boats!'

Unexpected visitors

Lucian was perfectly right. He did not know the way, and he could not find the boats. He was completely hopeless. He simply wandered here and there, making towards the sea, but arriving at a rocky beach where no boats could possibly lie.

'You're a mutt,' said Jack in disgust.

'Mutt!' said Kiki, pleased with the word. 'Mutty! Send for the doctor.'

Nobody smiled even at this. They were all too disappointed and disgusted with poor Lucian. He looked ready to cry.

'It's not my fault,' he said with a sniff. 'If I'd known it was going to be so important I'd have taken careful note of the way. But I didn't know.'

'Now, look here – if you start to moan again I'll push you down a rabbit hole, and stuff it up with seaweed,' said Jack in disgust. Lucian looked alarmed.

'I *would* remember if I could,' he said dismally. 'But I

do tell you this – nobody can come or go from these islands in a boat without a seaman who knows the way. There are hundreds of rocks just below the surface of the sea. Even an experienced seaman finds it difficult. I know because I've so often visited them with my uncle.'

Jack looked at him. 'Well – I believe you about that,' he said. 'I shouldn't care to navigate a boat myself without a sailor who knew the way. Gosh – we're really beaten now – no boats – and if we had them we'd probably wreck ourselves. A very poor outlook indeed!'

Lucy-Ann immediately had a vision of them and Mr Eppy and his friends remaining on Thamis Island for years and years! She sighed.

'I wish I'd never bought that ship in a bottle for Philip,' she said. 'If I'd known it was going to bring us such an adventure I'd have thrown it away!'

They began to make their way back to the city. As they went, Jack stopped and looked up at the sky. 'What's that noise?' he said. 'Sounds like an aeroplane!'

They all stopped then and listened, looking for the plane. Soon it came into sight, a small speck coming in from the north.

'Pity we can't make a signal of distress,' said Dinah. 'Anyway, I'm going to wave my hanky!'

She took out a small hanky and, much to the others' amusement, waved it wildly in the air.

'Do you really suppose for one moment that the

plane can see your dirty little hanky, and would come down here if it did?' demanded Philip.

'You never know,' said Dinah, still waving vigorously.

'You're daft,' said Philip, and Dinah gave him one of her best scowls. Leaving her waving madly, the others went on, still keeping an eye on the plane, which by now was over the island. It flew over it – and then made a wide circuit and flew back!

'It's seen my hanky!' shrieked Dinah. 'It's coming back!'

'Don't be an ass,' said Philip. But the plane certainly had come back – and what was more, it was coming down low too, making another circuit of the whole island as it flew.

'There's a flat space over there. Look! Look!' screamed Dinah to the plane, as if she really thought it could hear her. 'Come down there! Oh, don't pass it!'

The plane swooped down still lower and came round again. It seemed to see the flat place that Dinah had yelled about, and it came down neatly, as slowly as it could. Its wheels touched the ground, and for one awful moment it looked as if the rough ground was going to tip the plane over on its nose. But it righted itself and came to a stop.

Dinah looked at the others with flushed cheeks. 'There you are! It saw my hanky – and it heard my yell!'

The others were staring in delight at the plane. 'It

can't be friends of Mr Eppy's!' cried Philip. 'It must be someone sent to look for us. Come on!'

Their feet flew along over the rough paths. They saw two men getting out of the plane. They waved to the children and went to meet them.

Lucy-Ann's sharp eyes recognized them first. 'It's TIM!' she squealed. 'Tim, Bill's friend. And isn't that Andros the boatman with him?'

She was right. It *was* Tim, and beside him was a rather shamefaced Andros. Tim hailed them.

'Hello, hello! Where's Bill? Are you all safe? Andros here came to me with such a wild story I had to come along and investigate!'

'Yes, Bill's all right!' cried Jack, and he pumped Tim's arm up and down in sheer delight at seeing him. 'I say, it's good to see you. Did Andros really come and tell you about us?'

'He told me a most extraordinary tale,' said Tim. 'He apparently chewed it over for a day or so, and then decided he'd better tell someone. When he saw me down at the quayside, trying to spot you all, he recognized me and came up. He said that he took you to Thamis and dropped you there. Then he fell asleep waiting for you.'

'That's right,' said Jack.

'And then someone came and woke him up in a hurry, and told him he'd no right to be there, and threatened him with prison,' said Tim. 'Andros replied that he'd left a party there, a man and four children, a parrot and a monkey – and this fellow raved at him, said it was his own island, and if Andros didn't clear out then and there he'd have him arrested straight away.'

'Mr Eppy in a rage, evidently,' said Jack.

'Andros then pointed out that he hadn't been paid and this fellow poured money into his hands and then pointed a revolver at him. So Andros fled, comforting himself by thinking that as the fellow had a boat somewhere he could at least bring you all off in his own good time. That right, Andros?'

'I do not understand all, Mister, sir,' said Andros. 'Bad man here. Very bad. Andros very sorry, Mister, sir.'

'Well, now *you* tell your tale,' said Tim to Jack. So between them the children poured out their story – and it was such an astonishing one that Tim listened open-mouthed. Good gracious – what a tale! He had never heard anything like it in his life.

He soon grasped everything, and grinned to think of old Bill standing patiently by the broken column, waiting for Mr Eppy or his men to come out and be dealt with.

'I wouldn't mind dealing with them myself,' said the young man cheerfully. 'Biff, thud, ker-plonk – very nice too!'

'Oh, Tim – you do make me laugh!' said Lucy-Ann with a giggle. 'I wonder if Bill has been doing any biffing.'

'Well, if he has, I hope it's Mr Eppy that's getting the

biffs, to say nothing of the ker-plonks,' said Tim, grinning. 'Well, now – what's our plan to be?'

'We've got to find the other creek and the boats,' said Jack. 'That's the first thing to do. Then we've got to get the two men out of the way – the ones who are with the boats. Then somehow we've got to get the boats going and sail off safely without being wrecked on the rocks.'

'Well, Andros will know where the creek is – in fact, I know myself,' said Tim. 'I saw it from the plane – and saw the boats there too. And Andros and I will see to the two men all right.'

'No. We know a better way than that to get them out of the way,' said Philip, and he told Tim his plan to send Lucian to them with a fake message. Tim nodded.

'Yes, that's better, really. Saves a lot of rough stuff. Not that I mind that, but I'm not sure about our friend here. He's not made of such stern stuff as he might be.'

'I think we'd better get back and see Bill before we do anything,' said Jack. 'And anyway, we don't want to get the two boatmen out of the way yet, and turn them on to old Bill. That wouldn't be a very good plan. Come on – let's get back to Bill.'

So off they all went, Kiki chattering merrily, knowing that the children were now feeling very much more cheerful. 'Mistersir,' she said to Andros. 'Mistersir, mister!'

They got back to the temple courtyard, and Bill stared in surprise to see Tim. 'Hello!' he said. 'Well, well,

well – so it *was* your plane I saw coming over the island. I couldn't see it come down from here, but I hoped it had. Bit of luck you meeting with the children. I suppose they've told you all the news.'

'Yes, rather,' grinned Tim. 'Pretty adventurous lot, aren't you? Any trouble with the chappies down the column?'

'Just a biff or two a little while ago,' said Bill. '*Not* on Mr Eppy's head, unfortunately – one of the other fellows, I fear. I haven't heard so much as the flick of an eyelid since.'

The sound of a bell came echoing up the ruined street. 'Dong-dong-dong!'

'Pussy's down the well!' screeched Kiki, suddenly remembering ding-dong-bell. 'Who put her in, who put her in?'

'What on earth's that bell?' asked Tim, startled. 'Are we late for school or what?'

'Don't be silly!' said Lucy-Ann, laughing. 'That's our food. It comes every day regularly at this time. And I'm jolly glad – I'm still hungry after our poor breakfast.'

Tim was amazed to see the imp of a boy coming along with the panniered donkey. Bill did not leave his post by the column, but handed out money to Jack to pay for the food. The boy emptied the panniers, winked at Tim and spat once more at Micky. The monkey immediately spat back, and his aim was a lot better than the boy's. 'Pah!' said the little imp in disgust.

'Pah!' echoed Kiki. 'Pooh! Dong-dong-dong, pop goes the pah!'

The boy gave her a look of amazement and climbed on his donkey's back. He sent a stream of comments at Kiki, who copied him at once, ending with one of her pistol shots. The donkey reared in fright, and then galloped off with the boy at top speed.

'You'll be the death of me one day, Kiki,' said Bill, weak with laughing. 'Now then – hand out the food, Jack – and I suppose we'd better throw a bit down the column, or our friends below will starve to death!'

Fortunately the boy had brought a great deal of food, so there was plenty for everyone. Bill yelled down the column in a stentorian voice:

'If you want food, there's some coming. But don't try any funny tricks, or you won't get any more!'

Somebody evidently came up to get the bread, cheese and meat that Bill threw down. He also threw some fruit, feeling that the men must be as thirsty as he was. There was no word of thanks from anyone in the column, and no sound after the food had been taken.

'Wonder if they found the treasure,' said Jack, munching hard. 'Wish I'd seen it! I bet I shan't now – and if I don't, it'll be the disappointment of my life!'

28

Escape!

Plans were made while they ate. 'Tim, I want you to take the two girls off in your plane,' said Bill. 'I don't want anyone exposed to danger here one moment longer than necessary. Andros, once we have got rid of the two men down in the boats, you are to take charge of the better boat of the two, and go off with the rest of us.'

'What, Bill? Do you mean to say we're going to leave a boat for those scoundrels to escape in?' cried Jack indignantly.

'No. I'm going to ask Andros if he will kindly remove some small thing from the engine of the other boat so that it won't start up when the men want it to,' said Bill with a laugh. 'I think it would be a very good thing to leave them here, prisoners, till we report them, and find out whether Mr Eppy has bought the island or not. If he has, he's in a strong position of course, and nothing we say will be listened to with much attention.'

'He's always buying and selling islands,' put in

Lucian. 'I expect he has bought this all right. He's well known for that.'

'You may be right,' said Bill. 'Do you want to come with us, Lucian, or stay and welcome your uncle out of the column?'

There was no doubt about what Lucian wanted to do. He was going with Bill and the others!

They all felt a lot better after the meal. Tim set off for the plane with the two girls, who hugged Bill before they went and begged him to keep himself safe.

'I shan't set off in the plane till I hear your motor boat starting up and going off,' said Tim. 'Goodbye for the present. Come on, girls. What people are going to say when I land with you at the airport I cannot imagine. You're too dirty for anything – regular little grubs!'

Andros, Lucian, Jack and Philip set off for the boats. It was decided that only Lucian should go right up to the boats and give the false message. He was to say that the men were wanted up in the temple courtyard, and give them directions as to how to get there. As soon as Bill spotted them coming he was to leave the broken column where he was on guard, and go to the boats, keeping himself out of sight of the two men.

'Then we'll be into one of the boats in a jiffy, and off and away!' said Jack joyfully. 'That will show Mr Eppy!'

Andros led the way. He knew the other creek well, though he did not consider it as good as the one he had landed in. When they got near to the boats, Lucian went on alone, while the others hid themselves behind bushes.

Lucian was nervous but tried not to show it. He went up to the boats and shouted loudly. 'Ahoy there – where are you?'

The two men appeared. Lucian began to say something loudly in Greek, and the two men nodded. They leapt from the boat to the beach, and made their way up the shore. Lucian was telling them where to go, pointing this way and that.

'Well, I hope he's telling them correctly,' thought Jack, remembering how hopeless Lucian had been at trying to find the way to the boats that morning. 'Let's hope he has been more careful at marking the way this time.'

The men soon disappeared. Andros raced to the boats. He chose the smaller one of the two as being the better. He went to the other boat and tinkered with the engine. He withdrew something from it and threw it into the other boat, where it fell with a thud.

He grinned at the boys. 'That boat no good now,' he said. 'Engine dead. We get in here quick.'

They all got in. Andros tinkered about with the engine there too. It started up quickly and he stopped it at once.

The boys wondered how old Bill was getting on. Had he spotted the two boatmen? Was he even now coming down to the boat, keeping himself unseen? They hoped so.

Suddenly they heard shouts, and they all sat up straight in their boat. What was that?

Bill was tearing down to the shore at top speed. Behind him were the two men, also running at top speed. Andros acted quickly. He started up the engine at once, and called to the boys to give a hand to Bill when he came.

Red in the face and panting hard, Bill raced up to the boat. Willing hands dragged him in, and almost as he touched the deck of the boat it was off and away, its engine making a terrific noise in the calm of the little creek.

The two men leapt into the other boat at once, shouting angrily. Andros gave a malicious grin. Bill saw it and knew what it meant. The other boat was useless!

No amount of trying would make the second boat start up. Its engine was dead. The two men realised that Andros must have tampered with it, and they stood up, shaking their fists and shouting unintelligibly. Jack and Philip enjoyed it all thoroughly, but poor Lucian was as white as a sheet.

'Well – we're off,' said Bill, getting his breath again. 'Gosh, I had a narrow escape. I was watching for the men, but they came on me unawares. They must have guessed there was some trickery about, because they suddenly made a bee-line for me and gave me a jolly hard run. I was glad I'd got all directions from Andros as to where the creek was. I nearly missed my way as it was.'

'Any sound from Eppy and Co.?' asked Jack. Bill shook his head.

'No, but they'll have heard the shouts and I expect they'll be out of the column by now and having a good snoop round. They'll join up with the other two men and then Mr Eppy will have a few choice things to say to the two men who left the boats, and so gave us the means of escape. I expect he is thinking of quite a lot of things to say to Lucian too, for giving them that fake message.'

Lucian gave a feeble smile. He was still very white. 'I shall get a fearful beating,' he said.

'You won't,' said Bill. 'I'll see to that. I'll give your uncle something to think about, when I get back to the airport island. He's going to find himself in hot water very, very soon. I don't care whether he's bought the island or not. He's a rogue.'

The sound of an aeroplane's engine attracted their attention. 'It's Tim's plane!' cried Jack, and he stood up in the motor-boat and waved. 'Ahoy there, Tim!'

The plane swooped down low, and Kiki gave a squawk of terror. Micky hid his head under Philip's arm. The boys cheered and yelled. 'Good-bye, good luck, Tim! Hello there, girls.'

At about six o'clock in the evening the motor-boat arrived at the airport island. The first thing they saw was the *Viking Star* in the harbour, still lying silent. The second thing they saw was Tim on the quayside – and the girls with him! They had landed a long time ago, had

had a good meal, and then had come down to the quay to wait for the others.

'I've been to the police,' said Tim. 'Told the chief you had something to report and would he please not go home till he'd seen you. He's all hot and bothered – it isn't often anything happens here!'

Bill laughed. 'Well, I expect the report will really have to go to the mainland to be dealt with – but as Andros comes from here, and Mr Eppy hired his boats from here, and presumably saw lawyers here if he bought the island, it's best to see the chief of police of this island.'

The chief was a small bird-like man with an intelligent face, and quick, darting eyes. He spoke English very well. He was very thrilled to think there might be some important news for him.

He listened intently to Bill's remarkable story, asking a few questions now and again. The children added little bits. When the inspector heard of the treasure he almost fell off his chair.

'We must find out if this man Eppy did buy the island,' he said. 'I know him. He is always buying islands and selling them. I do not like him. He is crazy.'

A good deal of telephoning then went on, with a few 'Hallos' from a rather bored Kiki, and some 'Mistersirs' and 'One, two, three, pops!'

At last the little man turned to Bill, his face beaming.

'Paul Eppy *did* try to buy the island. But it is not for sale. It is not his – it belongs to our government.'

'*Good!*' said all the children together.

'What a nerve Mr Eppy has!' said Dinah.

'I hope he will not get away with any of that unique treasure,' said the inspector. 'He is not an honest man.'

'He can't,' said Jack, with a grin. 'Andros tampered with the only motor boat there – he can't use it. He's a prisoner there, and so are all the rest of them.'

'Good. I think that is *very* good,' beamed the bird-like man. He turned to Bill. 'If you will be kind enough to put in a report, sir – a detailed one – for me to forward to the mainland – I would be very much obliged. The children should read it, and sign it. And Andros here should sign the part of it that refers to his doings in the matter.'

'Right,' said Bill, and got up to go. 'Well, that's that. I've had some thrilling adventures with these four – but this beats the lot. I only wish we could have a bit of that treasure!'

'Sir, you shall,' said the inspector earnestly. 'I will see to it personally. My government will be very honoured to allow you to choose what you want from it.'

'A carved dagger for me!' said Philip, at once. 'Gosh, what would the chaps at school say!'

'Come along,' said Bill. 'We'll go on board the *Viking Star,* and take Tim to dinner there with us. I want a good bath, a good shave, a good meal and a good sleep in a comfortable bed.'

And off they all went on board the *Viking Star*, happy and excited, talking nineteen to the dozen!

29

Happy ending after all!

In the night the *Viking Star* sailed once more. Bill did
not hear the engines starting up, nor did any of the five
children. Kiki woke up, poked her head out from under
her wing and then put it back again.

It was astonishing to find themselves at sea again.
They were making for Italy. 'Oh dear – we've left the
treasure island far behind,' said Lucy-Ann mournfully.

'Don't be a humbug,' said Jack. 'You know you're jolly
glad you escaped from it.'

'Yes, I know that,' said Lucy-Ann. 'But I just hate
leaving all that treasure.'

'I never even saw it,' Jack reminded her. 'I feel I've
been done out of something – all because that idiot of a
Kiki took it into her head to fly off my shoulder just as
we were going to look for the treasure. Nitwit!'

'Nit-wit,' echoed Kiki pleasantly. 'Tit-bit!' She flew
down and looked at a plate of grapes.

'No, you don't,' said Jack, and removed it from her.

535

'No titbits for a nitwit – and anyway, you've helped yourself to about two hundred grapes already. You're a greedy pig, Kiki.'

'I suppose the rest of this cruise will be as dull as ditchwater,' said Philip. He glanced at the little carved ship on the dressing table of his cabin. 'Golly – weren't we thrilled when we found the treasure map inside! Bill says we've got to give that up to the Greek museum, but we can keep the re-drawn map, the one we used – if we can get it back from Mr Eppy!'

'I wonder what Mother will say to all this,' said Dinah suddenly. 'She won't be a bit pleased with Bill, will she? She'll never speak to him again!'

'Well – that would mean we'd never even *see* him again!' said Lucy-Ann, horrified at the thought. 'I simply love Bill. I wish he was my father. It's horrid not having a father or a mother. You're lucky, you and Philip, Dinah, you *have* got a mother, even if you haven't a father.'

'Well, you share our mother with us, don't you?' said Philip at once. 'You call her Aunt Allie – and she treats you as if she was your mother.'

'Yes, I know. She's a darling,' said Lucy-Ann, and said no more. She was worrying about Bill. Suppose Aunt Allie really kept her word, and refused to speak to Bill again because he had taken them into danger? That really would be dreadful.

It was maddening to sail away from all the romantic little islands, just as they had had such an adventure – all the children longed to know what had happened after they had left. What did Mr Eppy do? What happened to him? How did he eventually get off the island – or was he still there? And what about the treasure, that fabulous, amazing treasure hidden in the round treasure chamber deep down in the heart of the old ruined city?

Bill promised to let them know all he heard – and he was as curious as the children! The *Viking Star* put in at Naples, and then went on to Spain. It was there that Bill got the first news. He came straight to the children.

'Well, you'll be glad to know that Eppy and Co. couldn't get off the island, and almost went mad with rage about it. Then that police inspector chap sent a boat there – and what's more went in it himself – and had the whole lot arrested then and there. What a shock for Mr Eppy!'

'What about the treasure?' asked Dinah eagerly.

'It's all been brought out of the round rock-chamber, and is being sent to the mainland to be examined and valued. A list of the things will be sent to us – and we are each to choose a memento!'

'Gosh!' said Jack. 'I'll have a dagger, like Philip, then. I bet the girls will have jewellery.'

'*Is* it the Andra treasure?' asked Lucy-Ann.

'They seem to think so,' said Bill. All their eyes went to the little ship on the dressing table. There it stood, its sails set, its Greek name showing on its side. The *Andra*. What a Ship of Adventure it had been!

'What's going to happen about Lucian?' asked Dinah. Lucian was still on the *Viking Star*, but with *them*, not with his aunt and uncle this time! His aunt, in hysterical tears, had remained on the airport island to be with her husband. Bill had offered to take Lucian back to England, and park him with a school friend till it was time for him to return to his school.

'Lucian is to go to other relations in future for the holidays,' said Bill. 'That is, unless *we* can occasionally put up with him. I feel sorry for that lad.'

There was a silence. 'It's awful when you feel you've got to do something you don't like doing just because you're sorry for someone,' said Lucy-Ann with a sigh. 'I don't know whether Aunt Allie will like to have him, anyway. And oh, Bill – do you think she's going to be very cross with you about all this? This adventure, I mean?'

'Yes. I think she is,' said Bill. 'I telephoned her from Italy, and told her a little. Perhaps I should have waited till we saw her. She wasn't at all pleased.'

'Oh, dear – we shan't have a very nice time the rest of the hols,' said Lucy-Ann. 'I don't like it when Aunt Allie is upset or cross. She'll be tired, too, after looking after her Aunt Polly. I do wish this adventure was going to have a nice end, not a nasty one!'

Everyone was quite glad when at last the *Viking Star* arrived at Southampton at the end of her long cruise. After the exciting adventure in the middle of it, things had seemed very tame and dull. It was lovely to be on firm land again, going home. Mrs Mannering was not going to meet them. She was leaving her aunt the day before and going home to get things ready for the family. Lucian was to be left with a school friend of his on the way. They were all going home in Bill's car.

The boy was sad to say goodbye when the time came. He stammered and stuttered as he held out his hand to each of them in turn. 'Goodbye – er – I do hope I'll s-s-see you all again. I've had – er – er – a lovely time – and er – I'm sorry for anything I did you didn't like – and – er . . .'

'Er-er-er,' copied Kiki in delight. 'Pah! Send for the doctor. Er-er-er-er-er-er . . .'

'Shut up, Kiki, and behave yourself,' said Jack, vexed. But Lucian didn't mind.

'I shall miss old Kiki,' he said. 'And Micky, too. Goodbye, Micky – er – think of me sometimes, all of you.'

He almost ran from them, and Lucy-Ann stared after him, rather distressed. 'Poor old Lucian – he was almost crying,' she said. 'He's really rather a nice old – er – nice old . . .'

'Nit-wit,' said everyone, and Kiki yelled out too. 'NIT-WIT! Send for the doctor!'

'Well, he's nice for a nitwit, then,' said Lucy-Ann. She settled down in the car again. 'Now for home – and dear old Aunt Allie. I've got a frightfully big hug saved up for her!'

Mrs Mannering was delighted to see them all, though she was rather cool to Bill. She had a wonderful tea ready for them, and Kiki screeched with delight to see a plate laid for her and Micky, with a lovely fruit salad.

'One, two, three, GO!' she said, and settled down to eat, keeping an eye on Micky's plate, hoping she could snatch a titbit from it.

After tea they all sat in the comfortable sitting room, and Bill lit his pipe. He looked rather gloomy, the children thought.

'Well, Allie,' he began. 'I suppose you want to hear it all – the hunt for the Andra treasure – and all that happened.'

'We had some jolly narrow escapes,' said Jack, stroking Kiki. 'And you'll be glad to know, Aunt Allie, that Kiki got two grand nips at Mr Eppy's ear!'

They began their tale. Mrs Mannering listened in amazement. Her eyes went continually to the little carved ship on the mantelpiece, put proudly there by Philip as soon as he reached home.

'There!' said Philip when they had finished their tale. 'What do you think of that?'

Mrs Mannering did not answer. She looked at Bill. He would not meet her eyes, but knocked out his pipe very hard on the fender.

'Oh, Bill,' said Mrs Mannering sadly. 'You promised me – and you broke your word. I shall never trust you again. You promised faithfully not to lead the children into any kind of adventure again. I wouldn't have asked you to look after them if I hadn't trusted you. I can't trust you any more'

'Aunt Allie! What do you *mean*, you can't trust Bill any more?' cried Lucy-Ann indignantly, and she went to Bill and put her arms round him. 'Can't you see he's the nicest, most trustable person in the whole world?'

Mrs Mannering could not help laughing. 'Oh, Lucy-Ann – you're very fierce, all of a sudden. It's just that every time I leave you alone with Bill you get into horrible danger. You know you do.'

'Well, why can't you and Bill always be with us together?' demanded Lucy-Ann. 'I don't see why you can't *marry* each other – then we'd always have Bill, and you could keep an eye on him to see he doesn't lead us into adventures.'

Bill exploded into an enormous shout of laughter. Mrs Mannering smiled broadly. The others looked at one another.

'I say!' said Philip eagerly, 'that's a wizard idea of Lucy-Ann's! We'd have a father then – all of us! Gosh, fancy having Bill for a father. Wouldn't the other boys envy us?'

Bill stopped laughing and looked soberly round at the four beaming children. Then he looked at Mrs Mannering. He raised his eyebrows enquiringly.

'Well, Allie?' he said in a curiously quiet voice. 'Do *you* think it's a good idea, too?'

She looked at him, and then smiled round at the eager children. She nodded. 'Yes – it's really a very good idea, Bill. I'm surprised we've never thought of it before!'

'That's settled, then,' said Bill. 'I'll take these four kids on – and you'll see to it I don't lead them into any more adventures, Allie. Is that agreed?'

'*Well!* This adventure had a wonderful ending after all!' said Lucy-Ann, drawing a deep breath. Her eyes shone like stars. 'Good old Bill! Oh, I'm so happy now!'

'God save the Queen,' said Kiki excitedly. 'Polly put the doctor on, send for the kettle. Pop goes Bill!'

The *Island* of adventure

and

The *Castle* of adventure

Something very sinister is happening on the mysterious Isle of Gloom and the children are determined to uncover the truth!

But Philip, Dinah, Lucy-Ann and Jack are not prepared for the dangerous adventure that awaits them in the abandoned copper mines and secret tunnels beneath the sea.

Why is everyone so afraid of the castle on the hill, and what dark secrets lurk inside its walls?

When flashing lights are seen in a distant tower, Philip, Dinah, Lucy-Ann and Jack decide to investigate – and discover a very sinister plot concealed within its hidden rooms and gloomy underground passages.

The of adventure

and

The of adventure

Who are the two strange pilots, and what is the secret treasure hidden in the lonely valley where the children land?

Nothing could be more exciting than a daring night flight on Bill's plane! But Philip, Dinah, Lucy-Ann and Jack soon find themselves flying straight into a truly amazing adventure.

A mysterious trip to the desolate Northern Isles soon turns into a terrifying adventure when Bill is kidnapped!

Marooned far from the mainland on a deserted coast, Philip, Dinah, Lucy-Ann and Jack find themselves playing a dangerous game with an unknown enemy. Will they escape with Bill and their lives?

The **Mountain** of adventure

and

The **Ship** of adventure

Surely a peaceful holiday in the Welsh mountains will keep the children out of trouble! But the mystery of a rumbling mountain soon has them thirsty for more adventure.

Philip, Dinah, Lucy-Ann and Jack are determined to explore the mountain and uncover its secret, but first they must escape from a pack of ravenous wolves and a mad genius who plans to rule the world!

An amazing voyage around the beautiful Greek islands becomes an exciting quest to find the lost treasure of the Andra!

Philip, Dinah, Lucy-Ann and Jack are plunged into a search for hidden riches – with some ruthless villains hot on their trail! Will they find the treasure before it's too late?

The *Circus* of adventure

and

The *River* of adventure

Why did Bill have to bring the babyish Gustavus with them on holiday? Jack knows he'll only be trouble . . .

But when Gustavus is kidnapped, along with Philip, Dinah and Lucy-Ann, Jack bravely sets out to rescue them, leading him to a faraway land and the discovery of a plot to kill the King!

A river cruise through ancient desert lands becomes a mysterious adventure when Bill disappears!

While Philip, Dinah, Lucy-Ann and Jack are desperately searching for Bill, they become trapped beneath a forgotten temple where no one has set foot for 7,000 years. What dangers lurk within, and will they ever escape?

A selected list of titles available from Macmillan Children's Books

The prices shown below are correct at the time of going to press. However, Macmillan Publishers reserves the right to show new retail prices on covers, which may differ from those previously advertised.